I0674311

The Blue Rose

Terry Toler

The Blue Rose
Published by: BeHoldings, LLC.

Copyright ©2020, **BeHoldings, LLC**
Terry Toler
All Rights Reserved

All rights reserved. No part of this publication may be reproduced, stored in a retrieval system, or transmitted in any form, or by any means— electronic, mechanical, photocopying, recording or other-wise—without prior written permission.

Cover and interior designs: BeHoldings, LLC

Editor: Jeanne Leach

For information, address terry@terrytoler.com

Our books can be purchased in bulk for promotional, educational, and business use. Please contact your bookseller or the BeHoldings Sales department at: sales@terrytoler.com

For booking information email: booking@terrytoler.com

First U.S. Edition: October 2020

Printed in the United States of America

ISBN 978-1-7352243-7-4

This is a work of fiction. All of the characters, organizations, and events portrayed in this novel are either products of the author's imagination or are used fictitiously. Any resemblance to actual persons, living or dead is entirely coincidental.

BOOKS BY TERRY TOLER

Fiction

The Longest Day
The Reformation of Mars
The Great Wall of Ven-Us
The Eden Experiment
The Late, Great Planet Jupiter
Save The Girls
The Ingenue
Saving Sara

Non-Fiction

How to Make More Than a Million Dollars
The Heart Attacked
Seven Years of Promise
Mission Possible
Marriage Made in Heaven
21 Days to Physical Healing
21 Days to Spiritual Fitness
21 Days to Divine Health
21 Days to a Great Marriage
21 Days to Financial Freedom
21 Days to Sharing Your Faith
21 Days to Mission Possible
7 Days to Emotional Freedom
Uncommon Finances
Suddenly Free

For more information on these books and other resources
visit TerryToler.com.

PRAISE FOR THE TERRY TOLER NOVELS

"Terry Toler books are so riveting!"

"When you think you've got the plot worked out, he puts a twist on it and surprises you."

"I couldn't put them down and kept reading one after another."

"Never a dull moment in a Terry Toler novel."

"I love them. Every book has plenty of action and conflict."

"Terry Toler is my new favorite author."

"I love the new style of writing he has invented."

"Not everyone can write an ending like Terry Toler."

"Great writing style! Every novel captures me in the first chapter and then I can't put them down."

"I love all the twists and turns."

"I don't even like fiction, but I love your books."

"You really know how to draw an audience into your story, and I am a perfect example of that."

"I have to force myself to quit reading, so I can get some work done."

"Every time I finish a chapter, I say it's going to be my last, and the intrigue doesn't let me. I have to keep reading one more chapter!"

"Your cliffhangers are epic."

"I recognize a Terry Toler book from the first page."

"Your books have it all. Romance. Intrigue. Mystery. Suspense. And endings that make you come back for more."

"I'm hooked on Terry Toler books."

"The Eden Stories are revolutionary. You've created your own new genre of fiction."

"Wow! That's all I can say."

"When I finish a book, I think about it for days which is the characteristic of a great author."

"I can't wait to see what you come up with next."

"I love the characters. They draw me in, and I find myself rooting for them."

Dedicated to my sister Charlotte. The real Cat.
The inspiration for so many of the good things in my life.

Prologue

Los Angeles California
December 24, 1983

The gains women made in the workplace in the seventies and early eighties had not found their way to the southern California offices of Miles Fire & Casualty insurance company. Case in point, Catherine Ann Tolliver's boss, Harold Dawkins, was a world-class male chauvinist pig, and so far, no one had had the courage to do anything about it.

Cathy was not going to be the first.

Being the only female insurance claim's adjuster in the office, Cathy took the brunt of Dawkins vitriol and snide, sexist remarks but was determined not to file a complaint. She wouldn't have that in her otherwise impeccable file. Mostly, she kept her nose to the grind and tried not to do anything to upset him.

The Christmas holidays were upon them and Cathy had ten days away from the man. Her coworkers convinced her to join them at *Willy's* country bar for a drink and to celebrate the welcomed respite from the stress that can be insurance adjusting. Cathy reluctantly agreed but only because they chose *Willy's* for her benefit.

Cathy was from Houston, Texas, and *Willy's* was the only country bar in southern California. They assumed she'd like it, being a Texas girl. She would've preferred a quiet, art deco café. Going home was her real preference. The number of times she'd been in a bar could be counted on one hand.

Nevertheless, once there, she was glad she went. Everyone had a good time and laughed so hard, Cathy could feel the tension of another year in the office slowly leaving her body. Her friends took turns riding the mechanical bull. Cathy only rode it once, and once was enough. She could still feel the soreness in her tailbone when she sat down gingerly on the chair.

Still, she was having a great time.

Until her beeper went off.

Dawkins! What does he want?

Even though officially on vacation, as the senior claims adjuster, Cathy was always on call. Hopefully, he just needed help finding a file. The bar had a pay phone, and she dialed the direct line into his office.

Dawkins said, "I have a case for you. I left the file on your desk. You need to meet the fire investigator at the scene tomorrow morning."

Her worst fears were realized. "It's Christmas Day!" Cathy didn't often push back against her boss but couldn't control the urge or the rage building inside of her. She knew exactly why he was giving the case to her and she resented it.

"You're always on call," he said roughly.

"I'm on vacation. Give the file to someone else."

"You're single," he said.

Her mouth flew open in disbelief that he'd actually had the audacity to say the words she knew he was thinking. She could almost see the huge grin on his face as he said it.

"I'm sure you don't have any other plans. Everyone else in the office is married with kids. I can't give the case to them. That's where you belong Cathy. At home. Taking care of a husband and kids. Not working some insurance claim. I can't take the men away from their kids on Christmas morning. It's not fair."

Not fair? This was over the top even for him. Why did he think she didn't have plans?

The fact that she didn't was beside the point. She wanted to slam the phone down and hang up on him but didn't have the courage. Better yet, she wanted to quit on the spot. If she hadn't bitten her lip to prevent the words from coming out of her mouth, she might've quit. Dawkins had been wanting to fire her for the entire twelve years he'd been her supervisor.

When Dawkins was hired, she'd already established herself as the best in the office. He wanted to bring in his own team, but somehow, she survived. He couldn't fire her without a reason, and she never gave him one.

She thought about giving him one then and there. Her hand moved the phone away from her ear, while she tried to catch her breath so she wouldn't say something she regretted.

Instead of telling him off, she did what she always did.

Gave in.

"I'll come by later tonight and get the file," she said.

I

Six months later

Cathy sat in Dawkins office fidgeting nervously. Dawkins had called her in to discuss a claim she was working on—the Wanda Rose file.

"This case should've been closed months ago!" Dawkins said, not holding back his frustration or anger. While he didn't need a reason to act like a jerk, when he had one, it brought out the worst in him.

He was right, and she knew it. She'd been working on the case for more than six months. It should've been closed sooner, but Cathy had a gut feeling there was fraud behind the claim. An intuition. Something she developed over her twelve years on the job. A sudden urge to defend herself rose up from deep inside of her.

"It doesn't feel right to me," Cathy retorted, knowing her response would set him off further.

Dawkins leaned forward in his chair and glared at her from across the desk. "Are you a psychic now?" he said mockingly. "Is that how I taught you to investigate claims? With a crystal ball? I don't pay you to have feelings! I pay you to investigate facts. When you know the facts, you make a decision. Pay the claim or deny it. The facts are that we owe this claim. Pay it and move on to the next one. You've spent six months on a simple Christmas tree fire."

The Wanda Rose file was a simple case. Any junior-level claims adjuster could've handled it. A Christmas tree caught fire on Christmas Eve and caused extensive damage to Rose's luxurious townhome in a wealthy area of Beverly Hills. Nothing unusual about it at first. All Cathy had to do was assess the damage and cut her a check.

Some similar cases were closed on the same day. In the matter of Wanda Rose, other factors had made it more complicated.

Cathy should've never had the file to begin with. Had it not been Christmas Eve, Dawkins would've given it to one of her male counterparts. That's why she was as mad at him as he was at her. Subconsciously, maybe passive aggressively, she was making Dawkins pay for giving her the file in the first place. Or maybe her instincts were right, and something was amiss. At the moment, she didn't have time to decide which.

The room got uncomfortably quiet as Dawkins started flipping through the file leaving Cathy to her thoughts.

Truthfully, she loved her job. In some ways, Dawkins was the best and the worst boss she'd ever had. Granted, she'd only had a few. Miles Fire & Casualty was her first job out of college. The man who hired her left to take a job at another office.

Dawkins was hired and taught her the ins and out of the business. How to build a file. Things to look for in an investigation. How to spot fraud. He always taught her to follow her instincts, which were good; he had said so on more than one occasion. Ironic, considering the conversation they were having now.

Cathy forced her thoughts back to the issue at hand. Now that she was on the Wanda Rose case, she was determined to do her job. The fire investigator report said they found traces of a possible accelerant. Cathy decided to make that point to Dawkins as he was still looking down at the file.

"Possible accelerant?" Dawkins looked up immediately and shouted so loud Cathy winced. She shouldn't have said anything. The other employees in the bullpen outside his office could hear as she saw several look their way. Even then, they turned their heads away quickly. While Dawkins was hard on her since she was a woman, the men were also the recipients of his wrath from time to time as well and knew what she was going through.

When Dawkins got like this, no one in the office could stand him.

"I have plenty of evidence," she insisted. Over the years, she had become more courageous to stand her ground.

"Like what?"

"The expert I hired said that the extent of damage could not have been caused by Christmas tree lights," Cathy argued.

"She'll hire an expert saying the fire was caused by the lights. You know how the game works."

At least he had lowered his voice. Raising hers had worked to defuse the situation some. Now he tapped his pencil on the desk like she was wasting his time. Cathy wasn't sure which was worse—his anger or his dismissiveness. Now he treated her like she didn't know what she was doing.

He looked her up and down. Not in a sexual way. That was the one thing that would've made the situation worse, even intolerable. Sexual advances and innuendoes were something he never did.

Thankfully.

Cathy adjusted the collar of her pant suit. Dawkins matched her movement by adjusting his shirt collar. His dress was as boorish as his behavior. White shirt. Loosened tie dangling from the neck. The sleeves of his shirt were rolled halfway up his forearm. His salt and pepper hair was mussed.

A contradiction in style.

Cathy was immaculately dressed, and her hair and makeup were perfect. Dawkins insisted on it. *Women should always look their best* he told her often. While he almost always looked disheveled, he would never allow it from her. Another double standard she resented.

Stay focused, Cathy.

"One week later, Wanda Rose claimed that a necklace was missing," Cathy said, making her strongest argument. "A hundred-thou-sand-dollar necklace!"

"I'll give you that," Dawkins said, as he shook his head from side to side. "It is suspicious."

Cathy took the bait and walked through the opened door. "She says one of the firemen stole it."

"They may have for all we know," Dawkins retorted, as he closed the door as fast as he had opened it.

She wouldn't go down without a fight. "I interviewed every person who entered the premises," Cathy said. "There's no way anyone stole the necklace. I'm not even convinced the necklace ever existed."

"There's an appraisal in the file."

"But no pictures."

"Underwriting didn't require a picture."

"That was a mistake."

"No doubt. But we can't do anything about it now."

"The lady has pictures all over her townhouse. With dozens of celebrities. Billie Holiday. Count Basie. Frank Sinatra. Bob Hope. Pictures of her with all these famous people. Autographed. Inscribed to Wanda Rose. They were the first things she saved in the fire. She wasn't wearing the necklace in any of them."

"Did she have an explanation?"

"She always has an explanation for everything. She said she rarely wore it outside of the house. It was kept in a safe."

"How did firemen get in the safe?"

"By chance, she was cleaning the necklace when the fire started. She says she left it on the bathroom counter."

"And only noticed it gone a week later? I don't buy that."

"Exactly."

"Did you ask her for a purchase receipt?"

"Of course. She claims it was an anniversary gift from one of her ex-husbands."

"Did you talk to the company who did the appraisal? Maybe they have a picture."

"Out of business."

Dawkins kept tapping his pencil as he stared off into the ceiling.

"She's as famous as the people in the pictures," he finally said. "Wanda Rose is the foremost jazz singer of our time."

"She's the only female jazz singer to sell a million albums," Cathy added. She wanted Dawkins to know she had done her homework.

He didn't acknowledge it. "You saw her townhome. The woman's rich. Why would she run an insurance scam over a measly hundred thousand dollars?"

"Maybe she ran into financial trouble. I can't find anything on her finances."

"Let it go, Cathy. If you deny the claim, she'll sue us, and she'll win. You can't take that before a jury. They hate insurance companies to begin with."

That was true. Miles Fire & Casualty avoided the courtroom like it avoided the plague. Most of these cases settled. Which was why it was easier to just pay the claims and save the attorney's fees.

"I think the woman is lying," Cathy said.

"Do you know how much we paid out in claims last year?" Dawkins asked in a condescending voice.

Here we go.

This was always his closing argument. She'd heard this speech too many times to count.

"No sir," she replied. She knew the answer but decided to humor him.

"Three billion dollars!"

"That's a lot, sir."

"Damn right it is. And some of them weren't legitimate claims. That's part of the business. We don't always find what we're looking for. You've done a good job on this, Cathy. Very thorough. As usual. You've covered all your bases. It's time to move on."

She threw a grenade into the center of the conversation, ignoring the compliment even though they were few and far between. "I want to interview the ex-husband."

"No way!"

"Somehow I feel like he's the key to this story," Cathy argued. "He needs to fill in the missing pieces."

"The woman has five ex-husbands."

"And four of them are dead. That's suspicious in and of itself. I want to interview the one who's still alive. Norman T. Hurst. He lives in Fort Worth, Texas."

"I'm not flying you to Texas."

"I've already booked my ticket. If I don't find anything, I'll close the file. I promise."

With that, Cathy picked up the file and headed for the door before Dawkins could say anything more. When she saw his mouth open in disbelief, she decided not to look back again.

2

Fort Worth, Texas

When Cathy arrived at the home of Norman T. Hurst, it wasn't what she expected. The massive, white, four-columned *Gone with the Wind* house on a hundred sprawling acres had seen better days. As did the feeble old man who came out the front door and down the steps to greet her before she got out of her car.

Despite the strenuous effort, Norman had a smile on his face and a bounce in his step. Having a visitor seemed to have energized him. Especially one who wanted to talk about what she could tell on the phone was clearly the love of his life—Wanda Rose.

"I'm so glad you came," Norman said. "I understand you want to talk about Wanda." The moment he said her name, his wide grin penetrated the deep lines and wrinkles stretching them to places they probably hadn't been in a long time.

Yep. He loved her.

Norman was Wanda's fourth husband. Wanda was his third wife. He never remarried. She married once more. Perhaps he still held some animosity toward her, but Cathy couldn't tell it from his demeanor. She had hoped for an angry and bitter ex-husband ready to spill all of Wanda's worst secrets. Instead, she was immediately concerned that she had found a heartbroken lover still pining over his lost love.

That threw Cathy off track for a moment and she stopped to rethink her strategy. Making the two-hour drive from DFW airport to his house south of Fort Worth had given her the time to crystallize her questions. She needed to get Norman on her carefully laid track quickly.

He invited her into the house and offered her a glass of tea, which she declined. She followed him into his formal dining room, and they sat down at the table.

"Have you seen Wanda?" he asked with quickened breath and eyes twinkling with anticipation.

"Yes sir, I have," Cathy responded. "Several times over the last few months."

"How is she doing?" he asked hesitantly, almost as if he was afraid to, even though he obviously was desperate to know.

"She seems to be doing well. When was the last time you talked to her?" Cathy wanted to take control of the conversation and direct the questions back at him. She had to be careful, though, so he didn't lose his enthusiasm.

"February 4, 1967," he said, almost solemnly like he was giving her the day she died.

Cathy's heart sunk to the bottom of her stomach which was already feeling queasy from her nervousness. That was the day their divorce was final. Seventeen years ago. She had looked up that information, and it was in her file.

He hasn't talked to her. This is going to be a waste of time.

Along with that, he didn't show the least bit of anger in his voice. The actual divorce settlement was confidential, but Cathy knew Wanda had purchased her condo in Beverly Hills a week after the divorce became final. For ten million dollars. Cash at closing. Obviously, from the proceeds of the divorce settlement. Whatever had gone down between them, and despite costing him a large sum of money, Norman didn't appear to be holding a grudge.

"She asked about you," Cathy said, thinking she'd play into his vulnerabilities. "I told her I was coming to interview you."

His eyes lit up like a Christmas tree. Cathy found it ironic that his response would remind her of the reason she was there—to investigate the Christmas tree fire. Actually, the theft of the necklace. The fire loss on the luxury condo was actually greater than the necklace. It's just that Cathy was convinced the necklace never existed and was determined to prove it. If just for her boss's benefit. To prove she was right to keep pursuing it.

"She said to tell you hello," Cathy continued. "She speaks very highly of you."

Seeing Norman's response made her feel a twinge of guilt. He choked up. Cathy thought she saw a tear form in his eye.

What she said was the truth. Wanda did ask about him and told her to tell him hello. And with the same level of affection. Why was this line of question bothering her? Manipulation generally didn't. This was an interrogation and an investigation. *All's fair in love and insurance interrogations*, Dawkins said often in her training.

This didn't have the feel of an interrogation. In reality, Cathy felt more like a middle-school, girl passing messages between a boy and girl in school who liked each other.

Technically, insurance adjusters didn't do interrogations, or investigations for that matter. They were called evaluations of claims. However, Cathy liked the other terms better. It made her feel more important. Dawkins used them, so she did as well.

Wanda did seem terrified when Cathy mentioned she was coming to see Norman. When Cathy first questioned her when she dropped the bombshell that the necklace was missing, she had insisted that she didn't remember which ex-husband had given her the necklace. Something Cathy found impossible to believe. When Cathy mentioned that she was coming to see Norman, Wanda suddenly remembered that her third husband, Dick Lawlor, gave her the necklace and not Norman.

She was sure Wanda told her that so she wouldn't bother making the trip. It hadn't worked though, and she was determined to find out what Norman knew about it, using all her cleverness to pry it out of him. Whatever Norman was feeling was not going to get in the way of her doing her job.

"Did you ever give Wanda a necklace?" Cathy asked abruptly, trying to catch Norman off guard. "For one of your anniversaries?" she asked.

A puzzled look came on Norman's face as his eyes narrowed and he shrugged his shoulders.

"I'm sure I did. I gave her many gifts."

"This is a specific necklace. Oval shaped. With blue sapphires. It had five large diamonds in it totaling fifteen carats. It's worth about a hundred-thousand dollars."

Norman let out a chuckle. "I was rich but not that rich."

Cathy knew that wasn't true. Norman, at one time, was one of the hundred richest men in Texas. An oil tycoon, he made his money during the boom years. What money the three divorce settlements didn't take from him, the oil crisis of 1973 and the even bigger oil crisis of 1979 did. Most of the Texas oil men lost half their wealth in the first crisis and another half of what was left in the second one.

Norman's first two wives got much bigger settlements than Wanda. It was estimated that Norman was nearly a billionaire when he divorced his first wife of twenty-three years. In Texas, a wife got half her husband's wealth unless there was a prenuptial agreement. A mistake Norman didn't make the third time with Wanda, which was why she didn't get as much as the first two wives.

A sudden empathy came over her. Norman clearly didn't even have enough left to provide basic upkeep for his estate while Wanda was living in luxury in Beverly Hills. She put the feelings aside and got back to the questions.

"Did you ever see the necklace?" Cathy asked. "Did Wanda ever wear it out to events? Keep it in the safe."

"No," Norman said, rubbing the slight stubble on his chin. "I don't remember ever seeing it. I think I would remember if I had."

A bolt of excitement shot through her as her heart started racing and face flushed. She was already nervous and doing everything she could to keep her hands from shaking or her voice from cracking. This was good information. If Wanda said she got it as a gift from her third husband, then Norman would've seen it. He was her fourth husband.

"Maybe she kept it in a safe deposit box," Norman said pensively. "It was a gift from her ex-husband. She might've thought it hurtful to wear it around me."

In a matter of seconds, Norman had shot holes all through what she thought was a major development in the case.

"I think I *will* have that glass of iced tea," Cathy said out of the blue as her throat suddenly felt parched.

She needed to make the conversation more casual. Get Norman to open up. That last response seemed guarded. Like something Wanda would say. Sharing a glass of tea might do the trick.

Was he covering for her? Did he know more than he was letting on? Had she called and talked to him and asked him to lie for her?

So many questions ran through her mind. She hadn't broken through Wanda's guarded exterior. Maybe she could break through Norman's.

He struggled to his feet and walked out of the room. The formal dining room was just off the kitchen. Cathy took the opportunity to stand and stretch her legs, stiff from the flight and the drive over. She walked around the expansive room like she was touring a museum.

While the outside of the house was dilapidated and in disrepair, the inside was almost immaculate. Perfectly clean. Cleaner than her condo. Not a thing was out of place. The hardwood floors were polished. The drapes were old but elegant.

He must have a maid. There's no way he cleans this big house by him-self.

Yet, the room felt noticeably sparse. Several expensive pieces of furniture lined the walls but not much in the way of accessories. Things like pictures, paintings on the walls, vases, lamps, end tables, coffee tables, and chairs were missing. Was Norman selling his valu-ables one at a time? Maybe to pay the bills?

The room was sterile. Lifeless. Like there had been no laughter in it for years. It suddenly gave Cathy an eerie feeling. So, she walked out of the dining room and into the kitchen. "Can I help you with the tea?" she asked.

Norman was leaning inside the opened refrigerator door and pulled out a full pitcher of brown tea. He pointed to a cabinet with his free hand once he managed to straighten himself.

"There are glasses in that bottom cabinet. Get two of them, please."

Cathy did and walked back over to the counter where Norman had placed the pitcher.

"Would you mind filling them up with ice, dear?" he said as he grasped the counter to steady his balance.

"Not at all."

Cathy filled the two glasses with ice and then sat them both on the counter and filled them with tea. She took them in her hands and followed Norman as he took a different route back to the din-ing room. Down a hallway, Norman stopped in front of a big room with double doors at the entrance. It looked like a study.

It was the only room she had seen that seemed to still be in its original state. Everything was perfectly adorned and filled with fur-niture and effects. Above the fireplace was a large portrait of a younger Wanda Rose. A painting. Obviously commissioned. Wanda was in a blue dress. Her hair was up, not in a traditional sixty's hairdo, but more like the look of a princess or queen posing for a royal portrait. Whoever the artist, he was good.

Interesting that Norman still kept it.

Cathy noticed immediately that Wanda was wearing a necklace. Not *the* necklace. This one was more understated than the one she'd filed a claim for. She made a mental note to ask Norman and Wanda about that necklace.

"This is a beautiful room," Cathy said. "That's a stunning picture of Wanda."

"Why don't we continue our conversation in there?" Norman asked, holding out his hand out like he was inviting or perhaps directing her into the room.

Cathy hesitated.

The file was back in the dining room. She quickly dismissed the idea of going back to get it. That room gave her the creeps anyway. This one would be more comfortable. The file was etched in her mind, and she could get by without it. A pen and pad to take notes would be nice to have, but she didn't want to ruin the moment. Norman seemed like he was willing to talk, and the study would be a perfect setting to ask the questions.

Cathy knew from experience, people let their guard down in familiar settings. She almost always tried to conduct her interviews in the person's home. It made them feel like they were in control even though they weren't.

"Wanda was very beautiful," Norman said almost to himself. Regret and affection dripped from the words to such an extent that Cathy almost felt sorry for him again. Wanda had obviously charmed him the way she had tried to charm her. He had obviously fallen for it. She did at first as well. Until the inconsistencies became too great to ignore.

"She still is," Cathy said, not sure why she said it that way. Maybe she wanted him to feel even more regret. That might make him open up more. The truth was that Wanda was beautiful. Even stunning by the depiction on the wall. If possible, she was even more charming than beautiful.

She got five men to marry her and make her a wealthy woman. She had something going for her.

So had Norman. Cathy studied the man closely.

At one time Norman was one of Fort Worth's most eligible bachelors. His first two wives were Dallas socialites. From old money. His third wife was the most famous jazz singer of all times. He had to have something going for him to land those women. And it was more than just money. He had a certain charm that was disarming.

Cathy could see why the women had fallen for him as well. Behind the years, the Texas sun, the divorces, and the obvious signs of alcoholism, were ruggedly handsome good looks. Life had taken a toll on Norman. He'd aged beyond his years. Like his house. Years ago, the Hurst estate was probably one of the most prestigious in all of Fort Worth. Now it was a shell of its former self. Norman was like a valuable collectible sitting off in the corner of an antique store. Only someone who knew the provenance and history would know its real worth.

Cathy genuinely liked the man.

They settled into two high-back, plush, wing back, red chairs sitting in front of the fireplace.

Cathy couldn't take her eyes off of the painting.

* * *

Eventually, Cathy got to her questions. They only took twenty minutes. She rattled off every question on her list that she could think of without her notes. At the end, the frustration had overwhelmed her to the point that she had given up. Resigned to the fact that proving her case was a lost cause.

Norman didn't know anything about a missing necklace. That was obvious. Cathy was almost kicking herself.

Why would he know? He's an ex-husband. He hasn't spoken to her in seventeen years!

The trip had been a complete waste of time. She didn't know which was worse, wasting her time flying there or having to face the *I told you so* back at the office from Dawkins.

Totally exasperated, Cathy decided to close the interview and the file for good. Finding an opening to end the conversation wasn't easy. Norman still wanted to talk.

"I called her 'The Blue Rose,'" Norman said affectionately.

"Why is that?" Cathy asked. "I've never seen a blue rose before."

"She sang the blues. Wanda's most famous for her jazz, but her blues albums were her best, in my humble opinion. I still have all of them."

Norman got up from his chair and walked to an old phonograph that Cathy hadn't noticed was sitting in the corner at the back of the room. He pulled a vinyl record out of a sleeve, placed it on the turntable, and turned it on. He made it back to his chair and sat down as the music started filtering through the surround-sound speakers in each corner of the room.

The rich, deep, sultry, soulful voice of Wanda Rose filled the room and echoed off the high ceilings which provided perfect acoustics. Cathy followed Norman's lead and laid her head back and allowed herself to relax as the powerful bluesy tones penetrated deep into her soul. She loved music. All kinds. She preferred the hard seventies rock of Led Zeppelin, Black Sabbath, and the Who, but she did appreciate Wanda's skills. She could see why Wanda was the premier singer of her day.

Music moved her. Deep down. In her heart. Wanda Rose's singing did that for her. The blues song matched her mood, although making her feel surprisingly better. An interesting dichotomy. Of all the things she could say about Wanda Rose, the woman could sing. At one point, Cathy could see the huge chandelier hanging from the ceiling begin to shake.

How did that much power come from such a small frame?

It became apparent that Norman would not turn off the phonograph unless Cathy took the initiative. If she hurried, she could still catch a flight back to LA. Cathy stood to her feet and said, "Thank you for your time, Mr. Hurst, but I'd better be going."

He didn't move. Norman kept staring at her painting. "She's an amazing singer, isn't she?" he said barely above a whisper.

Cathy wasn't sure if it was a question or a statement or both. "She really is," Cathy responded warmly. She had no proof that Wanda was a liar and a cheat. It was time to give the woman her due. "I guess the best there ever was."

"You want to hear something funny?" Norman asked, still sitting down.

"What's that?" Cathy glanced at her watch trying not to be too obvious.

"I never heard Wanda sing," he said.

"I don't understand what you mean."

They were listening to Wanda sing right then.

"We were married for twelve years," Norman continued with a strange inflection in his voice. "Not one time did I ever hear her sing in person."

"You mean at a concert?"

"Anywhere."

Cathy sat back down and consciously closed her mouth, so it wasn't gaped open.

"You're telling me that you never heard Wanda sing? Ever?"

Cathy found that hard to believe and wasn't sure how to process this new information. All she knew was that alarm bells were going off in her head as a sudden rush of adrenaline shot through her like streams of pulsating water.

"That's what I'm saying," he said, nodding.

"She never sang in the shower?" Cathy asked. "Or in the car? She never sang along to her records?"

"Nope. Never."

"In twelve years?"

"No, Ma'am."

"How is that possible?"

"She always had an excuse," Norman said.

"Did you ever ask her to sing for you?"

"Many times. She'd say her voice was scratchy. Or she had a cold. She didn't feel like it. No matter how hard I tried, she would never sing for me."

Cathy settled back into her chair. A whole lot more questions had suddenly formed in her mind. This was going to take a while.

"Let's start at the beginning," Cathy said. "Tell me about the first time you met Wanda Rose."

3

1955

New Orleans, LA

Norman T. Hurst stared intently into his glass of scotch, oblivious to everything except the marvelous jazz music filtering through the smoke-filled Bourbon Street bar. Although one of Texas's wealthiest men, loneliness permeated his soul like the melted ice had overrun his mostly untouched drink.

The bar was full of patrons, yet he felt like the only person in the room. No one had given him a second look. Thankfully. The bartender had given up asking if he wanted his drink refreshed. At one point, the steward of the sauce tried to strike up a conversation, but Norman shut it down as quickly as it had started.

The music was the only thing that brought him solace. The standup bass player created a rich low tone with intricate finesse. It almost felt like Norman's heartbeat was synchronized to the band. The four-piece ensemble made up of a drummer, bass player, piano player, and a sax/clarinet/flute/trumpet player, alternated their set between jazz and blues songs. Norman couldn't make up his mind which he liked more. He loved them both.

The band suddenly burst into the jazz tune, *I Want to Be Happy*, a popular radio song made famous by Doris Day. He raised his head and looked their way. The clarinet player wistfully maneuvered his fingers through the intricate melody with precision. Norman actually smiled.

Until he remembered the words.

I won't be happy, till I make you happy too.

He hadn't made anyone else happy in years. Except maybe his banker. And his two ex-wives when he paid them millions of dollars in their divorce settlements. That almost made him chuckle. When the two women received their money, that was the happiest he'd seen them since their wedding day. As far as he was concerned, every day after the wedding had been worse than the one before it. He wasn't sad because the marriages were over. He was sad because he wasn't good at anything but making money.

And getting women to fall for me.

He was good at that. Norman knew how to wine and dine the ladies. It helped that he had plenty of money. That reminded him he needed to pay for his drink. He pulled out his wallet bulging with wads of cash and clumsily grabbed a few dollars to buy another. Then he realized he hadn't even taken a sip of the last one, so he shoved the money back into his wallet after slapping a five-dollar bill on the counter.

His life desperately needed to change. Not that he wanted to be married again. He was a great boyfriend but a terrible husband. When dating, he lavished a woman with gifts to get her to want to marry him. Once married, he worked eighty hours a week and complained incessantly at her excessive spending.

After so many years in the Texas oil business, Norman had built an impressive empire and had acquired a large amount of wealth. Cash he was willing to spend on the next woman, although he was determined not to marry her. That had been decided. His lawyer had suggested a prenuptial agreement, which was a new concept to him. His first two wives had taken a large chunk of his money, and a prenup would protect that from happening again.

Norman rued the fact that the prenup didn't exist when he divorced his first wife. She got nearly a half a billion dollars. *More than she deserved*, he fumed. He'd almost replaced that fortune when he remarried and lost half of it again in the second divorce.

This much was clear. He could save himself a fortune if he'd simply date the women and buy them gifts rather than marry them. Rather than a prenup, he suggested to his lawyer that he draw up an agreement stating that he would shoot Norman if he ever wanted to get married again.

Some men are just not meant to be married, he'd said.

For Norman, the chase was more fun than the kill, so to speak. He needed to extend the chase out, so it lasted longer. That's what he loved. Falling in love. Not being in love. The next time, he'd guard his heart to keep from falling for her. If he played his cards right, the chase might even last longer than his two previous marriages. He only needed to find the right woman. One who didn't want to get married.

At his age, that was hard to find.

So, most Friday nights he was on the prowl. But that had gotten old quick. At fifty-nine years old, he hadn't been able to find a younger woman he wanted to be with who was willing to only date him. He'd almost given up. Maybe he had. That's why he was so depressed. Tonight, he wasn't even looking for a woman to hook up with. For whatever reason, he wanted to be alone.

Norman lowered his eyes back to his diluted drink.

I need to get out of here.

When he had decided to leave, a noise grabbed his attention. A buzz suddenly filled the room. He looked around to find the source of the room's attention.

A woman.

In a sparkling red dress.

Sauntered through the front door as the crowd gasped.

Who is she?

He stretched out his long legs and used his expensive Lucchese cowboy boot heels to push his bar stool back against the wall. Teetering on the two back legs, he leaned back to see what was happening.

Even the band was looking her way.

She was mesmerizing.

Her skin flawless.

Her features perfect.

Norman reached up to stroke his own face, acutely aware of the tracks on his forehead.

Her curved body formed melodious lines. The jewels embedded in the cloth fabric picked up every reflection of the stage lights and created a sparkling aura around her.

The manager rushed to the door, took her hand, and escorted her to a table up front near the stage.

Norman had never seen anyone make such an entrance.

His demeanor and spirits immediately changed. He looked around to see if there were any empty tables near him and wondering deep down if she would even notice him.

His decision was made... He wasn't leaving.

I have to meet her.

The manager pulled out a chair and invited her to sit. She waived whimsically to her adoring fans before she elegantly did so. Norman wondered how everyone knew who she was. The manager flagged the waiter to bring her a drink as everyone continued to stare admiringly at her. Seeming to enjoy the attention, she acknowledged the individuals at the other tables with a nod and a smile. He could tell this intriguing woman enjoyed the attention.

Norman was kicking himself. He wanted to be the first one to buy her a drink. The manager had beat him to it. He scoured the room and sized up his competition.

What can I do to get her to notice me?

Putting his stool legs back on the floor, Norman sat up straighter, buttoned his expensive suit coat, and tightened his silk tie. He considered putting on his Stetson Diamante cowboy hat but decided he might have a better chance of catching her eye with his thick silver wavy hair which still looked good and at one time women thought was sexy.

Not losing sight of her out of his peripheral vision, Norman motioned to the bartender and ordered a fresh scotch on the rocks. He worked a woman better with a drink in his hand.

The manager suddenly went up on stage as the band stopped playing. He took one of the microphones, and after seeking applause for the band, announced that the bar had a *very* special guest in the room. He motioned to the woman to join him onstage.

"Wanda Rose!" he said excitedly as she made her way up the stairs and stood next to him. It seemed like everyone in the room already knew her name. The reaction from the crowd was immediate as everyone applauded and whistled.

The Wanda Rose?

Norman suddenly remembered. Everyone who loved jazz knew who Wanda Rose was. This must be the famous Wanda Rose who had entertained millions with her incredible voice by singing back in the day with some of the jazz greats like Dorsey and Ellington. Her songs were still played on the radio.

"Wanda, would you like to say a few words?" the manager asked, extending the microphone toward her.

Wanda noticeably blushed when catcalls and whistles went up from the crowd again.

The manager held the microphone to her mouth. She wrapped her long fingers around it.

"Thank you so much," she said in a sexy voice.

"I love you!" someone shouted from the crowd.

"I love all of you too," she said. Her tone was deep, smoky, and sultry.

Like her singing.

"Thank you for the kind welcome," she added.

"Would you sing something for us tonight?" the manager asked with a look of starstruck anticipation.

The crowd roared enthusiastically.

Before Norman realized it, he was clapping and whistling with everyone else.

"You're all so sweet. Ordinarily I would love to sing for you all... but... the doctor has told me that... I need to rest my voice. I'm so sorry.

Definitely next time."

A slight groan permeated through the room.

At that precise moment, Wanda Rose looked toward Norman.

Their eyes met.

Wanda smiled.

Norman returned the smile.

In an instant, Norman was certain he had just met his next wife.

* * *

Of all the men in the bar, Wanda only saw one she thought held any promise. He looked to be six-foot, one. Tall. She liked that. Ruggedly handsome. The room was dark, and the bright lights on the stage were in her eyes, but she thought she saw a Stetson Diamante cowboy hat sitting on the bar counter next to him.

You can tell a lot about a man by his hat.

He definitely had money.

Maybe lots of it.

He was definitely from Texas. A rancher perhaps. Texas men had a certain look about them. A swagger. The Texas sun could be seen on a man's face. He was in his late fifties. About twelve years older than she.

Most importantly, he had the look. His eyes were glazed like he was mesmerized. She could tell when a man was infatuated with her.

Don't let him know you're looking at him.

The urge to move too fast was overwhelming. Wanda was feeling a greater sense of urgency and was doing everything in her power to control it. The money from her divorce settlement would run out in about a year. She'd grown accustomed to a certain lifestyle and was not going to go back to the way things were before.

Money doesn't buy happiness, the saying goes, but neither does poverty as Wanda knew all too well. She'd been rich and she'd been poor and preferred rich much better. For the past six months, she had scoured the bars for a suitable husband. With no success. Maybe she was getting older and not as attractive. Music was changing so not as many people knew who Wanda Rose was. Perhaps she was getting pickier and setting her sights too high.

Whatever the reason, she had little to show for her efforts. Someone always bought her a drink, and usually she could get a free meal out of it. A few men had given her some expensive gifts, but those items weren't always easy to turn into cash. The two, all-expense paid vacations were nice but wouldn't pay the bills.

"Would you sing something for us tonight?" the manager said, jolting Wanda back to reality.

She knew just what to say. "You're all so sweet. Ordinarily I would love to sing for all you all... but... the doctor has told me... I need to rest my voice. I'm so sorry. Definitely next time."

A groan went through the crowd.

Now!

Look at him.

Time to make her move.

Wanda turned slowly toward the man in the far-left corner of the bar. She smiled and batted her eyelashes.

Made direct eye contact.

Don't overdo it.

He returned the smile.

Good.

Wanda turned away with perfect timing.

She blew a few kisses to the crowd and returned to her seat. When the band began playing again, Stetson man didn't come right up to her, which was disappointing. Most men who were interested made a move right away. A number of men did, and she had to politely get them out of the way. A few wanted her autograph which she dutifully gave them.

But others wanted to buy her a drink. That wouldn't work. If she accepted, that meant she had to talk to them. They'd sit down next to her. She had to avoid that scenario. Stetson guy might get impatient and leave.

Finally, a plan formed as the men didn't get the message and didn't disperse as quickly as she would've liked.

"Excuse me, gentlemen, but I need to use the restroom," Wanda said in a sweet voice.

One of the men helped her with her seat. Wanda stood, and slowly, seductively, walked across the room and into the lady's restroom, making sure to keep Stetson man in her peripheral vision. To her delight, his gaze followed her every step.

In the restroom, she looked in the mirror and nervously fixed her hair and makeup, although not much effort was needed. Mostly, she wanted to wait long enough for the men to clear away from her table.

When she exited the restroom, she took a different route back to her seat, one that took her closer to the man at the bar. He was there and still had that same puppy-dog look. Stetson guy was clearly interested which warmed her heart and sent a chill through her spine. Wanda was energized when she got closer to him and saw that he had on an expensive suit and Lucchese cowboy boots.

The man definitely had money.

When she neared him, Wanda stopped and said, "I like your boots, cowboy."

Stetson man looked down at them and then back at her. She got the immediate impression that he only bought Lucchese because they were the most expensive. Fashion was Wanda's area of expertise. She loved shopping for expensive things. Ideas were already running through her head as to what she could buy Stetson man to make him look even better.

Suddenly, a bolt of panic ran through her. Maybe he didn't buy them. What if Stetson guy was married, and his wife bought these things for him as a gift? He didn't have a ring on his finger, but that didn't mean anything. Many men didn't wear wedding rings anymore. Especially in a bar where they were looking to pick up women while they were traveling and away from their wives.

Wanda didn't want an affair. She wanted a husband. A married man was a deal breaker. She wouldn't share his wealth with another woman.

This might be a waste of time.

She decided to go for it anyway and see what she could learn about the intriguing man.

"Hi, I'm Wanda Rose," she said as she extended her hand.

He took her hand, raised it to his lips, and kissed it in a charming way. Then he said, "My name's Norman. It's a pleasure to meet you. Can I buy you a drink?"

"I'd love one," she said as she took a seat on the bar stool next to where he'd been sitting. Through her peripheral vision, she could see the disappointed look on some of the other men's faces as they left her table and skulked back to their seats.

"What're you having?" Norman asked her in a Texas drawl.

"I'll have a gimlet," Wanda said to the bartender who placed a napkin in front of each of them.

"Make it two," Norman said. "Except, make mine with vodka and not gin."

"I'm impressed that you know your drinks," Wanda said shyly.

Norman shrugged his shoulders. Rather than sitting down, he put his elbow on the counter and leaned in closer to her. Wanda sat up perfectly straight with her legs crossed and her hands in her lap. Ladylike. She knew men liked that.

After a few minutes of idle chitchat, Wanda got right to the point. "Are you a Texas rancher?"

She'd already learned that Norman was single and from Texas.

"Oil man. For most of my life." *Even better.*

The band started playing again, and the music helped with the ambiance and the atmosphere Wanda hoped to create. She could tell Norman was interested. He nursed his drink, and constantly looked down to stir it, even fidgeted, while he tried to maintain a calm and cool demeanor. She countered by acting aloof but alluring. A subtle balance she perfected over the years. The emotional dance they played seemed to be work for both of them as they grew more comfortable with each other.

"Why isn't a man like you married?" Wanda asked.

"I *have* been married," he said with a slight grin. "I just wasn't very good at it."

Wanda's laugh was deep and sultry. She touched his arm and said, "My ex-husband wasn't very good at it either."

They both shared a laugh.

Wanda decided to change the subject. Marriage wasn't the best topic for either of them. She already knew everything she needed to know. Norman wasn't married. He was wealthy. Divorced. Not a good husband, which suited her aims fine. A decent guy, so she was safe with him. Most importantly, he was totally into her. This relationship had more potential than any she'd seen over the last few months.

She decided to turn on the charm and let him know she was interested as well. Wanda uncrossed her legs and moved in closer. She kept touching his arm and laughing at his funny remarks. The conversation turned to music, and she spouted off Wanda Rose's resume, hoping he'd be impressed.

Whether he was or not, she couldn't tell because he seemed so impressed with her anyway that he was already putty in her hands. And she genuinely liked him, which was a bonus. What was not to like? Norman reminded her of the Marlboro man in the cigarette ads. Tall, dark, and handsome as they say.

"Do you want to get out of here?" he asked.

Surprising but a welcomed question, even if it was forward.

A rush of excitement shot through her veins. Wanda looked around the bar, not wanting to sound too eager. When she believed enough time had passed, she stood up, straightened her dress, took one last drink to calm her nerves, and said, "Definitely. I'm ready to go."

Norman pulled out a wallet bulging with cash and left a hundred-dollar bill on the counter for the bartender.

"Keep the change," he said.

It took every bit of self-control Wanda could muster to keep her mouth from gaping open.

Her last thought as they were leaving the bar was, *I think I just found my next ex-husband.*

4
1984

"We got married three weeks later," Norman said to Cathy with a huge grin on his face like he was proud of himself.

He told her about the night he met Wanda Rose in a bar in New Orleans. Now, he dropped the bombshell that they were married three weeks after they met. Cathy had their marriage certificate and knew the date but hadn't known that it had been a whirlwind romance of lightning-fast speed.

"What took you so long?" Cathy asked jokingly. She felt more comfortable around Norman now. So far, she hadn't asked a single question he didn't answer. He joked with her as much as she joked with him.

"I would've married her that night, if I could've."

"Why didn't you?"

"My attorney wouldn't let me. The same one I told to shoot me if I ever wanted to get married again." They both let out a laugh.

"He didn't shoot me, obviously, but he insisted that Wanda sign a prenuptial agreement." Norman got a faraway look as he remembered. "Also, Wanda couldn't find her birth certificate or social security card.

That took time to find."

Cathy nodded her head. "I couldn't find her birth certificate as well," she said. "I've looked everywhere for it."

"You won't find it."

"Why not?"

"Because Wanda Rose is not her real name," Norman said.

"What?"

Cathy couldn't believe what she heard, and she slapped her forehead with the palm of her hand. This was huge.

"Her real name is Wanda O'Neil," Norman said. "Wanda Rose is her stage name."

Now Cathy wished she had that pen and paper so she could write down this new information. They were still in the study, in the chairs in front of the fireplace.

Actually, no way would she'd forget that important fact. It opened an entirely new line of investigation.

The large painting of Wanda above the fireplace suddenly seemed even bigger. Cathy had a weird sensation that Wanda was right there in the room. Her picture hovered over them like the proverbial fly on the wall.

Wanda O'Neil. Her mind raced like a stallion that had been let out of his stable. She tried to process all of the ramifications but there were too many.

What did it mean for the claim? Was the policy invalid if it was in the wrong name?

That would be a technicality, but many claims were denied for lesser reasons. Could she deny it on those grounds?

Probably not.

Maybe.

That would be a question for legal to answer.

She continued to sort through all the possibilities. Cathy could deny the claim and let Wanda fight it. But would her boss, Hawkins, sign off on it?

Probably not.

The thought of her boss sent a bolt of anger through her. He had taught her to look for any reason to deny a claim. However, Miles Fire & Casualty wasn't as unscrupulous as some insurance companies. The worst ones denied every claim that was filed and fought them until they had no other choice but to pay them. Most people weren't willing to fight. The adjusters were trained to look for the ones who would give in easily and deny those claims even if they were legitimate.

Thankfully, her company wasn't that way. She could look for technicalities, but they had to be reasonable. Fraud was the best way to deny a claim.

Was this fraud?

The name on the policy was Wanda Rose. She wasn't Wanda Rose. Her name was Wanda O'Neil. Legally.

If she weren't really Wanda Rose, that would be fraud.

Cathy dismissed the ridiculous thought immediately. The possibility that she wasn't Wanda Rose had been ruled out long ago. One look at an album cover, and anyone could see that the woman who filed the claim was, indeed, the famous Wanda Rose. Every picture was a perfect match.

Even the painting on the wall. The artist drew an exact likeness of the woman she had met back in LA who lived in the townhouse and filed the claim. Cathy wanted to shake her fist at Wanda but didn't because Norman was there. Desperation was building inside of her that she wouldn't be able to find anything to justify not paying the claim.

The possibility that Wanda Rose was an alias had never crossed her mind. A rookie mistake. Many stars used an alias. Admittedly, less common back in the early 1900s, but it did happen. Doris Day's real name was Doris Mary Ann Kappelhoff. Most famously, Marilyn Monroe was Norma Jean Mortenson. When she couldn't find Wanda's birth certificate, she should've thought of that possibility.

Maybe she did and just didn't remember to follow up. Either way, she was on the right track now. She'd find that birth certificate before she made a final decision on the claim.

"I have a copy of her birth certificate," Norman said calmly.

A jolt went through Cathy like she had just taken a large gulp of strong coffee.

"May I see it?" she asked.

"Of course. But it's upstairs."

Norman let out a groan as he put both hands on the arms of the chair and pushed himself to his feet. Cathy wanted to reach out and help him but didn't think it appropriate. Norman was a proud and self-sufficient man. He'd probably resent the help. So, Cathy waited for him to catch his balance as he held his arms out to steady himself. Then she stood along with him. He took the cane off the table next to his chair and started to walk out of the study to the front entrance.

Cathy assumed he wanted her to follow him.

He stopped at the bottom of the stairs in the foyer, right inside the huge double doors. The ceiling in the entrance had to be at least thirty feet high. A massive marble staircase was the centerpiece of the entrance hall. Cathy had seen it when she first entered the house. Twelve feet wide, it curved in a backward crescent moon to a landing at the top where a railing overlooked the foyer. A huge chandelier illuminated the area. Noticeably, there were no pictures on the wall, although the faded paint told Cathy there had been at one time.

More items that were probably sold for less than their value.

Norman took a second to catch his breath.

Cathy wondered if he suffered from asthma. He clearly didn't smoke. Maybe chemicals from the years in the oil fields had damaged his lungs. An occasional wheeze could be heard behind his words. How would he make it up the steps?

"Upstairs is a large bedroom," Norman said. "That was Wanda's room. Second door on the left. You can't miss it... At the top of the steps turn right. Then it's the second left. In the closet is a box. On the outside of the box is Wanda's name. The birth certificate is in that box."

Cathy hesitated. Norman clearly expected her to go and get it by herself. Not that she minded, but she wasn't comfortable walking around his upstairs without him. It didn't seem appropriate. If something ended up missing, she could be blamed for it.

That seemed like an unnecessary worry.

Norman must've sensed her reluctance. "It's okay," he said, and waved his hand dismissively. "You won't hurt anything. You can see the rest of the house. Tell me if my housekeeper keeps it clean."

Norman let out a chuckle which turned into a full-blown cough.

"I'd be more comfortable if you went with me," Cathy said.

"Honey. I haven't been up those stairs in ten years. I don't intend to start now. The stairs are too steep and too slippery."

Cathy started to object further.

Norman shook his head and let out a tsk. "I'll go to my grave and never see that upstairs again," he said bitterly. "Doesn't matter. Nothing but bad memories up there anyway."

"Are you sure?"

Norman raised his cane and swung it like he planned to playfully swat her on the backside but stopped short as she scooted away from him.

"Do you want the birth certificate or not?" he said roughly like he was done playing. "It doesn't matter to me. I'll go back to the study to sit down.

You can do whatever you want."

With that, Norman abruptly turned and walked slowly away.

Cathy looked up the stairs then at Norman, and then turned her gaze back to the top of the stairs. For whatever reason, she felt fear.

Of what, she didn't know. What she did know was that she wanted that copy of the birth certificate. She had to overcome her fear to get it.

It'll be all right.

Her boss would be infuriated if he knew she did something so reckless.

What he doesn't know won't hurt him.

She willed her feet to move and took the first step. Then another. She clutched the rail and looked back to see the backside of Norman as he walked out of sight and down the hallway. Emboldened, she headed up.

Norman was right. The steps were slick. She gripped the railing like a vise. The housekeeper had clearly kept them polished which was why they had such a bright shine, almost a glow. Norman was smart not to go up there by himself.

At the top of the steps were two long hallways going two different directions. The upstairs of the house was as big as the downstairs except for the area in the high ceilings of the foyer.

Cathy took the hallway to the right as Norman had instructed. Once she got out of the light of the chandelier, the hallway grew dark.

Her fear had turned to suspense. A mix of anxiety and anticipation.

The door to the second room on the left was slightly ajar, and she pushed it the rest of the way open. The only thing in the room was a queen size poster bed. The floor was hardwood but bare of the usual furnishings. The bed was neatly made with an old, but plush, red velvet blanket with an N and a W embroidered into a heart in the center. Probably representative of Norman and Wanda.

This might've been their bed. Cathy felt like an intruder. Her heartbeat pounded in her ears.

She looked around before proceeding further. She could honestly report back that the maid kept the room immaculate. There wasn't a cobweb or a speck of dust anywhere. Even the windows were clear and clean on the inside.

When she saw the closet, she quickened her step. The door was open. She flipped on the light. A large walk in, completely empty except for one box on the shelf above bars to hang the clothes.

The words, *Wanda Rose*, were written in faded, black, magic marker on the outside of the box, and sent a chill through her all the way down to her toes. Cathy reached up and pulled the box forward until she could get a good grip on it and bring it down. The box was heavier than she expected it to be.

It didn't seem appropriate to open it there, so she flipped off the light and carried it back downstairs.

Norman wasn't in the study. He'd gone back to the dining room. The table was a better place to spread out the papers. As much as Cathy hated that room, she also wanted her file to take notes.

With the box now on the table, Cathy waited for Norman to take the lead. She didn't feel like it was her place to open it.

Norman removed the lid. "Let's see what secrets we can find in here," he said mischievously.

Secrets? What did that mean?

Cathy placed one leg up on the chair and leaned over the table like a kid might sit.

She couldn't remember the last time a case held this much excitement and intrigue.

* * *

The copy of the birth certificate was old and faded but readable.

Name of Child: Wanda O'Neil

Sex: Female

Color: White

Date of Birth: November 5, 1912

Father's Name: Andros O'Neil

Father's Birthplace: Ireland

Father's Age: 22 Years

Father's Occupation: Iron Finisher

Mother's Name: Rose O'Neil

Mother's Name before Marriage: Rose Kennedy

Mother's Birthplace: New York City

Mother's Age: 17 years

Mother's Occupation: Embroiderer

Signatures. P. Miller. Attending Physician.

Rose Kennedy. Mother.

The signature line for the father was noticeably blank.

Cathy's hand shook as she held the birth certificate in her hand. In some ways, she felt like she did something wrong. Like she invaded Wanda's private space, even though the document was public record and she could easily get it herself now that she knew Wanda's real name.

Why had Wanda kept it a secret from her?

Or did she really?

To give Wanda the benefit of the doubt, she had gone by Wanda Rose for so long, she probably didn't even think about her old identity. The whole world knew her as Wanda Rose. That name was on her marriage certificate and every other document Cathy had ever seen, including the policy application.

Norman poured himself another glass of tea and took a big sip. He seemed uninterested, except for a slight smirk as he seemed to take pleasure in Cathy's response. He'd obviously seen the document before, probably a long time ago, but he undoubtedly wondered the same thing Cathy also questioned.

What difference does it make?

The birth certificate intrigued her, but Cathy didn't know how it affected the claim other than it was proof that Wanda didn't use her real name in the application for coverage. Cathy didn't really think that argument had merit. Wanda paid the premiums and was well-known as Wanda Rose. Her boss probably wouldn't want to go down that road.

Still... something about the birth certificate seemed off. Cathy couldn't pinpoint the uneasy feel.

Norman must've sensed it because he said, "That's not *the* Rose Kennedy."

The words startled Cathy. She looked back down at the certificate. Wanda's mother's name was Rose Kennedy. Cathy hadn't made the connection to the President's mother. That wasn't the source of her angst, but it interested her.

"How do you know?" Cathy asked. "They are about the same age."

"Wanda's mother died in childbirth."

"Oh... I'm sorry."

Why she said she was sorry to Norman, she didn't know. Except that an overwhelming sadness had suddenly come over her. She genuinely felt sorry for Wanda.

"Do you know why her father didn't sign the birth certificate?"

"No idea. Wanda didn't know either. She never knew her father."

"Who raised her?"

"No one. She went to an orphanage."

"What about grandparents?"

"Wanda never knew anything about her mother or father until she turned sixteen," Norman explained. "The orphanage gave her a copy of her file with the birth certificate when they released her. That's when Wanda changed her name from O'Neil to Rose, so she'd be named after her mother. Then she destroyed the birth certificate.

Burned the whole file and moved to New Orleans where she became a singer. At least that's what she said happened."

Why did Norman say that line sentence? Did he not believe her story?

"Did she legally change her name?" Cathy asked. If she did, then her application for coverage was definitely legitimate.

Norman just shrugged his shoulders. "I don't think so."

"Interesting."

"She did change her name to Hurst when we got married, but she changed it back after the divorce. I didn't care. Since we didn't have kids."

What is it about the birth certificate? Something's not right.

Cathy stared at it.

A question suddenly came to her mind. "If she burned her birth certificate, how did you get this copy?" For that matter, how did you get married without it?"

"My lawyer pulled some strings and had a copy expedited from the archives in Canton, New Jersey. It arrived a couple days before the wedding."

"I'm sure that was a relief to both of you."

"To be honest, the birth certificate was the least of our problems. By that time, I didn't think the wedding would happen."

Cathy set the birth certificate on the table and leaned forward. "Why not?"

"Wanda didn't want to get married."

"How come?"

"She didn't want to sign the prenup."

Cathy leaned all the way forward in her chair. "Tell me about that," she said.

5
1955

Fort Worth, Texas

Norman was happier than he had been at any other time in his life. Two weeks ago, he met Wanda Rose, who was the reason for the sudden change in his emotional fortunes. What started out as a fling had turned into a fast-tracked marriage now only a week away. Getting all the arrangements in place in that short of time was the biggest challenge. The task at the moment was choosing an engagement and wedding ring for Wanda.

Someone recommended *Sparks Jewelers,* and Zane Sparks, a Swedish immigrant who Norman thought had the perfect name for selling diamonds, was showing Wanda his high-end selection of options. After three hours, she had narrowed it down to three.

"I like that one," Norman said, pointing to the one in the middle. He didn't really care which one she got; he just wanted to get it over with.

The diamond-studded solitaire surrounded by clusters of diamonds in a yellow-gold setting, sat on a wool pad on his desk. Zane picked it up carefully, dusted it off, and then blew on it. After the big production was over, he put it on Wanda's finger.

For what seemed to Norman like the hundredth time.

Wanda let out a squeal. "It's beautiful," she said, holding her hand out away from her body so she could look at it from a distance.

"It brings out the color in your eyes," Zane said in a heavy accent.

Norman wasn't sure how that was even possible, considering the ring was a couple feet from her eyes. He chuckled to himself.

Mostly, he was trying to relieve the boredom. Ring shopping was not his thing. Wanda wanted to pick out a ring for him, but he shot that down in no time. He'd never worn a ring or any piece of jewelry and wasn't about to start now. Truth be known, he considered jewelry a racket. Diamonds and the like were a waste of money as far as he was concerned.

A sentiment he didn't dare express to Wanda who was having the time of her life.

"Let me try this one again," Wanda said, pointing at the biggest and what Norman assumed was the most expensive of the three.

Norman let out a sigh on the outside and a loud groan on the inside. At this point, he didn't care what it cost. He just wanted her to choose one.

"I love it," Wanda said. "This is definitely the one."

"How much is it?" Norman asked, even though he was afraid to know the answer. Anything over a few hundred dollars was too much for a ring as far as he was concerned.

Zane opened a book and turned several pages before stopping at one. His finger scrolled halfway down the page. "Seventy-five thousand dollars," he said.

"We'll take it," Norman blurted. That was more than he wanted to spend but less than he had spent on his first two wives, so overall, considering inflation, he was satisfied.

"Honey, are you sure?" Wanda asked. "That's a lot of money."

"I'm sure. You're worth it," Norman said, forcing a smile.

Wanda let out another cry of delight and kissed Norman right on the lips. A smack that echoed throughout the entire room. His heart skipped a beat at the gesture. That didn't make the expenditure worth it, but it sure made him feel good in that moment.

Wanda's smile was genuine and bordered on elation. It warmed his heart to see her so happy. He didn't know her whole life story, but it seemed like Wanda had had a lot of heartache in her life.

"We'll size it for you and have the ring ready tomorrow after three. Will that work?" Zane asked with a big smile on his face.

He seemed to be as excited as Wanda. Why wouldn't he be? A sale like that probably didn't come along that often.

"That'll be fine," Norman answered.

With that task completed, they walked out of the store hand in hand. Wanda had such a bounce in her step Norman could barely keep up as they walked toward the car.

"What now?" Norman asked once they reached it.

"I've got an appointment to pick out a wedding dress in thirty minutes."

Norman looked at his watch. He really didn't want to go. His mind raced to find an excuse to get out of it.

Wanda must've sensed it because she said, "You can't go with me. It's bad luck to see the bride in her dress before the wedding."

Norman tried to put a look of disappointment on his face, but he didn't know if he succeeded. Whether he did or not, Wanda didn't seem to notice. She was so excited, he imagined nothing he could say or do would dampen her enthusiasm.

He looked at her with deep affection and tried to savor that moment with Wanda. Sear it into his memory. From what he remembered about marriage things would never get better than they were right then.

"How long will it take for you to pick out a dress?" Norman asked, already knowing that she had no idea.

"All afternoon," she said.

Perfect.

A huge relief came over him. That meant that he was done with wedding stuff for the day. Honestly, he preferred they go to the Justice of the Peace and skip all of the expense of a big wedding. Since that wasn't possible, the least amount of time he had to spend on it, the better. Having been married twice before, he knew this was a waste of time. The rings.

Dresses. Reception. The whole production.

For him. Not for her.

He did his best to match her excitement.

"I'll meet you for dinner at six," Norman said. "*Alfredo's* restaurant. It's near where you're trying on dresses."

Wanda had said Italian was her favorite food. He preferred a big steak and a baked potato, but this was a special occasion. He had something to discuss with her. Between the expensive ring, trying on wedding dresses, and eating her favorite food, maybe that might soften the blow and help the conversation go better.

Norman was truly dreading tonight.

* * *

Alfredo's

Today had been one of the best days of Wanda's life. They had just finished dinner when a serious look suddenly came on Norman's face as his eyes narrowed and his eyebrows furrowed.

"There's something I need to talk to you about," he said.

His tone was so somber that it sent a jolt of anxiety through Wanda. *What could it possibly be?*

The day had been perfect. She'd picked out a ring and a dress, and Norman had proved his willingness to spend money on her. That was a big step in their relationship. More confirmation that she was making the right choice by marrying him. Wanda had met men in the past who acted like they had a lot of money but didn't. Others had a lot of money but wouldn't spend it on her. Norman was the perfect balance. He had a lot of money and was willing to spend it. Norman had spent more than a hundred thousand dollars on her today. Whatever he wanted to talk about couldn't be that serious. Not enough to affect the wedding at least.

"This sounds serious," Wanda said, trying not to be concerned.

Norman pulled some papers out of his inside coat pocket.

He stared at them before speaking. "These are some papers my lawyer wants you to sign."

His voice cracked slightly as he said it.

He's nervous. That was making her nervous. "What are they?" Wanda asked. She tried not to show it on her face or demeanor.

"A prenuptial agreement."

Norman set the papers on the table between them. Wanda didn't immediately pick them up. She didn't know what a prenuptial agreement was.

"You'll have to explain it to me," Wanda said. "I'm not good when it comes to legal stuff. Is it a will or something?"

"Not exactly. A prenuptial agreement defines how my assets are divided in case we get a divorce."

"Divorce! We're not even married yet, and you're talking about a divorce?"

Her reaction was instinctive and stronger than what she expected. She was passionate and impulsive that way.

"It's my lawyer's idea," Norman said defensively. "My last marriage only lasted three years. My ex-wife got almost three-hundred-million dollars."

Wanda's heart did a complete somersault. She thought she did okay, getting a quarter of a million from her ex-husband.

"What does that have to do with us, sweetie? I'm not your ex-wife."

"I didn't think it was fair that she got so much of my money."

Wanda swallowed hard, trying to get the lump out of her throat. She needed to agree with him, but that wasn't to her advantage.

"I guess I see what you mean," she said instead.

"This agreement specifies how much you would get if for some reason we got a divorce."

"Why would we get a divorce? I want to be your wife for the rest of my life."

Wanda tried to sound as sincere as she could when she said it.

"I know, and I want that too," he said. "I don't think we're going to get a divorce. But if we did, this agreement protects me from having to pay out too much in a divorce settlement."

Wanda debated on whether to be angry or hurt. She decided on hurt and reached for a tissue out of her purse. In a way, the tears were real. Depending on the amount, she may not want to marry him. Her hopes were being dashed before her eyes.

"Don't cry until you see the numbers," Norman said, picking up the papers from the table. "I think it's very generous."

With the papers in hand, he reached across the table to hand them to her. She took them but then slammed them down rattling the glasses.

Time to try anger. "Exactly how much do you think it's worth to get rid of me?" she said with a furious scowl.

"It's not like that. I promise. But think about it. We barely know each other."

"I know you well enough to know that I want to marry you. I've never wanted anything more in my life. If we're going to get married, I want it to be forever."

She choked back some tears as she said it... for effect.

The waiter appeared at the moment causing an abrupt pause in the conversation. Norman dabbed at his mouth with his napkin as the waiter took the plates away.

"Would you like any dessert?" the waiter asked.

"Can you give us a minute?" Norman said.

When he was gone, Norman leaned forward. "I want to marry you too."

"Then some stupid agreement shouldn't matter to you," Wanda said.

"It's just that my attorney..."

Wanda interrupted Norman and asked angrily, "Do you think I'm marrying you for your money?"

"If you aren't then some stupid agreement shouldn't matter to you," Norman said without hesitation.

He had a point.

The conversation was spiraling out of control, and she didn't know the best way to respond. Wanda was concerned that if she didn't play her cards right, the entire marriage was in jeopardy of not happening. At this point, she had nothing to show for her efforts. At the same time, depending on what the agreement said, the whole marriage might not be worth it anyway.

She didn't know what to say, so she turned her head to the side and dabbed the tears away from her eyes. "Maybe we should wait to get married," she said. Reverse psychology was always a good fall back strategy.

"I don't know that we need to postpone the wedding." Norman reached across the table and tried to take her hand, but she pulled it away from him.

"Like you said, we don't know each other very well," Wanda said bitingly.

She suddenly put her hand to her mouth and gasped. She opened her eyes as wide as they would go.

"What is it?" Norman asked.

"We've already ordered my dress," she said. "And the ring. Can you still get your money back?"

"Honey... I know you're upset. I'm sorry. Let's not do anything rash.

I want to marry you. Read the agreement, and then we can discuss it." Wanda picked up the papers from the table but didn't look at them.

"So how much do I get?" she asked caustically.

"Read the agreement."

"Just tell me."

"You get a million dollars a year for each year we're married. If we're married when I die, then you get it all."

Two weeks ago, Wanda would've jumped at that deal. Now, she was insulted. It wasn't generous at all!

He's worth more than half a billion dollars.

The oil business was booming. A million dollars a year was chump change for him.

"Let me think about it," she said coolly.

"Can we talk about it?"

"I said I'd think about it!"

Norman looked away, seemingly unsure what to do.

"Do you want any dessert?" he asked.

"I'm not hungry. I just want to go home."

Norman paid the bill, and they left. The half-hour drive home was torturous as the silence between them stretched on.

When they got back to the estate, they stood in front of the large marble staircase in the foyer. Wanda said she was going to bed. Norman had followed her that far and stopped her before she went upstairs.

He tried to hand her the papers. She wouldn't take them.

Wanda asked him, "What happens if I don't sign it?"

"I guess it means we aren't getting married."

"Okay. At least I know where I stand. I'll let you know. I'm going to bed." Wanda started up the stairs.

"I'll leave the papers in the study in case you want to look at them. I need to know something in the morning. Like you said... we need time to cancel the ring and the dress."

Wanda could no longer control the tears as they rushed out of her eyes and down her cheeks with the force of a sudden spring shower.

* * *

She tossed and turned all night. She had a lot on her mind. The conversation pulsed around in her head like a migraine headache. This was the last thing she expected. The day had been so perfect.

Ironically, Norman was everything she ever wanted in a husband.

Until this.

She cursed the stupid lawyer under her breath, trying not to wake Norman who was lying next to her. When she realized she wouldn't be able to fall asleep, she got out of bed and walked quietly downstairs trying not to disturb him. The last thing she wanted was for him to wake up and them start talking about it again.

She needed time to think. Impulsively, what she really wanted to do was leave that night. If she had transportation, she might've done so. As long as she was there, she might as well read the papers sitting on the desk in the study where Norman had left them.

She settled in one of the chairs in front of the fireplace. The terms were straightforward. Except for all the legalese. Wanda pushed aside the tears and choked them back so she could think clearly and without emotion.

The moon cast an eerie shadow over the room as she set the papers back on the desk and turned the lights off.

The pros and cons weighed on her mind.

Texas.

That was a con.

She was a city girl, and the thought of living out on the ranch wasn't appealing to her.

The house.

That was a definite plus.

Wanda loved the house. Norman's ex-wife decorated it and had spared no expense. The furnishings were nicer than anything she'd ever seen before. The only thing she didn't like was the picture over the fireplace.

That would have to be replaced.

The location.

A con.

The house was so far from everything. She wanted to pick it up and put it in downtown Fort Worth. Wanda was a city girl. The hustle and bustle of a big city energized her.

Norman.

A plus in so many ways.

Norman was a decent guy. She hated to hurt him.

Being married to him wouldn't be that bad. Norman said that he'd be working a lot and wouldn't be around that much. That was fine with her. Or at least it would be if she lived in the city. Out here all alone, she might go crazy with only the coyotes to keep her company.

She could envision being alone, a lot. Wanda craved attention. Men fawned over her in every bar in New Orleans. They all knew her and loved her. While most people in Texas had heard of Wanda Rose, they weren't starstruck like they were in other places.

Wanda's dream was to live in Beverly Hills. There she would get attention. The name Wanda Rose would draw the best seats at restaurants, concerts, and plays. She would impress men. They had money out there.

I'd have to stay with Norman at least five years before I could afford to move to LA.

Five years was a long time.

Definitely a con.

Maybe she should go there now. Cut her losses. If she already had the ring, she could sell it, and that would buy her an extra month or two. Wanda quickly dismissed that thought. Starting over in LA wasn't an option. Too expensive, and she didn't know anyone.

Norman was clearly her best option for now.

The money.

That was a plus.

A million dollars a year was a lot of money. And it wasn't just a million. She'd be able to spend all she wanted. Norman wouldn't say anything. She could buy more things. Clothes. Jewelry. Cars. Things she could take with her in the divorce settlement. She might be able to turn the million dollars a year into twice that.

Should she roll the dice and wait for a better offer?

A man in the hand...

An opportunity like this might not come her way again. And Norman wasn't that bad. She genuinely liked him. When he said that it was his lawyer's idea, she believed him. If she didn't, she might've definitely said no.

A thought suddenly occurred to her. Could she negotiate with him?

Make it two million dollars a year?

Then she could leave after two or three years if she wanted.

That might make him mad.

He'd think she was only marrying him for the money. Call the whole thing off. That wasn't worth the risk.

I have to do it.

No, I don't. I can go back to New Orleans. I found Norman. Someone else will come along.

She got out of her chair, walked over to the desk, and sat down.

Thinking.

She picked up a pen and tapped it nervously on the papers.

Then she decided.

Satisfied, Wanda walked quietly up the stairs and slipped back into bed. "Norman, dear. Are you awake?" she asked. He had his back to her.

"Yes. I couldn't sleep."

"Me either. I've been thinking about our conversation."

"And?"

"I made a decision."

He didn't say anything.

"I signed the papers."

"Really?" he said, turning over.

"Of course. It's not about the money. It's about being married to you. That's what I want."

"That's what I want too."

She kissed him passionately. Norman wrapped his arms around her and squeezed her close to him like he had just found something he thought he'd lost.

Maybe he really does love me, she thought.

Who knows? Maybe someday I'll grow to love him too.

6

1984

"Why would Wanda be so concerned about a prenup?" Cathy asked Norman. "She had lots of money."

Norman had just told Cathy the fascinating story of how he was able to get Wanda to sign a prenup. From the sounds of it, the marriage almost didn't happen.

Norman shook his head no to Cathy's question about the prenup. She didn't know what he meant until he explained it to her.

"When I first met Wanda, she barely had twenty-thousand dollars to her name," Norman said. "That was a lot of money back then, but not enough to keep her in the lifestyle she wanted. Certainly not for the glamorous star everyone assumed she was."

"How is that possible?" Cathy asked. "She had three divorce settlements by the time she met you. All of her ex-husbands were rich."

"She never talked about her first two husbands. I know that she did get $250,000 from her third husband. Dick was his name... I think."

"Dick Lawlor."

"Right." A look of remembrance flashed across Norman's eyes.

Cathy wasn't surprised that he didn't remember a lot of details about Wanda's exes. Even then, she was impressed with his recall. While his body was failing, his mind was still as sharp as a whetstone.

"Lawlor was in construction in New Orleans," Cathy explained, refreshing his memory, or maybe giving Norman new information.

"He built commercial bridges and the like," she continued. "I think there's even a bridge named for him in Louisiana somewhere. Anyway. . . from what I can gather, he was pretty well off."

"Wanda liked expensive things," Norman said. "She always wanted to project a certain image. The night I met her, she was down on her luck, although, I didn't know it at the time. My first clue was that the beautiful sequined dress she was wearing was being held up by a safety pin."

That seemed strange. Wanda had millions of dollars flow through her hands over the years. Apparently, when she moved to LA, all she had to show for it was the money Norman gave her in the divorce settlement. Now that money was probably gone except for the equity in the townhome in LA.

It did happen to the best of them. Cathy researched all the jazz and blues greats from Wanda's era. When Billie Holiday died, her estate had a thousand dollars in it.

That might explain why Wanda was trying to get the money for the necklace.

Why, though? Wanda's royalty checks every month should be enough to live on. Something wasn't adding up. Why was Wanda broke when she met Norman? Why did she need money now?

Maybe she was one of those who spent more than she made, regardless of the sum.

"What about her albums?" Cathy asked. "She made a royalty on those. Still does, I'm sure."

Cathy flipped over to her notes. Wanda had made fourteen studio albums, forty-three singles, and one live album. Most of them were big hits. That was a large number for someone in her era.

Norman shook his head again.

He started shuffling through the box. Cathy's curiosity was going through the roof to the point that it was hard to sit still. This whole conversation was fascinating to her, although it felt a little bit like gossip. She wasn't sure how it applied to her investigation, but her inquisitive nature didn't allow her to change the subject to something more relevant.

"Here's what I'm looking for," Norman said as he pulled a file out of the box and opened it.

"What's this?" Cathy asked as he handed her some papers.

The documents were old. Cathy was almost afraid to handle them. Gingerly, she sat them down in front of her and began reading. Within seconds, she recognized it as a contract.

Wanda's recording agreement.

Cathy knew her way around a contract, and even though some of the ink was faded, she understood the basic terms.

July 7, 1929.

That was the date of execution. Cathy did the math in her head. Wanda was sixteen.

Happy O'Brian Agency. In New Orleans.

That name was on the letterhead. This must've been when Wanda left the orphanage and found her way to New Orleans.

Wanda Rose, Employee.

Not a recording contract. This was a representation agreement with an agent.

Ten years.

That was the term of the agreement.

"A ten-year agreement is a long time," Cathy said, looking up at Norman who nodded his head. "I wonder how common it was to sign someone for ten years. Happy O'Brian must've known he had a special talent in Wanda. He was obviously right."

Norman said, "The agreement said that O'Brian could renew it at his option every ten years."

She looked down at the contract and turned to the fine print on the second page. She didn't see it right away. Norman reached over and pointed to it. Norman knew his way around contracts better than she did, she presumed, being an oil man for sixty-plus years. He probably had this one memorized since she was his wife of twelve years.

Cathy read the fine print out loud.

"Sixty days before the expiration of this agreement, Agent may, at his sole discretion, renew this agreement for additional ten-year terms at a compensation to be determined by Agent but no less than the original terms outlined in this agreement."

"That's not fair!" Cathy said. "Wanda should've never signed this. I suppose she didn't have an attorney."

The look on Norman's face clearly showed that he felt the same way. His nose was crinkled, and his lips curled in obvious disgust.

"Wanda was just sixteen," he said. "She didn't know what she was doing. Getting a recording deal was big at the time. She probably thought she was the luckiest girl alive."

"A long-term deal is good if the compensation is fair," Cathy said. "But this says the agent can set the compensation at anything he wants. If he wanted, he could really take advantage of her."

Cathy put her finger on the page and scrolled down each page trying to find where the terms were outlined. She found it in Addendum A.

Her mouth flew open like a shark going after a seal. She read it out loud for both of their benefit. "Employee will receive $100.00 at the signing of this agreement. $200.00 for each album recorded. $50.00 for each single." Cathy turned to her notes which had Wanda's number of album sales. Two hundred dollars times fourteen albums was only twenty-eight hundred dollars. Two-thousand, one hundred, and fifty dollars was the sum she was paid for the singles.

Add in the hundred dollar signing bonus, and Wanda made a grand total of five thousand and fifty dollars on her albums!

Cathy could feel the rage building inside of her from the injustice that was unfolding before her eyes. The fact that the agreement didn't pertain to her and was dated fifty-six years ago was irrelevant. Her personal animosity for Wanda Rose aside, this was highway robbery. Happy O'Brian was a despicable lowlife for taking advantage of a vulnerable sixteen-year-old girl in such an obviously deceitful way.

"That O'Brian guy was a shyster!" Cathy said.

"The Great Depression started in 1929. That's the year the contract was signed," Norman said. "It probably seemed like a lot of money to Wanda at the time."

"Happy O'Brian made millions off of her. How much does she get in royalties?"

Norman held up his hand and formed his thumb and index finger into a zero.

"No way!"

"That's the truth. You can read it yourself in the contract."

Agent retains all copyright and royalty rights.

The clause was right there in big letters. "That's got to be illegal!" Cathy said, raising her voice. "Aren't record companies required to pay royalties by law?"

"They did pay royalties. To Happy O'Brian. Wanda never saw a dime of it. His estate is probably still getting royalties from her records. Every time they are played on the radio, he gets a royalty. Even today. Or at least his kids and grandkids do. I assume Happy O'Brian is dead."

"I can't believe it!" Cathy said. "This contract cost Wanda millions of dollars. Was there any way for her to get out of it?"

"I had my attorney look into it."

"What did he say?"

"That what O'Brian did was perfectly legal. The contract was valid.

Wanda performed a service and was paid under the terms of the contract."

"But she was a minor when she signed it," Cathy suddenly remembered something she had read somewhere.

Norman pointed his shaky finger at Cathy in acknowledgment.

"Bingo! That was our best argument. Technically, contracts entered into by minors can be voided by the minor because they lack the mental capacity to enter into it."

Cathy waited for him to continue rather than asking another question.

When he didn't, she asked, "Why didn't you fight it?"

"Wanda didn't want to. For whatever reason, she was afraid to go down that road. I almost insisted. I agree with you. It was a bad deal from the very beginning. I think we could've won. Wanda didn't think it made any difference, since I was so rich. I thought it was the principle of the thing.

I couldn't convince her. She's stubborn that way."

A loud bang came from the kitchen.

It startled Cathy. The whole afternoon, the house had been so peaceful and quiet.

It sounded like the back door opened and closed. Norman didn't seem the least bit concerned, so Cathy calmed her already frayed nerves.

"That's Esmeralda," Norman said. "My housekeeper."

Cathy knew he had a housekeeper but hadn't heard her name. A few seconds later, a petite, older Hispanic woman entered the room. She stopped abruptly when she saw Cathy and Norman sitting at the dining room table.

"I'm sorry. I didn't mean to interrupt," she said.

"You're not interrupting," Norman said.

Esmeralda didn't appear to be that much younger than Norman.

Based on first impressions, she wasn't in any better shape to clean that big house than Norman was.

"Esmeralda, this is my friend Cathy," Norman said in a friendly manner.

"Nice to meet you," Cathy said unsure if she should stand or not.

Esmeralda walked the rest of the way into the room and reached out her hand toward Cathy.

Her grip was firm and strong, like the grip of an alligator holding its prey. When Esmeralda released the handshake, Cathy actually rubbed her hand against her leg to shake out the cramp that had suddenly formed.

"We were talking about Wanda," Norman said.

Esmeralda shook her head from side to side, almost disapprovingly. "I never liked that woman," she said, waving both hands in the air.

If Norman hadn't talked to Wanda in seventeen years, that meant that Esmeralda had been his housekeeper for longer than that.

"Are you staying for dinner?" Esmeralda asked.

Cathy didn't realize it had gotten that late. The time was flying by.

"I'm not sure...," Cathy said hesitantly looking at her watch. It was too late to catch a flight, and she suddenly felt her stomach growling. She hadn't eaten lunch. They were so involved in the discussion she had completely forgotten to eat something.

"Of course, she is," Norman said. He seemed to be enjoying the conversation as much as Cathy. "You have to eat Esmeralda's cooking. It's kept me alive for more than forty years."

Based on that statement, Esmeralda started working for him before he even met Wanda.

"I'll cook you up something special," Esmeralda said as she turned and walked out of the room, not waiting for a response.

"I guess I'm staying for dinner."

"You're welcome to spend the night," Norman said, startling Cathy with the nice gesture.

"I have a hotel room," she responded. That wasn't true, but it sounded like the right answer, and the excuse seemed to satisfy Norman.

"If it's all right with you, I'm going to lie down for a few minutes before dinner," Norman said, pushing himself out of his chair. This time, Cathy stood.

"Do you mind if I go through the rest of these documents?" Cathy asked.

"I don't mind at all. Restroom is down the hall if you need it or want to freshen up."

Cathy passed it earlier and made a mental note of its location. Like her hunger pains, she hadn't even noticed that she needed to go.

"I think I'll do that first," Cathy said, waiting for Norman to make his way out of the room. The uncomfortable dining room chair had clearly caused him to stiffen up. Cathy was half his age and her back was aching.

When Cathy returned to the dining room, she dug into the rest of the things in the box, anxious to see what else she might find and no longer feeling uncomfortable in the room.

* * *

Beverly Hills, California

Wanda was furious.

She slammed the pots into the kitchen sink so hard the sound echoed through the entire townhome.

Cathy Tolliver, that despicable woman from the insurance company, was ruining her life. The claim from the fire should have been paid months ago. The repairs to the townhome had to be paid out of her savings account which had already been dwindling at the time of the fire and would be gone soon.

If the matter went on much longer, she'd have to take out a loan. Or find a husband. Something she was determined not to do.

The last man she married, Frazier Webb, had been a bore to live with it. When he lost half his money to a bad investment in a gold mine in Costa Rica, she had to get out of the marriage before he lost everything. Even then, she got less than five million in the divorce settlement.

Five years of her life for a measly five million!

The thought of the man made her shudder.

Now the insurance shrew was talking to her other ex-husband, Norman T. Hurst. That made her almost come unglued. At least Frazier Webb was dead, or she would have probably tried to talk to him too. Thankfully, those secrets went to the grave with him.

When she learned that Cathy was flying to Fort Worth to talk to Norman, the first thing she did was call him. That took a lot of nerve. She hadn't spoken to Norman since the divorce. The conversation was cordial, but at the end of it, she wasn't sure if he would do what he said. She played it back in her mind for the umpteenth time.

"Norman, it's Wanda. How are you, sweetie?" She had tried to be as sweet as possible.

"Wanda Rose. What a surprise! Where are you?" Norman sounded the same to her, just a little weaker.

"I'm in LA. I moved to Beverly Hills."

"You always wanted to live in California."

"I see you still have your same phone number. You must still be in Texas. How is the old homestead?"

"It's still here. Like me. Kind of run down."

Wanda chuckled. "We're not getting any younger, are we? Are you in good health?"

"Something new hurts every day that didn't the day before. That's the only way I know if I'm still alive in the morning. When I wake up, if I feel something hurting, then I assume I'm alive and get out of bed."

Norman always had a witty sense of humor. She missed that about him.

Is he still angry with me?

She'd try and find out.

"It's been a long time," Wanda said. "I hate how things ended between us."

"That was a long time ago. Time has a way of healing old wounds."

"Not all of them," Wanda said, and she meant it. "I miss you and think about you often."

"What can I do for you?" Norman asked, clearly not wanting to go on that walk down memory lane. He hadn't said it in a mean way. Not like he was put out but like he sincerely wondered why she had called out of the blue.

"Do you remember that necklace I had? The one with the blue sapphires and diamonds?"

Wanda's heart started pounding as she waited for the answer.

"I can't say that I do," he said, after pausing for what seemed like an eternity but was only a few seconds. "Did I buy it for you?"

"No. I had it before I met you. I showed it to you. Don't you remember? It was a real expensive necklace. It's worth more than a hundred-thousand dollars."

"Did we put it on our insurance policy?"

"I don't... think we did." Wanda hadn't thought about that. Norman kept every paper. If she said they did, she wouldn't put it past him to dig through the papers and look. When he didn't find anything, he might mention it to the insurance adjuster.

Wanda shook her fist in the air.

"No. I had my own insurance policy on it," Wanda said the first thing that popped into her head. "I don't think we ever bothered to put it on our joint policy."

"I'm sorry, but I honestly don't remember it."

"Like you said, we're getting older every day, and our memories aren't what they used to be. I'm sure you'll remember if you think about it."

"My memory is still pretty good, knock on wood."

She could hear him knocking on something. Probably his desk.

Norman was likely on the phone in his study. She could picture it in her mind. It probably looked the same as the day she left. The portrait of her was probably still over the fireplace. She was afraid to ask. For years, she regretted leaving that behind. Norman said he wanted something to remember her by. That painting was by a famous artist. She could probably get a hundred grand for it in today's market.

"The reason I asked is because an insurance lady is coming to meet with you," Wanda said, wanting to stay on the real reason for the call. "She's going to ask you a lot of questions about the necklace. I was hoping you remembered it." She had to be careful. Asking him to say he did remember could be considered insurance fraud. Norman couldn't be trusted to not tell the lady.

"She's coming tomorrow," Norman said, and her heart sunk a few degrees in her chest.

That dreadful lady was looking for any reason to deny the claim. Wanda was terrified that Norman would say the wrong thing.

"Do you still have that box?" Wanda asked. "You know the one with my things in it."

The box had important papers and photographs. It had gotten left behind in the move and she hadn't had the guts to call and ask him for it. Now she was kicking herself. It would be a disaster if the insurance lady got a hold of it.

"I don't have it," Norman said. "That was thrown out a long time ago."

Wanda let out a sigh of relief with her hand over the phone so he wouldn't hear it, although she wasn't sure she believed him. In twelve years of marriage, she'd never seen him throw away one piece of paperwork.

Even if it was decades old. Now she had reminded him of it. Knowing Norman, he'd go look for it.

She almost wished she hadn't brought it up.

"Anyway, honey," Wanda said. "I was just hoping you remembered the necklace. That would be immensely helpful to me."

"I'm sorry, but I don't. Thanks for calling, though. Call me anytime."

Norman was abrupt that way. He never liked to stay on the phone for long.

Wanda slammed the phone down, almost breaking the receiver.

Norman wouldn't lie for her. She was sure of that. He was as honest as a Texas hound dog. One of his endearing qualities that was infuriating her at the moment.

Since she couldn't count on Norman, that left her no choice.

She'd have to take matters into her own hands.

7

Cathy and Norman finished eating and sat in the study. The sun had set, and nine o'clock was almost upon them. Cathy stayed much longer than she had intended. Esmeralda left several hours ago after cleaning the dishes from what was an amazing meal. Cathy couldn't remember the last time she'd had a home-cooked meal and never one as good as what Esmeralda had dished up.

Norman barely ate half of his. After a full meal, he probably weighed a hundred and sixty pounds. From pictures, Cathy presumed that in his heyday, Norman was well over two hundred pounds of solid muscle. Even then, she was impressed by his stamina. He seemed to be going strong and didn't seem like he wanted the conversation to end anytime soon.

For three hours after dinner, Norman entertained Cathy with stories from the past. They spent the first hour looking through the old photographs in the box—several dozen of them. They were all of Wanda. Some from before she met Norman. The camera loved Wanda as much as she loved posing for it.

Some pictures were of her on the beach in a swimsuit. Most of them were of her dressed to the nines. In cocktail dresses. Entertaining a crowd. A few were of her on stage singing. One was holding a plaque for some achievement in jazz.

Noticeably missing were baby pictures and the usual childhood photographs most people keep in their box of memories.

Norman filled in what information he could about the origin of the pictures. They enjoyed guessing Wanda's age and trying to figure out where she was and what she was doing when the pictures were taken. The photos had absolutely nothing to do with Cathy's investigation, but they were interesting, nonetheless.

Cathy couldn't understand why she was so obsessed with Wanda. A simultaneous sense of sadness and relief came in her heart when she realized the obsession was coming to an end. She'd have to close the file tomorrow when she got back to LA. If she accomplished anything on the trip, she now realized she had no reason to deny the claim. Soon, she'd be able to put this whole nightmare of a case behind her.

In her mind, this turned out to be the biggest failure of her career. The trip to Fort Worth had done nothing but reinforce the belief in her that Wanda was lying about the necklace. Her inability to find the facts to prove it frustrated her. While Norman enjoyed looking at the pictures and talking about Wanda, it grated on her nerves.

She wanted to leave.

Several times Cathy said she had to go, but Norman insisted she stay for another half hour. The half hour turned into an hour. Then two hours. She would've left already, but she felt bad for Norman. He seemed to be relishing the company.

When they were done looking through the box, Cathy began to feel better. The lights were dimmed and one of Wanda's albums played softly in the background. The mood would've been perfect except for the painting on the wall. The ever-present Wanda hovered over them like a hawk circled roadkill.

She got the impression that this was probably how Norman spent every evening.

Alone.

Wanda's songs playing in the background.

Him staring at her picture.

What a sad life to lead.

Actually, she decided, this was probably the only thing left in his life that brought him some comfort. If Wanda couldn't be there in person, then this was the next best thing.

Nothing was said for several minutes as she let Norman savor the moment.

"What are you going to do now?" Norman finally asked.

"I guess I'm going to pay the claim," Cathy said, sighing. "I don't have any proof that Wanda ever owned a necklace, and I can't prove she didn't. So, there's nothing else for me to do."

"I'm sorry I wasn't more help to you."

Cathy waved the comment away even though Norman wasn't looking her way. His gaze was fixed on the image above the fireplace.

He looked her way and said, "Wanda called me yesterday."

"What?" Cathy said, bolting up in her chair. Her heart started doing jumping jacks in her chest.

"First time in seventeen years. I was as surprised as you are now."

"What did she say?"

Was it okay to ask?

She'd soon find out.

"She asked if I remembered the necklace." Cathy almost flew out of her chair.

She's good.

Wanda clearly asked the question in such a way to manipulate a response. Cathy listened carefully to see if Norman revealed anything that could be considered fraud.

"What did you tell her?" Cathy asked.

"I told her what I told you. I didn't remember a necklace."

"Did she ask you to lie?"

"Not in so many words."

"What words did she use?"

"It would be extremely helpful to me if you remembered the necklace." Cathy bristled.

That's just how Wanda was. Evasive and crafty. She was too smart to come right out and ask him to lie for her.

Do you remember the necklace?

Of course, he didn't! There was no necklace.

Wanda already knew the answer to that question but tried to put thoughts in Norman's head. Manipulate the memory of an old man who she hadn't given a second thought to in seventeen years. The contempt for the woman reared its ugly head again just as it started to fade away into a closed case file.

"Was that all she said?" Cathy asked.

"That was it. Mostly. Then the conversation was over."

"Did she even ask how you were doing?"

"She did. Sort of. At first. You know... surface stuff. I got the impression she was just calling about the necklace. So, I ended the call right away."

"I'm sorry you even had to take that call."

"It was good to hear her voice, actually."

Cathy settled back in her chair. She wanted to rip Wanda to shreds and might've if the woman had been in the room. She fought back the urge to say something she might regret. What good would that do? Wanda Rose was the love of Norman's life. He never got over her. That much was clear.

For whatever reason.

It didn't matter how badly Wanda had treated Norman in the past, he was still in love with her. Would be until he died. What place was it of hers to ruin that fantasy?

As if she could.

The call was enough to raise suspicion again but not proof of any wrongdoing on Wanda's part. She wouldn't bring it up to her boss or he would yell at her again. Rightly so. Cathy had nothing but suspicion. No proof whatsoever. This case was over. In some ways, she was glad. This was starting to weigh her down. She had to move on to other things.

Her boss would be happy. Even the slightest attempt to argue her case would result in him raining his full wrath and fury down on her. She didn't think she could handle it. Cathy wished she were back in LA already so she could close the case right away.

Then she shuddered and squirmed in her chair. She'd have to see Wanda one more time. To give her the check and let Wanda take her victory lap. She could see her smug look now. Maybe she could courier the paperwork to her. No. Wanda had to sign a release.

Neither of them said anything for several minutes. Norman got up to start another album. Cathy wanted to get out of there as soon as possible.

"You know, deep down, Wanda does really have a good heart," Norman said.

She turned to him. She most likely wouldn't be leaving anytime soon. She settled back into her chair. "I can tell that you really did love her," Cathy said warmly. The more she focused on Norman and not Wanda the better she would feel. She genuinely felt sorry for him. "She didn't deserve someone as good as you."

"I still love her." Norman's voice cracked as he said it. "I'd take her back tomorrow, if she'd come back."

"Even after all these years?"

"So many times, I dreamed of her walking through that door. I wish I could've gone back in time and done things differently. Don't grow old like me, Cathy, still holding on to regrets. It's a painful way to live."

The sudden urge to give Norman a hug came over her. She despised Wanda that much more. She probably had no idea the pain she'd caused this man.

"I knew at the time that Wanda was marrying me for my money," he said soberly. "But I didn't care. I was tired of being alone." Norman let out a soft chuckle. "Do you want to hear something funny?"

She'd been leaning back against the chair but lifted her head to look directly at him.

"I was going to tear up the prenup," Norman said. "That same night. If Wanda had refused to sign it, I would've torn the damn thing up. That's how bad I wanted to marry her."

Cathy laughed.

Maybe Wanda didn't win after all. She got twelve million dollars in the divorce settlement but could've gotten thirty times that. Cathy couldn't force herself to say anything mean about Wanda, even though it took all her willpower not to do so. Instead, she tried to be understanding and comforting to Norman.

"I think she loved you too," Cathy said, warmly. "She stayed married to you for twelve years. She wouldn't have done that if she didn't feel something. She could've left earlier and become a millionaire."

"I think she did... love me. To the extent that Wanda is capable of loving anyone."

Norman was overcome with emotion as he sunk deeper in the chair. He bit his lip which told her he was fighting back tears. At night, when no one else was around, Cathy wondered if he maintained such self-control.

"Are you going to be all right?" she asked, suddenly feeling badly that she may have opened old wounds.

"I'm glad you came," Norman said, ignoring the question.

"So am I. I'm so glad I got to meet you. You're the only good thing that has come out of this case. Thanks again for dinner, by the way. I don't remember a meal that good."

"We don't have many guests around here. I'm glad we were able to give Esmeralda something to do. She loves to cook. It's boring for her just cooking for me. She likes you."

"I like her too."

"Sorry I didn't know any more about the necklace."

He'd already said that several times. Maybe Norman was starting to lose a little of his short-term memory.

"You were a big help," Cathy said reassuringly. "If nothing else, I think I know Wanda a lot better now. She's lying about the necklace, but at least now I understand why."

One of Wanda's most famous songs started filling the room. A soft, bluesy tune, *I Never Stopped Loving You*. Afraid that the song might cause Norman to sink further into a deeper depression, Cathy decided to change the subject.

"I love this house. It's so big. Do you plan on staying here?"

"I'll die here. Although, not any time soon apparently. My doctor says I'm as healthy as a horse," Norman said. "I've got another ten years left in me."

"At least."

"That's one good thing that did come out of my divorce."

"What's that?"

"I quit drinkin'."

Cathy had noticed Norman hadn't offered her a drink the entire time she was there. She wouldn't have accepted it, but she did find it strange.

"Really?" Cathy said, sitting up in her chair.

The movement gave her a slight burst of energy which was a good thing. She could feel herself starting to fall asleep. The drive to the hotel was at least an hour, so it'd be awhile before she was able to.

"As soon as Wanda was out the door, I walked into my study. Right over there." Norman pointed to a liquor cabinet on the far wall. Cathy had noticed it before, but it hadn't registered to her that it was empty.

"I took all my bottles and poured them down the drain. Haven't touched a drop since."

"That's amazing."

"I'd be dead by now if I hadn't."

The song ended.

Cathy thought she saw a tear escape from his eye and run down his cheek.

"I love that song." Norman said.

"It's beautiful."

There was no steady rhyme or reason to the conversation. It kept jumping around to different topics, but it always seemed to come back to Wanda.

"What I wouldn't give to see her again and hear her voice one more time," Norman said.

Cathy laughed, changing the mood.

"After I give her the settlement check, I hope I never hear her voice or see her face ever again."

Norman wiped the tear away with his sleeve and laughed with her.

"I guess I should be going," Cathy said. "I can't thank you enough for dinner and for showing me the box."

"Do you want to take the box with you?"

It sat on the floor next to the fireplace.

The question startled her and thrust her back into business mode.

Would that be appropriate?

She had wanted to make copies but was hesitant to ask. While the information was interesting, it wouldn't affect the claim.

"Sure. If you don't mind."

"I'd like to be rid of it anyway. I kept it, hoping she'd come back for it, and I could see her one last time. I don't guess that's going to happen."

"I'll take it if you're sure you don't want it."

"Take it! I want it out of the house."

While Norman still loved Wanda, he still had some underlying animosity. Even after all these years. It probably would be good for Norman to purge the box out of his life. The painting and records too. Seventeen years was a long time to pine over a lost love who wasn't coming back.

Maybe Norman's last years would be more enjoyable if he could think of something else besides her. Cathy really shouldn't be making such observations. She'd broken the cardinal rule of insurance adjusting—don't get emotionally involved with the parties.

She couldn't help it. Norman had touched a nerve. One of sadness and empathy. In a way, she felt the same mixed emotions Norman obviously felt. Not at as deep a level, but part of her felt sorry for Wanda and the other part hated what she'd done to him. The thought that he would die alone broke her heart.

Wanda gave him the best and the worst years of his life.

Cathy felt a sudden sadness for Wanda too.

Empathy for Wanda rushed through Cathy like a raging river. Maybe pity. Cathy settled on compassion. Compassion was one of her best qualities. One of the reasons she went into insurance adjusting was to satisfy that longing to help people. When a family lost everything to crime or natural disaster, Cathy liked being right on the spot to help them recover through the pain.

That's how she felt for Wanda at first. A fire on Christmas Eve was devastating for anyone. Losing all the presents under the tree.

Presents.

Wanda didn't have any presents under her tree. Or at least didn't file a claim for any. At first, Cathy thought that was strange. A major inconsistency in the story. Now she knew the truth. Wanda was alone. She had no one to give a present to or anyone in her life to give one to her.

Wanda was an only child. Her mother died in childbirth, and she never knew her father. Cathy had a sister and a brother she loved dearly. Wanda had no siblings. Life without any family must've been horrible.

Then Wanda moved to New Orleans and was discovered. The incredible gift God had given her, that angelic singing voice, became a source of great hardship for her as a ruthless man took advantage of a naïve child and stole all her money.

Cathy looked up at the painting.

A sudden guilt rushed over her like a flood.

Cathy had made it worse for Wanda, dragging out the claim. Making her pay for the damages herself and wait for reimbursement. Cathy was one more person who had made Wanda's life worse.

The whole thing was a sad, sordid affair.

No one could do anything about it. This wouldn't end well for either of them.

* * *

Norman stood outside on the porch until Cathy's headlights faded in the night. He walked back into his study, picked up his phone, and dialed a number he knew by heart.

His attorney Winfred Rawlings answered the phone on the first ring. Norman knew he wouldn't be asleep yet.

"Hello."

"Win, it's me, Norman."

"Is everything okay?" Rawlings asked.

Norman could hear the concern in his voice. He should've waited until

in the morning but didn't want to. "Everything's fine," Norman answered. "I'm sorry to call you so late."

"You can call me anytime. You know that."

Win Rawlings had been his personal and business attorney for more than fifty years. He owned one of the biggest law firms in Fort Worth. Even though the firm had grown to a staff of more than a hundred lawyers, Win always insisted on handling Norman's personal matters himself. When Win retired several years ago, he still maintained an office at the firm and came in once a week just to handle clients like Norman.

Win was not only his lawyer, but Norman considered him a lifelong friend.

"What do you need Norman?" Rawlings asked.

"I want to change my will."

8

Los Angeles, California
The next day

Closing an insurance case file was not as easy as it should be. Particularly, one with as much paperwork as was in the Wanda Rose folders. While Cathy preferred being in the field, she was good at the details of processing a claim. Her boss, Harold Dawkins, demanded it of her. Being a stickler for details, he'd send the file back to her in a second if every "i" wasn't dotted and every "t" crossed to his satisfaction.

The last thing she wanted was the file coming back to her. Six months of her life had gone into this dead end, and she was determined to get the closing right on the first try. By the end of the day, hopefully, this matter would be closed and the file off her desk forever.

Cathy let out a big yawn and stretched her arms over her head. When she left Norman's last night, rather than going to a hotel, she found a red-eye flight that got her back to LAX airport at three in the morning. Thanks to the two-hour time change, she was able to go home, sleep for four hours, take a shower, and still get to work on time. While she was able to sleep some on the plane, she still felt the effects of the overnight flight.

She could've taken the day off, but getting the file closed was giving her the energy to keep going. Her hope was to meet with Wanda today. The first thing she did when she got to work was to call and leave her a voicemail message.

"Ms. Rose. This is Cathy Tolliver at Miles Fire & Casualty. I'm pleased to inform you that your claim has been approved for payment. Please call me back at your first convenience so we can set a time to meet and sign the paperwork. I should have a check for you later today. We can meet early this evening if it is convenient for your schedule."

A glance at the clock confirmed it had been more than three hours since she left the message. Surprising, considering how anxious Wanda had been to get the matter closed and the check in her hands. Hopefully, she'd hear from her soon.

The second thing she did was tell her boss in passing that she was closing the Rose file. Dawkins walked down the hallway in a hurry. All she got from him was a grunted, "About time."

"I'll put it on your desk. Sign off on it, and I'll get a check cut," she said.

He waved while walking away with his back to her. Fine by her. His rudeness was the best possible scenario. The trip to Fort Worth hadn't come up, and she hadn't offered any details. The expense report wouldn't be turned in until the end of the month, so all she needed to do was get the check to Wanda, close the file, and her boss might not ever mention it again. If he did, it'd be a month from now, when they would move on to other things for him to yell at her about.

Cathy furiously worked the calculator. Adding. Double checking the numbers. Making sure she included all the damages. Wanda didn't have receipts for everything, which made her job harder. Some costs had to be estimated.

When she was finished with the column of numbers, she stared at the green figure on the calculator screen.

$736,472.56.

Including the necklace.

Insured for the appraised value of $101,500.00, even.

To be sure her numbers were correct, she added them three more times. They came out the same each time. Wanda would be happy. That was probably more money than she was expecting. Miles Fire & Casualty would have another satisfied customer. Cathy wished she were satisfied, but the feelings of the employee were irrelevant. This was an injustice as far as she was concerned, but she was slowly making peace with it. At least it wasn't her money, although, she took her job so seriously sometimes it felt like it was.

A check request form was already in the file.

Pay to the Order of.

All she had to do was fill in the name.

Cathy let out a loud laugh that would've carried outside her office had the door not been closed.

Should I make the check out to Wanda O'Neil or Wanda Rose?

Imagine the look on Wanda's face if she were to put O'Neil on the check. Of course, she would never do that. Dawkins would send it back to her so fast with a reprimand that it would make her head spin. Humor and insurance claims adjusting rarely crossed paths.

Dawkins wouldn't even get the joke. Cathy hadn't put that information in the file. The box Norman had given her was at home sitting on her kitchen table. Now, she wasn't even sure why she hauled it all the way back from Fort Worth.

Cathy filled in the check request form in her best printed handwriting.

Pay to the Order of <u>Wanda Rose</u>

Amount $ <u>736,472.56</u>

Claim NO. <u>R4165302</u>

Claim NO. <u>R4165303</u>

One claim number was for the damages to the townhome. The other for the theft of the necklace.

She stood from her chair and walked the paperwork down the hall to bookkeeping.

"Laura, can you expedite this check request?" Cathy asked.

"Oh, of course," she said facetiously. "It's not like I have anything else to do."

Laura was only kidding. She'd been there longer than Cathy, and they'd been friends since the day Cathy had started working there. They were two of only six females in the entire office, so they stuck together. Cathy was authorized for anything up to a million, so all Laura needed was her approval, and the fact that the check request form came from her was enough to get the check cut.

"You're a doll," Cathy said." I'll pick it up in a couple hours."

"Don't worry about it. I'll put it on your desk."

Cathy went back to her office still wondering why Wanda hadn't called.

* * *

At ten minutes to five, the phone rang.

Cathy had already packed her things and was heading home. She'd planned her whole night. Take-out Chinese food, a hot bath, and then go directly to bed. *Do not pass go and do not collect two hundred dollars* her dad used to say when he ordered her off to bed when she was a child. A reference to Monopoly. A game she loved playing with him as a child.

Cathy answered in her usual manner even though she hated her fake telephone voice.

"This is Cathy Tolliver. How may I help you?"

"Cathy, this is Wanda. I'm home now if you'd like to stop by." A sudden hesitation came over her.

Tiredness had come upon her so fast that all she wanted to do was go home and go to bed. The drive to Beverly Hills was twelve and a half miles. Thirty minutes with moderate traffic. An hour in five o'clock traffic. It would take her more than two hours to drive there, go through the paperwork, and drive home.

I can get this case closed for good.

That argument won the day.

"I'll be there about six," Cathy said.

"Perfect, darling," Wanda said in her most syrupy-sweet, annoying voice.

* * *

An accident slowed her progress, and Cathy didn't get there until six thirty.

Already tired and cranky, she could barely put on her best face and behavior. The thought of closing the file provided the adrenaline needed to get the job done.

When she handed Wanda the check, her eyes lit up in obvious delight.

"I'm sorry it took so long to process this," Cathy said, with as much sincerity as she could muster. The truth was that she really was sorry it had taken so long. More for her sake than Wanda's, but the statement was truthful, nonetheless.

"Me too," Wanda said. "It shouldn't have taken this long."

Cathy ignored the snarky comment and put all of the signed paperwork in the file, leaving one copy for Wanda's records. Before giving Wanda the check, Cathy explained to her that she had to sign the "release of all claims form." That meant that she released Miles Fire & Casualty from any further liability on the claim.

The insurance company was still allowed to go after her for fraud if uncovered, but Cathy hadn't seen that in all her years of claims adjusting. Once the paperwork was signed and the check cashed, the matter was closed as far as her company was concerned.

With the signature secured, Cathy packed up her things like she was ready to go. A suitcase was sitting on the floor around the corner, barely in plain view. She tamped down the urge to ask about it. In a matter of seconds, she'd be rid of the woman forever. Idle chitchat would only delay the relief Cathy knew she'd feel in just a few seconds when the weight of the file was off of her shoulders.

Get me out of here.

Before she could stand up to leave, Wanda said, "Tell me about your meeting with Norman."

None of your business, she wanted to say.

"It was good," Cathy said instead. "Norman was delightful. I enjoyed meeting him."

"What did he say about the necklace?" Wanda asked.

We paid the claim. That should tell you everything you need to know.

Cathy decided to take the highest road possible. "He said he didn't remember it."

"I'm not surprised," Wanda said. "He's nearly ninety. I would expect him to have lost a mental step by now. He wasn't the sharpest knife in the drawer, even back then."

Wanda let out a laugh at her own joke, but Cathy didn't join in. The remark made her mad. It took everything in her power not to show it.

"No," Cathy said. "Norman still seemed pretty sharp to me."

"Oh well... I guess it doesn't matter now," Wanda said, waving her check in the air.

Cathy couldn't resist the sudden urge to go back into investigator mode. "Ms. Rose. I've been such a fan of yours for so many years. I really have." Cathy put on her own fake syrupy-sweet voice for effect.

Wanda smiled.

"I wanted to ask you for a favor," Cathy said.

"What's that, honey?"

"Would you sing for me? Just a few notes. How about that song, *I Never*

Stopped Loving You? I just love that song."

Wanda put her hand over her mouth and started coughing. "I have a cold, or I would."

"Just a few bars. Maybe the chorus."

"I don't think I could even remember the words."

"Would you try? Please." A side of Cathy came out she'd never seen before.

"I haven't sung that song in years," Wanda said.

Cathy began humming the tune. She sang a bit back in the day. Mostly in the church choir. Since she'd just heard the song at Norman's, it was fresh in her mind.

"I had so many songs. Hard to remember all of them."

"It doesn't have to be that song," Cathy insisted. "Sing anything. Sing Happy Birthday if you want. I just want to hear the great Wanda Rose sing. Just one time." The words were dripping with such sarcasm, Wanda clearly had gotten the motive behind them. Cathy was no longer hiding her disgust for the woman.

Wanda folded her arms and clenched her jaw. "No!" she blurted.

"Why not?" Cathy said roughly.

"Because I don't want to."

"I don't understand why not."

"Do I have to have a reason?"

Cathy couldn't resist the urge to turn up the heat in the conversation.

"How come you never sang for Norman?" she said accusingly.

"Is that what he said?"

"Yeah. That and a lot of other things."

"I did sing for him."

"He said you didn't."

"He's lying."

"Why would Norman lie?"

"Why would I lie?"

Cathy didn't want to answer that. They both knew the reason Wanda would lie. She decided to try a different line of attack.

"What about the mole?" Cathy asked.

"What mole?" Wanda said.

Both women were standing now.

"Wanda had a mole on her face. It's in all her pictures. Why don't you have a mole?"

"What business is it of yours?"

"A mole doesn't just disappear."

"I had it removed."

"When?"

"None of your business."

"I don't believe you."

Wanda's eyes got so big it looked like they were going to pop out of her head. If looks could kill, Cathy would've already died a thousand deaths.

"How dare you call me a liar!" Wanda shouted at the top of her lungs.

"Did you have the birthmark removed as well?" Cathy asked, keeping her demeanor calm but firm. She'd been wanting to have this confrontation for months. Now she couldn't help herself. All self-control was out the window.

"What are you talking about?" Wanda said.

"Wanda had a birthmark on her leg," Cathy explained. "I saw a picture of Wanda in a swimsuit."

"Where did you see the picture?"

"Norman had it in a box."

Wanda swallowed hard several times. She was pacing around now.

"How dare you go through my things!" she said when she finally stopped walking.

"They weren't your things. They were Norman's."

"That box had my stuff in it."

"Show me your birthmark!"

"I will do no such thing."

"Show it to me, and I'll walk out that door and never bother you again."

"I will not!" "Why not?"

"I think you should leave."

"Are you afraid to show me?"

"I'm not afraid of anything."

"Then show it to me."

"Never. I don't owe you anything."

"You owe me the truth."

"I'm going to report you to your supervisor."

"You do that."

Cathy wrote down the name and phone number of Dawkins and threw it at Wanda. Something she knew she could eventually regret but couldn't stop herself. The tension from the last six months came out all at once, and it felt good.

"I've never been spoken to in this manner in my entire life. You are an impudent fool."

"And you are a liar," Cathy said. "There was no necklace. Never was. I just couldn't prove it."

There. She said it. Everything was out in the open now. At least Wanda would know that Cathy knew.

Wanda's entire body convulsed as she tightened her fist and raised her shoulders. "Get out of my house." For a moment, Cathy thought Wanda was going to hit her.

"Show me your birthmark," Cathy said calmly.

"If you don't leave right this minute, I'm going to call the police." Wanda walked across the room and picked up the phone.

Cathy grabbed her things and stormed to the door slamming it behind her.

* * *

When Cathy got to her car, she threw the file in the backseat. Her heart beat so fast, it felt like it was going to come flying out of her chest.

"Oh! That woman. She's so infuriating," she said.

A couple deep breaths did nothing to calm her. Her hand was still shaking when she put the key in the ignition and started the car. Her eyes started filling up with tears. She wiped them away roughly.

The drive home was long enough for deep regret to sink in.

How could I have been so stupid?

All Cathy had to do was go to the woman's house, give her the check, and leave. Never to see her again. Instead, she had to taunt her. Ask her to sing. Obviously, she'd refuse which would lead to a confrontation. She'd noticed the mole and the birthmark when she was going through the pictures with Norman but decided to ignore it and pay the claim anyway.

Even if the woman wasn't the real Wanda Rose, that didn't necessarily mean the company wasn't on the hook for the claim. The only way it was really fraud was if the necklace didn't exist or Wanda started the fire herself to collect the insurance. Cathy never found proof of either. That's why the whole confrontation was foolish. What good did it do? The file was closed.

The claim was paid.

All she had to do was walk away. Why couldn't she just do it?

By the time she got to her condo, she was as mad at herself as she was at Wanda. She put everything on the counter and collapsed onto her couch. She kicked off her shoes and thought through the ramifications of her actions.

She might lose her job.

At least I'm done with the woman.

I'm not really done if she calls my boss.

Dawkins will be furious.

A letter of reprimand might be put in her file.

Wanda doesn't have the guts to make the call.

If she were right about Wanda, and the case was a fraud, there would be no way she'd complain. That would be a mistake and draw attention back to her and the false claim. They might even investigate her. Cathy would get a chance to plead her case to someone besides Dawkins. If it went to court, all they had to do was ask Wanda to raise her dress and show her upper thigh. Either there was a birthmark or there wasn't. Case closed. One way or the other.

She suddenly felt better. Wanda probably wanted this matter closed as much as, if not more than, Cathy did.

What if Wanda did have the birthmark?

I'd get fired.

I don't even care.

It didn't matter. What was done was done. If Wanda complained, Cathy would just have to deal with the fallout. If she got fired, then all the better. Maybe it was time for her to consider a new career. Having to deal with Dawkins, and the emotional stress of dealing with real life claims might be getting the best of her. How she had reacted had been totally unprofessional. Even if she was in the right.

All the thoughts were giving her a headache. The one thing she could say was that she was no longer tired. The rush of adrenaline had her wide awake.

The phone rang, startling her. Another rush of adrenaline pulsed through her as she wondered who was calling.

Dawkins?

Could that be her boss already? Did Wanda complain that fast?

The police?

Did Wanda call them? She wouldn't put anything past her.

Or did a neighbor hear them shouting and called the police?

Cathy considered letting it go to voicemail. Instead, she picked it up right before it did.

"Hello," she said hesitantly.

"Is this Cathy Tolliver?" A familiar woman's voice was on the other line. Cathy couldn't quite place it.

"Yes. This is Cathy."

"This is Esmeralda."

A lightning bolt of panic flashed before Cathy's eyes. *How did she get my number? Why is she calling me?*

"Hi, Esmeralda. Is everything okay?"

The woman was crying.

"No. Everything is not okay," she said. "Norman is dead."

9

"Esmeralda, you need to calm down and tell me what happened," Cathy said.

Between the sobs, the heavy accent, her broken English, and the hysterical speed in which Esmeralda was speaking, Cathy couldn't understand a word she said. All she had gleaned from her was that Norman was dead.

Her first thought was that Wanda killed him, but that was just an emotional leap with no basis in fact to back it up. Norman was eighty-eight years old. He could've died from any number of causes. More information was needed, but Esmeralda would have to calm down before she could get anything out of her.

"Take a deep breath," Cathy said, "and start from the beginning. Take your time."

Seconds later, Esmeralda let out an audible exhale. Cathy took in a deep breath and did the same.

"I came to the house this afternoon," Esmeralda said. "Like I do every day. I call out to Mr. Norman, but he doesn't answer me. I go to his bedroom. The door's open. He not sleep in his bed."

Esmeralda took in another deep breath and another noticeable exhale. Her voice was shaking. Cathy could tell she was on the verge of breaking down again.

"Go on," Cathy said softly. "What happened next?"

"I find Mr. Norman on the floor. By the big staircase. He not move. I try to shake him, but he not wake up. I say, 'Are you all right, Mr. Norman? Can you hear me?' Nothing. He not say anything. I could tell he was dead. His body was cold."

Cathy shuddered at the thought of touching a dead body. Even someone you've served for forty years. That probably made it worse.

Esmeralda started sobbing hysterically again. Cathy didn't try to stop her. She needed the time to process what she 'd just heard. While she'd only known Norman for a little more than twenty-four hours, his death hit her like someone had just told her a family member had died.

"I... don't... know what... to do." Esmeralda choked out the words.

As hard as she was trying to tell Cathy what had happened, the words weren't coming out clearly. Cathy stood in the kitchen having just come home from her confrontation with Wanda. Her emotions were already frazzled, and now they were swirling around inside of her like an eddy. She needed to maintain her composure, if only for Esmeralda's sake.

The cordless phone allowed her to walk around the house freely. She walked over to the couch and sat down, trying to calm herself.

A number of questions kept circling around in her mind. How did Esmeralda get her number? Did she call the police? Did they suspect foul play? Theoretically, Cathy was the last person to see Norman alive. Would she be questioned? The sadness of the news transformed into grief at the thought that Norman's last moments on this earth were with her. In the study. Listening to Wanda Rose songs.

He at least seemed happy and content, which brought her some comfort. Cathy wondered if he suffered. Did he have a heart attack? Maybe she should've stayed longer. She could've been there to help him.

"Mr. Norman's cane was at the top of the stairs."

"What?" Cathy was shocked into reality. She bolted up from the couch.

"They say he fell down the stairs and hit his head."

"That's impossible. Norman never went upstairs."

Norman had told Cathy he hadn't been upstairs in ten years. How did his cane get up there? Cathy started pacing the condo. Trying to make sense of what she was hearing.

"I know," Esmeralda said. "He was afraid to go up there."

"Who are *they*, Esmeralda?"

"What you mean?"

"You said that *they* said he fell down the stairs. Who are they?"

"The policemen. I call 911," Esmeralda said. "The policemen come. One ask me what happened. I not know."

"You did the right thing, Esmeralda."

Cathy heard a gasp.

Then more audible cries.

"What's wrong, Esmeralda? Are the police still there?"

Dead silence.

"Oh..." she finally heard Esmeralda say in a pained voice. The phone seemed to be away from Esmeralda's mouth, but Cathy could hear commotion in the background.

"They take... Mr. Norman away," Esmeralda said between sobs.

"Esmeralda. Is the policeman still there?"

"Yes. But he's getting ready to leave. They are putting Mr. Norman in a truck and are driving away."

"Esmeralda. Pay attention. Listen to me carefully. I want to talk to the policeman. Can you put him on the phone?"

"Hold on."

A few seconds later, Cathy heard the phone rustling. Then a man's voice.

"Officer Stone speaking."

"Hello Officer Stone. My name's Cathy Tolliver." Cathy hesitated.

How should she describe herself to the officer? *Am I Norman's friend?*

Investigator?

Instead of identifying who she was, she just said, "What happened to Mr. Hurst?"

"He fell down the stairs and hit his head. I'm sorry to say he's deceased. Are you a relative?"

"Friend."

She thought Norman would consider them friends.

"I'm sorry for your loss."

Officer Stone had a deep, southern, Texas drawl. It reminded her of Norman's.

"I'm sorry too. That's strange that Norman fell down the stairs because he never went up there."

"His cane was at the top of the stairs. I guess this time he did."

"I don't think he had any reason to go up there. The stairs are too slick for him."

"That's for sure. I almost fell myself. But he'd been drinking. That probably contributed to the fall as well."

Cathy could feel her mouth gape open. "Did you say Norman had been drinking?"

"Yes. Ma'am."

"But Norman doesn't drink."

"There's a half empty bottle of Vodka in his study and a glass sitting by the chair. He smelled like alcohol to me."

Cathy tried to process all this information. Was Norman lying about his drinking? He certainly did seem depressed last night when Cathy left. She wondered if she was to blame in some way. Did stirring up all the memories of Wanda cause him to fall off the wagon? After her confrontation with Wanda, she could've used a stiff belt, even though she didn't drink. That woman could drive any man to turn to the bottle.

That's probably how he survived twelve years with her.

The memories of her confrontation with Wanda flooded through her mind. Suddenly, she remembered.

The suitcase.

When she was in Wanda's apartment, she saw an unopened suitcase in the room just off where they were sitting. Almost out of view, but still plain as day.

Was it possible that Wanda was in Fort Worth?

She didn't return my call.

It had taken Wanda all day to call her back. That was suspicious. Where was she all day? Wanda always returned her calls immediately. A scenario was becoming clear in her mind. Wanda knew Cathy was going to meet with Norman and was concerned about what he might say.

What was she so afraid of?

Worried about what Norman would say to Cathy, Wanda flew to Fort Worth and confronted him.

What did Norman not tell me?

He did seem evasive at times. Like he had a secret he wasn't willing to share.

Should I say anything?

The suitcase could be anything. Wanda might've been at the hair salon all day. Or visiting a friend. There were many reasons why she didn't call her back right away. The policeman might think she was foolish if she brought it up.

It didn't matter. Norman deserved justice.

"Have you considered foul play?" Cathy blurted out to the policeman.

"And who are you exactly?" he asked.

"I'm an insurance claims adjuster with Miles Fire & Casualty. Out of Los Angeles. I'm investigating an insurance fraud claim filed against Norman's ex-wife, Wanda Rose."

Cathy should've said a potential insurance fraud claim. She didn't want to mislead the police into thinking it was actual fraud, even though Cathy was convinced of it.

"I was with Norman last night," Cathy continued. "I interviewed him for the claim. I may have been the last person to see him alive." The phone was eerily silent for a few moments.

"The coroner has already ruled the official cause of death was an accidental fall."

"I understand. Hear me out. I think his ex-wife might've killed him."

Cathy couldn't believe the words coming out of her mouth. They bordered on defamation. Wanda might've lied to collect a hundred grand on a necklace, but murder was a huge leap. She needed to walk back her words. Before she could, the officer did it for her.

"Whoa! What are you talking about?" he said. "I don't have any evidence that he was murdered."

Cathy couldn't help herself. Just like she couldn't control her tongue when she was meeting with Wanda. She had to ask her to sing. If she hadn't, the confrontation would've never happened. Now she was going down another road she might regret getting on.

"You should at least look into it," Cathy said trying to be more nonchalant about it.

"Why would his ex-wife kill him? What was her motive?"

The policeman at least seemed interested. He probably wouldn't be when he learned she was his wife seventeen years ago. Cathy could hear her argument in her head, and it already sounded foolish to her. She was afraid it would sound even worse when she actually said the words.

Don't do it.

"To cover up the insurance claim." Cathy put her hand to her forehead as she said it and immediately regretted it.

"But you said you interviewed Mr. Hurst. Did he incriminate his ex-wife in some way?"

"No sir. He didn't."

"That doesn't sound like much of a motive to me."

"But she didn't know he wouldn't incriminate her."

"Where does his ex-wife live?"

"In LA."

"How long have they been divorced?"

"Seventeen years."

"When was the last time Mr. Hurst saw or talked to his ex-wife?"

"The last time he saw her was seventeen years ago. He talked to her two days ago."

The policeman let out an almost mocking chuckle.

"What was her name?"

"Wanda Rose."

"The jazz singer?"

"Yes sir."

"Look lady. Anytime there's a death, I always consider foul play. Even if it obviously isn't. But what you're telling me doesn't make any sense."

"I know. His ex-wife is very clever. She's shrewd. I can't pin the insurance fraud on her, even though I know it's true."

"So, he hasn't seen his wife in seventeen years. She lives in LA. Has no motive. I don't see anything here to investigate."

"I saw a suitcase in her house earlier tonight," Cathy said not willing to let it go. Her shoulders were as tense as a tree stump. The pent-up anger and frustrations toward Wanda were driving her to not drop it. If she couldn't get justice with Wanda, maybe a policeman could.

Cathy continued to make her argument. "I also couldn't get Wanda on the phone today. I think she flew out to Fort Worth and killed Norman and flew home the next day. It should be easy to verify whether she was on a flight or not. Don't they have records?"

"I don't even have probable cause to ask for those records. There was no sign of forced entry."

"There wouldn't be," Cathy said, almost pleading for him to consider her side. "If she showed up at his doorstep, Norman would let her in the house. It's his ex-wife. He still loved her."

The Officer's tone turned sarcastic. "You're trying to tell me an ex-wife, who he hasn't seen for seventeen years, flies to Dallas, drives to her ex-husband's house, gets him drunk, and then pushes him down the stairs."

"That's the thing: Norman doesn't drink. I mean he did. He used to. He hasn't had a drink in seventeen years."

"How do you know? You said you just met him yesterday for the first time."

"I know. I'm just telling you what he told me."

"Look, Miss. What's... your name?"

"Cathy Tolliver."

"Look Miss Tolliver. This isn't some episode of Columbo, and I'm not Peter Falk. This is real life. You need to have proof before you start accusing people of things like murder."

"Just think about it. That's all I'm saying. It's suspicious."

"The coroner said the death was accidental. He hit his head falling down the stairs and died. Case closed."

"They need to do an autopsy."

"Are you crazy? That ain't gonna happen. The man was nearly ninety years old. The scene is consistent with a fall. He had too much to drink. Tried to walk up the stairs. Made it to the top and fell. Or maybe he was already at the top and dropped his cane. He reached for it and stumbled down the stairs. Either way, this case is closed."

"But... If you would just look into it. I'm not sure his ex-wife is even the real Wanda Rose..."

"How big is this ex-wife?" the policeman asked roughly.

"I'm sorry."

"How old is she?"

"Seventy-two."

"How much does she weigh?"

"A hundred and twenty pounds I would guess."

"How does a hundred and twenty-pound, seventy-year-old woman carry a grown man up the stairs?"

Cathy had no answer. She couldn't. That thought hadn't occurred to her.

The policeman was no longer on the line. He didn't wait for Cathy to answer.

A few seconds later, Esmeralda was back on the phone, more composed than before.

"I don't think Norman would've gone upstairs," Cathy said.

"He wouldn't have," Esmeralda agreed. "He was afraid to walk up there. And there's nothing up there. Just that box. And it's gone."

"I have the box. Norman gave it to me."

Cathy looked at the box on the kitchen table. Now she wished she hadn't taken it with her. A gnawing feeling inside prompted her to continue the conversation with Esmeralda who'd be a more sympathetic ear.

"Have you ever seen Norman drink?" Cathy asked.

"Not in years. He used to drink a lot. After Miss Rose left, he poured out all the alcohol. He hasn't touched a drop since the day she left."

"That's what he told me."

Esmeralda let out another sigh, but it seemed like she was stronger and able to keep the tears at bay. She said, "I don't know what to do now."

"I guess, just go home. There's nothing you can do."

"I'm going to clean up the place. There's blood at the bottom of the stairs. I clean the floor."

"Norman loved you, Esmeralda," Cathy said sincerely. "He appreciated all you did for him."

Cathy could hear her choke up again, even over the phone. Before she let her go, she had to ask, "Esmeralda. How did you get my number?"

"Mr. Norman wrote it down by the phone. I didn't know who else to call. I think maybe Ms. Rose do this, and so I call you."

"I'm glad you did. You can call me anytime. I'm so sorry for your loss."

* * *

Cathy hit the red *end* button on the cordless phone and slumped back into the couch. Stunned.

Her mind started playing a game of checkers. One side was grieved by Norman's death. Tired from the emotional trauma of the day. Frustrated by six months of dealing with Wanda Rose. The dark side of the board was having all kinds of sinister thoughts. A scenario had even formed in her mind. She kept jumping to conclusions.

One was an answer to the policeman's question, "How did Wanda carry Norman upstairs?"

She didn't. He followed her up there.

Cathy had the ability to picture her thoughts. The house and study came into view. Her investigative mind had allowed her to retain information so that she remembered every detail of her surroundings.

Wanda was hiding in the shadows, waiting for Cathy to leave. Cathy tried to remember if anything seemed odd or out of place. Sometimes she got a feeling when they were.

As soon as Cathy drove away, Wanda went right up to the door.

Knocked on it. She imagined Norman would be shocked to see her. Cathy could see his face as his eyes widened as big as a Texas drink coaster.

Wanda was dressed to the hilt, like she always was. Smelled good. Talked sweet to him. She had alcohol with her. Of course, she had no idea he didn't drink anymore. They went into the study, and she poured two drinks. It took some coaxing, but she got him to drink a toast with her.

"Let's have a drink for old time's sake," she had said.

Norman was so glad to see her, he couldn't resist.

Wanda didn't want to see Norman. She wanted to get the box. Or at least see if he still had it. Also find out what he had said to Cathy.

She had to come up with an excuse to search the house to see if the box was still there. Probably asked to see their old bedroom, thinking it might still be in the closet.

"Come with me, darling," Cathy imagined Wanda saying.

Norman probably resisted and said he never went up there anymore. The stairs were too slick. She sweet talked him. Kissed him on the cheek. How could he resist her feminine wiles?

In her mind, Cathy could see Norman struggle up the stairs. One hand on the rail and the other held the cane. Maybe Wanda was helping him. At the top of the stairs, she pushed him. It was a long drop. He hit his head several times.

Wanda rushed down the steps to make sure he was dead.

He was.

She picked up his cane and put it at the top of the stairs to make it look like a fall. Then went in the study and got her drink glass which she stuck in her purse. Then she wiped everything clean of fingerprints.

Left, went to the hotel, and flew home the next day. Her flight arrived in the afternoon which was why she didn't return Cathy's call until later in the day.

It all made sense.

Maybe it didn't happen exactly that way, but it was something like that. Cathy was sure of it.

What do I do now?

That was the same question Esmeralda was asking.

What *did* Cathy do now?

There was only one thing she could do.

First thing tomorrow morning, she'd go to the office and stop payment on that check.

IO

Despite running on fumes and getting little sleep for two straight nights, Cathy got to the offices before everyone else. The case for stopping payment on Wanda Rose's settlement check had to be laid out for her boss in specific detail in order for her to have a shot at convincing him to do so. Something, she now felt was a long shot.

At home, when she was formulating the arguments in her mind, she felt confident. She practiced her presentation in front of her bathroom mirror a couple of times and thought she was convincing. Now that she was in the office of Harold Dawkins, every ounce of conviction was gone and had left her knees wobbly.

Fortunately, she was sitting down.

"I want to talk about the Rose file," Cathy said with her hands crossed over the file so Dawkins wouldn't know they were shaking.

"Okay," he said in a pleasant manner. He held a cup of coffee and took a long sip. Cathy could see the steam rising. In a few minutes, she was afraid she might see steam rising from his head. The visual caused her to inwardly smile and her nerves calmed slightly.

Dawkins seemed like he was in a good mood. A rare occasion, one she was thankful for, although, she wasn't sure how long it would last. Dawkins' office was sterile and cold. The temperature a few degrees lower than the other offices. Cathy always wore a sweater or a coat to meet with him. On this occasion, a pant suit. She brought out her best outfit for the occasion.

Cathy took a quick glance around the room even though she knew it as well as she knew her own apartment. He didn't display any personal pictures. No awards or plaques, even though Cathy knew he'd received numerous ones over the years. He didn't seem moved by personal accolades, so he didn't give them out except on rare occasions. She didn't expect any from him today.

One picture of a wave crashing over a lighthouse hung behind his desk. Cathy felt a little bit like the lighthouse.

"Everything I know about claim's adjusting I know from you," Cathy began. "You are the best in the business at spotting inconsistencies, and you've taught me to follow my instincts. I appreciate that."

She thought buttering him up at first might be the best approach.

"What do you want, Cathy?"

His look was one of total indifference. He looked like he was about to yawn. Maybe buttering him up wasn't a good idea. At least speaking words out loud without her voice cracking had settled her nerves enough to continue.

Everything inside of her told her to say, *I don't want anything,* and just stand up and walk out the door. Before his wave of fury came crashing down on her like the huge waves in the visual behind him.

"There are too many inconsistencies in the Rose file to ignore," Cathy said slowly and deliberately.

"I thought we already paid it." "I think we need to reopen it." She braced for his reaction.

Surprisingly, he remained calm. "Why is that?"

"Her ex-husband is dead. The one I went to see in Fort Worth."

That statement should at least raise some curiosity and hold off his wrath for a few minutes. Who could resist a good murder mystery in an office that handled generally boring and mundane insurance claims?

"And you know this, how?" Dawkins said, leaning back in his chair. That was his textbook move when he was interested in what she had to say.

"That's a fair question." Cathy decided to answer him direct and to the point. "His housekeeper called to tell me. She was concerned that the circumstances surrounding his death were suspicious. She felt that Wanda

Rose might be behind it."

That wasn't exactly true, but it wasn't a lie either. This part of the conversation was carefully scripted. While a seven-hundred-thousand dollar pay out on a claim was on the lower side of the scale for Miles Fire & Casualty, it still warranted scrutiny. A death in the middle of a claim would always raise some suspicion. If for no other reason than Dawkins would expect her to thoroughly document it, for the file.

Dawkins' body language changed from boredom to cynicism as he folded his arms in front of him and furrowed his brow. "Why would Wanda Rose kill her ex-husband?"

"To keep him from revealing damaging information to me."

"You said he died after you talked to him. Did he reveal anything damaging?"

"He said that Wanda *did not* have an expensive necklace when they were married. Wanda said she was given the necklace by her third husband. Norman was her fourth. Supposedly, she had the necklace when they were married. I don't believe her. I don't think there ever was a necklace."

That's not exactly what Norman had said, but Cathy didn't mind spinning it to meet her ends. That was the gist of what he said. And she had to throw in her opinion. After all, that's the reason they were having this discussion. A case for fraud had to be made, and she was allowed to have her interpretation of the facts. He may not agree with them, but he would think she wasn't doing her job if she didn't reach some conclusions. His job was to poke holes in her theory and see if withstood the scrutiny. She was prepared for that inevitability.

"Maybe he just didn't remember it," Dawkins said. "I don't know what necklaces my ex-wife had when we were married."

"Would you know, if it was worth a hundred grand?"

"That's a good point."

"Also, would you insure it?"

"I would."

"It was not on their policy. That he was certain of."

Dawkins didn't say anything; he just nodded in agreement. He leaned further back in the chair and stared at the ceiling like he was deep in thought.

Cathy took a deep breath. This was going surprisingly well. He hadn't asked the more difficult questions yet. The ones in which she had no definitive answers.

Emboldened, Cathy said, "I think this might be a case of stolen identity." She braced for an eruption that never came.

Instead, Dawkins calmly said, "You lost me there."

"I don't think this woman is the real Wanda Rose. If she's not, then her claim is not valid."

"Is that what her ex said?"

"Not in so many words. But he seemed suspicious."

The only good thing about Norman's death was that he couldn't refute her impressions of their conversation.

Dawkins leaned forward and put his elbows on his desk. Not a good sign. "But did he say it outright?" he asked.

"What he said was... that in twelve years, he never heard his wife sing. Imagine that. You're married to a famous jazz singer, and not once does she sing for you. That would be like being married to a professional golfer and never seeing him swing a golf club. That's too unbelievable to be true."

Cathy knew Dawkins was an avid golfer and used that analogy on purpose.

"My ex never saw me play golf."

"Maybe not. But she saw your clubs in the garage. Or wherever you kept them. She did your laundry and washed your dirty golf shirts, pants, and socks. She at least saw some evidence that you were a golfer. Mr. Hurst never saw one bit of evidence that she was a professional singer."

"I've met the woman. She looks just like the Wanda Rose on the album covers."

"They are not identical." Cathy could tell that this line of discussion had his undivided attention. Above all else, Dawkins was a claim's investigator. He would like a juicy story even if it turned out not to be true. That's what she was counting on anyway.

"The Wanda Rose on the album covers has a mole on her cheek. This Wanda doesn't."

"She could've gotten it removed."

"That's what she said."

"You confronted her about it without proof!" Dawkins said, raising his volume level considerably.

Cathy expected an outburst sooner rather than later and was ready for it. "Wanda is having financial troubles. Her money is running out."

"Doesn't she own her townhome free and clear?"

"She does. And it's worth ten million dollars. But she's cash poor."

"What about the royalties on her music?"

"She doesn't get any. I saw her contract. Her compensation was per album she recorded. Wanda Rose doesn't make a dime in royalties."

Dawkins let out a chuckle. "A lot of famous people were taken advantage of in that way."

"I agree. While I feel bad that she did get taken advantage of, it still doesn't change the fact that she had motive to set fire to the townhome and fake the theft of the necklace. She needed the money."

Dawkins took a deep breath in. Desperation or greed, one or the other, or both, was always behind false insurance claims. Proof of either always got Dawkins attention.

"You need more than that," he said.

"I saw a suitcase in her townhome. She didn't return my call right away. She seemed tired like she had been traveling. Her eyes were bloodshot."

Dawkins stared at Cathy. That made him hard to read. He didn't seem convinced but hadn't summarily cut her off which meant he wanted to hear more.

Cathy continued with a greater sense of urgency. "Norman... her ex-husband's body was found at the bottom of the stairs. His cane was found at the top of the stairs. He told me he hadn't been upstairs in ten years. Why would he all of a sudden decide to go up there? The stairs were too slick. He was an older man. The risk of falling was too great."

Cathy was speaking faster now. Spouting out the facts as fast as she could remember them. She was off script now. That didn't matter. With her last statements, the conversation had turned. By the look on Dawkins face, she was losing the argument. It was time to put all of the cards on the table or fold her hand.

She continued. "The policeman said he'd been drinking. Norman didn't drink. The fire investigator said the fire couldn't be caused by the lights. There was an accelerant present. She has no proof the necklace even exists. No pictures. Just an appraisal from a company that she knows is out of business."

Dawkins held his hand in the air to quiet her. Cathy realized she had been speaking so fast she was rambling.

"Hold on for a second."

He paused and Cathy used the opportunity to catch her breath.

Then he said with a shrug of the shoulders, "Let's assume for the sake of argument that you're right, and it is fraud. What do you propose we do about it?"

When Cathy ran all the scenarios in her mind, she never expected to get this far with him. That question was not something she ever imagined him asking. She was prepared anyway.

"I think we should stop payment on the check," she said emphatically.

"That's not going to happen."

"Once she cashes the check, the money will be gone. You know that. The chances of us ever getting our money back go way down."

"If we stop payment on the check, then we are the ones who committed fraud. We processed the claim, signed a release, gave her a check which she assumed was good, and then we stopped payment on circumstantial evidence at best."

"It's not circumstantial evidence—"

"Hear me out," Dawkins said. "What if she is not *the* Wanda Rose?

That's still not a basis to deny the claim. Have you ever heard the term unjust enrichment?"

Cathy shook her head.

"It's a legal term. It means that even if the contract is void for some reason, we can't unjustly benefit from it. The lady paid premiums to us for ten years."

"I thought about that. We could refund them. That would still be less than the amount paid out in the claim."

"Did she ever tell you she was Wanda Rose, the singer?" That question stopped Cathy in her tracks.

"No. Not in so many words. She had pictures on her wall. I just assumed she was."

"Miles Fire & Casualty did not rely on her representation that she was Wanda Rose the singer when we entered into the contract. We only relied on the value of the townhome and the appraisal on the necklace and her paying the premiums on time. I don't see where we would prevail legally."

This was why Dawkins was the supervisor and Cathy a lowly claim's adjuster. She hadn't thought about that argument at all. She ran through her conversations and couldn't remember a time when Wanda actually claimed to be the singer. She certainly implied it but never said it outright.

Dawkins continued. "The police might be interested if she stole Wanda Rose's identity. That's criminal. They aren't going to be interested in anything we have to say unless we can prove that the necklace didn't exist or that she started the fire on purpose. Nothing I've heard today is enough evidence to prove that. I'm sorry, Cathy, but you just don't have the goods."

"I think I have proved my case," Cathy said raising her voice and intensity.

Dawkins exploded. "You allowed yourself to get emotionally involved in the case. That's why I don't like women claims adjusters."

Until then, Cathy had been able to control her anger. That last statement was condescending and arrogant.

"This has nothing to do with me being a woman," Cathy said. "I resent you insinuating that it does."

"Are you telling me you haven't gotten emotionally involved in this case? It's all over your face. Women can never hide their emotions."

"At least we women have some."

Cathy fought back the tears. The last thing she wanted was for him to see her even more emotional.

"I'm a professional, doing my job," Cathy said bitterly. "I do it better than any of the men in this office. You and I both know it. If I get emotional about a case, it's because I care. I care about Norman who is dead. Someone I met just twenty-four hours ago. Likely killed by the woman I'm investigating. I'm sorry if I get emotional about that. I'm not a robot. I can't turn my emotions on and off like most men."

These were words she'd been wanting to say for years but didn't have the guts. Once they started spewing out like a geyser, she couldn't stop them.

"When you get emotional, you lose your perspective," Dawkins countered. "You've done that on this case, Cathy. You and I both know it. You've wasted valuable time and resources because you couldn't control yourself. I suggest you get up out of your chair and go back to your desk before you say something emotional that we both will regret."

Cathy stood to her feet, so she towered over him. "You are a pompous and arrogant fool! There I said it. And I won't regret it."

Dawkins chin started free-falling to the floor and would have, if not attached to his face.

He started to say something. Cathy held out her hand to stop him.

"You don't have to fire me. I quit!"

Just as she said it, the intercom on Dawkins phone buzzed. They both jumped.

"Mr. Dawkins," his secretary said. "You have a call on line three."

"Can you hold my calls? I'm in the middle of something." he said roughly.

"Take the call," Cathy said, rising to leave. "This conversation is over.

I have nothing more to say."

Before she could leave, the secretary said to Dawkins, "It's Wanda Rose. She wants to speak to you."

Cathy turned around, walked back to her chair, and sat down. This time it was her mouth wide open.

She may have quit, but she wasn't leaving that office until she heard what Wanda Rose had to say to Dawkins.

II

Harold Dawkins put the call from Wanda Rose on speaker phone so Cathy could hear both sides of the conversation. Cathy's heart pounded in her chest like a bass drum. even though she'd just quit her job, the thought of Wanda telling her boss about last night's confrontation was embarrassing, bordering on humiliating.

Her boss would almost certainly take Wanda's side. Wanda would only tell one side of the story, but whatever she said would only reinforce Dawkins' belief that Cathy had acted out of emotions. Maybe she had. She certainly behaved unprofessionally, and no amount of defensiveness on her part would get Dawkins to sympathize with her point of view.

Why did she care what her ex-boss thought? The fact was, that she still did. For twelve years, she'd been trying to earn his approval. The call with Wanda would only reinforce in his mind that he was right about her all along. Who did she blame? She had no one besides herself. Her emotions had gotten out of control, and now she'd have to pay the price for it.

Her contempt for Wanda ran as deep as a river canyon. Unfortunately, she could do nothing about it but listen and take it. No way would Dawkins let her speak up and defend herself to contradict whatever lies Wanda told on the phone.

Actually, Wanda didn't even have to tell any lies for it to sound really bad. Cathy was out of line, and she knew it. If she could, she'd skulk out of the office and never look back, wishing the Wanda Rose case file had never crossed her desk.

Too late. The conversation had started.

"This is Harold Dawkins. How may I help you?"

Dawkins smiled at Cathy as he said it.

What was that all about?

Adding insult to injury, she assumed. Like he was toying with her emotions.

A familiar voice began speaking on the other line. Syrupy sweet to start out with. Cathy would not have expected anything less. "Mr. Dawkins. My name is Wanda Rose. I've been a long-time customer of your company. Do you know who I am?"

"Yes Ma'am, I do. And thank you very much for your business. What can I do for you today?"

Cathy had heard Dawkins interact with customers many times. His motto that he mentioned many times was "the customer is always right." A strange motto for a fraud investigation unit that wanted to prove the customer was not only *not right*, but a thief to boot. In this case, she had no doubt that Dawkins was going to take Wanda's side. She wished they'd skip the pleasantries and get on with bashing her good name.

Her anger was so strong in Cathy it felt like water boiling on a stove.

"I'm calling to complain about one of your employees... Cathy Tolliver. Do you know her?"

Even though Cathy was expecting as much, the words still cut through her like a knife. The nerve of the woman to call and complain about her. Cathy had never expected her to actually do it, which was why she foolishly gave the shrew Dawkins name and number.

Dawkins presented a highly professional demeanor. "I'm Ms. Tolliver's direct supervisor. We were discussing your case earlier today. I understand that she brought you a check yesterday and paid your claim. I hope everything was settled to your satisfaction"

"Yes, she did. And no, I'm not satisfied. Ms. Tolliver's behavior toward me was totally unacceptable. I bet she didn't tell you that. The woman should be fired immediately."

Dawkins had a mischievous grin on his face. Cathy didn't know quite what to make of it. He was probably enjoying making her listen to this conversation and watching her squirm.

"Ms. Tolliver is the best claim's adjuster in our office."

Cathy almost blushed. Those were the last words she expected to come out of Dawkins' mouth.

Wanda was quick with a retort. "After I tell you what she did, you won't feel the same way about her."

"Ms. Tolliver investigates fraud claims. I admit that she may be overzealous sometimes, but I can assure you that she is just doing her job."

While Dawkins was giving her a backhanded compliment, it felt like she had been slapped in the face with the back of his hand. *Overzealous.* He taught her to be aggressive and to not hold anything back when she was investigating fraud. Early in her training, more times than she could count, he scolded her for not being tough enough.

Her emotions were going up and down like a roller coaster at Knotts Berry Farm. While she didn't appreciate the characterization, she did appreciate the spirit in which it seemed to be given. Ultimately, it didn't matter. Her remaining tenure as an employee of Miles Fire & Casualty could be measured in minutes, not hours. If she hadn't already quit, Dawkins would fire her after he heard Wanda's version of events.

"This is not a fraud claim," Wanda retorted. "This is a legitimate insurance claim. This is why I paid premiums to your company all these years. Why in the world would Tolliver think this was a fraud claim? I had a fire on Christmas Eve. Can you imagine how horrible that was? Your employee has made me relive it over and over again for months."

"The fire department said that there was a possible accelerant that contributed to the fire. Can you explain that? Can't you see why that would raise suspicion to Ms. Tolliver?"

"I can't explain it because it didn't happen. There was no accelerant."

"Why do you think the fire inspector would say that?"

Cathy was shocked to hear Dawkins somewhat making her case.

"Why would I burn my own house down? All you did was reimburse me for what it cost to repair it. What did I have to gain except months of inconvenience?"

Wanda had a point which Cathy had considered on several occasions. The only conclusion she could come to was, that Wanda staged the fire in order to claim that the necklace had been stolen by one of the firemen. Cathy admitted that the whole scheme seemed far-fetched. But, so did stealing the identity of a famous singer. Wanda was obviously a sociopath who had lived a lie so long that she thought she could get away with anything.

"There's also the matter of the stolen necklace," Dawkins said getting right to the heart of the case as far as Cathy was concerned. "That's even more suspicious."

Wanda responded in a huff. "What is suspicious about it? I told Ms. Tolliver that I was cleaning the necklace in the bathroom. I left it on the counter. The next thing I knew it was gone."

"You didn't report it missing for a week. Why is that?"

"I didn't notice it. You have to remember that I had just had a fire in my home. I was traumatized."

Cathy rolled her eyes.

Wanda continued. "It wasn't until later that I noticed the necklace wasn't in the safe. Then I remembered I was cleaning it. I searched the whole house, and it was gone. I presume that one of the firemen took it."

"Ms. Tolliver interviewed the firemen and couldn't find any evidence of that."

"Maybe Ms. Tolliver took it. She was in my house the next day."

Cathy could feel her mouth fly open.

"Why are you questioning me about the necklace anyway? I already went over all of this with Ms. Tolliver."

"I'm just trying to explain why she was suspicious. If I were working the case, I would be too. Like I said earlier, Ms. Tolliver was just doing her job."

"Is it part of her job to tell me to take off my clothes?"

As if Cathy's mouth couldn't open any further. She let out a sound of exasperation so loud, Dawkins motioned for her to keep quiet. It was all she could do to keep from coming out of the chair and yelling at Wanda through the phone. If Wanda had been in the room, it would've taken every bit of self-control to not wring her neck.

"I didn't tell her that," Cathy whispered.

Dawkins motioned with both hands for Cathy to keep quiet.

"Can't I defend myself?" Cathy said in disgust, not caring if it was loud enough for Wanda to hear.

"Not now," Dawkins mouthed.

Cathy sat back in her chair, folded her arms roughly, and pursed her lips on purpose, for effect. To let Dawkins know that she wasn't happy. This wasn't fair that she couldn't at least defend herself.

"I find it hard to believe that Ms. Tolliver would tell you to take off your clothes."

"She demanded to see my birthmark," Wanda said. "It's on my upper thigh. How else was I to show it to her without taking off my dress? And what right does she have to come into my house and demand that I strip off all my clothes so she can inspect my body?"

Cathy sat forward in her chair and whispered, "Wanda has a birthmark. I wanted to see it. That way she could prove she was really Wanda."

"Ms. Tolliver just wanted to be sure that you are really Wanda Rose. If you aren't, the whole policy is invalid."

"Of course, I'm Wanda Rose. Who else would I be? Look at any picture, and you'll see that I am Wanda Rose."

"I have an idea," Dawkins said. "Take a picture of your birthmark and mail it to me. That should prove once and for all that you are Wanda

Rose."

"What are you, some kind of pervert?" Wanda's voice reached an almost shrill level. "Do you get your kicks looking at old lady's legs?"

Cathy almost burst out laughing. She could see Dawkins holding back his amusement as well. This conversation was good. Dawkins was seeing firsthand what she had been dealing with all these months. Wanda Rose could be incredulous when she wanted to be, which was most of the time.

Behind that charismatic and sweet exterior, was a cold and calculating liar.

"I can assure you that I have no interest in seeing your legs," Dawkins said sarcastically. "However, it's a way for you to prove who you say you are. I would think you would be anxious to do so."

"I had the birthmark removed several years ago. I told Ms. Tolliver that."

"No, she didn't," Cathy said trying to keep it below a whisper. "She said she had a mole removed. She didn't say anything about a birthmark being removed."

"What was the name of the physician who removed your birthmark? We can call his office and confirm your story, and that should close the matter."

"I don't remember his name. It was years ago."

Dawkins didn't respond. He had his own disgusted look on his face, a slight frown, and rubbed his eyes roughly.

Wanda continued her diatribe. "I demand to know if you intend to fire

Ms. Tolliver."

"I do not," Dawkins said emphatically.

"Then you're a bigger idiot then she is," Wanda said as the line went dead.

Dawkins reached over and pushed the button to disconnect the call.

Cathy didn't know what to say, so she waited to let Dawkins speak.

He leaned forward in his chair, clasped his hands together and began speaking slowly and succinctly.

"The woman is obviously lying," he said.

"That's what I've been trying to tell you."

"Here's what we're going to do. I want you to reopen the file."

"You're not going to fire me?" Cathy asked.

"No."

"But I quit earlier. What about that? I said some things I can't take back."

"Ahh... I'll pretend that conversation never happened. You can't quit because I need you."

For a moment, Cathy wondered if she even wanted her job back. As quick as the question came in her mind, she answered it with a resounding yes. She thought about pushing for an apology but decided not to press her luck.

Instead she said, "Did you really mean it when you said that I was the best claim's adjuster in the office?"

"Yes. But don't let it go to your head. And don't tell anyone else. If they ask me, I'll deny I said it."

"Thank you for sticking up for me," Cathy said sincerely. "It means a lot to me."

A sly smile came on Dawkins face. An almost sheepish grin as the left side of his mouth curled to the side. "I can criticize you all I want. But I'm the only one. You need to know that about me. I'm intensely loyal to my people. If someone else is criticizing you, especially unfairly, I've got your back."

"I appreciate that."

"As I was saying, reopen the file. I want you to nail this woman. Don't leave any stone unturned. I believe she started the fire. I don't believe there was a necklace, and I don't believe that she's Wanda Rose. Your job is to bring me proof."

"I'm on it."

"There are two new files on your desk. One is another jewelry claim. Another is workman's comp. It shouldn't take you long to get those off of your desk. After you do, I want you to spend every waking moment on Wanda Rose."

"What about stopping payment on the check?"

"We can't do that. If we're wrong, that will open the firm up to its own fraud claim."

"We're not wrong."

"I agree. You bring me proof. Wanda Rose is going to rue the day that she called me an idiot."

Cathy stood to walk out of the office, thankful her boss's anger was turned on someone else for a change.

That's just what she was going to do. Make Wanda Rose rue the day that she ever turned in that fake necklace claim.

* * *

That same day

Vinny Giordano came from a long line of firefighters. His grandfather was a fireman and his father was a fire chief in Queens, NY, for twenty-five years before he retired and moved to LA. Vinny didn't want to be a fireman, but it was in his blood, and after high school, he chose putting out fires to going to college.

He loved the work more than he expected, except for the pay. That's why he found another way to make extra money. Fence items from the houses while he was putting out the fires. It turned out to be a highly lucrative endeavor and easier than he ever imagined.

The firemen, for obvious reasons were the only ones in the house. The homeowners were not allowed in until the fire was put out. Vinny had a cardinal rule that he only stole items from fires where it was clear that the structure was going to be so severely damaged that most of the contents wouldn't be recovered.

A rule he broke for the first time about six months ago.

He walked into the Easy Pawn Gold & Jewelry shop on East 17th Street in downtown Los Angeles.

"Hello Mustafa," he said to the Pakistani immigrant standing behind the counter.

No customers were in the store. Mustafa walked to the front door, turned the sign from open to closed, locked the door, and then came back to where Vinny stood.

"What do you have for me today?" Mustafa said as he greeted him with a firm handshake and a shoulder hug.

He'd been Vinny's go-to guy to get rid of the stuff.

Vinny reached into his pocket and pulled out a royal navy-blue cotton bag. Inside was a necklace. He gingerly pulled it out and laid it on the counter in front of Mustafa who now stood on the other side.

"Ooh," he said with an approving smile. "This is nice. Where did you get it?"

"I fenced it from some rich bitch over in Beverly Hills."

Vinny liked getting fire alarm calls to Beverly Hills. He found all kinds of valuable stuff there to steal. When he was called to a townhome on Christmas Eve, he found the necklace on the bathroom counter. In plain view. Normally, he wouldn't be so brazen as to take something that was out in the open, but he couldn't resist. They were also successful in putting out the fire, so it never affected the bathroom.

When an insurance lady came to the fire station and started interviewing everyone who had worked the fire, he almost wet his pants, he was so nervous. Somehow, he answered all her questions, and she seemed satisfied with his answers because she never came back. He held onto the necklace for six months, anyway, knowing that the first place they'd look would be pawn shops. It seemed like enough time had passed to where he could safely move the necklace and not get caught.

Mustafa inspected the oval-shaped necklace carefully. "This is the nicest thing you've ever brought me," he said.

"An insurance lady said it was worth over a hundred grand."

"What insurance lady?"

"The woman I stole it from turned in a claim. Said it was stolen by a fireman. The insurance company sent somebody to the station to question all of us. I denied it. No big deal. She couldn't prove anything anyway."

Mustafa seemed more nervous at that information as he started inspecting the necklace again with furrowed eyes like he was concerned about buying it. Vinny was afraid for a moment that he'd said too much. He didn't have any other source that he trusted to give him a fair price for such an expensive item.

"She said it was worth a hundred G's?" Mustafa asked.

Vinny nodded.

"I can see why. It's got sapphires and diamonds. I'd say it's at least fifteen or sixteen carats. I'll give you ten grand for it."

"Are you kidding me? Come on, man. You and I both know it's worth way more than that. I want at least fifty."

Mustafa shook his head. "This item has some heat behind it. You said insurance people are looking for it. Maybe the cops too. I'm going to have to pay someone to tear this apart and make it into a different looking necklace. "I'll give you twenty, but that's the best I can do."

Vinny didn't know what to do. Twenty was a lot of money, but he was counting on fifty. He wanted to buy a new truck with it.

"Give me forty, man. I got to have at least that. I'm the one with my neck on the line taking all the risk."

"Can't do it. It'll take me awhile to move this. It's not everyday somebody comes in here looking for a hundred-thousand-dollar necklace."

"I'll take it somewhere else then."

Vinny was bluffing. The question was if Mustafa knew it. If he had to, Vinny would take the twenty, even though he didn't want to. Twenty thousand dollars was nearly a half a year's pay.

Mustafa called his bluff. "Be my guest. Shop it around and see what you get. I'll bet you'll be back."

"Come on, Mustafa. I need the money. I've brought you a lot of good stuff. There's more where that came from. I'm doing more and more fires in the Beverly Hills area."

Mustafa put his hand to his chin. "I tell you what I'll do... since you're such a good customer of mine. I'll give you thirty. But that's my final offer. Take it or leave it."

"I'll take it."

Mustafa left the room. A couple minutes later, he returned with three large bundles. Each bundle had ten thousand dollars in it according to Mustafa.

"Do you want to count it?" Mustafa asked.

"No. I trust you," Vinny said. He stuffed the bundles into the pockets of a large coat he was wearing. "Nice doing business with you," he said as he headed for the door.

Mustafa met him there and unlocked it so he could exit.

Once on the street, he let out a huge sigh of relief. Every night for six months, he worried about cops bursting into his home and finding the necklace.

He was glad to finally be rid of it.

12

Two weeks later

The two files Dawkins left on Cathy's desk took longer to dispose of than either of them had anticipated. That was often the case in the world of insurance claims adjusting. In both situations, Cathy suspected fraud, and that always took more time than just processing a normal claim. Consequently, there hadn't been time to do anything on the Wanda Rose file, much to her consternation.

Hopefully, enough progress could be made on both cases today that she could get them off of her desk and get back to the mystery that kept trying to dominate her every thought.

Halsey Geis, a freelance private investigator for Miles Fire & Casualty, had just provided Cathy with the evidence needed to prove her suspicions of fraud in both cases. The two of them were in the conference room, waiting on the first of the two claimants to arrive so Cathy could spring Halsey's evidence on them, hopefully enticing a confession so she could close the cases.

While they waited, Halsey brought up the Wanda Rose case file. Halsey and Cathy had worked on many cases over the years, and Wanda Rose was one of them.

"Did you ever close the Wanda Rose file?" Halsey asked.

"Still working on it," Cathy replied.

His eyes widened in surprise.

"So, I guess you never could prove fraud?"

"Like I said, I haven't given up yet. I know the reason why you never found her birth certificate, though," Cathy said.

"I've got to hear that. I almost felt bad billing you for all my hours and not being able to find it."

"Almost?" Cathy said and they both laughed, easing the tension in the room. Anytime Cathy was about to confront a person on a fraud claim, her insides were wound as tight as the inside of a baseball.

"Wanda Rose is not her real name," Cathy continued. "It's Wanda O'Neil."

Halsey's lips contorted. "Oh... I figured it had to be something like that. Without the right name, I'm shooting darts in the wind. There's no way to find it."

"Any suggestions on what I should do now? I'm kind of stuck."

"You can find her birth certificate in the county and state where she was born if you know it."

"That's not what I meant. I have the birth certificate."

"There you go. You're well on your way then."

"Now that I have it, I don't know what to do with it."

"That's because you haven't answered the question."

"What question?"

"The only one that matters."

Before Cathy could ask what that one question was, the secretary interrupted them and said on the intercom that her first appointment had arrived.

"Send them in," Cathy said.

Cathy said to Halsey, "What question?"

"We can talk about it later," Halsey said as Cathy could see the couple coming around the corner.

"Don't forget!" she blurted. "Don't you dare leave here without telling me what that one question is. I'm dying to know."

* * *

In walked Percy Cunningham and his wife, Fiona. Both dressed like they were going to have dinner at a country club. Percy had on a dressy, skin-tight, black, V- neck tee shirt with a huge gold chain around it, black pants, and black sandals. Percy was an NFL player with the San Diego Chargers and had on his left hand a massive NFL AFC Western Division Champion ring from 1979.

Fiona was a model. Cindy Crawford beautiful, including the mole on her cheek, which reminded Cathy of Wanda Rose. Everything those days reminded her of Wanda. Fiona had rings on at least half of her fingers, solid-gold loop earrings, and an expensive necklace providing the only covering to her plunging neckline, which barely covered her surgically augmented breasts.

They both obviously loved jewelry. That indulgence was what would get at least one of them in serious trouble today.

For Cathy, this was the worst part of her job. In a matter of minutes, this couple's lives would be turned upside down. Percy probably had no idea what his wife had done. Some investigators lived for the moment when they outed the crime. Cathy hated it. The two unsuspecting, stunningly beautiful, and successful, world-class professionals at their trades, were probably really good people, deep down.

In her research, she found that Percy donated his time speaking at schools, telling the story of how he used football to drag himself out of the ghetto and through hard work and perseverance made it to the NFL.

Fiona was a spokesperson for various women's causes. They donated money to women's shelters and children's orphanages. The main vice was that Fiona liked expensive things. She had spent them to near bankruptcy, even though they made hundreds of thousands of dollars a year. They had a modest home in San Diego where they lived during football season and a beach house in Malibu which was why the case was even in her office. When a fire tore through the

Malibu house, they had to provide receipts for the items they claimed were destroyed in the fire.

For whatever reason, Fiona had altered a receipt. From $1,000 to $10,000 dollars. Something as simple as adding one zero was about to change their lives as they knew it.

Halsey found the original receipt. The evidence was incontrovertible.

A deep breath did not help Cathy. Dropping the bombshell was her job, and in this case, she dreaded it. She couldn't force herself to look up and make eye contact with them.

"I was going through the receipts for the items you submitted, and I found a discrepancy," Cathy said.

Fiona changed positions in her chair. Noticeably.

Cathy kept her head down focused on the papers in front of her.

"What kind of discrepancy?" Percy asked.

She pulled the receipt they had submitted out of the file and laid it on the table in front of them.

"This is the receipt for the watch from Luxe department store in Santa Monica. As you can see the receipt says you paid ten thousand dollars for it."

Percy shrugged.

Fiona started fidgeting even more nervously.

Cathy shoved the original receipt across the table, so it was in front of them.

Percy's eyes widened.

When the receipts were side by side, the alteration was obvious.

Cathy continued. "Mr. Halsey Geis is a private investigator for our firm. He went to *Luxe*, and they pulled the original receipt."

Percy picked it up and stared at it in stunned silence. "There must be some mistake," he said as he laid it back down.

"There's no mistake, Mr. Cunningham. Your wife altered the receipt. That's insurance fraud. I have no other choice but to deny your claim and refer the matter to the police."

"I don't believe my wife would do such a thing," he said, looking at her. "Maybe the store altered the receipt. Or Mr. Geis. There must be some explanation."

Cathy didn't respond.

"Tell him you didn't do this," Percy said to his wife.

Fiona burst into tears. The tears started flowing so hard and so fast that her black eyeliner leaked down her cheeks like a branch of a river. "I did it..." Fiona said between sobs. "I'm sorry. I really am." Fiona buried her head in her hands.

Percy made no move to comfort her.

"Why would you do such a thing?" Percy shouted at Fiona. "Over nine thousand dollars!"

"I didn't think anyone would notice."

"I'll deal with you later," Percy said roughly as he turned his attention back to Cathy. "Is there something we can do? Just take that receipt out of the claim. Pay us for the rest of our damage."

"I'm sorry, but I can't do that," Cathy said. "Your wife willfully and blatantly tried to defraud our company. We take insurance fraud very seriously. If you read your policy, we can deny the entire claim if you submit even one piece of fraudulent information. Plus, it's a felony in the state of California to defraud an insurance company."

Cathy pulled another piece of paper out of the file and slid it across the table to them as Fiona clearly tried to regain her composure.

"What's this?" Percy asked in a voice of resignation.

Cathy answered, "This is a letter denying your claim. I'm sorry. I really am."

She stood. This was the most awkward moment. Did she shake their hands? She had just ruined their lives. Percy might even lose his job with the team. Cathy knew that every NFL policy had a personal conduct clause. This would probably make the papers if the DA decided to press criminal charges against an NFL player's wife. Fiona might never work again in the fashion industry. Her endorsements would dry up. All over a stupid receipt. Greed. Maybe even a momentary lapse of judgement. Perhaps a sense of entitlement. With her beauty, she'd been given free things all of her life.

More than likely, she wouldn't go to jail since this was a first offense. Halsey had pulled her criminal record, and she didn't have one. She could probably cop a plea to a misdemeanor and pay a fine. Cathy wondered if their marriage would survive it, though. Thankfully, they didn't have kids.

Cathy didn't extend her hand. That seemed inappropriate. The couple walked out of the room slowly.

"I hate that," Cathy said to Halsey after they left, almost feeling sorry for them. This wasn't like the Wanda Rose case. She'd draw great satisfaction for bringing that woman down.

Halsey had a smug grin. "I love it. They'll get what they deserve."

Halsey, a retired Los Angeles county cop had seen it all and was hardened to it she supposed. Normally, he wasn't in these meetings, but he had insisted.

Cathy could feel the emotion welling up inside of her. "I know," she said. "I shouldn't feel that way. I can't help it. They made a mistake. I'm glad you found it. It saved my company a lot of money. It's still sad."

"Pull yourself together," he said, "because we got another one right after it." Halsey's demeanor was cold and calculating. She was glad he was on her side.

"I'm going to the restroom." She abruptly stood and walked out of the room, needing a minute to compose herself.

When she returned, the other claimant was already sitting in the same chair as Percy Cunningham. Unsuspecting. About to have his life shattered by Cathy.

It was his own fault.

That didn't make it easier.

* * *

Roger Walton worked for Signet Packaging out of Glendale, a suburb of Los Angeles, a little north of their offices off of Highway 2. Walton filed a workman's compensation claim against the company, attesting that he was injured on the job.

Cathy studied him closely. A white brace circled his neck, even though the supposed injury occurred more than eight weeks before. He appeared to be in considerable pain. Each time he moved in the chair, he let out a painful moan.

"Are you okay?" Cathy asked him. "Can I pour you a glass of water?"

"I can get it," Walton said as he reached out to grasp the pitcher of water which sat in the middle of the table.

Walton winced and let out another groan. And then reached his hand up to his neck brace like it was too painful to lift the pitcher and cup.

Halsey seemed like he could barely contain his laughter. A smile came on his face which he quickly covered by a fake cough.

"I'll get it for you," Cathy said almost mockingly, although if Walton noticed, he didn't let on.

"Do you want one, Mr. Geis?" Cathy asked Halsey. She gave him a stiff glare. Her way of telling him to behave himself. They'd get to the good stuff shortly.

"I'm good," Halsey said with a wave of the hand as the other covered his mouth again to cover his urge to laugh with another fake cough.

"Do you mind if I record this?" Cathy asked as she sat a portable tape recorder on the table in front of Walton.

"I don't mind." Walton nodded and then seemed to realize that his neck was not supposed to have that range of motion. Just in time, he caught himself and immediately went back into character, wincing and carrying on for dramatic effect, even though his audience wasn't buying it for one second.

The previous couple should've been recorded, but Cathy didn't have the heart in case Fiona were to break down and confess, which she did. That confession wasn't needed to prove the case, and Cathy didn't want it on tape to bolster the DA's case and make it even worse for them. Also, if a confession happened, she didn't want to relive the heartbreaking moment again if she didn't have to.

In the matter of Roger Walton, Cathy didn't have the same misgivings.

Another look over at Halsey confirmed that he appeared to be relishing the moment. He was on the edge of his seat. Like a panther about to pounce on a prey. This was what he lived for. The fruits of his good work. Busting the bad guys. He was loving every minute of it.

In this instance, he had video evidence of Walton's deception and fraud. Halsey appeared to be itching to have his work on display like a movie producer on the release of a new film.

Cathy went through all the formalities for the benefit of the tape recording. State your name. Occupation. Date of birth. Address. Phone number. Cathy read the case file number aloud and the nature of the claim. After about five minutes, she was ready for the questioning. They came out rapid fire like a machine gun.

"Mr. Walton, I see that you're wearing a brace on your neck. Is that from the injuries you sustained from the incident on May fourteenth?"

"Yes, Ma'am."

"Can you describe the injuries?"

"I have a sprained neck and back."

"Do those injuries prevent you from returning to work?"

"Yes, Ma'am they do. I can't work now. I don't know if I'll ever be able to work again."

"Are you in constant pain?"

"Yes."

"In what way does this injury affect your normal everyday life?"

"It's horrible. I mostly have to stay in bed all day. Or on the couch watching TV."

"Do you go outside much?"

"Not much. I can't really. It's too painful."

"Can you exercise?"

"No. That's impossible. As you can see, I'm almost an invalid." "Do you own a boat?" Walton paused.

"Yes. I own a boat."

"You were once a professional water skier, weren't you?"

"Yes. I was pretty good in my day."

"Can you still water ski?"

"No, unfortunately, those days are over."

"Can you at least go for a ride on your boat?"

"No. It would be too hard to get in and out of it."

"Do you play any sports?"

"I used to play basketball and softball. But I can't anymore. My playing days are over as well."

Walton feigned a tear. Cathy wanted to get to the video tapes to save him the trouble but had a few more questions for him. If she could, she'd reach across the table and rip off the brace from his neck.

Cathy continued her questioning. "Are you married?"

"I am."

"How does this injury affect your marriage?"

"I'm not able to perform my husbandly duties, if you know what I mean."

"I do know what you mean," Cathy said, trying to hold back a smile. She flipped through her notes. "I think I'll turn this over to Mr. Geis. He has a few questions for you."

A television and tape recorder were on a rolling stand at the end of the conference table. Halsey stood, walked over to it, and turned them both on. The VCR tape was already cued and ready to go.

The screen crackled and then came into focus.

An image of a man water skiing came into view. Even though the camera angle was from a distance, the image was close up and they could clearly see Walton's face.

He turned sheet white. As white as the brace around his neck.

"Is that you Mr. Walton?" Halsey asked.

"That must be an old tape of me," he said.

"Do you see that date at the bottom?" Halsey pointed at the screen.

7-04-1984

"That was last weekend," Halsey continued. "I took this tape myself. You were out on the lake water skiing. You don't appear to have any injuries there."

Walton was seen doing all kinds of tricks. Skiing backward. Back flips.

Jumping over the wake.

"The tape is doctored somehow," Walton said. "That's not me."

Halsey hit a button on the remote and the tape fast forwarded to a man playing basketball at a local playground.

"Is that you, Mr. Walton?"

"I don't think so. It's somebody that looks like me."

The man on television was twisting and turning. Jumping and running. Slashing back and forth with no effort. The close up on the man's face told the whole story. Clearly, he was the same man sitting across from them. Walton was a good basketball player.

Cathy always marveled at how Halsey could get these close-up pictures, undetected.

"You said you were married," Halsey said.

"I am."

"Is this your wife?" Halsey asked.

The screen was now on an image of a man in front of a motel. With a woman. He picked her up and carried her into a room.

Whereas Walton's face was white seconds before, now it was beet red. He didn't bother answering. Halsey had him dead to rights, and he knew it.

"That isn't your wife, is it?" Cathy said.

Walton still didn't answer; he simply glared at her. He pulled the brace off his neck, threw it on the table, and stood to his feet.

Halsey stood as well to make sure he didn't try something stupid.

"I was injured. I have a doctor who verified that I had a sprained back and neck."

"Is the doctor a cousin of yours?" Cathy asked.

"I don't have to answer that question. I'm getting out of here."

Cathy buzzed her secretary. "Can you send the officers in?" Cathy said.

Halsey walked over to the door and stood in front of it so Walton couldn't leave. "You're not going anywhere except to jail," Halsey said.

Two officers suddenly appeared at the door, and Halsey opened it.

"You're under arrest, Mr. Walton," one of the officers said. The speaker phone was on in the conference room, so the officers heard everything that was said from Cathy's office.

After they handcuffed Walton and read him his rights, Cathy said to the officers, "I'll see the DA copies of the VCR tape and the cassette tape of the interrogation."

"I'll get you, you bitch!" Walton said, as they dragged him out the door.

Halsey immediately shouted out, "I believe you just threatened bodily harm to Ms. Tolliver. Add criminal threatening to his charges as well. I witnessed it."

With those last words, Walton and the two officers disappeared from view.

Cathy gave Halsey a side hug of appreciation. "Good job, Halsey," She said exuberantly. "The look on Walton's face was priceless."

"That felt good. I wanted to nail that guy. I knew he was dirty from the first time I laid eyes on him."

"I can't believe you got pictures of him with his mistress."

"That brace was in the back seat of his car. And he was carrying her across the threshold like they were just married. He's going to jail for a long time."

Halsey started packing up his things.

"Wait a minute," Cathy said. "You were going to tell me something about the Wanda Rose file."

"Oh yeah," he said as he sat back down.

"I'm all ears. I know Wanda Rose is dirty as well. I just can't prove it. What's the one question I need to answer?"

13

Halsey barely hesitated before answering Cathy. "The question you have to answer is what happened to the real Wanda Rose?" "How could I possibly know?" Cathy asked.

"I have no idea, but you'll never know for sure that this woman is not Wanda Rose until you find out what happened to the real one?"

"That makes sense."

"And if this lady's not Wanda then who is she?"

"I don't know."

"Exactly. That's why it's a question you have to answer. Your gal can't just impersonate someone as famous as Wanda Rose without getting rid of the real one."

"Are you saying that *my* Wanda murdered the real Wanda Rose?"

"That's the question you need to be asking. The real Wanda is either alive somewhere or dead. If she's alive, then she must not be aware that someone has stolen her identity. And how did this Wanda get away with it for so long? If the real Wanda is dead, then she was probably murdered by your lady who covered up the crime. Otherwise, the world would know about the death of the famous Wanda Rose."

"I haven't really thought about it that way. Where do I start?"

"You start at the beginning. Track Wanda Rose's life from birth to today. Find out everything you can about her. You find out what happened to Wanda Rose, and you'll have your answers."

"Will you help me?"

"I can't."

"Why not?"

"I just retired. Those were my last two cases."

"No! You can't retire on me."

"I've got a bad ticker. Doctor says the stress is making my blood pressure go up too high. Just like today. I wanted to come across the table and strangle that Walton guy. If I don't retire, I'm going to keel over one of these days. Probably right here in your office. Sorry kid. You're on your own. I wish you luck though."

With that, he was gone. His last words still lingered over the room. *What happened to the real Wanda Rose?*

* * *

Cathy hadn't been home from work for more than thirty minutes when the phone rang, startling her. It didn't ring very often at night. Either her mom was calling or a telemarketer.

"I'm calling for Cathy Tolliver. Do I have the right number?" the man asked.

She started to say no, but it could be work related. Even if it wasn't, she was curious as to who would be calling her this late at night with a Texas drawl.

"This is Cathy," she said.

"Ms. Tolliver, my name is Win Rawlings. I'm an attorney in Fort Worth, Texas."

An attorney?

"How can I help you Mr. Rawlings? I don't know any attorneys in Fort Worth, Texas."

"I'm Norman Hurst's attorney."

Why would Norman's attorney be calling me?

"I'm calling to let you know that Mr. Hurst has passed away."

"I'm aware. Esmeralda called me."

Cathy assumed that if he was Norman's attorney for forty years, he knew the housekeeper. Maybe he was the attorney who drew up the prenup for Norman and Wanda. Perhaps the one Norman told to shoot him if he ever wanted to get married again. She wondered what light he could shed on the situation. Would he know if this lady was the real Wanda Rose? Did he have suspicions? She was suddenly elated that he called, although she still had no idea what he could possibly want.

A sudden question popped into her head. "How did you get my number, if I may ask?"

"Norman gave it to me. The night he died."

"Why would he do that?"

"He wanted to change his will."

"I still don't understand what that has to do with me."

"Let me get right to the point. I am the executor of Mr. Hurst's estate. Can you come to Fort Worth on Tuesday of next week for the reading of Norman's will? I will send you a plane ticket and provide a rental car and hotel."

"Why would it be necessary for me to come to the reading of his will?"

"Because Norman named you as a beneficiary."

Cathy sat down on the couch just in case her legs didn't hold her up from the stunning news.

"I barely knew him. I spent about six hours with him."

"Be that as it may, he called me the night he died to make an amendment to his will. It's signed and legal. As his beneficiary, I'm notifying you of that fact. I can't make you come. If you don't want to be here, then I'll have a public reading of the will and will notify you of what he left you. It doesn't affect your inheritance. You'll get whatever is specified in the will."

Inheritance!

Cathy regrouped. "I'll be there. I'm sorry if I sound bewildered. This has just come as quite a shock to me."

"I understand. If you'll give me your name and address, I'll overnight a plane ticket, and all of the travel arrangements to you."

She gave him all the information and then wrote down his address and phone number. After she hung up from the call, she wondered if it was all a scam. Somebody calling to get her personal information. But all she gave them was her address. That sent a chill through her. Did Wanda hire a hit man to call Cathy and get her personal address so he could come over there and kill her like she killed Norman?

That caused her to laugh out loud. She was being paranoid.

Even so, that night, she didn't sleep as well as she usually did.

* * *

The law offices of Rawlings, Crawford, Langston, & McDonald, took up the entire tenth floor of the Petroleum Building in downtown Fort Worth. Cathy was early and a secretary led her into a large conference room. She felt like a deer out of the woods.

A far cry from anything in southern California, the room was gaudy. Ostentatious even. The walls were covered with thick, custom, red cherry wood panels. The table was at least twenty feet long and four feet wide and made of rich mahogany. A dozen red high-back office chairs surrounded it, and Cathy melted into one of them near the head of the table when she sat down.

She had barely settled in when the door to the conference room opened, and an older gentleman who reminded her of Norman walked through the door and set some files down at the head of the table. Then he extended his hand and welcomed her with a friendly smile.

"Win Rawlings," he said more formally than was his demeanor.

"Cathy Tolliver," she said in her most businesslike voice.

After he sat down, his tone turned even friendlier. "I hope you had a good trip in," he said.

"I did."

"Is your hotel satisfactory?"

"Very much so," she said. "I travel a lot for business, and I'm not used to such nice accommodations."

She consciously told herself to loosen up a little.

A knock at the door interrupted their chit chat.

"Come in," Mr. Rawlings said.

Esmeralda walked through the door. Her face immediately lit up when she saw Cathy. But when they made eye contact, she looked petrified.

Cathy assumed she'd be there. It made sense that Norman would leave her something. Certainly, a lot more than he left Cathy. Esmeralda had served Norman faithfully for years. Cathy knew him for a few hours. To say she felt out of place would be an understatement. There's no way she deserved to be named in the same will as Esmeralda.

Esmeralda gave Mr. Rawlings a slight wave and sat down next to Cathy. They hugged slightly, and Cathy could feel Esmeralda's body shaking nervously.

"It's good to see you again, Esmeralda," Mr. Rawlings said. "As always."

She nodded.

"If you've never had a meal cooked by Esmeralda, then you don't know what you're missing," Rawlings said.

"I have had the pleasure," Cathy said, smiling approvingly at Esmeralda who seemed oblivious to the compliment. A squeeze of Esmeralda's hand seemed to calm her slightly.

Suddenly, Wanda Rose sashayed into the room, and the tension in the room exploded.

"What's *she* doing here?" Wanda said, pointing directly at Cathy.

"Hello, Wanda," Mr. Rawlings said. "It's been a long time." He extended his hand and Wanda shook it but kept eyeing Cathy warily.

"It's good to see you, Win," Wanda finally said. "The last time I saw you was in this same room. When we were signing the divorce papers."

"I remember that day well," Win Rawlings said in a warm but businesslike manner. "It's hard to believe that was seventeen years ago. Time sure flies." Wanda took a seat next to Win and across from Cathy and Esmeralda.

"Like I said, why is that lady here?" Wanda pointed her skinny little finger Cathy's way a second time.

Point it again and I'll rip it off your hand.

Mr. Rawlings replied, "I invited her." Before Wanda could say another word, he said, "That's everyone, so we can get started."

He shuffled a few papers and put on a pair of reading glasses. "We are here this afternoon for the reading of the final last will and testament and codicil of Mr. Norman T. Hurst. Does anyone have any questions before I begin?"

They all shook their heads, even though Cathy had a lot of questions.

Mr. Rawlings continued, "Norman's will is dated February tenth, nineteen fifty-five."

That was the day before Norman and Wanda were married.

Interesting.

"There is one codicil. That's dated June twenty-third, nineteen eighty-four."

Even more interesting.

The day Cathy met with him.

"Mr. Hurst called me at fifteen minutes after nine on that date and told me he wanted to change his will. I had him write out the changes, sign it, and fax it to me. Being familiar with his signature and having discussed it with him on the phone, I had my secretary notarize it the next day."

He held up a copy of what was a one-page codicil which Cathy knew was an amendment to a will.

Nine fifteen was right after she left his house that night.

Right before Wanda Rose killed him.

The plot thickened.

If Cathy were writing a novel, she couldn't have written a more twisted and sordid tale. Before today, this was already the most interesting insurance claim case she'd ever worked on. Now there's no way it could ever be topped.

"I will read the codicil first," Mr. Rawlings said.

Tension filled the room like smoke filled a beaker in a science experiment.

"To my dear Esmeralda."

A tear formed in her eye. Cathy wanted to reach over and hold her hand reassuringly but didn't think it appropriate.

"For all of your years of service, I leave you whatever monies are in my investment accounts, and the Cadillac in my garage."

Esmeralda let out a slight gasp. Wanda looked on with a permanent scowl etched on her face.

Mr. Rawlings continued, "When we liquidated all of his accounts, stocks, bonds, and money markets, the sum comes to one million, seven hundred thousand, two hundred and forty-five dollars, and sixty-five cents. After all of his debts, taxes, and burial was paid."

Dual gasps went throughout the room as both Wanda and Esmeralda let one out at the same time.

Good for her. Norman wasn't as bad off as I thought.

If anyone deserved it, Esmeralda did. She just became a millionaire in a matter of seconds.

Mr. Rawlings pulled out a piece of paper and a check out of the file. "Esmeralda, if you do not wish to contest the will, then sign the form in front of you. Attached to the form is a check made out to you from my trust account."

Esmeralda took a pen out of a cup in the center of the table and signed her name.

"You may want to hear the rest of the will before you make a decision," Mr. Rawlings said.

Esmeralda shook her head no. "If this is what Mr. Norman wanted me to have then I'm fine with it. I didn't take care of him for the money."

"She already signed it anyway," Wanda said. "That makes it official."

"If she wants to change her mind, I'm the executor, and I will tear up that form," Mr. Rawlings said strongly and firmly with a hint of anger in his tone. "Do you understand that, Esmeralda? If after I read the rest of the will, you want to challenge it for some reason, then that form you signed will be null and void."

"I won't," she said meekly.

"That's fine. But if you want to, you can."

Mr. Rawlings turned his attention to Cathy. "Ms. Tolliver," he said.

"Mr. Hurst also named you in his will which is why you are here today."

"What about me?" Wanda said.

Mr. Rawlings seemed to be losing patience with her. "I want to read the amendment first. Then I'll get to you, Wanda."

Cathy's heart started racing, even though her expectations were low. He probably left her some token gift for the night they spent together. Of course, there was always the possibility that he had left everything to her. The house, furnishings, everything except the money he left to Esmeralda. Perhaps Wanda was getting the token gift.

She almost snickered at her absurd thoughts but held herself back.

That would make me so happy.

Cathy never allowed her mind to go there until now. The satisfaction she would get from seeing Wanda's face if Norman left her everything. That would be worth more to her than all of his possessions. She'd probably sell everything and donate the proceeds to charity anyway.

If things were tense before, they had become excruciatingly so.

"To Miss Cathy Tolliver, I leave..." Mr. Rawlings started coughing before he finished.

Hurry up.

Not wanting to sound impatient like Wanda, Cathy bit her tongue.

"To Miss Cathy Tolliver, I leave the painting of Wanda Rose that is above the fireplace and all of her albums in my collection."

Cathy laughed out loud.

"What?" Wanda exploded. "That painting is mine! He gave it to me when we were married."

The gift was Norman's idea of a joke. That night, she said she never wanted to see Wanda's face or hear her voice ever again. So... he left her the painting and her albums.

That's too funny.

Cathy barely heard Wanda's objections. That was almost better than if he had left her everything.

"That painting is valuable," Wanda whined. "I deserve it."

"If you would like to contest the will, you have that right."

"Norman was obviously not of sound mind when he made it. Why would he leave my painting to *that* woman?"

"I can assure you that Mr. Hurst was of sound mind, and I will testify to that fact in a court of law."

He held out his hand to quiet Wanda. She immediately shut up. Cathy wished she had that same power.

"Ms. Tolliver, I will tell you that Wanda is correct. Margaux Lefebvre is a famous artist from France. His paintings are valuable. It has been insured and appraised for slightly more than two hundred and fifty thousand dollars."

"I'll buy it from you," Wanda said.

"It's not for sale," Cathy said out of spite. Truthfully, she'd love nothing more than to walk out of there with two hundred and fifty thousand dollars and never look back. She wouldn't give Wanda the satisfaction.

"Maybe I will contest the will," Wanda said as Mr. Rawlings handed Cathy what looked to be the same form he handed to Esmeralda.

"Wanda, you never could keep your mouth shut, could you?" Mr. Rawlings said.

That was probably unprofessional, but he was getting up in years and probably didn't care anymore.

Cathy took one glance through the form and signed it. She didn't care what he gave to Wanda.

Mr. Rawlings continued with his lecture. "Just listen to what I have to say. If you still want to contest the will when I'm done, then be my guest. As the executor of the estate, I will fight you tooth and nail and make you wish you'd never done so." He looked at Wanda when he said it.

"Are you threatening me?" Wanda asked.

"It's not a threat. It's a fact."

"Just tell me what he left me."

"Everything else."

Her demeanor suddenly changed. The frown changed to a smile. Her eyes widened and began to sparkle.

"That's what the will said?" she asked.

"As you know, Norman changed his will when you were married. Right here in this office. You were there when he signed it. He never changed it after you divorced. Except for the amendment which I've already read. Everything he owned now belongs to you."

It was clear that Wanda hadn't anticipated Norman leaving her anything. Why would he? They were divorced. Cathy knew why, having spent the evening with him. He still loved Wanda. Why? Cathy hadn't a clue. Who knows why the heart wants what it wants? Whether Wanda deserved it or not, Norman wanted her to have it.

"Do you still want to contest the will?" Mr. Rawlings asked Wanda.

"No," she said with resignation in her voice probably just for Cathy's benefit.

Wanda signed the form.

That gave Cathy an idea. Wanda's signature. She could compare it to the recording contract Wanda Rose signed. If they didn't match, that would prove her theory. Cathy couldn't wait to get back to Los Angeles and look.

Brilliant.

Wanda didn't hang around, which was fine by Cathy who purposefully lagged behind. For one, she needed to arrange to get the painting and the albums. How she was going to get them back to LA was a concern she'd have to discuss with Mr. Rawlings. More importantly, she had another question for him.

When they were alone, she said, "I'm an insurance claim's adjuster in Los Angeles. I've been investigating a potential fraud claim regarding Ms. Rose. That's why I came to Fort Worth to talk to Mr. Hurst.

"You must've made an impression on him, for him to name you in his will."

"We hit it off for sure. I liked him almost from the moment I met him."

Cathy took a deep breath. "Could you answer a legal question for me?" she asked.

"I'll try."

"Theoretically, if Ms. Rose was responsible for Norman's death, would she still be entitled to the inheritance."

"Have you ever heard of the slayer rule?" he asked.

"I have not."

"A murderer may not profit from his or her crime. Theoretically, if Ms. Rose was responsible for Mr. Hurst's death, then she wouldn't be entitled to his inheritance."

Perfect. I just have to prove she killed him before she spends it all.

14

When Cathy returned to her office in LA after the reading of Norman's will, she went to the Wanda Rose file and pulled out the application for insurance dated in 1974 and the claim submissions form dated in December 1983. The idea had occurred to her to compare those signatures. Careful inspection of the two showed that the handwriting appeared to be identical. The same person wrote both. At least to the extent she could surmise with her limited experience in handwriting analysis.

Then she compared the insurance application form with the agreement Wanda signed in the attorney's office just a few days before. The agreement not to contest the will. They also appeared to be the same handwriting.

That meant that if Wanda's identity was stolen, it happened before 1974. Not surprisingly. Cathy was certain the crime happened before she married Norman. Sometime before they met in 1955.

From the box Norman had given her, she pulled out the agency representation agreement Wanda signed in 1929 with Happy O'Brian. A bolt of excitement went through her when she saw they weren't the same signatures. Or at least they didn't appear to be to her.

Cathy immediately went to Dawkins' office to show him the four documents. Fortunately, he didn't have an appointment and could see her.

She didn't know if she could contain her excitement if he were to make her wait.

He wasn't as impressed as she thought he'd be.

"This is a good start," he said.

"A good start?" Cathy retorted. "This proves it! Those signatures are clearly not the same. Two different people signed those documents."

Dawkins lifted them up again, one in each hand, and compared them a second time.

Then he said sarcastically, "I didn't realize that you had a forensic science degree?"

"I don't. Anyone can look at the two signatures and see that they aren't the same."

"I agree that they don't look the same. That doesn't mean they weren't written by the same person." Cathy started to object.

Dawson held up a hand. "Here me out before you jump to any more conclusions."

Jump to conclusions!

If Dawkins said anything about her being a woman, hinted at her being too emotional, or said one word about PMS, which he'd done before, she was going to become unhinged. Before she realized it, her fists were literally balled together. Her jaw was clenched, and her shoulders raised.

She was ready to go to battle if need be.

Calm down. Hear him out.

After telling him off the week before, she realized how easy it would be to do it again. The last thing she wanted to do was get fired. Proving this case was too important to her. Once she proved she was right about Wanda Rose, she could sell the painting, quit her job, and take a year or two off. Then Dawkins would be out of her life forever. For now, she had to put up with him until she could get her evidence. These documents brought her one step closer.

Dawkins must've sensed her angst because he noticeably softened his tone. "The person who signed this document." He waved the 1929 agency agreement in the air. "That person was only sixteen."

He then waved the other one in the air with his other hand. This agreement she signed this week is fifty-five years later. People's handwriting changes from a child to an older adult."

"Yeah, but not that much. These two don't even look anything alike."

Dawkins laid the papers back down on the desk. "I doubt my signature looks anything like it did when I was a kid."

Cathy's heart sunk. A few minutes before, she thought she'd broken the case wide open. Dawkins, in his usual form, shot holes all through it in a matter of seconds.

"Cheer up," he said. He must've seen the disappointment on her face. "Keep digging, and you'll find something."

Without saying anything more, Dawkins began flipping through his rolodex. When he stopped, he said, "Call Sigmund. Let him look at these and give us his opinion."

Sigmund Douglas was a forensic document examiner. A handwriting expert Miles Fire & Casualty had used for years. His opinion and court testimony helped them win several big cases. Cathy had thought of that, but in her zeal, couldn't wait to show the documents to Dawkins. In retrospect, it clearly would've been better if she had taken them to Dawkins along with a letter from Sigmund backing her conclusions.

Why do I need his approval so much?

More than likely it had to do with her relationship with her own father. The two men were similar in a lot of ways. Both were perfectionists. Each demanding and uncompromising in his own way. Cathy's dad was more loving and supportive, though. If Dawkins were to pay her a compliment and say she was right, he probably would cringe.

As usual, she tried to see his side of the argument. Truthfully, he just wanted to make sure she did a thorough job.

Why do I defend him?

Ultimately, he was right. If she was going to prove her case, especially to the point of taking it to the authorities or even filing a civil lawsuit, Sigmund's opinion was all that mattered. Nobody cared if she thought the two signatures didn't match. No court of law would even allow her testimony to that effect. She needed the forensic analysis and was kicking herself for not getting it first.

He could at least say good job for thinking of it. Was that too much to ask?

Before Dawkins could say anything to make her feel worse, she skulked out as quickly as possible, emboldened by the fact that at least he agreed with her that the signatures didn't match. Sigmund would too. She was sure of it. They couldn't match. They weren't the same person.

Her job was to prove it, something she was more determined than ever to do.

* * *

Sigmund Douglas ran a one-man shop. By the look of his office, no one could tell he was the foremost handwriting expert in southern California— maybe the whole United States. A former retired FBI agent, he'd spent the last twenty years working with insurance companies and police agencies putting people behind bars. His testimony was the gold standard in the legal world, and he was in great demand. So much so that he only worked with existing clients, which was good for Cathy. Even then, it took more than three excruciating weeks for her to get an appointment with him.

She had five sets of documents that contained Wanda's signature to show him. The 1929 agency representation agreement, Wanda and Norman's wedding license, the Miles Fire & Casualty insurance application form, the claim form for the fire and theft of the necklace, and the release she signed in Fort Worth, agreeing not to contest the will. Win Rawlings had given her a copy at her request.

Cathy organized each document by date and had a facsimile copy so they could discuss it.

She set his file in front of him and said, "It looks to me like the 1929 is a different signature from the 1974 and 1984 documents. What do you think?" she asked.

"I never express an opinion based upon my naked eye. The eye can play tricks on you."

"I think it's pretty obvious from looking at them," Cathy said, a comment Sigmund ignored and instead rifled through the documents.

The room wasn't so much an office but had more of a feel of a laboratory. He had a microscope on his desk and another on a table behind him. A large bookcase along the side wall was full of books. Old and new.

They looked to be on the subject of forensic science.

"I'll look them over and let you know what I think."

"Should I come back?" Cathy asked, hoping he said she could wait.

"No. You can stay. It should only take about half an hour."

Sigmund placed the documents under the microscope on his desk, one by one. A notepad sat next to the microscope along with a pair of reading glasses and a pencil. He would look through the lens, let out some kind of sound, put on his reading glasses, and write something down. Then he'd repeat the process. Again, and again for a good thirty minutes.

Except for the anticipation of learning the results which she had waited three weeks for, Cathy would've been bored. From the sounds Sigmund made, she couldn't tell if they were good or bad for her case. Every noise was different, the meaning unclear. His mannerisms were identical each time.

Sigmund was wiry and his hair almost white. If she had to guess, she'd say he was in his late seventies. Although, as he said, the eye can be deceiving, so basing an opinion as to a person's age based on what her eye saw might be a mistake.

Somewhere between sixty and a hundred.

The thought made her smile.

After nearly an hour, Sigmund pushed the microscope aside.

Cathy got the impression he was done. At least she hoped he was, as she got out her own pad and paper for taking notes. She preferred a pen so the notes couldn't be altered. A couple of times in court, an aggressive defense attorney accused her of changing her notes after the fact. The pen didn't completely solve the problem, but it did help.

Sigmund looked up at her. "I have good news and bad news."

That made her heart flutter as she wasn't expecting anything but good news. "Give me the good news first," Cathy said.

"The documents dated 1974 and 1984 are all in the handwriting of the same person, in my opinion."

Cathy already assumed that.

"I look for seven things," Sigmund said. "The first is pressure. Someone trying to duplicate another person's signature, will press down harder than someone just writing their name naturally. The 1974 and the December 1984 documents are all written in normal pressure by someone comfortable with her signature. The most recent document, the June 1984 release of contestation of a will, is a facsimile. That makes it more difficult to assess the pressure. But it is consistent with the other signatures."

Cathy wondered if he was going to go through all seven things. That wasn't necessary if he had already concluded Wanda wrote those documents. She'd already concluded the same thing. His opinion on the 1929 document was what she was dying to know the results of.

Perhaps, Sigmund sensed her impatience, because he flipped the pages on his notes and said, "As to the 1929 document... that's where I might have what you would consider good and bad news. Pressure is inconclusive. The 1929 document was clearly signed by someone comfortable with her own handwriting as to the name Wanda. However, that person was not comfortable with signing Rose."

That got Cathy excited. She had information Sigmund didn't have.

"Wanda Rose was an alias. Her real name was Wanda O'Neil. That would explain it."

Sigmund let out a sound of understanding.

Cathy was starting to figure out what his noises meant.

He rubbed the stubble on his chin slightly. "That would be consistent with my findings. Changing her name probably happened around the time the contract was signed. That's a problem."

"Why is it a problem?"

"The handwriting attributes of the *Rose* in the later documents are not the same. But that's not surprising now that you've told me about the name change. Let me point out the differences. In 1929, there's no slant. The signature is straight. In present day documents, the slant is slightly to the left. That can also signify deception, although judges won't let me testify to that effect."

"Are there other differences?" Cathy asked.

"Many. One thing I look at is the size of the letters. In 1929 they are noticeably smaller. Also notice how they are written right on the line. The later documents are written in larger letters and are above the line."

Cathy could clearly see the differences now. She knew something was off before, and now she knew what it was.

"Fascinating," she said.

"Also, the space between the letters are different. In 1929 they are farther apart. As you can see, in 1974 and 1984 the letters are closer together."

"Why is that not good news?"

"Because as far as the last name goes, any forensic examiner worth his weight in salt would spot the discrepancy between the first name and the last name in 1929 right away. So, any discrepancies related to the last name in the present-day documents would be inconclusive. It would be normal for someone to alter the last name through the years if it wasn't something they grew up signing from the time they started writing."

Cathy's heart sunk a few spaces in her chest.

"What about the first name? What can you conclude from it?"

Sigmund looked down at his notes. "In my opinion, they were not written by the same person."

"That's good news."

"In comparing the *w* in the documents, they are conclusively different," Sigmund explained.

"You mean in the 1929 and the present-day documents?"

"All of them. I should say none of them are consistent."

"In the 1929 document, the *w* is wavy. In 1974, it's wide. In 1984, it's narrow, and the middle lines of the *w* cross at the top."

"What does that mean?"

"I think it means deception. The person writing it is not really Wanda Rose."

Cathy's heart rebounded to the point of elation until she noticed the frown on Sigmund's face.

"What's wrong? That's what I wanted to hear."

"The problem is that none of the four people who signed any of these documents are actually Wanda Rose."

"How is that a problem? I explained to you the name change that occurred in 1929."

"It raises doubt though. The defense will argue that the accused never got comfortable signing a fictitious name. So, the signature varied throughout the years. A normal person's signature varies between sixteen and sixty. Usually, they retain some characteristics. Maybe not, if all that time it really wasn't her name to begin with."

"But you said that they were not written by the same person. That's all I need to know."

"I said that it's my *opinion* that they are not the same person. Proving it in a court of law is another thing."

"Would you be willing to testify to that effect?"

"I don't think you would want me to," Sigmund said.

"Of course, I would."

"I'd have to admit that my findings aren't beyond a reasonable doubt."

"Can you at least give me a letter stating it's your opinion that they aren't the same person? That way if I get more evidence, then I can use that as supplemental proof."

"I can give you a letter with my findings. I don't know how helpful they'll be."

Cathy had to ask. "Forget for a minute about being in a court of law. Just between the two of us. Is the person who signed the 1929 and 1984 documents the same person?"

Sigmund paused for a good thirty seconds. He looked down at his notes. Then at Cathy and then back down at his notes.

Finally, he said, "In my opinion, they are not the same person."

"That's all I needed to know," Cathy said. "Now look at these photos."

Cathy handed Sigmund copies of the photos hanging on Wanda's wall that were signed by celebrities. "Can you tell me if these signatures are real?" she asked.

* * *

It took nearly a week for Sigmund's letter to arrive. When it did, it wasn't nearly as definitive as Cathy would've liked. Still, she brought it to Dawkins along with her arguments, fully prepared to defend her position to what she thought was its logical conclusion. The woman she knew was not the real Wanda Rose.

"Here's the letter with Sigmund's findings," Cathy said, taking it out of the file and laying it in front of Dawkins.

Without looking down he said, "Summarize it for me. So, I don't have to read the whole thing."

It's only one page, Cathy wanted to say sarcastically, but changed her mind. This was actually better. She could put her own spin on it.

"He agrees with me that our client is not the singer who signed the document in 1929," Cathy said.

A half-smile formed on Dawkins' face. She thought that meant he was pleased but couldn't be sure.

She continued. "He also said that the celebrity signatures on the photos hanging in Wanda's house, all appear to be authentic. Although, he wasn't examining the originals, so they could be copies."

"Good work. Now what does that have to do with our claim?"

"I'm sorry?"

"Okay. So, it's not the same person. So what?"

"It means we've proven that she's a fraud. She's going around pretending to be Wanda Rose the singer."

"You need more."

"How much more?"

"A lot more than what you've got. My bosses aren't going to sign off on a lawsuit based on that information, as interesting as it may be. Keep digging. See what else you can find."

"Any suggestions on what I do next?"

"Yes. Come with me to the conference room."

"Why?"

"Because everybody in the office is there."

"I don't understand."

"Happy birthday," he said less than enthusiastically. "They have a cake and everything for you."

Cathy didn't think anyone remembered.

Dawkins asked, "How old are you now?"

"I'm not saying. Don't you know it's rude to ask a woman her age?" "I'd guess forty or forty-five," he said with a sly grin.

"Thirty-seven," Cathy quickly answered. If he was going to guess high, then she'd tell him her real age.

"Ah... To be thirty-seven again. Oh well. Age is just a number."

"Yes, it is."

"Your biological clock is ticking. You'd better hurry up and get married if you're going to have kids. Soon, you won't be able to."

Cathy's shoulders shuddered in anger. She didn't think it possible for Dawkins to say something that would shock her, but he managed to. It seemed like every conversation with Dawkins ended on a sour note. Somehow, he managed to throw a sexist remark into the dialogue at some point. That almost spoiled the thought of the birthday party. She tried not to let it. Her heart was warmed as they walked toward the conference room.

Right before she got there, something hit her.

A thought.

Her birthday reminded her of something.

What is it?

"Act surprised," Dawkins said as they rounded the corner and got to the conference room door, which was shut, and the blinds to the windows were closed.

Something about Wanda's birth certificate seemed off, she remembered. Suddenly she knew what it was.

15

The birthday party for Cathy went on for more than thirty minutes and didn't seem like it would end anytime soon. Much longer than she would've liked. Not that she didn't appreciate her coworkers' gesture, but she desperately wanted to get back to the Wanda Rose files. Her birthday had sparked a memory, and her curiosity was distracting her from anything else.

Something about Wanda O'Neil's birth certificate didn't seem right when she saw it for the first time at Norman's estate. Try as she might, she couldn't figure out what it was.

Now she knew, or at least she thought she did, and was dying to confirm it. After the problems with the handwriting analysis, she needed a new line of investigation. With the birth certificate, she might very well have one. She could find out quickly and had to get back to her office.

First, she had to endure a cake, a couple presents, and several toasts. One of the ladies prepared a pink punch, which Cathy was sure one of the men had spiked as a joke, knowing that she didn't drink. The crew had clearly started drinking before Dawkins and she even arrived, evident by the buzz in the room, and by the good mood everyone seemed to be in, considering it was the middle of the workday, and no one would be going home for several hours.

Cathy tried her best to put on a smile and a friendly face and avoid drinking too much of the punch. When she got back to the office, the last thing she wanted was to have her senses dulled by alcohol.

Such had become her life and obsession with Wanda Rose—she'd rather be working the file than celebrating her birthday.

When Dawkins raised a glass to toast Cathy, she had a second reason why she wanted to be anywhere else but there.

"A plane is about to crash," Dawkins began, confirming to Cathy that a distasteful joke was forthcoming. "A woman stands up and says, 'I want to feel like a woman one last time before I die. Is there any man on this plane who is man enough to make me feel like a woman?'"

A chuckle went through the room with everyone but the six women, including Cathy who glared at Dawkins. Only he could figure out a way to ruin her birthday celebration. He must've known she was angry because he kept his gaze on the room and clearly tried not to make eye contact with her.

He continued. "A man stood up, took off his shirt, and handed it to the woman and told her to iron it!"

The men in the room turned their chuckle into a boisterous roar.

Cathy was appalled that a few women laughed, even though the joke was demeaning and undeserving of such brown nosing.

"Seriously," Dawkins said when the room quieted down. "If we must have a woman as a claim's adjuster, Tolliver is as good as they come. Here's to you," he said, looking at her smugly and raising his glass in the air.

Even his compliments were backhanded.

Everyone raised their glasses, and they all toasted to what Cathy thought was his sick humor undeserving of a toast. So, Cathy didn't raise her glass. Noticeably. Something that wasn't lost on Dawkins as the veins in his neck throbbed and his jaw clenched. A glaring standoff suddenly ensued.

"You see it in all the animals, the female in the species is deadlier than the male," he said waving his hand toward her with a challenging stare.

Cathy wasn't sure if he was trying to defuse the situation or escalate it.

If he could use her last name as a sign of disrespect, so could she.

"Dawkins, I'm glad to hear that you think women are superior to men." "I said deadlier, not superior. There's a big difference."

The men guffawed. By the looks on the women's faces, they were secretly cheering her on. Although, some seemed shocked that she dared to challenge the lion in the room. Obvious, as their collective eyes were as wide as the punch glasses. Cathy presumed the women were vacillating between nervousness for her and anticipation as to what Dawkins might say or do next. No one had ever stood up to him like this before.

No woman anyway.

Drawing on their encouragement, Cathy retorted. "A woman put a *husband wanted* classified ad in the newspaper. She got hundreds of responses from women who said, 'You can have mine!'"

The laughter in the room raised another level. Cathy had been saving her own jokes for the right moment. Now seemed like as good a time as any.

Not to be outdone, Dawkins fired back, "For all the guys who think a woman's place is in the kitchen, remember that's where all the knives are kept."

Cathy retorted, "Women will never be equal to men until we can walk down the street with a bald head and a beer gut and still think we're sexy!"

The entire room applauded. Even the men appreciated that joke. Dawkins raised his glass in surrender. Then he ordered everyone back to work, reminding them who was in charge.

It seemed her duty, so Cathy stayed a few minutes longer to thank everyone as they filed out. Dawkins stormed out of the room without saying anything to her. As much as she would've preferred being in her office and working on the Rose file, she did feel a certain satisfaction from the exchange.

The birthday party was enjoyable after all.

* * *

When she returned to her office, Cathy got Wanda's birth certificate out of the box from Norman's house. The birthdate had piqued her interest.

November 5, 1912.

The time of birth was 12:04 a.m.

The place was St. Francis Hospital, Canton, New Jersey.

For some reason, Cathy remembered that the birthdate on Wanda's insurance application was November 4, 1912. It wouldn't take long to confirm if her memory was correct.

The application was near the top of the file because she had taken the original to Sigmund to analyze the handwriting. A bolt of excitement shot through her when she saw the birthdate Wanda had put on the application.

Date of birth. November 4, 1912.

Her body twitched as the adrenaline pulsed through her veins.

What did that mean?

The date on the application didn't match the date on the birth certificate. How is it possible that Wanda didn't know her own birthday?

Cathy gathered the two documents and stood to go into Dawkins office but stopped herself. He'd just shoot her down with some snide remark. Especially since he was probably still mad at her for showing him up at the birthday party.

I need more information.

Think.

What were some possible explanations? A couple came to mind.

Maybe Wanda was told she was born on the fourth. After all, her mother died in childbirth, and she was sent to an orphanage. It's feasible she was given the wrong day. The time of day was just after midnight. The nurses might've told the director of the orphanage the wrong date or the wrong time. Perhaps Wanda had been celebrating it wrong all these years.

If she gave Wanda the benefit of the doubt. Something she wasn't prepared to do. Everything related to Wanda Rose was met with skepticism as far as she was concerned.

And... it didn't make sense.

Norman said the orphanage gave Wanda her file with the birth certificate in it when she was sixteen. According to him, she burned the file. Which seemed strange in and of itself. One would think she would've at least looked through it. Wouldn't she have noticed the discrepancy on her birthdate?

Certainly, she would've seen the correct date when the birth certificate arrived so they could get their wedding license. Is it possible that no one noticed? Norman seemed to be sharp when it came to details. What date did they celebrate Wanda's birthday? They were married for twelve years.

Cathy could easily explain it away. Norman had only known Wanda for three weeks when they were married. He might not have known her birthdate. When they did celebrate her birthday, he might not have even remembered the date on the birth certificate. Cathy was trained to look for discrepancies. Most people would never think to. Still... it seemed infeasible that it never came up.

More questions than answers surfaced in her mind.

She found the marriage license and took it out of the file. It didn't have a birthdate on it.

What else would have a birthdate on it?

Driver's license.

When Wanda made her application for insurance, a copy of her driver's license was put in the file. Cathy would have to search for it. By this time, Wanda's complete file took up four large folders.

After much digging, Cathy found it. The picture was from over ten years ago. Wanda was still beautiful in her picture, even though she would've been around sixty at the time. Cathy felt a twinge of jealousy. Her own driver's license picture looked hideous.

Focus on the date.

DOB: November 4, 1912.

That's strange.

Wanda put the fourth when she applied for her California driver's license, and the fourth on her insurance application. Why the discrepancy from her birth certificate? That had to prove deception. No one transitioned back and forth between two different birthdays.

Which was right? The birth certificate or the driver's license and the insurance application? Most likely neither. The imposter's birthdate was probably a different date altogether which was why she couldn't keep it straight.

Cathy wasn't sure what to do. If she talked to Dawkins, he would think it was interesting, but not proof of anything. How could she prove it with her limited information?

Only one way came to mind.

With the decision made, Cathy packed up her file and headed out of the office. Before she did, she stopped by Dawkins office to see his secretary. The last thing she wanted was to see him.

"Tell Mr. Dawkins that I've gone to Canton, New Jersey. I'm working a lead on the Wanda Rose file. I'll call him when I have something."

Before the secretary could respond, Cathy was already down the hallway, hoping she hadn't made a big mistake by leaving without his permission.

* * *

This was Cathy's first trip to the northeast part of the country. Born and raised in Houston, Texas, she took a job right out of college with Miles Fire & Casualty. When they offered her the opportunity to transfer to southern California, she felt like a fish out water. Twelve years later, she had completely bought in to the laid-back lifestyle of beaches, lattes, and art deco cafés.

Now in New Jersey, she felt like a fish out of water again. Her flight was actually into Philadelphia, Pennsylvania, where she was greeted with billowing smokestacks that put off a stench unlike any she'd ever smelled before. The drivers were aggressive and rude, and the roads narrow and filled with cars darting back and forth between lanes in far too big a hurry.

Philadelphia was the *City of Brotherly Love*, but she didn't experience any of it in the short time she was there.

It never felt like she left the city limits. When she crossed the Ben Franklin Bridge over the Delaware River and left Pennsylvania and crossed into New Jersey, she went from one concrete jungle to another. Camden, New Jersey, was the skyline on the other side.

New Jersey was called the Garden State, but Cathy didn't see one.

To make matters worse, she got lost in downtown Camden, and the maze of one-way streets took her around in circles. Once she did find the courthouse, she had to park six blocks away and pay ten dollars for the privilege. Dawkins would never believe she had paid that much for parking, so she demanded a receipt, and the attendant reluctantly and rudely finally gave her.

She blamed her frustrations on Wanda Rose, and that made her feel better.

Until she got inside the building.

The courthouse was old. The historical registry sign out front read 1826. From the outside, it looked every bit that old and more.

Inside was slightly better in that the marble floors were polished, and the stoned walls cleaned. Except for the musty smell of an old building, Cathy thought it was kind of cool. She'd never been in a building that predated the Civil War.

The archives department was downstairs. One look at the elevator, and she decided to take the stairs.

A woman named Violet, based on her name tag, greeted her at the counter inside the door that said *Public Records*. Although, she wouldn't call it a greeting. It sounded more like a *What do you want and why are you bothering me?* kind of address.

Cathy skipped the greeting and got right to the point. In her short time in the northeast, she'd already learned that the locals weren't much on small talk. Cathy said, "I'm working on a fraud investigation, and I'm looking for a birth certificate dating back to 1912."

"That's in the dungeon," Violet said.

"I beg your pardon?"

"We keep the archives in what used to be the old prison." *Great.*

"Follow me," Violet said.

They got on the old elevator, much to Cathy's reluctance. Inside was worse than it looked on the outside. It appeared to be as old as the building, even though Cathy didn't think that was possible. She scanned through her memory trying to remember when elevators were first invented.

As if Violet was reading her thoughts, she said, "This was the first elevator in New Jersey. Dates back to 1853."

Great.

The contraption creaked and moaned, and Cathy could hear the gears grinding as it lurched downward. When it suddenly stopped, her heart skipped a beat. Violet didn't seem alarmed, so she took her cue and didn't say anything. But when the doors finally opened, she took a deep breath that she hadn't realized she'd been holding.

When she did, an overpowering mixture of moldy air and mildew filled her lungs and she almost gagged.

"We don't get a lot of people down here," Violet said. "Although, you're the second one this week."

They exited the elevator into a dark and dank room with makeshift fluorescent light fixtures attached to the ceiling. They walked into a big room with a lot of small ones around the edges where the prison cells had been. The bars were removed so each room had a twelve-foot wide opening into it.

Violet walked toward the last room on the left, while Cathy tried to keep up. People moved a lot faster in New Jersey than they did in California.

"The rooms are organized by decades," Violet explained. They also talked faster. "We house all the records up to 1930 in this building. Everything else is kept in Trenton. A birth certificate from 1912 would be in this room."

"What about death certificates?" Cathy asked. She was also looking for Wanda's mother's death certificate.

Violet answered, "Same room. All the public records are stored in here. Birth certificates. Marriage licenses. Death records. Let me know if you need anything. I'll be upstairs."

Great.

I can't believe you're leaving me alone in this dungeon.

Cathy didn't expect the lady to help her search the files, but she had envisioned a large room like a library where the attendant would be a few feet from her. She didn't expect to be left by herself in a dungeon where the walls suddenly seemed to be closing in on her.

It's all Wanda's fault.

At least she could keep blaming her for the hardships. The only other consolation was that she was feet away from information vital to her case.

She entered the room carefully. It still felt like a dungeon even though it was filled with files with the dates clearly identified on the outside which would make her job a lot easier. Cathy was obsessed with detail, and so she appreciated the effort it took to get the records in this condition.

She'd seen worse. Except for it being a dungeon, Cathy was glad she didn't have to go through a lot of dusty files that were in random order. More times than she could count, she'd had to find the proverbial needle in a haystack.

This would be easy. She'd start with the November 5, 1912 birth certificate. Since she already had a copy, she knew it existed. On the outside of one of the cabinets was *Birth Certificates, 1910-1915*. They were organized by date.

That's good.

When she found 1912, she flipped to November fifth. Wanda's should be one of the first on that date since her time of birth was 12:04 a.m.

Turns out they weren't organized by time, but alphabetically. Cathy flipped through the files carefully, not wanting to damage the older documents. When she got to the 'O's, there were only two. Neither of them said Wanda O'Neil.

"What?" Cathy said out loud.

She checked and doubled checked the files.

November 5, 1912.

Thinking maybe it was misfiled, she flipped through the entire collection of files for November fifth.

Nothing.

She looked on the fourth. Still nothing.

On the other side of the wall were the death certificates. Cathy found November 1912 and rummaged through it. There was no death record for Rose Kennedy O'Neil on November fourth or fifth.

She even checked the entire week, thinking that maybe her mother lived a few days before passing. A sense of urgency suddenly came upon her. She had come to Camden with so much expectation only to have them dashed against the concrete walls when she couldn't even find any record of anything.

Cathy couldn't fathom all of the consequences of what that meant. After a futile search that lasted for more than an hour, she finally gave up and rode the elevator upstairs.

Violet was still at her post. "Did you find what you were looking for?" she asked.

"I did not."

Cathy pulled out a copy of the birth certificate in her file. Violet took one look at it and handed it back to her without comment.

"That's what I'm looking for," Cathy explained. "It's not in the cabinet."

"It should be."

"It's not. I looked everywhere for it."

"That's definitely one of ours. It should be there."

"I know it should be. Can you help me look?" Cathy hesitated to ask because it meant another ride down the elevator into the dungeon.

Violet's response was not helpful and bordered on impolite. "If you couldn't find it, what makes you think I can? It's not hard. Everything is organized by date. Did you look in the right year?"

Cathy made what she hoped was a noticeable frown. "Of course, I did."

"Must be misfiled then. That happens. When somebody pulled the birth certificate... the one you have, they probably didn't put it back in the right place. No telling where it is."

"The death certificate is missing as well. The mother died giving birth to her daughter and that death record isn't there."

"That's strange."

"Yes, it is," Cathy said, waiting for a solution.

"I don't know what to tell you."

Cathy put the certificate back in the file. Totally deflated. The entire trip had been wasted. Dawkins wouldn't let her hear the end of it. She hadn't even gotten permission to come there. Now she wasted all the time and money on a dead end. She walked away in a huff. Not mad at anyone in particular. Just unsure what to do next. Then a thought hit her. She walked back to the counter. Violet didn't seem happy to see her.

"You said that I was the second person this week to look at the archives. Could you describe the other person?"

"Woman. Late sixties. A bit overdone with her makeup and jewelry. She was probably pretty at one time. Had a silly looking feather in her hat."

Cathy's heart started racing, and her hand shook as she pulled a picture of Wanda out of her file. "Is this the woman?"

Violet's eyes lit up in recognition confirming her suspicions.

"Yes! That's her."

"Thank you very much. You've been extremely helpful."

16

Wanda sat in the bar of a Philadelphia hotel, nursing her third glass of gin and tonic. Satisfied that she had dodged a bullet. The little trip to the courthouse in Camden had done the trick, and she had safely removed all evidence of her past that could be used against her.

Probably unnecessary, but she had not gotten this far without being overly cautious.

That insurance lady, a despicable woman, was ruining her life and forcing her to go to these lengths. Perhaps she was being too cautious. More than likely, the Cathy lady wouldn't come to Camden, but Wanda wasn't going to take any chances. After learning that Norman had given her box to Cathy, she realized she'd probably seen the birth certificate.

Those are my things. What right does she have to them?

Nevertheless, she did have them. That might raise questions and make her want to snoop around further. It wouldn't be hard for her to write to the archives in Camden, New Jersey, and request more information. Keeping her skeletons safely buried in the closet all these years had taken tremendous effort and manipulation. She wasn't about to let the truth come out now.

As chance would have it, a not-so-fortuitous fire was almost her downfall and had started the chain reaction that had become this nightmare.

Her mind wandered back to that fateful night.

Christmas Eve.

All alone.

The sadness had overwhelmed her to the point that she'd had too much to drink. That was true far too many nights. She'd just poured herself a third glass of gin when she suddenly smelled smoke. She went to investigate, and to her horror, the Christmas tree was on fire. Without thinking, she threw her drink on the flames to put them out, which only made things worse, as the gin splashed the flames against the wall and ignited it.

Within a couple minutes, the whole room was ablaze.

Fortunately, the firemen got there quickly and put the flames out before it destroyed everything.

Then the necklace went missing.

Damn fireman.

She knew which one of them did it. The blond-haired boy with shifty eyes had come out of her bathroom, startled that she had seen him. If only she'd remembered the necklace right away. From the trauma of the fire, it took a full week before she realized it was gone.

The insurance adjuster didn't believe she even had a necklace and wouldn't quit asking questions.

Of all the nerve. Accusing me of lying.

It went on for six long months. When she finally got the check from the insurance agency, she thought that was the end of it.

But the woman got her painting.

Wanda balled her hand into a fist and hit it against the bar counter.

Why did Norman give it to her?

Revenge probably.

He was no doubt laughing in his grave.

She needed to get that painting back. But how? She had no idea where the painting was. How could she know? By the time she got to Norman's house, *my house*, after the reading of the will, the painting was already gone.

Did Cathy sell it? Ship it to her house? To an auction house? In any of those scenarios, she couldn't think of a viable plan to get it back.

"Do you have a phone?" she asked the bartender.

He reached under the counter and pulled out a desk top phone with a long cord.

Wanda dialed Cathy's home number which she had memorized.

Somehow, she had to get that painting back before Cathy Tolliver found out the secret behind it.

* * *

Camden, NJ

The prudent thing for Cathy to do would be to go back to LA. Wanda Rose had been one step ahead of her from the beginning. At some point, she'd have to accept defeat and go back to her life.

Something she wasn't prepared to do yet.

Since she was already in Camden, Cathy thought she should pay a visit to the hospital. They would have a record of Wanda's birth. Wanda probably thought of that too, but hopefully the hospital wouldn't be stupid enough to leave her alone with the records. The archives of Camden, New Jersey, should change that policy. Stealing or changing historical documents was easy to do when the records were left unattended. Getting someone to work full time in that dungeon might be a challenge, but something needed to be done. She'd bet this wasn't the first time, records had suddenly gone missing. She could think of several scenarios where that might occur. Particularly in a divorce, or a contested will, or an insurance fraud claim.

The thought of Wanda stealing those documents made her insides boil like a cauldron. At some point, the Wanda Rose case had crossed over the line from a professional fraud claim investigation into a personal vendetta. Wanda was a fraud, and she was going to prove it if it were the last thing she did as a claim's adjuster. Which might very well be the case if she didn't prove it soon. Dawkins wasn't going to put up with her insubordination for much longer without some results to justify it.

She only got lost twice going to the hospital which was better than she did in finding the courthouse. The new wing of St. Francis hospital, dedicated in 1953, sat in the same location as the original, which dated back to the late 1800s. It appeared that only a small part of the original structure still stood.

Cathy called ahead and set an appointment with the administrator, Prudence Flowers. A name she thought was unique and interesting, so she told her so. "I really like your name," she said to the perky woman about her age, maybe a little older.

Prudence answered with a warm smile, "My mother was Welsh, and my dad was German."

"It's pretty."

"It's Latin. It means, cautious."

"I assumed it had something to do with the word *prudent*."

She nodded in agreement. "An interesting anecdote, if you have a minute?"

"Of course," Cathy said.

"Mia Farrow, the famous actress has a sister named Prudence. I'm named after her. That's where my mom got it."

Cathy suddenly remembered, "John Lennon also has a song called *Dear Prudence*."

"The song was named after Farrow's sister." The warm grin had turned into a full-blown smile.

They both laughed at the same time. Cathy said, "That *is* interesting. I love John Lennon and the Beatles."

"I cried when he died. Such a senseless tragedy," Prudence said as her voice cracked slightly.

"I remember where I was when I heard the news. December 8, 1980."

"You have a good memory."

"I remember dates."

Cathy did have an uncanny gift for remembering important dates in history. Not just history, but everyday life as well. She never forgot a birthday, anniversary, or a significant date to someone important to her. The fact that it had taken so long for her to discover the discrepancy on Wanda's birth certificate was surprising.

"I'm impressed," Prudence said.

Prudence Flowers was different than the other people she'd met in the northeast. She was warm and friendly. She intended to try and be as cordial as possible, hoping that the effort might curry her favor. It didn't seem to be necessary with Prudence. If Cathy read her right, she was the type of person who would help her in any way she could.

Hopefully.

As if on cue Prudence asked, "What can I do for you today?"

"I'm looking for information about a baby who was born in your hospital in 1912." Cathy had rehearsed the speech several times in her head. "Do you still have those records?"

Please say yes.

"We keep all of our records in the basement of the old wing of the hospital."

The basement. Ugh.

Cathy shuddered inside. It couldn't possibly be worse than the dungeon, or at least that's what she told herself.

She responded without letting Prudence know her angst. "Excellent. The baby's name is Wanda O'Neil. It's possible that Wanda might have recently dropped by looking for the same information."

Prudence shook her head. "No one has been here, as far as I know."

A sense of relief flooded through her. Maybe she was one step ahead of Wanda this time. "May I research those records," she asked.

"May I ask your purpose? Are you a private investigator?"

"No, ma'am. I work for *Miles Fire and Casualty* out of Los Angeles California. I'm a claim's adjuster, investigating a fraud claim." Cathy said the words as sweetly as she possibly could without coming across as insincere.

"I'm sorry Ms. Tolliver, but I can't let you see the records. Patient privacy issues and what not."

Cathy had noticed that people in the northeast said "what not" a lot. She wasn't sure why. Ignoring it, she asked, "What privacy issues are there, dating back seventy-two years ago?" trying not to sound argumentative.

"All medical records are private. The only way we can let some-one view those records is with a court order. Or if you are a physi-cian licensed in New Jersey, which I assume you aren't." Prudence's voice had replaced the friendly demeanor with a professional tone. Still polite, but more businesslike than before.

"I'm not either of those, but I can tell you that the information is extremely important."

"Short of a court order, I can't help you. Have you tried the courthouse?

They should have the birth records there."

They should have. But they don't.

And would have if Wanda hadn't stolen them. Now was not the time to make that accusation. If Prudence knew all the facts, there's no way she'd let the hospital get involved in a mess.

"What about death records?" Cathy didn't miss a step. "The mother died in childbirth. Surely there aren't any privacy issues re-lated to someone who is deceased."

"Unfortunately, the only person who can have access to those records would be the guardian of the estate. So theoretically, a close relative could view the records. I assume you're not a close relative."

"I'm not," Cathy said with obvious disappointment in her voice. Although the thought occurred to her that Wanda could view the records if she could prove the records were hers or her mother's. Maybe she couldn't which was why she hadn't tried.

"I'm sorry I can't help you." Prudence clearly seemed sympathetic.

"I understand that you have rules."

"The coroner's office might keep the records. You could go to the county morgue."

A chill went down Cathy's spine as she imagined what their dungeon must look like. She wasn't that desperate for the records.

There has to be another way. So, she asked, "If a mother died in childbirth, and the father wasn't in the picture, what would happen to the child?"

"I presume she would go to the next of kin."

"My understanding is that she went to an orphanage. Any idea where she might've gone?"

"The only orphanage I know of that has been around that long is the *Sisters of Charity* in Pennsauken."

"Is it still in existence?"

"Yes, it is."

Cathy could feel the blood rush to her face.

"I don't think they take in children anymore," Prudence continued. "But the nuns still live there. The files are probably still kept there. Although... you'll probably run into the same privacy issues."

If it was even possible, Cathy felt the color drain from her face as quickly as it had rushed into it. "I suppose I will."

Of course, they had privacy issues. Orphanages might even be stricter than hospitals if that was possible. Going there would be an even bigger waste of time.

"May I make a suggestion?" Prudence asked.

"Sure," Cathy said, as she prepared to leave and get on the first plane back to LA.

"Check the baptism records at the orphanage," she said. "Those aren't private. If the baby went to *Sisters of Charity* orphanage, she would've been baptized within eight days of arrival."

"That's a good idea. Thanks. Do you have a phone number for them?"

Prudence picked up the phone on her desk. "Let me call them on your behalf so they'll be expecting you."

Turns out Cathy was right. Prudence did do everything she could to help her.

* * *

Sister Angelica was as friendly as Prudence but in a more solemn and dignified manner. Every sentence was deliberate and measured, carefully constructed, with every word economical by design. By the looks of her, she was a good ten years younger than Cathy. Only her face and hands were showing, and they appeared to be as soft as a baby's bottom as if no care in the world had ever come across them.

The office was understated with nothing but religious artifacts on the wall. Cathy felt compelled to speak in a quiet and reverent tone without even realizing it until she was well into the conversation.

With her Protestant upbringing, it seemed strange calling the woman sister, but she did anyway. "Sister Angelica, thank you for your time today."

She bowed her head slightly. Her hands were folded in front of her on top of the desk. It looked like the scene from a movie, although, she couldn't place which one.

"I'm looking for any information you can give me regarding a Wanda O'Neil. I believe she came to your orphanage in November of 1912."

"I hope I can be helpful to you."

When Cathy spoke slowly, she reverted back to her southern drawl. "I sure do appreciate it."

Sister Angelica had a large book open in front of her. Prudence had told the Sister on the phone what Cathy was looking for, so she was prepared. The book had lines and columns on each page with handwriting on most of the lines. Cathy strained to see them without being too obvious.

"I looked through the baptism records and there is not a Wanda O'Neil listed," the sister explained.

Cathy's heart sunk as she had reached another dead end. Norman said that Wanda was born at Saint Francis hospital in Camden New Jersey and went to an orphanage right after her mother died and stayed there until she was sixteen. The conversation was embedded in her memory.

According to Prudence, this was the only orphanage in the area at that time.

Cathy asked, "Is it possible that she came here and wasn't baptized?"

"Every baby who comes into our care is baptized into the faith."

"I'm told she was here until her sixteenth birthday. Then she was given her file and released."

"The girls stay until they are of age, which is eighteen, or they are adopted. We don't give them their file. It is kept in our possession."

"So, do you have a file for Wanda O'Neil?"

"We do not. I checked before you came."

"Is there anyone still alive who was here during that time?"

"Sister Rita has been here for many years."

"May I speak to her? Perhaps, she would remember Wanda."

"I'm afraid that Sister Rita is in failing health. Her memory is not what it used to be."

"I really need to talk to her. Could you ask her if she would see me?"

Sister Angelica stood to her feet and Cathy did as well. "Please wait here," she said politely but with authority.

Several minutes later, she returned.

"Sister Rita will see you in the garden."

Cathy was surprised. She had expected another dead end. *I hope she knows something.*

* * *

The first garden Cathy had seen in the Garden State consisted of a gazebo with two chairs and a small table. Two blue hydrangea bushes provided the only color. An elderly nun sat in a wheelchair with her shoulders slumped. Cathy followed Sister Angelica cautiously and only sat in the chair next to her once she was invited by a hand outstretched toward the chair.

Sister Angelica began speaking in a loud voice into Sister Rita's ear. "Sister Rita, this is Ms. Tolliver. She wants to ask you some questions."

The delicate woman lifted her head slightly and nodded. "How are you, dear?" she said weakly to Cathy.

"I'm very well, thank you."

"When am I going to have lunch?" Sister Rita asked Angelica.

"You've already had lunch, Sister Rita," she answered respectfully.

Then she said to Cathy in a whisper, "Her short-term memory is what has faded the most. Her long-term memory is still good. Hopefully, she'll be of help to you. I think she'll enjoy the company. I'll be right over here if you need me."

Sister Angelica turned and walked a distance away. Cathy guessed to give them privacy, though it wasn't necessary. Or maybe to keep a watchful eye on the sister.

"Who are you?" Sister Rita asked looking directly at Cathy like she was sizing her up.

"My name is Cathy. I wanted to ask you about Wanda O'Neil."

A faraway look came into her eyes as she looked toward the sky like she was thinking.

"I don't know a Wanda O'Neil," she eventually said in a labored voice.

"She came to your orphanage in 1912."

"What year is it now?"

"1984."

"When am I supposed to have lunch?"

Cathy looked over at Sister Angelica who just smiled. They were still within earshot, but clearly Cathy was on her own. "You already had lunch," Cathy answered.

"Oh. I hope I liked it," she said with a chuckle at her own joke.

Cathy laughed with her. "I'm sure it was. Do you remember a baby who came to you in 1912 from St. Francis hospital? Her mother died giving birth to her."

"I remember Bea."

"Her name was Wanda. Not Bea."

"We never had a girl named Wanda. A sweet baby name Bea came to us around that time. That girl was a handful. Her poor mother died during childbirth."

"Was that in 1912?"

"Heavens, I couldn't remember the year. But I do remember Bea. She could sing like an angel. A handful though," she said, repeating herself. "Honey, would you tell them to bring me my lunch?"

Cathy felt like she'd just had a B-12 shot.

Could it be the same person?

What seemed like a million questions suddenly came into her mind to ask the nun.

"I'm tired," Sister Rita said.

Angelica walked toward them and stood beside Rita and leaned in and said, "Are you ready to go back in?"

"I'm ready for lunch."

"Okay. I'll take you back inside."

"Please wait here," she said to Cathy

Sister Angelica wheeled Sister Rita away, leaving Cathy with more questions than answers. At first, she tried to put it out of her mind. Clearly, she couldn't count on the memory of a woman who couldn't remember the lunch she'd had a few minutes before. The name Bea didn't sound anything like Wanda. The fact that she was a beautiful singer hardly meant anything. They probably had plenty of girls come through there who could sing.

Another dead end.

Clearly, Wanda had lied to Norman about going to an orphanage. Maybe she even lied about her mother dying.

Who knows?

Cathy had already caught Wanda in more lies, than she could count. This was just one more.

When Sister Angelica returned, they walked back toward the office, and Cathy asked for her own piece of mind, "Would you mind looking at the baptism registry one more time?"

"When I looked before I saw a Beatrice. But her last name wasn't O'Neil."

"What was it?" Cathy asked, taking a stab in the dark.

"Her Christian name for the baptism was Beatrice Rose Kennedy."

That was Wanda's mother's name. Rose Kennedy. That couldn't be a coincidence.

"You have made my day, Sister."

17

New Orleans, Louisiana
Louisiana Vital Records

"What are you looking for?" the cute boy at the counter in the Department of Health & Hospital building in downtown New Orleans asked Cathy.

He wasn't really a boy. By the looks of him, he was probably only four or five years younger than Cathy. She called all men "boys" who were younger. A defense mechanism she formed many years ago. That made them undatable in her mind. Her last serious boyfriend was in college and broke her heart. He was selfish and immature, so she vowed to never date someone younger than her.

Older men had their own drawbacks, though. Men her age were usually divorced, with kids. That wasn't an option either. She wasn't going to raise another man's children or deal with a scorned ex-wife. That pretty much classified every man on earth as undatable. Which was why it had been five years since she'd been on a serious date. A fact she didn't want to be reminded of at the moment. Her total focus had to be on finding out the identity of Beatrice Rose Kennedy.

Cathy realized she let the boy's question, *what are you looking for*, linger in the air too long, so she said, "I don't know what I'm looking for." A comment which made him laugh.

Even his laugh is cute.

"We have millions of documents in this building," he said. "Good luck finding what you're looking for if you don't know what it is."

The truth was that she didn't know. The only thing she knew was that she wasn't going to find out anything more in Camden, New Jersey. So, she left to come to the scene of the crime. New Orleans. Or at least that's where she suspected the crime happened. That's where Wanda Rose lived until she married Norman and moved to Fort Worth. If she were to find anything, it would be there. What it might be, she hadn't a clue.

Not wanting to keep letting too much time lapse again before she answered, she said, "I'm looking for information regarding Wanda Rose."

"The blues singer?"

"You've heard of her?"

"Of course. I think everyone in New Orleans has heard of Wanda Rose. I love her."

Cathy bristled. The name Wanda Rose raised the hair on her arms. She thought her contempt for the woman couldn't be greater until she learned that she stole the documents out of the New Jersey archives just to keep Cathy from finding them.

"Have you ever heard of Beatrice Rose? Or Beatrice Rose Kennedy?"

"Can't say that I have." She liked his folksy, southern, sing-song manner of speaking.

"Where would I start looking to find information on her?"

Cute boy scanned the room. She followed his eyes. This room was the antithesis of the dungeon in New Jersey. The structure still had that "new car smell" about it. Clearly, they had just moved in because some workers were hanging pictures on the walls.

A dozen or more people were searching files in various parts of the room which—a stark contrast to the desolate prison in Camden. They had microfiche readers throughout the room. Cathy had worked with those many times before. All she had to do was find the film and scroll through to find what she was looking for. Hopefully, the documents were organized well.

Once she knew what documents to find.

Cute boy answered her after a short delay of his own. "It depends on what you want to find. We house birth, marriage, and death records in this location."

"I don't need birth. I'm not sure about the others."

"I'm sorry, ma'am. But I need more information."

That settled it. Anyone who called her ma'am was definitely un-datable. That and the fact that he lived nearly two thousand miles away from Los Angeles.

Why am I thinking about dating?

Maybe because it had been too long.

Cathy tried to get her focus back on the task at hand. "Why don't I start with marriage records? Where would those be?" she asked.

"Under the sign that says marriage records," cute boy said with a shy grin. He didn't say it sarcastically, and he didn't seem to be making fun of her. The banter was said jokingly, like a friendly discussion which made him even cuter.

Made the *boy* cuter, she reminded herself.

Not datable.

"Oh right," she said, embarrassingly when she realized what he meant. She began looking for the first opportunity to exit the conversation as gracefully as possible. Embarrassed by her thoughts as much as by her inability to carry on a sensible conversation with the cute boy.

"My name's Matt, by the way. Let me know if I can help you."

"Thanks, Matt. I should be fine. I may also look at the death records. I assume they are under the sign that reads, *Death Records*."

"You catch on fast," Matt said with a wide smile.

For a moment, Cathy thought the *boy* was flirting with her.

*** * ***

The marriage records of Wanda Rose weren't hard to find because Cathy already had the dates and copies of the marriage certificate. She wrote for those when she first began her investigation several months before.

In 1931, at age nineteen, Wanda married Norris Booth a record producer. A man thirteen years her senior. That marriage lasted eight years, and they were divorced in 1939.

That raised a question for Matt. Cathy trudged back over to the counter. "Where would I find land records? Deeds of property and such?" Cathy wondered if the couple had owned property together.

"In the Office of *Lands*," he answered in the same joking manner enunciating the lands part of the sentence.

"I know that," Cathy said somewhat roughly, growing tired of the banter. "I meant, where is *that* office? Its physical location."

"In the courthouse. Three blocks from here."

"Thank you."

She resolved that she was not going to ask Matt any more questions.

She returned to her research and she confirmed that, in 1940, one year later, Wanda married Caldwell Lee. A New Orleans socialite who came from old money, she remembered from her research. He was six years younger. The marriage only lasted two years.

See, all men are undatable. It doesn't matter if they're older or younger.

As Wanda Rose found out the hard way.

She was suddenly glad she'd never been married. Wanda had two divorces by the time she was thirty. The question of whether she had kids was still unanswered.

Where would I find those records?

Cathy looked over at Matt who caught her eye and smiled at her. She wasn't going to ask. Not if her life depended on it. Then she noticed a sign that read *Birth Records* with an arrow pointing out the door into another room.

She'd look at those later. After finding all the marriage certificates. There should be one more.

The third marriage wasn't until 1946 when Wanda married Dick Lawlor. The husband the LA Wanda said gave her the necklace. That marriage lasted six years. In 1955, Wanda met Norman, and they were married three weeks later.

So far, she had been there all afternoon and hadn't learned anything new. She needed to ask Matt a question, so she gave in and approached the counter.

"How would I find a marriage license if I don't know the date? I only have the name." Cathy wanted to see if Beatrice Rose Kennedy ever married in New Orleans.

"The only thing you can do is go through each year."

"That would take forever!"

Matt just shrugged. "There's no other way until we get them organized alphabetically as well. Which will also take forever." "What about death records?" Cathy asked.

She had a suspicion Beatrice was really Wanda. The lady at the orphanage said Beatrice could sing like an angel. Wanda Rose became her stage name when she moved to New Orleans and signed the record deal. The imposter in LA killed Beatrice and assumed her identity which was easy to do since she looked like Wanda Rose.

She still hadn't reconciled who Wanda O'Neil was. That birth certificate had her confused. Her working theory was that Beatrice Rose Kennedy was the Christian name given to Wanda O'Neil by the Catholic church at her baptism. That's the only explanation that made sense.

If Beatrice was murdered so the imposter could assume her identity, it would've been there in New Orleans. That's why Cathy came to Louisiana. To find a death certificate or even a grave site if there was one. She just didn't know where to begin looking.

"When did she die?" Matt asked the obvious question.

"I don't know," Cathy answered sheepishly.

Matt let out a noticeable sigh. "Do you know approximately when she died? Can we narrow it down to a decade?"

"I don't even know if she's dead. Or if she is, that she died in New Orleans."

Cathy realized how stupid she must sound to Matt, still obviously trying to be nice. Dawkins would've laid into her by now. She'd started to call him before she left Camden but decided against it. Now she was glad she didn't. He would've ripped her theory apart, thrown away the scraps and demanded that she come home immediately.

Fortunately, Matt was nicer. He didn't make a joking remark. He just smiled in a friendly manner like he wanted to keep being helpful.

"That's a tough one," he said. "I don't know what to do other than have you go through every death certificate by year and see if you find one. You can do it. It'll just take some time."

Cathy looked at the clock. "What time do you close?"

"Four thirty."

That was in ten minutes.

"Oh... I'd better start packing up my stuff then," Cathy said, thanking him as she walked away with a wave of her hand.

They were the last two people left in the room. It took Cathy time to put all of the microfiche back in their proper place. Matt waited and then opened the door for her and locked it behind them.

She waited for him because she had a question. "Do you have a recommendation for a good place to eat?"

"Do you like Cajun food?"

Cathy crinkled her nose. She associated Cajun food with crawfish. The only time she'd had the nasty creatures, she nearly threw up. The thought of them still repulsed her.

"Italian?" he asked.

"I was thinking a good steak and potatoes. I'm from Texas. We like our beef."

"I know just the place. How about I take you there? My treat." Cathy was suddenly without words.

All the reasons why she shouldn't go were trampling through her head.

Only one thought kept coming against them.

Why not? It's not really a date.

So, that's what she said. "Why not? Except we'll go Dutch."

A wide smile formed on his face. "Okay then. It's a date."

He thinks it's a date. I hope he's not a serial killer.

* * *

For the first half hour and all through dinner, Cathy related to Matt the whole sordid Wanda Rose tale. If he was bored, he didn't show it. Usually she could tell if a guy was fake listening because he had ulterior motives. Matt didn't seem like that type of guy.

For that matter, Matt wasn't like any guy she ever dated before. He was thoughtful and mannerly. Even pulled out her chair when she sat down. That wasn't something she was used to from the guys in California, who were all into themselves and their pretty boy looks.

He even offered her a suggestion, which she wished she'd thought of before she left Camden, New Jersey.

"Did you look at the newspaper notices?" Matt had asked.

Cathy slapped the palm of her hand on her forehead. *Birth announcements.* The local newspapers posted births in the paper at least once a week dating back decades. Why didn't she think of that? That would've proven things one way or the other. There was no way Dawkins would let her go back to New Jersey to look.

Matt continued. "You could also look at the obituaries. Wanda's mother's death would be in there as well. Her children would even be listed as survivors."

"You're so smart," Cathy said sincerely. It seemed like he might've even blushed when she said it.

Cathy was now officially flirting.

When there was a lull in the conversation, she said, "Let's talk about something else. I'm sure you're tired of our whole date being about Wanda Rose." She figured he'd welcome the opportunity to change the subject.

Instead, he said, "I don't mind. It's a fascinating story. Full of all kinds of mystery and intrigue."

"So, what's your favorite movie?" Cathy asked as she took a sip of water. Next to her water was a glass of wine, but the glass was still half empty.

Matt had just finished his second one.

"*Somewhere in Time*," Matt said.

Cathy almost spilled her water as she tried to hold back a laugh. "Are you serious? You liked that movie? It was horrible."

"What was horrible about it? A classic love story. Christopher Reeve went back in time to find his one true love."

Cathy pushed back harder than she intended. "The film was sappy and predictable! Too romantic for me. And of course, it had to have a happy ending. I hated that movie."

"So, what kind of movies do you like?"

"Action and adventure. I prefer movies like *The Poseidon Adventure*."

"That has a happy ending."

"But not until a bunch of people die," she said emphatically, realizing how calloused that sounded.

"Not everyone died. There were survivors. That's what made it a happy ending."

Neither of them said anything for what seemed to be a minute.

Cathy broke the silence. "You know, I don't think we have anything in common. I had steak and a baked potato, and you had a salad with chicken on it. You've had two glasses of wine. I've barely touched mine. We obviously don't have the same taste in movies."

"It's like the saying goes, opposites attract."

For some reason Cathy felt argumentative. She wanted to stop herself but couldn't. Or at least, didn't. "That may be true," she said, "but I think you have to have something in common to build a meaningful relationship."

"I tell you what," Matt said, with a sly grin. "If we can find one thing that we have in common, then we'll go on a second date. If by the end of the evening we can't, then it was nice meeting you."

Cathy laughed. "Of course, we have one thing in common," she said. "I'm sure I have something in common with every person in this room."

"I'm not so sure. Let's see."

Matt raised his wine glass. "Half empty or half full."

"Both. It's half a glass."

"Oh... so you're neither an optimist nor a pessimist."

"I'm a realist. I base everything on logic."

"I'm an idealist. I like to look at things at how I wish them to be."

"So, you wish your glass was half full."

"No. I wish it was completely full. Waiter!" Matt waved his hand in the air to signal the waiter to come right over.

"Could you refill my glass?" he asked, looking at Cathy with a spirited grin.

When the waiter had obliged, Matt said, "I propose a toast. May your glass always be neither half empty nor half full. May it always be full."

Cathy picked up her glass of wine and after clinking glasses, she took a big sip of hers. She was going to need it. It might take all night to find one thing they had in common. Even then, as opposite as they were, she enjoyed his company and sense of humor.

"Maybe we should've started with something a little easier," Cathy said. "Not something so philosophically deep. How about... I know. What is your favorite ice cream?"

"You, first. I don't think we're going to have that in common."

Cathy answered right away. "That's easy. Vanilla."

"You really do like to play it safe, don't you?"

"It's the best ice cream. What about you? Let me guess. Chocolate." He shook his head no.

Cathy tilted her head in surprise. "Not chocolate. Rocky Road." She listed off several others. They were all wrong.

"Strawberry," he finally admitted.

"You're kidding."

"I am not."

"There's not a person in the world whose favorite ice cream is strawberry."

"There's one," he said pointing his finger back toward his chest. "It worked out great in our family. I had a brother and a sister. Do you remember Neapolitan ice cream?"

"Yes. You ate the strawberry?"

They both laughed so hard they had to shush each other. The restaurant was more upscale than a typical steak house, and some of the patrons were looking their way along with the waiter.

"Favorite football team," Matt asked.

"Oilers."

"Cowboys."

"Ew. I hate the Cowboys."

"I hate football."

"I don't. I love football. What's your favorite color?"

"You first," Matt said.

"Why do you always want me to go first?"

"Because you're going to laugh at me."

"I won't laugh at you. I promise," Cathy said.

"My favorite color is salmon."

Cathy let out the biggest laugh of the night. "That's not a color. It's a fish."

"It's also a color."

"What does it look like?"

"I don't know. It's hard to describe."

"Look around the room and point out one thing that is a salmon color."

"That lady over there," he said. "That dish she is eating is salmon color."

He pointed toward a table slightly behind them but close. Cathy turned her head slightly to look without being too obvious.

"She's eating salmon."

"I know. That's where they get the color. It looks like a salmon." They both were doing everything they could to contain their laughter. Cathy didn't know if it was the wine or the company, but she was feeling giddy. The tension was leaving her body and it felt good.

"I give up. I guess we don't have one thing in common," Cathy said.

"That's too bad. I would've liked a second date."

"Better luck next time."

After another half hour of pleasant conversation, Matt called for the check and paid it against Cathy's objections.

They walked back to her hotel only a couple of blocks away.

"I had a good time," Matt said, facing her.

"Me too," Cathy crossed her arms in front of her. She wasn't cold, just nervous.

Out of the blue, Matt leaned in and kissed her. Softly. She could feel his lips quivering. Maybe they were hers.

"That was nice," Cathy said.

"I liked it."

"So did I."

Matt's eyes widened. He pumped his fist in a victorious and triumphant fashion.

"What?" Cathy said.

"That's one thing we have in common. We both liked the kiss."

"You're right," Cathy said warmly. "I guess that means there'll be a second date."

They kissed again. This time more passionately.

Cathy liked all the kisses.

18

Hotel Regency
Camden, New Jersey

The elation Cathy felt from her date with Matt was short-lived.

When she got back to her hotel room, she made the mistake of calling her message machine.

"Nine messages," the robotic voice on the machine said.

What?

How is that possible? Cathy didn't get nine messages in a month.

She halfway expected them to all be from Dawkins.

"Tolliver. What the hell are you doing in New Jersey on a wild goose chase without my permission? Call me as soon as you get this."

She hit *next message*.

"Hi. Cathy, it's your mother. I've started planning Christmas already. I know it's only July. I hope you can come home this year. Your brother will be here. Call me. Love you."

Of course, he will. He's the good child.

"Hello Ms. Tolliver, this is Wanda Rose." Cathy almost dropped the phone and dropped down onto the bed, her mouth agape. "I hope you're doing well. I'd really like to work out something with you on the painting. Could you call me back please? Thank you."

The messages were coming so rapid fire, she didn't have time to process the one from Wanda.

The familiar gruff voice rang in her ears and made her cringe.

"Tolliver! If you want a job when you get back in town, you'll call me right now!" Dawkins said rudely.

His words cut through her soul like a knife through soft butter. For whatever reason, he still struck fear in her. Even with her new-found backbone.

The next message was almost a welcomed reprieve.

"Honey, it's your mom. Where are you? I left you a message earlier. Call me. I love you."

Then a disappointing message.

"Ms. Tolliver. This is Francois Noel with the art gallery. We received your painting of Wanda Rose. Our appraiser has looked at it, and he put the value at about seventy-five to a hundred thousand dollars. I'm sorry I don't have better news. I know you were hoping to get closer to two fifty for it. This particular artist's work has gone down over the years. Call me to discuss our next step."

Another annoying message from her mom only added to her mood which had turned completely sour.

Then the most shocking voice mail she'd ever received.

"Ms. Tolliver, this is Wanda calling again. I know you probably don't want to talk to me, but I'm prepared to pay you five-hundred-thousand dollars for the painting. That's twice what it's worth. I think that's more than fair. Please call me as soon as possible so we can work out the details. You have the number."

Cathy barely heard the last message from her mother that came before the long annoying beep signifying the end of the messages.

"This is your mother! I'm worried about you. Call me. Love you."

A half a million dollars!

Cathy stood from the side of the bed, hung up the phone, and started pacing her hotel room. The information was almost too much to process at once. The first cogent thought was that Wanda's message made Dawkins' messages moot. With five hundred thousand dollars she could quit her job. Take a year or two off. Travel. Maybe move back to Houston.

No! Dallas. I don't want to go back to Houston.

While she loved her family, she didn't want to be that close to them. In some ways, she wondered if that was why she moved so far away. Dallas seemed like a good compromise. When she met Norman in Fort Worth, she noticed how much she liked the city. It had sports teams. Concerts. Good restaurants. A big airport.

The best part was that it was far enough away from Houston that her mom and dad couldn't drop in without notice. But close enough that she could go home for Christmas and a couple of other times a year.

The cost of living was cheaper.

It was closer to New Orleans.

Don't even go there.

The unfolding events had caused her to forget the good time she'd had with Matt. She quickly put the thought of seeing him again out of her mind. He had no bearing on this decision.

Her thoughts turned back to the money. Cathy still couldn't believe it. A half a million dollars was more money than she thought she'd ever see at one time in her lifetime.

Why am I not more excited?

Probably because it was Wanda making the offer. Anybody else and she'd be dancing through the streets of New Orleans. The thought of the money should be enough to overcome the disgust from hearing Wanda's voice.

Her message was also timely. The appraiser said the painting was only worth seventy-five to a hundred thousand dollars. Wanda would be paying five times the value, not double. She smiled at the thought of getting the best of her.

This was her way to extract revenge for all the heartache and trouble Wanda had put her through over the last seven months. And the best thing about it was that Wanda was clueless. She had no idea what the real value was. That caused an exuberant feeling to come over her like a tsunami.

She made the decision and picked up the phone to call Wanda back, ignoring the fact that the long-distance call would cost a fortune. Once she finalized the deal, money wouldn't matter. She'd be rich.

Suddenly, her hand began shaking from the nervousness. Or the excitement. Maybe both. Anxiety began pulsing through her like the streams of water from a car wash. She didn't have enough time to analyze the source. Before she knew it, the phone stopped ringing. The call went to a message machine. Wanda must not be home. That was good that she didn't have to talk to her directly.

What do I say?

There hadn't been time to prepare her words. She wasn't good at leaving messages anyway.

Say... I accept your offer!

Then she heard Wanda's voice and instinctively hung up the phone. The call was disconnected before she even realized it in her mind and certainly before she could process the ramifications of what she was doing. Cathy searched for the source of her hesitancy.

A conversation with herself erupted, breaking the eerie silence in the room.

"Why would Wanda pay five times what the painting is worth?" Cathy said out loud while looking at herself in the mirror on the wall.

"She doesn't seem like the sentimental type."

"It's her painting. If I were in her shoes, I'd want it too."

"No, it's not! It's a painting of Wanda Rose. She's not Wanda. The painting has no sentimental value to her. There must be another reason she wants to pay me."

"She'll make me drop the investigation!" Cathy said, raising the intensity of her voice. She suddenly realized that the people next door could hear her when she got that loud, so she softened her tone.

"The nerve of that woman," she said barely above a whisper but with the intensity of a small earthquake inside of her.

"Why do I care?"

Of course, Cathy would drop the investigation. She was going to quit her job. There was nothing to investigate.

The conversation with herself erupted again. This time in her thoughts. *Was that why Wanda was willing to pay five times what the painting was worth?*

Because I'm getting too close.

The fire is getting too hot. Cathy smiled at her own pun.

Norman.

An intense sadness came over her and overwhelmed the thoughts.

The image of Norman sitting in the study staring at Wanda's painting flooded her memory. Then she saw Wanda pushing him down the stairs.

If she quit now, Wanda would get away with murder.

Norman wanted her to have the painting, not Wanda.

He could've given it to Wanda in his will. He gave her everything else.

For whatever reason, Norman didn't want Wanda to have it.

It felt like a betrayal.

Somehow, she would feel like she was selling out. She'd be complicit in Wanda's deception.

And what about the real Wanda Rose? She was likely dead too, at the hand of the imposter. Didn't she owe it to her to bring her murderer to justice.

"I have no proof she's a murderer," she said out loud again. Maybe she got away with faking the robbery and starting the fire, but murder was a huge leap.

Cathy rubbed her head and eyes roughly trying to shake the confusion, hoping the right thing to do would loosen in her mind.

Seventy-five thousand dollars is still a lot of money.

Half a million is a lot more.

But would she be able to live with herself? Her peace of mind was worth more than all the money in the world. Maybe she couldn't quit her job with seventy-five thousand in the bank, but she could always look for another one. And start over somewhere else.

It's not seventy-five thousand. She had to pay the art gallery a commission.

It didn't matter. Turning it down was the right thing to do.

Impulsively, she picked up the phone and dialed Wanda's number, unsure of what she was going to say.

Do I accept the offer or not?

At the right moment, she'd know what to do. She always trusted her instincts, even when she acted impulsively. Sometimes, what came out of her mouth without a plan was what was deep in her soul. She had to trust that.

A huge sense of relief came over her when it went to the voice mail machine again. She tried to tune out Wanda's voice and listened for the beep. When it came, she said, "Wanda, this is Cathy. I got your message.

As I said before, the painting is not for sale."

She slammed the phone down into its cradle for emphasis. *I hope I didn't just make a big mistake.*

* * *

The next morning

At quarter to nine, Cathy arrived at the Office of Vital Records. Matt said he would get there at nine. Her plan was to arrive shortly after him, so she didn't seem too anxious to see him. Actually, telling him about what transpired with the painting was fueling her impatience, which was why she arrived earlier than planned.

For a moment, she thought about going somewhere out of sight and watching for him but then realized how schoolgirl that sounded. Maybe she should go get them both a cup of coffee. That would buy some time. The problem was that she didn't know him well enough to know what he liked. He might not even drink coffee.

Before she could consider another plan to leave and come back, Matt appeared from around the corner of the building.

Cathy burst out laughing.

He pointed at his shirt.

"See... salmon really is a color," he said when he got within earshot.

As it turned out, the fact that she was there waiting was better. He got to surprise her which by the boyish grin on his face clearly made him happy.

"That's actually pink," Cathy said jokingly.

Matt looked down at his shirt and then at her as his shoulders drooped slightly.

"I thought this was salmon."

"It is. I'm joking." She kissed him on the cheek, and he seemed to instantly feel better.

"Does this mean I win the bet?" he retorted playfully.

"I don't remember betting. I just remember talking about it."

"We bet a second date."

"That was for finding something in common."

"Oh... right."

Cathy's impatience was growing now that she had seen him. "Hurry up and open the door. I can't wait to tell you what happened to me last night."

"I already know. You got kissed by me."

"Better than that!"

"What could be better than being kissed by me?"

A half a million dollars.

"Just wait until you hear!" she said.

* * *

"You turned down a half a million dollars?" Matt said incredulously

Cathy was biting on her nails because she had just finished relating to him the entire story and had braced for his response.

"I know," she said. "That was really stupid, wasn't it?"

Matt rolled his eyes. "I would've taken the money."

For some reason, a blaze of anger flashed through Cathy's body like a rapidly spreading wildfire. It felt like he had just judged her. As if he had any right to do so. They just met.

"It was the principle of the thing," Cathy said defensively. "It was hush money."

"I still would've taken it," he said, probably more smugly than he intended.

"Is that because you don't have any principles?" she countered angrily.

Mostly, he seemed to ignore her rising anger which made her even madder.

"I do have principles. It's just that to get a chance to have that much money would be too hard to turn down."

"I have to sleep at night," Cathy retorted. "I don't care if it's a *million* dollars. I'm still not compromising my integrity."

"I would buy a very expensive bed with the money, and I'd sleep great!"

To keep from saying what she was really thinking, Cathy bit her lip to the point that she thought she tasted blood.

The pause in the conversation allowed her to gain some perspective. The truth was that most people would take the money. She wasn't even convinced that she did the right thing. Making an issue about it with someone she had just met and had no future with was bordering on self-righteousness.

And it didn't matter anyway.

This morning her plan was to make a halfhearted effort to look for Beatrice Rose Kennedy's death records. Matt had pointed out that she was looking for the proverbial needle in a haystack. Without a year, it would take her days to go through everything, and she didn't even know if one existed. By noon, she expected to say good-bye to Matt, check out of her hotel, and catch the next plane home. She was prepared to renege on the promise of a second date.

Matt had other ideas.

"I thought of a way we could narrow the search for the death certificate," he said with the glimmer of excitement back on his face and in his eyes.

"What's your idea?" Cathy asked.

"When did Wanda record her last album?" Matt said excitedly,

"I don't know. Why?"

"That gives us a starting point. We start looking for death records in that year."

"Because she had to be alive to record the last album," Cathy said, thinking out loud. "That makes sense. But she could've lived for many years after that record."

"Not likely. How many albums did she make over her whole career?"

"Fourteen studio albums. Forty-three singles, and one live album," Cathy said without hesitation. For whatever reason she had a gift for remembering numbers. She would've remembered the date of the last recorded album, but she didn't think she ever knew it. Doing the math in her head, she estimated it to be about 1944 or 45.

"That's another clue," Matt said eagerly, like he was ready to start looking.

"Why do you say that?"

"The woman recorded fifty-eight records, in what... twenty years?"

"More like fifteen."

"Okay fifteen. That's almost four a year. She was at the height of her career. Why would she suddenly stop recording?"

"Unless something happened to her." Cathy said as the light bulb came on. "Somebody took her out of the picture."

That somebody was Wanda Rose. Rather the lady impersonating her in LA.

"The library is a block over from here. Go there and look up Wanda Rose in an encyclopedia. They'll have a list of all of her albums. They might even have some other useful information."

A good idea. While a part of her didn't like being told what to do, she kept her mouth shut, repacked her things, and was off to the library with Matt's simple directions on how to get there.

The encyclopedia section was easy to find, and the workers were just as nice as Matt. The south was a lot different than the northeast when it came to friendliness. The young boy, in his late twenties who offered to help her, even pulled out several different editions and opened them to the Wanda Rose pages.

Either he was just being helpful, or he was flirting with her as well.

Maybe I should move to New Orleans. Easier to find a man here.

She consciously told herself to shut up. One romantic entanglement in New Orleans was enough for one trip, so she tried to maintain a cool and businesslike manner with the new kid. He got the hint and left her alone with the books. Or he wasn't really interested and didn't see a need to nursemaid her. Either way, she was glad to be alone with the books.

With them opened in front of her, she began pouring through them with a sense of excitement and anticipation building.

Wanda's last album was in 1944, she wrote on a pad, confirming what she already suspected. *Lady Sings the Blues* was her biggest-selling album to date. That was important. Matt was right. Wanda was at the apex of her career. Why would she stop recording then? Unless she had met an untimely demise and couldn't anymore.

With the real Wanda Rose out of the way, the imposter could assume her identity but not her singing career since she couldn't sing like the real Wanda Rose. She'd be spotted as a fraud the second she opened her mouth.

Amazingly, she had gotten away with the perfect crime for forty years.

Reading through the other encyclopedias gave her no new information, so she prepared to pack up. One of the volumes had a picture of Wanda singing with Tommy Dorsey in 1943, so, Cathy made a copy of it for the file. Then she rushed back to tell Matt what she found.

"You were right," she said to him. "Her last album was in 1944. It was her best-selling album. There's no reason for her to quit singing then. I'm thinking she died shortly thereafter."

"You take 1944 and I'll take 1945."

She was surprised that he was going to help her. Once again, she didn't appreciate him taking charge of her investigation and ordering her around, but she let it go because she could use the help and didn't want to dampen his enthusiasm. The truth was that all men had a little bit of Dawkins in them. Even the good ones thought that they should be the leaders.

Cathy took some leadership and told him what names they were looking for. Even wrote them down for him.

Wanda Rose. Wanda O'Neil. Beatrice Rose. Beatrice O'Neil. Beatrice Rose Kennedy.

Three hours later, they had found nothing. The work was tedious, and Cathy needed a break.

"Do you want to go and grab some lunch?" she asked Matt. "I never ate breakfast, and I'm starting to feel weak."

"I can't. I have to stay here and watch the archives. There's a sandwich shop just around the corner on the way to the library. That's what I would recommend."

"I saw it when I was walking. Can I bring you a sandwich?"

"I brought my lunch, so I'm good. But go ahead. It'll give me a chance to catch up on some of my other work."

Cathy felt much better after she ate. When she returned, Matt was standing at the counter with a frantic look on his face.

For a moment, Cathy thought something bad had happened. Then she saw a piece of paper in his hand.

As soon as she was to the counter, he said, "I found the death certificate!"

"For Wanda Rose?"

"No. For Beatrice Rose. January 7, 1945."

"That's amazing!"

"There's more."

"What is it? Don't keep me in suspense."

"Her cause of death was mercury poisoning."

Cathy's head started spinning so fast from the shocking revelation, she had to put her hand on the counter to brace herself.

She wouldn't be catching an early flight home.

19

"Let me see the death certificate," Cathy said to Matt who was still holding it in his hand.

The document was old and delicate. Matt had obviously found the original after discovering it on the microfiche.

"Be careful with it," he said.

Cathy laid it on the counter, so she didn't even have to handle it any more than necessary. She scanned through it for the most important information.

Louisiana State Board of Health Vital Records Certificate of Death

City of New Orleans

Name of Decedent: Beatrice Rose

Date of Death: January 7, 1945

Sex: Female

Date of Birth. Nov. 1912

Birthplace: Camden, New Jersey. Another incontrovertible clue.

Divorced

Occupation: Singer

"Oh my gosh!" Cathy said. "Her occupation was singer."

The sober realization hit her all at once. The mystery was unlocking before her eyes. Cathy looked up at Matt. "This confirms it. Beatrice is Wanda." A sense of accomplishment came over her for the hard work it took to get to this point.

Disease or condition: Mercury poisoning

An overwhelming sadness came over her. "Poor Wanda," she said.

"What a horrible way to die. To be poisoned."

Physician's certification: The name on the signature line was illegible.

"Look at this part," Matt said, pointing to the bottom of the document which would be the top and upside down from his point of view on the other side of the counter.

Cathy read it aloud. "Informant's Certification." Next of kin was under the signature line. Handwriting was on the line but was illegible as well.

She looked up at Matt. "I can't read the signature. Can you?"

Matt responded. "It's almost as if the person didn't want us to be able to read it."

"Wanda! She was there and signed the death certificate. How did she weasel her way into that?"

The intensity in Cathy's voice raised several decibels and got higher in pitch. The mystery was so close to being solved. But every time she answered a question another one emerged.

She stepped back away from the counter and walked back and forth. Moving helped her to think better.

"What are you thinking?" Matt asked. He didn't know her well enough to know that he needed to let her mind fully process the facts before asking.

Finally, she answered, "Somehow Wanda met Wanda." Matt's lips contorted into a confused look.

"I know. It's confusing," Cathy said. "For the sake of discussion, let's call them, Wanda One and Wanda Two. Wanda One is the real Wanda

Rose. Wanda Two is the imposter. The one living in LA."

"You look cute when you're like this," Matt said.

Cathy ignored the comment. Not that she didn't appreciate it, but her mind couldn't process two things at once. Right now, she was in full-on investigation mode and didn't need any distractions from a guy no matter how handsome.

She continued. "Wanda One is Wanda O'Neil, born on November 5, 1912 in Camden New Jersey. Her mother died in childbirth, so the hospital sent her to an orphanage. They baptized her and gave her a Christian name— Beatrice Rose Kennedy."

"I'm with you so far."

"Beatrice Rose is such a pretty name," Cathy blurted as the thought came into her head.

Matt only nodded, which she was glad for. Better to not interrupt her when she was on a roll, even with a compliment.

Cathy said, "Sister Rita from the orphanage remembered a Bea who could sing like an angel. That confirms Bea or Beatrice is Wanda One. The famous singer."

"Sounds logical to me." Matt placed his elbow on the counter and rested his chin on it.

"Wanda One moved to New Orleans at sixteen and signed a record deal and started recording albums."

"Right."

Cathy preferred that Matt not say anything until she finished her thought. It was distracting that he said something after every sentence. Cathy continued with her train of thought. "Somehow, Wanda Two entered the picture. She's the spitting image of Wanda One."

Matt jumped in. "She probably saw her on television or in a club down on Bourbon Street and realized how much she looked like her." "Exactly!" Cathy pointed her finger at Matt.

Matt continued. "So, she devised a plan to steal Wanda's identity. Wanda One."

"The problem with her plan was that she can't sing," Cathy added. "How do you assume a singer's identity if you can't sing a lick?"

"You can't. You also can't assume her identity unless she's out of the picture."

A somber fog suddenly came over the conversation.

"So... Wanda Two killed Wanda One to get her out of the way," Matt surmised.

"Poisoned her with mercury. How horrible is that? Then told the authorities that her name was Beatrice Rose. That way she could continue on as Wanda Rose, the singer."

"Her singing career was over. But she would get all the royalties on her songs."

"Wanda Rose didn't get any royalties."

"I wonder if Wanda Two knew that when she killed her."

"Whether she did or didn't, it didn't matter. Wanda Two was able to turn Wanda Rose's fame into a lot more money than she would've ever made as a singer. Wanda Two went on to marry three rich men and got huge divorce settlements that made her a rich woman." Cathy made sure to emphasize the huge part.

"It really is a sordid tale of lies and scandal. You are some investigator to have uncovered it," Matt replied supportively.

"Thanks." She smiled at him to let him know that she appreciated the compliment. Then she got right back to the story. There was still more to think through.

"I wonder if they did an autopsy, or if the police investigated Wanda's death as murder?" Cathy said, thinking out loud.

"They might have," Matt said. "But if they did, they didn't come to that conclusion. Otherwise, the death certificate would say that the cause of death was homicide."

"I need to talk to an investigator and tell him what I've discovered. Maybe they can reopen it."

"There is no statute of limitations on murder in Louisiana."

"Now look who's the smart one," Cathy said affectionately.

"I watch *Hill Street Blues*."

Cathy didn't know what he meant. She never watched television.

As if he suspected he said, "It's a crime drama on TV. You can learn a lot watching that show. I watch all of them. *Magnum PI* is another one."

"That I've heard of. Tom Selleck. He's handsome."

Now she was trying to get a rise out of him. The other part of the conversation about Wanda was over, so she felt like bantering with him. As far as Cathy was concerned, the mystery of what happened to Wanda Rose was solved. Now it was just a matter of proving it.

"I don't see it," he said. "Tom Selleck is not handsome. But... whatever. I also like *Remington Steele*. And there's a new one that just came out this year, called *Miami Vice*. You probably think Don Johnson is handsome too."

Cathy shrugged her shoulders. She didn't know who Don Johnson was. "Growing up, I watched *Perry Mason*."

"There you go. These shows are like that. Only better."

As much as Cathy was enjoying the banter, she'd rather be working. She looked for an opportunity to exit the conversation. The last thing she wanted to be doing was discussing stupid TV shows. At the same time, she didn't want to offend Matt. Finding the death certificate was a godsend. It probably saved her job.

She'd have to thank him properly later with a wet kiss.

"Where is the nearest police station?" Cathy asked.

"What are you going to do?" Matt asked.

"I'm going to expose Wanda Rose for the fraud and murderer she is, once and for all."

* * *

New Orleans Police Station, Precinct 4

Bruno Zampizi, who everyone called "Champ," was a former prize fighter-turned policeman, now detective for the New Orleans police department. Information he readily offered in the first two minutes of their conversation as an introduction.

By first impressions, Cathy was disappointed. She expected him to be all brawn and no brain. Evident by his nose, contorted in several different directions, no doubt a result of being hit in the head too many times either in the ring or on the street. If Cathy needed protection on Bourbon Street at two in the morning, Champ would be her guy. He looked as though he had thumped a few heads in his day. Cracking a murder seemed like a stretch and out of his wheelhouse, but he was the hand that was dealt her, and she needed to give him a chance.

"How can I help you, honey?" Champ said.

I'm not your honey.

One of her pet peeves was when men she didn't know called her honey, dear, darling, or babe. A flash of anger shot through her. What right did he have to call her honey? She wasn't his honey and never would be. While she was used to dealing with being a woman in a man's world, her experiences with Dawkins were testing her willingness to put up with it.

Now is not the time to get on your soapbox.

Since she didn't answer right away, he said, "I understand you want to report a murder."

Cathy felt a little embarrassed. She had assumed that she wouldn't get past the front door with her story as it was. When she told the person at the front desk that she wanted to report a murder, she got through right away. Now that she had an audience, she had to make the best of the opportunity.

"I'm an insurance fraud adjuster out of Los Angeles. There's a woman there who is posing as one of your famous residents, Wanda Rose. Are you familiar with her?"

"Of course. She's the jazz singer."

Cathy was surprised Champ knew of her. He didn't strike her as someone who listened to jazz or blues music. Of course, in New Orleans, music was a way of life. She supposed, everyone was exposed to the genres in some form or fashion.

"I discovered a death certificate for Beatrice Rose."

She handed Champ a copy.

She also had a picture of Beatrice's headstone. Before she came to the station, she bought an instant camera and went to the cemetery. He looked at the picture first, then the death certificate. Looking at the two barely took ten seconds. Cathy hoped it was because he knew his way around a death certificate and not because he had taken one look at the date and dismissed her out of hand. Either way, he didn't say anything, which Cathy took as a sign that he was willing for her to continue so she did.

"I've discovered that Beatrice is actually Wanda Rose," Cathy said. "I discovered her birth certificate and baptism records up in Camden, New Jersey. The woman in LA claims to be Wanda Rose the singer. That's impossible. Wanda Rose is dead. She died on January 7, 1945. She died of mercury poisoning."

"I saw that," Champ said matter-of-factly.

"After 1944, Wanda Rose never recorded another album. That's because the woman in LA can't sing. But after she murdered the real Wanda Rose, she carried on her life and used the identity of the famous singer to make a fortune."

He still didn't say anything. As good at Cathy thought she was at reading people, her skills weren't helping her with Champ. He was probably a good poker player because his face didn't give away anything. Probably a good skill to have when interrogating suspects. She could've used more of that ability when she was dealing with Wanda Rose. Cathy wore her heart on a sleeve. Everyone always knew what she was thinking. And feeling.

"Look at this marriage certificate," Cathy said. "It's dated 1947. The bride is Wanda Rose. That's impossible. Wanda Rose died in

1945. How could she marry someone two years later?"

"She couldn't if she was dead," Champ said.

"Exactly."

Cathy didn't want a lull in the conversation, so she said, "My lady in LA poisoned the real Wanda Rose and has been living her life all these years." "Now you lost me," Champ said.

"The death certificate says that Beatrice Rose died of mercury poisoning."

"I know. I saw that."

"Beatrice Rose is Wanda Rose the singer."

"I got that."

"The woman in LA assumed her identity. The marriage certificate is proof. The woman in LA claims she was married to Dick Lawlor. He's the man listed on the 1947 marriage certificate under the name of Wanda Rose."

"How does that prove that your Wanda murdered Beatrice?"

"It's obvious. She had to get rid of the real Wanda Rose to assume her identity."

"It may be obvious to you, but won't be to the DA, or to a jury. Not that it would ever get that far."

Disappointment and anger were competing for domination inside Cathy. Her logical mind overrode the feelings for the moment.

"It's what you call a circumstantial case. That means it's deduced or inferred. You can get a conviction with what is a logical explanation."

Champ sat forward in his chair. His demeanor hadn't changed from the moment he quit talking about himself until now. "I know what a circumstantial case is. Rarely in a murder case do you have all the facts. It's nice to have a confession or an eyewitness, a video tape, or a murder weapon. Most murderers cover up their crime in some way. So, we almost always have to infer some of the evidence."

"I think we have a lot of evidence that doesn't have to be inferred."

Champ shook his head. "The case is too old. Nobody in this office is going to be interested in it."

Cathy started to object. He held out his hand to stop her. "The death certificate doesn't list homicide as the cause of death."

"It says she was poisoned. That implies something sinister to me."

"Even if it did, how are you going to prove that the Wanda in LA was the one who gave her the mercury?"

"She might confess."

"She'd lawyer up in a second."

"You could exhume the body," Cathy answered.

"Why? You already know it was mercury poisoning. Examining the body is not going to show anything else. Mercury can get in the body in a number of ways. She might've taken too much medicine with mercury in it. Who knows? There's no way to know. Sounds like you have a good case for identity fraud in LA."

"The fraud happened here in New Orleans. To one of your famous citizens. Couldn't you prosecute her?"

"When did she last live here?"

Cathy's heart sunk as she knew her answer would blow that argument out of the water. Champ was a lot sharper than she had given him credit for. "1955," she answered weakly.

"Statute of limitations ran out a long time ago."

"I guess it's run out in LA as well since she moved there over ten years ago."

"Not if she's still impersonating Wanda Rose. The fraud statute would run from the date it was discovered and the time she last claimed to be Wanda Rose. Sounds like she's still committing the fraud. Good luck. I wish you well with your case in LA. I'm sorry I couldn't help you."

That was Cathy's clue to leave. She didn't want to.

"Can you close the door on the way out?" Champ asked, making it clear she had to leave.

Cathy bristled. That sounded like something Dawkins would say to her. Men were the same everywhere. Why did they always think they could order her around? To make matters worse, Champ didn't stand or offer to shake her hand. He clearly would've given that courtesy to a man.

Suddenly, she didn't like him. Maybe men in general were who she didn't like.

Unfortunately, she had a long list of men she'd have to deal with ahead of her. Tomorrow, she'd go to Fort Worth and have the same discussion with an investigator there about Norman's death. At least that death was still recent. Her anticipation was that the investigator there would dismiss her, thinking she was just a foolish girl, conjuring up all kinds of imaginations in her limited girlish mind.

The truth was that she had no proof Wanda pushed Norman down the steps. What she did know was that Wanda went to Camden and stole the birth certificate. She had proof of that. Sort of. A woman identified Wanda as having been there. The certificates were missing. The other thing she knew was that the real Wanda Rose was dead. This lady had to be an imposter.

Put two and two together, people.

How hard is it?

That wasn't the worst of it. Back in LA, she'd have to deal with Dawkins. The worst of the male species. For a moment, she wondered if it was worth it.

The only consolation was that Matt was waiting for her. They were to meet for dinner in a few hours. While he had his own preconceptions about women, they were minor. He was better about it.

She vowed not to bring Wanda up. She couldn't stand the thought of him shooting down her theory as well.

* * *

The entire dinner, all Cathy could talk about was Wanda Rose. By the time dessert came, Cathy was tired of talking about it, and she could tell Matt was tired of listening as well. At least he'd been supportive and hadn't said anything negative.

"Let's go do something fun," Matt said. "Take your mind off of Wanda for a few minutes."

That was a good idea. Tomorrow, she was leaving. She thought about going to her hotel, packing her bags, and getting on a plane before dinner, but she had promised Matt a second date. It would be extremely rude to renege. While men were more than willing to cast women aside on a whim, she couldn't do it. Matt had been really nice to her, and she didn't want it to end on a down note.

"What did you have in mind?" she asked.

"Let's go down to the French Quarter," he said.

"Oh no! That will just remind me of Wanda. There's a jazz bar on every corner."

"I already thought of that. I was thinking we go to the city park. It's really nice at night."

"Is it safe?"

"You have me to protect you."

Matt wasn't Champ, but that was all she had. And she didn't want the date to end, but she didn't want to go near the blues bars. The park sounded nice.

And it was.

A large statue stood in the center of the park. There they shared their first kiss of the night. One that was more relaxed. It felt even better than the ones the night before as they were growing comfortable with each passing moment.

Even with Matt there, Cathy felt uneasy as there were a number of unsavory people around.

"Let's get out of here," Cathy said and started walking. "That woman over there is scary looking," Cathy said pointing to a lady just ahead of where they were headed.

"They are harmless," he said.

"Who are they? They look creepy."

That particular woman was sitting on a bench staring off into space. She had on a colorful robe. Her hair was long and stringy, and she appeared to be chanting something.

"They practice voodoo and claim to be witches. Supposedly, they can put hexes on people?"

That caused Cathy to shudder. "Let's get away from her."

As they turned to walk away, the lady let out a frightening scream.

Cathy jumped. Her arm was already clutching Matt's and she cowered into him further. The woman stood from the bench and was in Cathy's face before either of them could react.

"You are deeply troubled," the witch said in voice that could only be described as evil.

She threw her hands in the air.

Cathy was frozen in fear.

The woman turned her gaze back toward Cathy and their eyes met. The look shot through Cathy like a fiery dart.

"Child... You are in great danger." Her voice was more subdued as she said it. Solemn. Almost sounded normal if that was possible.

Then she started shrieking again at the top of her lungs. Matt put his arm around Cathy and started directing them away from her.

The crazy woman followed them. "You are in grave danger," she kept saying over and over again to Cathy.

When she caught up to them, she forced something into Cathy's hand. "Drink this," she said. "It will protect you."

Cathy instinctively threw it to the ground and wiped her hand on her pants. She didn't want it and didn't even want to touch it.

"What have you done? You foolish girl! Now you will surely die," she cried out as she bent down on the ground and tried to pick up the vial that had broken and spilled its contents on the sidewalk.

Cathy and Matt ran away.

The woman's screams could still be heard several blocks away.

She kept saying over and over, "Things are not what they appear."

20

As Cathy had expected, the Fort Worth investigator wasn't willing to consider reopening Norman's case without more evidence. When it became apparent that she was about to make him angry, she backed off and left, certain Wanda had gotten away with murder.

The investigator had several good points. Cathy had pleaded her case, and he had a rebuttal for every one of her arguments.

"You could pull airline, hotel, and rental car records and prove Wanda was in Fort Worth on the night of the murder," Cathy had argued.

"That's not a crime. She's free to travel to Fort Worth if she wants. There's nothing to link her to the house."

"What about DNA or fingerprints?"

"Easily explained. She owns the house now. Her DNA is all over it."

"What about the identity fraud? I think we can prove she's not the real Wanda Rose."

"That needs to be handled where she lives. I'm not going to extradite the woman all the way to Texas for identity fraud when I don't have a victim who lost money here. For there to be identity fraud, the perpetrator has to have gained financially in some way."

"Norman was a victim. She stole all of his estate. That's financial gain."

"He left the money to her in his will! She didn't steal anything."

Cathy continued to grasp at straws, but he shot each of them down, summarily.

"Your best bet, honey, is the District Attorney in LA. He might very well be interested in it."

When he called her honey, she cut off the conversation and left in a huff.

* * *

The DA in LA, Flavio Toro, was running for re-election and had made a name for himself going after celebrities. The Wanda Rose case was interesting to him. It had all the ingredients for a case the public would be interested in, which was all he seemed to care about. It had money, sex, murder, and mystery.

He needed more evidence.

Detective Bernie Lawrence was assigned to the case. He was like a dog going after a bone. Within two weeks, he had determined that Wanda had indeed flown to Fort Worth the day of Norman's murder. She had also flown to Philadelphia, the week before Cathy went there in search of the birth certificates. There was nothing to link her to Camden, New Jersey, but the working theory was that she was the one who stole the birth and death certificates out of the archives.

Unfortunately, the *New Jersey Gazette*, the local Camden newspaper which operated in the early 1900s, didn't have a birth announcement for Wanda O'Neil on November fourth or fifth of 1912. They did have a one line obituary for Rose Kennedy O'Neil, who died on November 5, 1912, but no surviving kin were listed. Andros O'Neil, the father listed on Wanda O'Neil's birth certificate, died three weeks before Wanda was born while working on a subway line in Philly. He was crushed by an earth mover. Rose Kennedy was listed as his surviving wife in the obituary. There was no mention of a daughter.

So, while some facts were being pieced together, they were still sketchy at best. No one could confirm that Beatrice Rose, Wanda O'Neil, and

Wanda Rose were the same person, but that was the theory everyone was proceeding under. The Wanda in LA knew nothing of the investigations as Detective Lawrence was keeping things low key until he had enough to arrest her.

Then he dropped a wild idea on Cathy.

"I'd like for you to meet with Wanda," he had said.

"What for?" Cathy asked.

"I want you to wear a wire."

"A wire?"

"Get her to say something incriminating. If we get it on tape, then we can arrest her on the spot."

"Is it safe?"

"We'll be outside listening to everything. If she makes one move on you, we'll be right there."

"She won't meet with me."

"She'll meet with you. Tell her you've reconsidered and want to talk about selling her the painting."

Cathy reluctantly agreed, although she didn't think it was a good idea.

* * *

Detective Lawrence finished rigging Cathy with a wire and asked her to test it. They were sitting in an unmarked police van outside of Wanda Rose's townhome.

Cathy spoke the words nervously into the microphone hidden under her blouse, "Testing. One, two, three. Testing. Can you hear me?"

The sound technician gave the detective a thumbs up, which Cathy assumed meant the wire was working. She hoped so because she was about to be alone with Wanda, and the fear factor sent her emotions to the precipice of a panic attack.

Wanda was excited on the phone when Cathy had called and said she was willing to sell the painting. Cathy felt a twinge of guilt for misleading the woman in that way. She had no intention of selling her the painting and actually intended to use the guise to bring her down.

Cathy was literally shaking in her shoes as the time of the meeting neared. The words spoken by the voodoo witch in City Park in New Orleans were adding to her trepidation.

"Things are not as they appear," the crazy woman had said. "You're in grave danger," she cried out when she gave Cathy a vial and demanded she drink it.

When Cathy threw the vial to the ground, the woman had cried out in a shrill voice, "You foolish girl! You're going to die."

Were the disturbed woman's words about to come to pass?

Cathy didn't believe in voodoo, witches, or hexes but that didn't mean that the situation she was walking into wasn't dangerous. If she let it, Cathy's imagination could run a mile in her head in only seconds.

"Are you sure this is safe?" she asked the detective again, almost trembling inside. "Wanda's already killed two people. What makes you think she won't kill me as well?"

The detective answered calmly, "She wants the painting. I think she'll play nice with you. Besides, we'll be outside the front door, listening to every word."

Nothing the detective could say or do took away the risk completely. They might be just outside Wanda's door listening in, but Wanda could kill Cathy in less time than it could take them to rescue her. In fact, they might not even know it was happening if Wanda poisoned her drink or suddenly pulled a knife or gun on her.

"I have a bad feeling about this," Cathy said, with her upper lip quivering.

"You'll be fine," Detective Lawrence said. "We haven't lost one yet, have we, Morris?" he said to his sound technician with a sly grin.

Morris gave a thumbs up sign and Cathy a reassuring smile. It did nothing to calm her frayed nerves.

"Why do we even need this?" Cathy implored. "We already have enough evidence to put her away for a long time."

The detective replied, "You never have enough evidence if you can get more. That's my motto."

Cathy gave him a halfhearted grin.

"Is everybody ready?" he said.

Everyone seemed like they were.

"Then let's rock and roll," the detective said it like a daredevil about to jump out of an airplane. He seemed to be loving the excitement.

Cathy wished she had his confidence. She couldn't get the voodoo lady's voice out of her head.

* * *

When Wanda opened the door to her townhome, Cathy immediately could tell that something was off. Wanda's hair was disheveled, her eyes blood shot like she'd been crying or drinking a lot, or both. Her dress was impeccable as always—a flowery, light-green chiffon dress that went below her knees and a white sweater that covered her arms.

But she seemed depressed.

Melancholy.

Not her usual smug self.

Probably the alcohol. Even though it was one o'clock in the afternoon, Wanda was already sloshed.

Cathy was taken aback and stumbled right out of the gate. She suddenly went blank on what she was supposed to say or do.

Especially when Wanda locked the door behind them sending a lightning bolt of fear through her.

Then she unexpectedly gave Cathy a hug.

Did she feel the wire on my back?

To accommodate the wire, Cathy had a different look as well. Instead of her normal tight-fitting pant suit, she wore black slacks and a loose-fitting blue blouse. The detective had said that blue was a calming color and conveyed trustworthiness.

Green was another calming color he had recommended; however, Wanda's green dress was doing nothing to calm Cathy's nerves.

Cathy's blouse was sheer on purpose. She never anticipated Wanda touching her. There was no way she didn't feel the wire. Cathy felt her hand brushing against it. The tape even ripped off her skin and she winced but tried to maintain her composure. Every bit of common sense inside her wanted to go running out the door and never come back.

What have I gotten myself into?

When Cathy got the first words out without her voice cracking, she felt a little better, "Hello, Wanda," she said. "It's good to see you. Under better circumstances than the last time."

"I felt bad about that for days." Wanda seemed in an agreeable mood. "Please forgive me for being so rude. I was distraught over the death of my husband."

Wanda seemed sincere when she said it, although Cathy had believed several of Wanda's lies before they had been proven false.

Cathy decided to get right to the questioning. The detective said to be careful not to make it sound like an interrogation. Just work the prearranged questions into the normal course of discussion, he had advised.

"Speaking of Norman, how long had it been since you saw or talked to him?" Cathy said lowering her head slightly, so she was talking in the direction of the microphone. She tried to stay close to Wanda so they would pick up her words as well.

"At our divorce, I guess," she said. Wanda was subdued in her speech. Talking quietly. "I sent him Christmas cards for a few years, but we lost touch."

"I figured you'd call him after I told you I was going to see him," Cathy said nonchalantly.

"I did call him," Wanda said, which surprised Cathy. "He said he didn't remember the necklace. It would've eased your mind if he had. Oh well. Memories fade."

Cathy hoped the detectives picked up on that discrepancy. Wanda said she hadn't seen or talked to Norman since their divorce. Now she admitted talking to him before he died. Norman had already told Cathy about the phone call, and Cathy was expecting Wanda to lie about it. The detective had said it was hard to keep all the lies straight, so Cathy decided to try and trick her.

"It must've been devastating when the necklace was stolen," Cathy said, trying to match Wanda's syrupy tone. "You said it was a gift from your second husband for an anniversary if I remember right. I can't imagine how heartbreaking it would be to lose something that valuable."

"Yes, it was. Bobby was a hopeless romantic."

Wanda was slurring her words, but it sounded to Cathy like she said the name Bobby. Norris was Wanda's second husband's name. Wanda had said that her third husband, Dick Lawlor, had given her the necklace.

It is hard to keep all the lies straight.

"Norris, you mean?" Cathy said, correcting her.

"What did I say?"

"You said Bobby."

Wanda started wringing her hands together like she was anxious. "I said Norris. You must've not heard me right."

"I suppose. Where do you want to sit and discuss the painting?" Cathy asked.

They were still standing at the entrance.

"Let's go in the dining room," Wanda said, and started leading her that way, even though Cathy had been there before. A few new pieces of expensive furniture were scattered throughout the rooms. Probably from the sudden windfall of money Wanda had received from the insurance settlement and the money she was getting from the sale of Norman's assets. Wanda hadn't accounted for the cost of bail and attorney which she'd need soon, a thought that made Cathy smile noticeably because Wanda said, "What's so amusing?"

"I'm just glad we were able to work out something on that painting,"

Cathy responded. "Can you imagine that painting in my little apartment?" "It's a big portrait. Norman insisted that we go all out."

Norman had said the painting was Wanda's idea, but that would be hearsay in a court of law and an irrelevant discrepancy in the case. But Cathy filed it away in her mind anyway, so she'd remember to write it down later.

They sat down at the dining room table.

The fire had started in that big open room. Cathy glanced over to where the Christmas tree once stood. A new armoire was now in its place.

"What will you have to drink, darling?" Wanda asked.

A chill went down Cathy's spine as she remembered Beatrice and the mercury poisoning. Probably given to her in a drink.

"I'm... good," Cathy said with a slight stutter. "Thanks. I'm not thirsty."

"Nonsense. You won't let an old woman drink alone. I'll fix you something special."

Before Cathy could object, Wanda was in the kitchen. She returned with two glasses and coasters which she sat on the dining room table. To Cathy's surprise, she didn't sit down but went back to the kitchen where she returned with a cutting board, a lime, and a large knife.

Wanda set them on the table and began cutting open the lime. She put one of the slices in Cathy's glass and another in hers.

"That's a large knife you have there," Cathy said for the benefit of her protectors who were hopefully listening. Wearing the wire left her with an eerie feeling. She really had no way of knowing if they could hear her or not. They certainly couldn't see her, so she had an almost irresistible urge to give them a play by play of the important happenings.

The thought suddenly occurred to her. *What if Wanda knocked the wire free, and they couldn't hear her?* They would've already burst in if that had happened, she surmised, which made her feel better if only temporarily.

Wanda squeezed the lime into the glass and then sucked the rest of the juice out of it. She then raised her glass and proposed a toast. Probably to force Cathy to take a drink out of her glass.

"To Norman," a tear came in her eye as she said it.

"To Norman," Cathy replied and took a small sip which had way too much alcohol in it for such a small glass.

Wanda downed hers in one gulp, and before Cathy knew it, Wanda was standing and walking back to the kitchen. She returned with a half-empty bottle of gin and poured herself another drink.

"Let's do another toast," Wanda said. "You say it, Cathy."

Cathy hesitated, not sure what to say. Finally, she blurted out the first thing that came into her mind. "To the fire, that brought us together." She wanted to slap herself upside the head for saying something so stupid. Giving a toast had never been a strong suit, especially on the spur of the moment and under this much pressure.

"That damn fire," Wanda said taking a drink. Her hand was shaking as she poured another.

"It's strange how fast that fire spread," Cathy said inquisitively.

"That was my fault," Wanda blurted out. "Stupid me. I poured my glass of gin on it."

The accelerant.

Cathy had to forcibly keep her mouth from flying open. Wanda had just unwittingly admitted to causing the fire. Wanda quickly realized what she had said as she raised her hand to her mouth and put it over it like she was trying to shush herself.

"I guess I shouldn't have said that," Wanda said between drunken giggles.

Wanda had just confessed to insurance fraud. The whole wire thing was a good idea as it turned out. If the detectives captured those words, that just made their case fool proof. Miles Fire & Casualty even had a basis to demand Wanda return the insurance proceeds.

Cathy decided to escalate the situation further. The more drunk Wanda became, the more likely she was to let her secrets spill out. For a moment, she wondered how much would be admissible in court, if Wanda was under the influence. Either way, she was dying to know Wanda's secrets and the fear in her was subsiding.

The only thing holding her back was the knife within Wanda's reach. Even if Wanda was planning to kill her with a knife or by poisoning, she wasn't in a physical condition to do so. Cathy could easily overpower her.

Going on the offensive seemed like a good idea while Wanda was vulnerable.

"How come you won't ever sing for anyone? You have such a beautiful voice," Cathy asked, trying to sound anything but confrontational.

"It's a long story. To be honest, honey, my life hasn't been so great. I don't much feel like singing."

"Norman told me you grew up in an orphanage and your mother died in childbirth."

Her eyes were instantly full of tears. Alcohol had that effect on people, Cathy knew. It brought out deep emotions.

"The past is better left in the past," Wanda said somberly.

"I'm so sorry that happened to you." Cathy said with as much fake sincerity she could muster, considering the contempt she had for the woman.

Wanda was obviously moved, and her face contorted as she visibly tried to hold back the tears. She reached out and took Cathy's hand. Cathy's natural instinct was to pull away, but she resisted the urge. She was gaining Wanda's trust. That was a good thing. Maybe she'd confide in her.

More than anything, Cathy wanted to ask Wanda about Beatrice, but the detective had warned her not to. They didn't want to alert Wanda that they were on to her. Cathy had to be careful about what she asked her next. So, she didn't ask anything.

The conversation had not gone like Cathy envisioned. From their past communications, Cathy was prepared for a knock down drag out verbal boxing match. She halfway expected Wanda to try and kill her.

"About the painting," Wanda said brushing away the tears that were running down her face.

"Yes. The painting. That's why I'm here."

"You must've made quite an impression on my husband for him to want to give that to you and not to me. Why do you think that is?"

The fact that Wanda kept calling Norman her husband did not escape Cathy's notice.

Cathy responded. "I have no idea why. I was as shocked as you were. All I did was sit in the study and watch him stare at your painting and listen to him go on and on about how much he loved you. Trust me. The last thing I ever expected was to be mentioned in his will."

"Did you discuss it?"

"No! Not at all." Cathy wondered if Wanda was insinuating that she somehow manipulated it. That caused anger to momentarily rise up inside of her.

"Strange that Norman would change his will on the same night he died," Wanda said pensively. The woman still had more of her wits about her than Cathy had realized.

Cathy responded defensively. "I didn't want to be named in his will. The thought never occurred to me if that's what you're implying."

"That's not what I meant."

"That's what it sounded like," Cathy said roughly as she felt the battle getting ready to erupt.

Wanda leaned in really close to Cathy. At first, Cathy cowered away. She looked over to see if the knife was still on the cutting board.

After confirming it was, she let Wanda come the rest of the way until her mouth was against Cathy's ear. The smell of alcohol was so strong, a shiver snaked down Cathy's spine. Maybe it was the fear that had returned.

"What are you doing?" Cathy asked. "You're scaring me." She wanted to warn the detective that something strange was happening.

Wanda's hand was on Cathy's back pulling her close to her. There's no way that she didn't feel the wire running down Cathy's back along with the broadcaster attached to her pants. Cathy tried to pull away, but Wanda was surprisingly strong.

"You foolish girl," Wanda said. "You think you know me. You know nothing."

A loud bang!

The sound of something big crashing to the floor.

The detective was breaking down the door.

There was another loud bang.

Then shouting.

Within seconds, guns were drawn and pointed at Wanda.

Wanda had already leaned back in her chair and took another drink as if expecting the intrusion. As if she knew the whole thing had been a set-up.

They maintained their stares as the detective shouted, "Wanda Rose, you're under arrest. You have the right to remain silent. Anything you say can and will be used against you in a court of law. You have the right to an attorney. If you cannot afford an attorney, one will be provided to you. Do you understand these rights?"

Wanda nodded her head but still maintained her steely stare. The eyes pierced through Cathy's soul like the sharp knife on the dining room table.

Then she saw relief on Wanda's face.

Her jaw relaxed.

Her shoulders slumped.

Maybe Wanda was glad the ruse was finally over after all these years.

They stood Wanda to her feet and handcuffed her. As they were leading her away, Wanda turned her head back and said to Cathy, "Things are not as they appear."

That is the exact same thing the voodoo witch said.

21

Later that afternoon

"Wanda Rose is out on bail," Detective Lawrence said to Cathy.

"Already?" she replied in dismay.

A quick glance at the clock confirmed that it had only been two hours since she wore the wire, and Wanda was arrested. The last person she expected to hear from when the phone in her office rang was the detective with that news.

"She has a good lawyer and no prior criminal history," Lawrence explained.

"And she murdered two people! Yet she gets out on bail in no time," Cathy said in exasperation.

His tone turned sarcastic. "She's a pillar in the community... Owns a ten-million-dollar townhome so she has roots in Beverly Hill. She's recognizable. There's nowhere for her to hide. She's not a flight risk... blah blah blah... Same old, same old. The typical arguments recycled. I've heard them a thousand times. The judge let her out on a ten-thousand-dollar bail."

"'Which is nothing considering she has several million dollars to work with now that Norman's out of the way," Cathy muttered.

"Anyway, I just thought I'd let you know."

"I appreciate it. Do you think I'm safe?"

"For sure. And for two reasons. One is that she wouldn't dare try anything against our star witness. She'd be the first suspect."

Cathy was not thrilled to hear that they considered her their star witness. She figured she'd have to testify but didn't know that the entire success of their case would rest on her shoulders.

"What's the second reason?" Cathy asked.

"Because the media is camped out at your doorstep. She'd never try anything with so much press around."

"What are you talking about?"

"The press is all over this. It'll probably even hit the national news."

"How do they know about me?"

"Somebody leaked it. You're the one who is bringing down *The Blue Rose*, as they're calling her. The lady who sings the blues. Anyway, I just wanted to give you a heads up. You might want to let your boss know as well. I suspect the paparazzi will show up at your work any time now."

"What do I tell them?"

"I can't tell you what to say. The best thing is no comment. Whatever you say can and will be used against you in the court of law by her defense attorney."

"Sounds like I'm the one on trial. And now I'm going to be locked in my house. I won't even be able to go to the store without being followed. It'll be like being in prison."

"I've been in the prisons. It won't be like that. Don't worry about it. It'll die down eventually. Get used to it. This is your fifteen minutes of fame."

"Fame, I didn't ask for. I'm dreading testifying." The reality and consequences of her dogged actions hit her.

"These things usually never make it to trial," Lawrence said. "Even if it does, the trial won't be for nine months to a year. You'll have time to prepare. Anyway, I probably won't see you again until closer to the trial.

So, good luck to you."

Cathy hung up the phone slowly.

How could she have known that she was opening a can of worms with no way to wiggle out of it.

* * *

The hits kept coming.

"I suggest that you wait to auction the Wanda Rose painting," the art curator said. "With all the publicity surrounding Wanda Rose, I can get at least a hundred and fifty thousand for it now. But depending on how the trial goes, you might be able to get five times that at our next auction." "When is your next auction?" Cathy asked.

"Not until next spring. That's the best time to sell the painting."

"Next spring!" Cathy had hoped to sell the painting now and quit her job. The stress was starting to get to her. The thought of having to work for Dawkins for ten more months was not something she would look forward to.

As if on cue, Dawkins stuck his head in the door.

"I've got to go," Cathy said to the curator.

"Congratulations, Cathy," Dawkins started out saying. "We did it. We brought to justice the great Wanda Rose."

We?

She suddenly realized that he was going to take most of the credit with the bosses. The fact that he fought her tooth and nail every step of the way will not be mentioned.

"We still have to win at trial," Cathy reminded him. "Better to not count our chickens before they hatch as the saying goes."

"It's not going to trial. We've already heard from her lawyer. Get this. They wanted to know if we would drop the charges if they repaid the insurance proceeds."

"That's great! We should take it." That might mean that Cathy would not have to testify, and she could put all this behind her.

"Our lawyer said no thanks."

"Why in heaven's name would he do that?"

"They want to make an example of her. A deterrent for others who might be thinking about defrauding us. They need to know that we mean business and will pursue fraud to the fullest extent of the law. The judge will order restitution anyway."

"That makes sense," Cathy said forlornly.

"Anyway. You did good. Better than half the men in this office could've done."

That statement infuriated Cathy. She did better than *any* of the men would've done. Better than Dawkins even. He would've paid the claim a long time ago. The company would've been out the entire amount of the claim, and Wanda would've gotten away scotfree.

He must've sensed her rising anger.

"I'm paying you a compliment," he said. "Just accept it. You proved me wrong. A *broad* really can do this job."

Before she could throw something at him in her mind, he was out the door.

He returned a few seconds later.

"Did you call the Morrisons?"

"I sent them a letter."

"You need to call them. It's common courtesy."

"Would you call them? I don't have the heart to make a call like that."

"Get some cojones, sweetheart. It comes with the job."

She would've thrown something at him if he wasn't already out the door.

"I hate my job!" Cathy said aloud after closing the door to her office. If it had a lock, she would've used it.

She held her hand to forehead to fight back tears then dialed the number for the Morrisons.

Mrs. Eileen Morrison answered the phone. Hearing her voice only made things harder for Cathy.

"Mrs. Morrison, this is Cathy Tolliver, with Miles Fire & Casualty. How are you doing?"

"As well as can be expected under the circumstances. But thanks for asking."

"I want you to know once again that I'm deeply sorry for your loss. I can't imagine what you're going through."

Tad Morrison was their ten-year-old son. A trucker who works for Harbor Nationwide Freight Services, struck her son, killing him. Miles Fire & Casualty insured the company. Mrs. Morrison witnessed the accident.

The problem with the case was that both the trucker and the boy were at fault.

The boy was riding his bike and pulled in front of the truck making him impossible to miss. The trucker was speeding. He was in a hurry to get his load to its destination on time. In addition, the trucker was tired. The law said that a trucker can't drive longer than twelve hours at a time without at least a six-hour break. Harbor's man had been going for eighteen hours without sleep.

His reaction time was impaired by his own admission. A re-creation of the scene by an expert concluded that the trucker would've hit the kid even if he wasn't impaired. What made the situation worse was that the boy didn't die instantly. He and his bike were dragged a good fifty yards under the truck before the trucker realized what had happened and came to a stop. The mom ran after the truck in horror, trying to get him to stop.

The boy was rushed to the hospital and lived for three weeks. Seven surgeries were performed to try and save his life. The medical bills alone were over a million dollars. Not to mention the pain and suffering the family had gone through.

Cathy was calling to deny the claim.

"Mrs. Morrison. I have reviewed all of the information, and I've taken a statement from the trucker and from all the witnesses. After careful consideration, I've denied your claim."

Cathy winced as she said it and put her free hand just above her eyes on her forehead, bracing for the reaction she knew was about to come.

As expected, Mrs. Morrison burst into tears. "I don't understand. Why would you deny the claim? The trucker admitted to the police that he was speeding. They gave him a ticket. He killed our son."

"Unfortunately, the state of Virginia has what is called contributory negligence," Cathy said with no emotion in her voice.

"I don't understand what that means," Mrs. Morrison said, her voice cracking between the sobs.

Cathy kept a calm and cool and businesslike demeanor even though she consciously tried to make her tone sound sympathetic.

"It means that if your son contributed even one percent to the accident then you can't recover any damages from the other party."

"That's not fair! What kind of loophole is that?"

"It's not a loophole. It's a law in the state of Virginia. I don't necessarily agree with it, but I don't get to make that call."

She didn't agree with it. There were only four states in the country with contributory negligence laws. Alabama, Maryland, North Carolina, and Virginia. Most states adopted a comparative approach. You can recover damages, but they are reduced by your percentage of fault. Cathy thought that was fairer.

Under the law, her company wasn't liable. Her job was to follow the law. The accident happened in Virginia. It was on her desk because the trucking company was in southern California. If it were up to her, she'd find a way to help them out. It wasn't up to her. She was just the messenger.

"We'll lose everything," the mother said. "We'll have to file for bankruptcy. We can't afford the medical bills."

Cathy knew their medical insurance was capped at half a million dollars per incident. The Morrisons would be responsible for any expense over that. Most people were like the Morrisons. They pay their insurance premiums and expect the insurance company to be there when tragedy strikes. In reality, most people are one accident or sickness away from ruin and don't even realize it.

Cathy continued. "I sent you a letter in the mail documenting our position."

"Do you have children?" Mrs. Morrison asked tersely having regained her composure which had turned to anger.

"No. Ma'am, I don't."

"If you did, you wouldn't be so cold."

Before Cathy could answer, the line went dead.

That's when Cathy knew.

She had to quit her job.

It had taken twelve years of her life. If she gave it any more years, it would take her heart and soul.

Cathy left her office and walked down the hall to bookkeeping. Laura was at her desk. She walked in and sat down across from her.

"Congratulations!" Laura said. "I hear Wanda Rose was arrested."

"Yeah. It happened this afternoon. But she's already out on bail."

"Being rich does have its advantages."

"Could I crash with you?" Cathy blurted. "The paparazzi is camped out in front of my house. I don't want to deal with them right now."

'Of course. My husband's out of town on business. We'll have the house to ourselves. We can celebrate."

"I'm afraid I don't feel much like celebrating," Cathy said.

"What's wrong, honey?" Laura asked.

"I don't want to do this anymore. This job. Dawkins. The tragedy in life we see every day. I've had enough."

"I'll finish what I'm doing, and you can ride with me," she said, suddenly moving things around on her desk.

"That would be great. I feel like I'm in a ditch, and I know you can help me get out of it."

"You know how I feel about that," Laura said. "God is the best person to get you out of a ditch. And I'll help. I promise."

* * *

"I feel overwhelmed," Cathy said to Laura, where they sat in Laura's cozy living room on the couch, her feet up under her and to the side.

The only light was from an adjacent room and cast calming shadows on the furniture and ceiling.

A cup of hot tea in her hand. Laura sat on the floor with her back leaning against an ottoman. After dinner, they had consumed several bowls of ice cream, which Laura assured Cathy would make her feel better.

Being with Laura did make her feel better. Laura was the person she turned to over the years for spiritual matters and direction when her life seemed to be getting off track. Laura had a way of bringing everything back to God which was what Cathy needed right then.

Cathy was afraid she was sounding like a pity party, so she said, "Then I think about Mrs. Morrison, and I feel stupid. Imagine what she's going through?"

Cathy had told Laura the whole story, leaving out some of the gruesome details.

"I can't imagine."

Laura had two girls. Twins. College age. One was in Costa Rica on a mission's trip. The other was starting college in the fall but was away with some friends on a class outing. So, they did really have the whole house to themselves for several days. Cathy could stay as long as she wanted. Even when her husband, Walter, returned.

"When I think about Mrs. Morrison," Cathy said, "I feel guilty. I don't have it nearly as bad as she does."

"That's how life is. You don't have to look far to find someone worse off than you."

They were quiet for what seemed like a couple minutes.

"I feel so alone." Cathy noticed that she kept saying how she felt. She always considered herself a thinking person. Feelings were for the weak. Right now, she felt weak which was confirming her assumption that when someone wallowed in self-pity, it's because they've allowed their mind to wander away from rational thought. She tried to will herself to snap out of it, but it wasn't working.

Laura broke the silence. "Have you ever heard the story about the footsteps?"

"I don't think I have."

"A woman was walking along the beach. Actually... she dreamed she was walking on a beach. I'm sorry. I don't know if I'm getting the story right."

"It's all right. I like the story. A beach sounds great right now."

"One day she was looking back over her life... That's what it was. She saw scenes from her life in the sky. Sometimes she saw two sets of footprints on the beach, other times she only saw one. The hardest times in her life were the ones when there were only one set of footprints."

"Because she had to go through the hard time alone?" Cathy asked hesitantly.

"That's what the woman thought. So, she asked God about it. 'God why did you forsake me during the hardest times of my life?'"

"What did God say?" Cathy asked, enthralled by the story but not understanding the point.

"God said, 'During those hard times, I carried you. Those were my footprints, not yours.'"

"Oh..." Now she understood.

Laura continued. "Things are hard right now. But God is with you, Cathy. He never left you."

"Maybe I'm the one who left him."

"You can't. Remember Jesus said he would never leave you nor forsake you. God is with you no matter what. Even if you get in a ditch. He can pull you out of it."

"I like that. I feel better already. Do you have any more pearls of wisdom for me?"

"Yes, I do."

"I knew you would," Cathy said with a smile.

"There's a verse that I always turn to when I'm feeling down."

"When are you ever feeling down? Your life is perfect."

Laura let out a chuckle. "A couple of years ago, I found a lump in my breast."

"I didn't know," Cathy said, sitting up.

"Every day I kept saying one Bible verse out loud. It's in Corinthians.

Let me see if I still remember it."

She looked up to the ceiling like she was thinking.

"Praise be to the God and Father of our Lord Jesus Christ, the Father of compassion and the God of all comfort, who comforts us in all our troubles, so that we can comfort those in any trouble with the comfort we ourselves receive from God."

"I like that. I want to memorize it. So, what happened with the lump?"

Laura gave Cathy a dismissive wave of the hand. "Turns out it was nothing. But for a couple weeks, things were really scary. I didn't know what was going to happen. The thought of never seeing my girls get married. Have babies. And Walter... Who was going to take care of him? I swear, sometimes he's like having a little boy around. Without me, he'd go to work every day with wrinkled clothes and peanut butter and jelly sandwiches for lunch."

They both laughed longer than the joke warranted, but it felt good to relieve some tension.

"Anyway..." Laura continued. "The lump was benign. A false alarm. But it makes you realize what's important in life. Sometimes, you need to go through hard times to bring you back to relying on God."

"That makes sense. So, God brings you trouble so you get back on track."

Laura immediately retorted, "No! God doesn't bring the trouble. Every good and perfect gift comes from him. That's another Bible verse I rely on. The troubles come from the enemy. God wants to comfort us through the troubles. Then we can comfort others, like the verse says. That's what's happening now. God comforted me, and now he's using me to comfort you. That's how the Christian life is supposed to work."

"Makes perfect sense. So, what am I supposed to do about Dawkins?"

Laura sat up straighter and got a mischievous grin on her face. "That boy needs to be hogtied and dumped in the middle of the ocean, never to be seen again."

"That's not a very Christian attitude."

"I didn't say I was perfect. God's still working on me."

"I guess I just have to feel sorry for him. He's too ignorant to know better."

"Actually, he's threatened by you."

"Threatened by me?"

"Most men are threatened by powerful and successful women. You need to stick to your guns. You are proving to him that you're his equal, and he can't handle it. You may not see a difference in Dawkins, but other women will benefit from your success."

"I suppose. The insurance industry has been a man's world for so long, I wonder if it'll ever change."

"It already has. Look at you. Bringing down *The Blue Rose*. No one else in the office could've done it."

That sparked a question in Cathy. The words of the voodoo witch still haunted her. "When Wanda was being led away in handcuffs, she said, 'Things are not as they appear.' What do you think she meant by that?" "What do you think she meant?"

Cathy told Laura all about the voodoo witch and how she spoke the same words.

"Don't listen to those words!" Laura said sharply. "The witch is of the devil. Listen to God and what the Holy Spirit is speaking to you. Do you really believe that Wanda is guilty?"

"I do. I know without a shadow of a doubt that she is impersonating Wanda Rose."

"No doubt in your mind?"

"None."

"There could be no other explanation? What if things aren't as they appear?"

That stopped Cathy dead in her tracks to the point that she didn't know how to respond, so she said, "I don't know what other explanation there could be."

"I don't either. But just be open to it. Don't be quick to judge her. Same with Dawkins. Did you know that he's going through a divorce right now?"

Cathy's heart skipped a beat. "I didn't know that."

"A messy divorce from what I hear."

"That explains a lot. Maybe I need to cut him some slack."

"He's still a cad. But it helps to understand that other people are going through things as well. There may be a reasonable explanation for Wanda

Rose that you don't know about."

"No. She's a cad like Dawkins."

"Remember the footprints, Cathy. Things are not always as they appear. The woman thought when she saw one set of footprints that God had forsaken her. There was another explanation. She was totally wrong. Maybe there's another explanation to the whole Wanda Rose story."

The peace Cathy had been feeling from Laura's words, was suddenly filled with trepidation.

What if I've been wrong about Wanda Rose all along?

22

Beverly Hills Courthouse
Ten months later

Was Cathy the only person in the courthouse that day who didn't want to be there? For ten long months, Cathy had prayed that the Wanda Rose case would plead out, and she wouldn't have to testify. As each month passed and it became apparent that it wasn't going to happen, her apprehension had turned into full-blown dread.

She blamed the prosecutor, Flavio Toro. From the outset, he clearly wanted this case to go to trial. This was his chance to try a high-profile case two weeks before his reelection bid. When he argued vehemently for cameras in the courtroom, his true motivations became undeniable.

The viewing public was mesmerized by the whole affair. What was billed as the "Trial of the Decade," had become the Spectacle of the Century as far as Cathy was concerned. Even Wanda seemed to be relishing the limelight. She entered the courtroom with the fanfare of a movie star. Waving to her fans, blowing kisses to the crowd of spectators who were congregated outside, and posing for pictures. Quite a show.

It'd been years since Beverly Hills had seen a celebrity legal scandal, and this one had captivated all of southern California. A television had even been brought into the offices of Miles Fire & Casualty so they could watch the proceedings and their colleague testify, which should be later today if everything went as planned.

The courtroom was abuzz with anticipation as the spectators and press filed in. The jury had been selected over the previous two days, outside of the presence of the audience and the cameras. The judge had remarked that this was the first trial in her memory in which the jury selection would last longer than the trial itself. According to the judge, the morning would be devoted to opening arguments, the afternoon to witness testimony, and closing arguments would begin the following morning. If all went as planned, the jury would have the case by tomorrow afternoon.

Cathy liked the judge. Eileen Kelley was fairly new to the bench. Toro said her presence was a disadvantage. He would've preferred a male judge. He didn't come right out and say it, but Cathy got the impression that he thought the judge might be biased toward Wanda since she was a woman. The only advantage he saw was that she had a hard time controlling her courtroom. She generally gave the attorney's a lot of leeway, which he planned to use to his benefit.

The sound in the room was almost deafening.

Suddenly, the Bailiff stood and shouted, "All rise."

In a matter of a split second, the noise turned to complete silence. The door to the judge's chamber opened. Woman or not, the power of a district court judge was immense, and Judge Kelley looked the part in her flowing black robe and perfectly coiffed hair.

"This is the case of the State vs. Wanda Rose." The judge's words were strong and firm and while she had a microphone, the acoustics of the room projected her voice throughout it with authority.

She looked up from her notes and said, "I see that counsel for the defense and the state are present. Bailiff, bring in the jury."

The four men and eight women filed into the courtroom, and Cathy saw them for the first time. She didn't know if it was an advantage or not that there were more women than men. All she knew was that the selection of the jury had been an epic battle between Toro and Wanda's attorney, Roy Douglas. Toro felt confident his side had won.

Once the jury was seated, the judge said, "Mr. Toro, you can begin your opening arguments."

The flamboyant Toro, who looked more like a playboy than a prosecutor, stood to his feet with the flair of a circus master. Before he spoke, he buttoned the middle button on his fancy Italian designer suit. He pulled the sleeves of each arm down in a dramatic gesture. Then he shook his neck to the side like he was cracking it and sauntered from behind the table so that he was standing in front of the jury.

"Ladies and gentlemen of the jury," he began. "I want to thank you for your service to the State of California. There's no greater or more noble honor than to serve your country in this constitutional capacity."

Cathy thought that line was over the top. Serving in the armed forces and fighting in a war were more noble. Even though she was on Toro's side, she didn't like the man. He was dismissive of women and a publicity hound. Two traits she despised. He also had a penchant for hyperbole and exaggeration. Being a facts person, Cathy despised those who took liberty with them.

The jury seemed to love him, though. Even the women, who Cathy watched closely. Toro was recently in the headlines for a well-publicized affair that ultimately led to his wife filing for divorce. His girlfriend entered the courtroom earlier and was sitting on the second row, right behind the prosecution's table, one row in front of her. In Beverly Hills, he could get away with such a discretion. In Houston, the jury would immediately be turned off by the man who seemed more like Hugh Hefner than a prosecutor.

He did have a way with juries, though. His reputation as an effective litigator was well known which was why he was predicted to win his re-election in a landslide and was the odds-on favorite to get a conviction in this case. Word was that he aspired to someday run for governor. Another reason why he didn't settle this simple matter. The more opportunity in front of the camera the better. He seemed to relish the opportunity.

After a few other remarks of minor importance, he got right to it. "I have a problem today," he said. "My problem is that I don't know what to call the defendant."

He walked over near the defense table, so he was standing right in front of Wanda. She sat in the chair all prim and proper. Straight back, hands resting in her lap, her face emotionless.

Toro pointed at her. "I can't call her Wanda Rose because she isn't Wanda Rose. That's why we're here today. This woman," he said, exaggerating his gesture as his arms rose high in the air and then ended in an accusatory finger pointing, "stole the real Wanda Rose's identity some forty years ago and has been using that identity ever since to make a fortune."

The jury watched his every move and tuned in his every word. Cathy had been in the courtroom at least a dozen times and knew that juries were most attentive in the opening arguments. After that, they were easily bored once the case got into the weeds.

"We have a saying where I'm from. If it looks like a duck and sounds like a duck, then it's a duck. This lady right here, looks like Wanda Rose, the famous jazz singer. The problem is that she doesn't sound like her. This woman can't sing. For twelve years she was married to Mr. Norman Hurst of Fort Worth Texas. You'll hear testimony that Mr. Hurst never heard his wife sing over the twelve years, even though he begged her to sing for him."

Wanda kept her gaze away from Toro.

"Can you imagine that?" Toro continued. "You're married to the world's most famous jazz singer, and she won't sing for you. Why is that? It's because she can't. The minute she opens her mouth, the ruse ends. The gig is up."

Toro walked over to the prosecutor's table and got a 16 x 20 canvas with Wanda's picture on it and held it up for the jury. Then he walked over to the defense table and held it up so the jury could compare the picture to Wanda.

Cathy was surprised that the judge kept letting Toro invade Wanda's space. Usually they were instructed to stay on their own side.

"I gotta admit that she looks like a duck. The resemblance is uncanny."

He kept the picture in the air, facing the jury for effect. With perfect timing, he took the picture and threw it down on the floor for further effect.

"But she doesn't sound like a duck. If you look like a duck, but don't sound like a duck, then you aren't a duck. So, let's call a spade a spade. This lady is not Wanda Rose."

Toro got a sudden look on his face like he had a revelation. He held a finger to his chin and rested his elbow on his other arm and looked to the side like the scarecrow on the Wizard of Oz did when he got his brain.

With his voice raised, he said mockingly, "I know! Problem solved. I'll call her a spade. Instead of Wanda Rose, for the sake of discussion from this point on, I will call her Ms. Spade. Because a spade is a spade. She's not a duck. She doesn't sound like one, and therefore, she can't be one."

Wanda's attorney, Roy Douglas, stood to his feet.

Toro stopped speaking.

"What is it Mr. Douglas?" the judge asked.

"Your honor, I generally do not make it a point of interrupting opposing counsel's opening argument. However, I can no longer keep my seat. My client, Wanda Rose, walked into this courtroom today with a presumption of innocence. With all due respect to Mr. Toro, he doesn't get to decide if she is Wanda Rose. Those twelve people over there get to decide," he said, pointing to the jury. "She is Wanda Rose until the good people of this jury find otherwise.

I would respectfully ask the court to direct Mr. Toro to refer to my client as Wanda Rose. That is her name."

"So, ordered. Mr. Toro quit the grandstanding and get to your evidence."

Deep down inside, Cathy cheered the judge. While she rooted for her side to ultimately win, Toro was grandstanding and playing for the cameras. He made a good analogy about the duck and had the jury riveted until he started mocking Wanda. Cathy noticed a couple of the women had their arms folded and glared at him.

Toro must've suspected it because he immediately changed his tone and line of attack. He went into the whole story of the fire and the missing necklace and the holes in Wanda's story. Waiting a week to report the stolen necklace and the like.

"The noted defense attorney for Ms. Rose and a worthy adversary does not plan on calling any witnesses," Toro continued. "You have to ask yourself why. I have a handwriting expert who will say that the signature of the Wanda Rose sitting in this courtroom does not match the signature of a contract signed by the real Wanda Rose on her sixteenth birthday."

Toro knew exactly when to pause and when to start up again. "The Fire Marshal's report says there was an accelerant that caused the fire to spread. You'll hear in Wanda Rose's own words that she started the fire and threw a glass of alcohol on it which caused it to burn out of control. I'm sure the defense will claim it was an accident. That she thought the gin would put the fire out. How ludicrous is that line of thinking? It doesn't hold water. No pun intended."

That got a slight chuckle from the gallery. Not enough to make the judge raise her gavel, so he continued.

Toro began wrapping up his argument at exactly the right time. The jury seemed to be getting bored. "What I want to keep bringing you back to is this—the woman can't sing. If she can't sing. She's not Wanda Rose. She's not a duck."

Toro went back into his entertainer mode. He flailed his arms in the air as he said, "I can sing. The judge can sing. Every member of the jury can sing. All the people in the audience know how to sing. But none of us can sing like Wanda Rose. Because we're not her. Neither is that woman."

Roy Douglas stood to his feet again. The judge looked at him with an annoyed glare like 'why are you interrupting?' He's about finished.

"Your honor. I must object again," Douglas said. "I've heard Mr. Toro sing at a party after a few too many beers. I think it's beyond the jury's constitutional obligation to be subjected to cruel and unusual punishment."

The entire courtroom erupted in laughter. Even the judge couldn't control herself and let out a laugh before catching herself. Toro looked at Douglas with admiration. The defense had scored some points with the jury during the prosecution's opening argument. Douglas was a formidable opponent not to be taken lightly no matter how strong their case was.

The judge responded, "So, ordered. Prosecutor shall not sing."

The sea of people burst into laughter again. Even the judge was getting in on the comedy act. If this was any indication, the whole trial was going to be one big circus.

"I'm finished, your honor," Toro said.

"We'll take a fifteen-minute break," the judge replied as she struck her gavel for the first time.

Cathy heard the command, "All rise!"

Then she tried to beat the rush to the lady's room.

* * *

Roy Douglas was the antithesis of Flavio Toro. In his early sixties, he looked like the grandfather on *The Waltons*. His silvery hair, wire-rimmed reading glasses, and understated suit and tie gave him a down-home, folksy feel that came across as trustworthy. Like a man of his character would never defend someone who was guilty. Both Toro and Douglas had advantages with the jury. It would be interesting to see who made the bigger impression.

Hopefully, the members would look past the lawyers and focus on the evidence. Unfortunately, in opening arguments, mostly what they got was the lawyers' views of the case and little evidence. This was the opportunity for the attorneys to make a good first impression on the jury and now was Douglas's opportunity.

He went through the obligatory thanking the jury and instructing them on their solemn vow to presume Wanda was innocent until proven guilty. He explained the ins and outs of reasonable doubt skillfully and with just enough information to keep it from becoming boring. His skill and years of experience were evident from his first words.

The meat of his opening was powerful.

"In my forty years of doing this, I've never had a trial where I did not call a single witness. Never. Not one time. Mr. Toro made a big deal about that. Here's the reason. I don't have to in this case. The prosecution witnesses are going to create reasonable doubt in your mind. How do I know this? Because the prosecution's witnesses have reasonable doubt themselves."

He paused to let that sink into the juror's minds.

Then he approached them and put his hands on the railing to prop himself up, so he was closer to them. Eye to eye. An effective technique.

"They're only going to call four witnesses. Probably in this order. The Fire Marshal is going to say that he can't say beyond a reasonable doubt that Wanda Rose started the fire. He'll testify that it could've been started by the Christmas tree lights. If he has reasonable doubt, then you must as well."

Another pause.

"Oh yes," he said, looking pensively. "The accelerant. The Fire Marshal will testify that there was a possible accelerant. So, he wasn't even sure beyond a reasonable doubt that there was an accelerant. But we'll stipulate that there was. The stimulant was a glass of gin. That exacerbated the fire and made it worse. You'll hear Wanda Rose admitting to throwing the glass of gin on the fire."

The jurors' attentions were glued to Mr. Douglas. When he was speaking, not a sound could be heard in the audience. Everyone hung on his every word. His manner was believable, almost as if he wanted to win the case right then and there.

"Now, Mr. Toro misrepresented what Ms. Rose said. I don't know if you caught it. But he said that she admitted to starting the fire. That's not what she said. She admitted to throwing her glass of gin on it. Mistakenly. You see, she had two glasses sitting on her table. A glass of water and glass of gin. When she threw the contents of the glass on the fire, she thought she was throwing the water."

Mr. Douglas was crossing the line into testifying for Wanda. The judge was letting him. Toro wasn't objecting. Probably because he didn't want the jury to think he was afraid of the evidence.

The other problem was that Douglas was right. Toro had misrepresented what Wanda said on the tape. A mistake. The worst thing an attorney can do in his opening was say something that turned out to be untrue. That made the attorney untrustworthy and could make the jury wonder what else he might've lied about.

Toro could recover, but it was one strike against him.

Douglas continued. "The second witness is the handwriting expert. He'll testify that he cannot say with certainty that the same person did not write the signatures. Keep in mind, one signature was from 1929. Fifty-five years ago. My signature today looks nothing like it did when I was sixteen. My hand shakes. My eyesight's not as good. I'm lazier than I was then and don't go to as much effort as I did when I was in school. For that matter, I've changed my handwriting several times over the years."

Toro should've objected. Douglas was getting his own testimony on the record. What his signature looked like was irrelevant. However, it was a logical argument that would make sense to any reasonable person. More points for Douglas. He discredited the witnesses before they even testified.

"Before I get back to the witnesses, let's address this issue of Wanda Rose not singing."

Douglas walked over and stood in front of Toro's table. A good move that broke up the visual and would get the jury's attention back if he'd lost it in his arguments.

"That was a very clever move, Mr. Toro. I have to hand it to you. That was a fine performance that was on display for the jury." Douglas chuckled.

Toro remained stoic.

"But it's a trick. It's like asking a man when he stopped beating his wife. How do you respond to that accusation in a way that proves you never beat your wife?"

He turned back around so he was facing the jury.

"Mr. Toro is trying to bait Wanda Rose into testifying and singing for you. He knows that if she sings, then she'll have to testify. The judge will instruct you later that Wanda Rose has a constitutional right not to testify. I can count on one hand how many times I've let my client take the stand. It's nothing more than a magician's trick. A sleight of hand to confuse you.

And as jury members, you should see it for what it is—a stunt by the prosecutor to try to get you to believe something that cannot be proven one way or the other. Wanda not singing is not proof. You don't convict someone on what they don't say or do."

He walked back toward the jury but stopped about five feet away. Another good move. Give them some space.

"Back to the witnesses. A detective will testify, but he won't have much to offer. He didn't investigate the fire or the theft of the necklace. He also won't offer any testimony as to who my client is. He may say that she's not Wanda Rose, but he doesn't have any clue as to who she might be. Even with all his skills as a detective, he was not able to find any evidence that will prove that my client is not Wanda Rose."

Cathy sensed that Douglas was winding down.

"Cathy Tolliver," Douglas said.

Cathy's heart did a complete somersault when she heard her name. She thought she was going to get through both openings without her name being mentioned.

"Cathy Tolliver is an insurance claim's adjuster for Miles Fire & Casualty. She's the one who supposedly broke this case open. Proved that Wanda Rose is not who she says she is. Ms. Tolliver... I will give her credit for her dogged tenacity. She badgered and pursued my client for six months, refusing to pay a claim that her company obviously owed. But why? Why did she pursue this matter so hard? That's a question to keep in the back of your minds."

Badgered?

"She will make accusations about birth certificates, baptism records, death certificates. Missing records. Once again, a magician's trick. To deflect your attention from the real crime. Ladies and gentlemen of the jury, Cathy Tolliver is not a normal insurance claim's adjuster. She is a calculating and scheming opportunist!"

What?

If she could, Cathy would bolt out of the courtroom like a bullet shot out of a gun. Many in the media had turned their heads and were looking her way.

"What insurance adjuster profits financially from a claim? Evidence will show that Cathy Tolliver made tens of thousands of dollars by scheming her way into Wanda Rose's ex-husband's inheritance."

Scheming?

"Further, remember those missing birth certificates. The evidence is going to prove that Wanda Rose didn't steal those certificates. Cathy Tolliver did! She went to Camden, New Jersey, and stole the evidence that would have exonerated Wanda and proven she is the real Wanda Rose!"

Did he just accuse me of stealing the birth certificate?

"She had opportunity! She had motive!" His voice reverberated throughout the whole room as Douglas was nearly shouting.

"Tragically, the very person she extorted the money from, Mr. Norman Hurst, is dead. He can't testify today. He died under suspicious circumstances. Who was the last person to see him alive? Cathy Tolliver!"

Did he just accuse me of murder?

At first, anxiety overwhelmed her. And fear. Her heart pounding almost drowned out the noise in the courtroom. Douglas clearly was going to go after her to deflect the heat off of his client. Her face felt flush and her stomach suddenly became queasy.

What if the jury believes him?

Then she got spitting mad which fought away the negative emotions like a big stick would fight away a rabid dog.

If he wants a war, I'm going to give him one.

23

Wanda's attorney, Roy Douglas, had thrown down the gauntlet in his opening statement and basically accused Cathy of several crimes. Clearly, he was going to try and go after her as the one who should be on trial. Cathy admitted to herself that their case was mostly circumstantial. A circumstantial case was effective if there was no other plausible explanation. Douglas was going to use Cathy as the misdirection to take the scrutiny off his client.

Cathy's anxiety she felt earlier turned to resolve. She knew the case backward and forward and was ready to go to war with Douglas. Twelve years had given her a great deal of experience testifying in court. This wasn't the first time she met a hostile defense attorney and, in the past, had comported herself well. Although, she had to admit that none of them were as formidable as the daunting Mr. Douglas.

After Douglas's opening statement, the court took another short recess, and now the proceedings were well underway. The District Attorney, Flavio Toro, was in the middle of his case in chief, and Cathy would be his last witness. Since Douglas had referenced in his opening statement what he thought would be the prosecution's order of witnesses and had gotten it right, almost like he was reading Toro's mind, the DA scrambled to change the order so it didn't appear to the jury that Douglas was in charge of the trial or that the prosecution was predictable.

So, he started with the weakest part of the case—the identity fraud charge. This part of the case was circumstantial at best, and

Douglas had plenty of ways to poke holes in it. He'd already done so in his opening argument.

Toro almost welcomed the change so they could get that part of the testimony out of the way and end with their strongest evidence. If they believe Wanda set the fire on purpose and there was no necklace, the jury might not have much of a stretch to believe that she was capable of stealing an identity, regardless how weak it might've seemed at the beginning. Like most people, jurors had a short memory and would focus on the most compelling evidence first.

Sigmund, the handwriting expert, was the first on the stand. His direct examination went longer than Cathy had anticipated. The testimony was tedious and detailed. While Sigmund was a notable expert, he over explained why he believed the signatures on the documents didn't match. The first few minutes several of the jurors were taking notes. By the end, they had all set aside their pencils and notepads.

In retrospect, Cathy would've preferred for Toro to start with a bigger bang. Kudos to Douglas for throwing the prosecution off its game right from the outset.

When Toro was finally finished with Sigmund, Douglas didn't even rise from his chair. He just asked one question. "Can you say without a reasonable doubt that the same person did not sign those documents?"

"No."

"I have no further questions for this witness."

That nearly hour of testimony was discounted in only seconds. Such was the ebb and flow of trials. Though a long way from being over, Cathy couldn't help but feel like they were behind.

Detective Lawrence was next. As Douglas pointed out, Lawrence had no direct knowledge about the fire and stolen necklace. Toro brilliantly asked him about them, anyway, effectively using him as another expert witness.

The detective explained, "The fire looked to me to be a classic set up.

A diversion."

"Can you explain what you mean?"

"Very often a perp… a perpetrator of a crime will start a fire to cover up the real crime. In this case the crime being covered up is the fake theft of the necklace."

"Why do you say that?" Toro asked.

"If I were investigating a fire, and the so-called victim suddenly had a valuable item missing, I'd immediately be suspicious. Especially when an accelerant like alcohol is thrown on the fire."

Defense counsel, Roy Douglas, rose to his feet to lodge his first objection.

"What are the grounds for your objection?" Judge Kelley asked Douglas.

"Foundation. No evidence has been presented about an accelerant."

"We were just getting to that, Your Honor," Toro said. "We have an audio tape to play for the jury that will clear that up."

"Get to it then, and I'll rule on the objection after I hear the tape."

The entire conversation with Wanda Rose in the townhome was played for the jury. Cathy found it strange hearing her own voice in the recording. Toro stopped the tape periodically to make a few salient points. The jury seemed enthralled, and Cathy saw some of them taking notes again.

The judge overruled the objection, and when the issue came up again, Lawrence was allowed to answer the question. He could discuss the accelerant because it was on the tape, and he did investigate that part of the case.

"You don't believe that Ms. Rose threw gin on the fire by accident, do you Detective?"

He said that he didn't and then explained effectively why he thought so from his years of experience as a detective.

Toro then used Lawrence to get his exhibits into the record. The birth certificates. The baptism record for Beatrice Rose. Her death certificate in New Orleans along with a picture of the grave. The insurance application and claim form were already introduced in the exhibits from Sigmund's testimony, but Toro asked Lawrence some questions about those, including the discrepancies with the birth dates.

This would save time when he got to Cathy's testimony. He wanted her time on the stand to be seamless and not interrupted by placing exhibits in the record which took time. The trial was like a chess match, and Toro was setting the board up the way he wanted before he really went on the offensive.

When he was done with Lawrence, Douglas surprised Cathy again by only asking three questions. As with the first witness, he didn't even bother to stand. A clever move. He was signaling to the jury that he didn't view the witness's testimony as being important enough to warrant the effort of standing or even trying to rebut it.

"Detective Lawrence, did you search Wanda Rose's apartment?"

"Yes, sir. We did."

"Did you find those missing birth certificates that my client allegedly stole from the public records in Camden, New Jersey?"

"No, sir. We did not."

"Did you search Cathy Tolliver's house for those records?"

"We did not."

"I have no further use for this witness."

Toro immediately stood for redirect and asked the detective, "Why didn't you search Ms. Tolliver's house for the records?"

"There was no probable cause to do so."

"Thank you, detective."

Even in the detective's testimony, Douglas tried to sow a seed of doubt in the juror's minds that Cathy might have stolen those documents. He didn't need to prove that she did, he just had to create reasonable doubt that maybe his client didn't, and it was within the realm of possibility that someone else did.

The Fire Marshal was next. His report was placed into the record, and Toro asked him a few questions about it.

"Explain what you mean by the phrase 'possible accelerant.'"

The Marshal answered, "An accelerant is simply a substance used to spread a fire."

"And you noticed something strange about the fire right away, did you not?"

"The fire was suspicious from the beginning. I've seen many Christmas tree fires. This one spread more quickly than those I've seen before."

"How did the fire spread differently?"

"It jumped from the tree to the wall and then spread quickly. Had it stayed on the tree, Ms. Rose might've been able to put it out on her own. Once it hit the wall, it had sheetrock and wood to fuel it."

"Is it conceivable..." Toro paused. "Do you believe that the accelerant was applied on purpose?"

"Yes."

"Why is that?"

"I don't buy Ms. Rose's story that she accidentally threw the alcohol on the fire."

"Have you ever seen that before in your more than twenty years of public service as a fireman and now as a Fire Marshal?"

"Never."

"So, it's your expert opinion that Ms. Rose set the fire on purpose?"

"That's correct."

Douglas stood to the podium and came after the Fire Marshal much harder.

"Did you find evidence that Ms. Rose set the Christmas tree on fire?" Douglas asked.

"I did not, but it's possible she did."

"It's possible. But you can't say with certainty, can you?"

"Not with certainty."

"Not even beyond a reasonable doubt, correct?"

"That's correct. But we can say beyond a reasonable doubt that Ms. Rose threw an accelerant on the tree that caused the fire to spread."

"Fair enough. But back to the origin of the fire. The evidence points to it being started by the lights, is that correct?"

"Without the accelerant, that would've been my conclusion.

Douglas raised the intensity of his voice like this was an important point. "Just for the sake of discussion, how would Ms. Rose set the fire on purpose? Would she stick a match to it?"

"That would be the most likely way."

"But you would see evidence on the tree if she lit a match. Isn't that correct?"

"Yes."

"Did you find such evidence?"

"We did not."

"So, what you want this jury to believe is that Ms. Rose was sitting in her townhome with a glass of gin in her hand, just waiting for the Christmas lights to catch the tree on fire. When it did, she rushed into the room to pour the gin on it. And she did all of this because she was smart enough to concoct a scheme to say a fireman stole a hundred-thousand-dollar necklace. A necklace which Mr.

Toro is now arguing doesn't exist. Is that your theory on what happened?"

The Fire Marshal got a slight grin on his face as did several members of the jury. For the fire to be a crime, the Prosecution had to prove criminal intent. That Wanda set the fire on purpose or poured the accelerant on the fire on purpose. All of which seemed ludicrous when put in that context.

"When you put it that way, it doesn't seem feasible."

A murmur went through the courtroom as happens when there was a pivotal moment in a trial.

The judge gaveled it down.

Cathy wasn't worried by that setback. There was another way of making it a crime. She was itching to get on the stand and spring it on Douglas and the entire courtroom. When both sides were finished with the Fire Marshal, the judge ordered a break for lunch.

After lunch, Cathy would get her chance.

* * *

Douglas objected over and over again to questions Toro asked Cathy in his direct examination. Especially as it pertained to her conversations with

Norman. This led to several sidebars with the judge, which Cathy was able to overhear because of her close proximity to the bench.

"Your Honor, her conversations with Norman are hearsay," Douglas pleaded with the judge.

Toro rebutted, "Norman is not available to testify because of his untimely death. A death we believe Ms. Rose had a hand in. We intend to introduce evidence to that fact."

"You can't be serious. There's no proof Ms. Rose was in any way responsible for Norman's death. Anything introduced would not be evidence but sheer conjecture."

"Ms. Rose traveled to Fort Worth the day of his death."

"It's not a crime to travel to Texas."

"It's just suspicious."

"Exactly. What the prosecution wants to do is divert the jury's attention away from the case they are losing. They want to make the jury think Ms. Rose killed her ex-husband so the jury will despise her and find her guilty even though the facts don't support it."

The judge interrupted. "I won't permit any evidence related to Mr. Hurst's death. This is not a murder trial. Ms. Rose has not been charged with a crime in his death. Let's stick to the facts of this case. As to Ms. Tolliver's conversation with Mr. Hurst, I will allow hearsay to the extent that it relates to personal or family history. However, Mr. Toro, you have a short leash. If you stray too far off course, I will use that leash to yank you back to what is relevant in this case."

The judge displayed backbone as the trial progressed.

"I want my objection noted on the record," Douglas said.

"So noted," the judge said. "Step back, and let's move this thing along."

That severely limited what Toro could ask regarding her conversations with Norman, but Cathy was confident she got enough in to raise the jury's curiosity if not suspicion.

In cross-examination, if Douglas opened the door by asking a question in the wrong way, then she would walk right through it and get some of their conversation in. Norman had said a number of things that would be incriminating to Wanda if only Cathy could tell the jury about them.

Cathy wondered if they might need that testimony to win. Douglas had effectively disrupted the flow of Toro's questioning of Cathy. At this point, in her mind, the outcome was still a toss-up.

When Toro finished with his direct examination, Douglas came right at her with his firepower on display for the jury's benefit.

"Your boss wanted you to settle this case a long time before you actually did, didn't he Ms. Tolliver?"

"Yes, sir." Cathy had learned to just answer yes or no. Don't offer any information not asked for. That was the quickest way to dig yourself into a hole.

For the next ten minutes, he tried to paint her as an overzealous agent who didn't follow normal procedures and even went against the directives of her boss. Cathy didn't think he scored many points, but it could put the idea in the back of their minds.

When he got to the documents, the cross-examination began in earnest.

"May I approach the witness, Your Honor," Douglas asked. He couldn't just hand Cathy a document to look at. He had to ask permission before approaching.

"What's the name on the birth certificate?" Douglas asked.

"Wanda O'Neil."

"What's my clients name?"

"I don't know," Cathy said, as the courtroom chuckled.

She quickly added, "She claims her name is Wanda Rose."

Cathy didn't want to evoke the wrath of the judge like Toro had earlier. She also didn't want to come across as a smart aleck, but she did want to stick with what she believed was true and the reason they were there.

Even then, Douglas wanted to use her words against her. "The judge has already acknowledged that we are to refer to my client as Wanda Rose." "I understand. But I'm under oath and I'm sworn to tell the truth. Truthfully, I don't know her real name."

Another chuckle trickled through the crowd. It felt to Cathy like she was coming across as sincere and not argumentative.

"You will acknowledge that Wanda O'Neil and Wanda Rose are two different names."

"Yes. I believe that Wanda Rose is Wanda's O'Neil's stage name."

"With all due respect, Ms. Tolliver, what you believe is not important. It's what you can prove. You have no definitive proof to that effect do you, Ms. Tolliver?"

"That was what Norman, Wanda's ex-husband, told me."

Douglas was livid.

"Objection! That's hearsay Your Honor. We just talked about that. Counsel should be reprimanded."

"He asked about personal and family history, Your Honor," Toro argued. "You said that was allowable."

"You may tell the jury what Norman told you about the birth certificate," Judge Kelley said to Cathy with a slight smile.

"He said it was Wanda's."

"Is it possible Norman was mistaken?"

"I would think that a man would know his own wife's birth date."

"Did Norman ever tell you that his wife was not the real Wanda Rose?"

"No. He did not."

"According to you, any man would know his own wife's birthdate. Right? That's what you said. "But you want us to believe that he lived with her for twelve years and didn't know her real identity? That seems like a stretch doesn't it?"

"Objection."

"I withdraw the question. Let's talk about that birth certificate. What is the birthdate on it?"

"November 5, 1912."

"What is the date on Wanda Rose's insurance application?"

"November 4, 1912."

"What is the date on Wanda Rose's driver's license?"

"November 4."

"November 4, 1912, correct?"

"That's correct."

"So, the name is different. And the birthdate is different."

Toro stood to his feet. "Does counsel have a question for the witness?"

"Withdrawn, Your Honor."

Douglas was smart not to open that door too far. Maybe Toro would get it in on his redirect.

Douglas continued. "Counsel for the State entered an exhibit earlier that are baptism records from *Sisters of Charity* orphanage in Camden, New Jersey. What name is on the baptism records?"

"Beatrice Rose."

"Thank you."

Douglas handed Cathy the photograph of Beatrice Rose's gravestone.

"What is the date of birth on that headstone?"

"November 5, 1912."

He didn't ask about the death certificate. Probably because he didn't want to draw attention to the mercury poisoning.

"You have a vivid imagination, don't you, Ms. Tolliver?"

"Objection, Your Honor. Argumentative."

"Sustained."

"Let me ask it a different way. You've made a lot of assumptions here, haven't you?"

"Objection."

Toro had obviously decided to start objecting more to use the same tactic on Douglas and break up his cross-examination.

"Overruled. You may answer counsel's question."

"I wouldn't use the word assumptions. I would say that I've connected the dots."

"But Wanda Rose was born on November fourth. Beatrice Rose was born on November fifth and doesn't have the same first name. Wanda O'Neil was born on November fifth and doesn't even have the same last name as Wanda Rose or the same first or last name as Beatrice Rose. You're not connecting dots. You're going way outside the lines to try and give the illusion that these are all the same person, when the connection is marginal at best, and there are not really any dots to connect."

"Is there a question in our future?" Toro stood and asked, not really stating an objection.

"What is your question, counsel?" the judge asked.

"It's possible you're wrong, isn't it, Ms. Tolliver?"

"I'm not wrong. Wanda O'Neil is Wanda Rose. Beatrice Rose is her Christian name. Wanda Rose died in New Orleans. This woman stole her identity. The reason the birthdates are different is because this Wanda Rose can't keep her lies straight."

"Like I said, you have a vivid imagination."

"Objection."

"Withdrawn."

Douglas stood at the podium now and looked through his notes.

"Ms. Tolliver, you testified earlier that you went to the archives building in Camden, New Jersey, looking for birth certificate records and death records. Were you ever alone with the records?"

"Yes. They were down in a basement. The woman who worked there took me to them and then went back upstairs."

"Did you look for birth certificate records on November fourth or just on the fifth?"

"I looked through the records on both days."

"And if you had found a birth certificate for Wanda Rose on November 4, 1912, that would blow your whole theory out of the water, wouldn't it?"

Cathy tried to diffuse the impact of the underlying inference by playing nice. "I go where the facts lead me. I would've loved nothing more than to prove that she really is Wanda Rose. I'm a big fan of the real singer. But there was no birth certificate for Wanda Rose on November fourth."

"So, you say," Douglas said almost to himself while looking down at his notes.

Here we go. The fireworks are about to begin.

Toro must've thought that wasn't egregious enough to object to.

From Cathy's perspective, she was holding her own. She had at least fought him to a draw.

"Ms. Tolliver," Douglas said. "When you went to Camden, New Jersey, you had already paid the claim, is that correct?"

A surprising turn in the questioning.

"That's correct."

"So, why go to Camden, New Jersey? Why keep investigating a claim you've already paid?"

"I still had my suspicions that there was fraud involved in the claim."

"So, by your own admission, you didn't have enough proof to deny the claim, so you went looking for more; is that your testimony?"

"Even after a claim is paid, if we find evidence of fraud, we can reopen a case."

"If you had found evidence that exonerated my client, that would reflect poorly on you with your boss, would it not?"

"Not necessarily."

"You admitted earlier that your boss was angry at you for not closing the case sooner, is that correct?"

"I didn't say angrier."

"Did he give you permission to go to Camden, New Jersey?"

"No."

"You went on your own, didn't you?"

"Yes."

"If you asked for permission, would your boss have granted it?"

"Probably not."

"Like I said, if you found Wanda Rose's birth certificate in the archives showing she was born on November fourth, that would have reflected badly on you, wouldn't it?"

"I didn't find any such certificate."

"Let's talk about the necklace for a minute. You didn't find any evidence that the necklace wasn't stolen, did you?"

"I didn't find any evidence it was."

"But you paid the claim."

"Yes, we did. Against my objections."

"Did your boss sign off on the payment?"

"Yes."

"By paying the claim, you were admitting that you had no proof that Wanda Rose made up the story about the stolen necklace, weren't you?"

"I had my suspicions and still do."

"With all due respect, we don't send people to jail on suspicions. Our system of justice demands proof. You have no proof that the necklace wasn't stolen. No proof that Wanda O'Neil is Wanda Rose. No proof that Beatrice Rose is Wanda Rose. The only testimony you have to offer this jury today are your suspicions. I'm sorry, Ms. Tolliver, but your suspicions do not meet the burden of proof."

"Objection. Argumentative."

"Sustained. Jury will disregard counsel's characterization of Ms. Tolliver's testimony."

Douglas barely noticed the slap on the wrist. He kept going.

"Ms. Tolliver let's talk about the fire and the glass of gin. Did Miles Fire & Casualty pay the claim for the fire?"

"Yes, we did."

"Isn't that an admission that you had no evidence to deny the claim?"

"At the time, yes."

"So, you couldn't prove that Wanda Rose set the fire on purpose, so you paid the claim, isn't that correct?"

The question jolted Cathy like she had just been struck by lightning.

Douglas just made a mistake and didn't even realize it.

"It doesn't matter," Cathy said with a sudden burst of confidence.

Before that question, it seemed like they were about to lose the case. If she handled this right, the entire case was about to turn in their favor.

24

Roy Douglas, by his own admission, wasn't well versed in insurance fraud claims. He made his reputation defending white-collar criminals for banking and wire fraud and celebrities for serious felonies like murder. In the sunset of his career, he had intentionally taken cases that were less stressful—like the Wanda Rose case.

Trials that lasted longer than a couple of days zapped his energy, so he gravitated toward those that could be settled without going to court or would only take a day or two in trial. In this trial, not calling any witnesses had meant less work for him and also turned out to be a good strategy.

A bout with the flu the week before the start of the trial, had put him on his back and cut into his normal preparations. Still, the case was going surprisingly well, considering he wasn't as prepared as he would've liked to be.

As easy as it had been, he was still starting to feel tired. The final witness in the trial was on the stand, and it would be over soon. A nagging feeling inside told him that he needed to get Ms. Tolliver off the stand as soon as possible. The cross-examination had gone as well as could be expected, and he was confident that his client was going to get off on all the charges. An old saying among trial lawyers was *don't snatch defeat from the hands of victory*. When you have a case won, get it to the jury as soon as possible.

Douglas glanced down at his notes. He'd checked off everything on his list except the fire. There really was no need to ask Ms. Tolliver about it.

The Fire Marshal gave him everything he needed and more.

Quit while you're ahead.

It seemed like an awkward stopping point. Ms. Tolliver just admitted her company paid the claim on the necklace. That clearly showed that even the insurance adjuster had reasonable doubt about her own theory. The insurance company had also paid the claim on the fire. That showed reasonable doubt as well. So, he figured he might as well get Ms. Tolliver on the record admitting it.

He looked over at the jury. One of his best skills was reading them. They seemed antsy, like they had heard enough and were ready to go back and deliver him a victory.

Douglas said to her, "One final question, Ms. Tolliver." The jury would be glad to hear those words.

He turned back toward the witness. "Did Miles Fire & Casualty pay the claim for the fire?"

"Yes, we did."

"Isn't that an admission that you had no evidence to deny the claim?"

"At the time, yes."

"So, you couldn't prove that Wanda Rose set the fire on purpose, so you paid the claim, isn't that correct?"

"It doesn't matter."

The answer almost caused Douglas to laugh out loud. The jury wouldn't like that response. He wanted to see if he could coax more absurdity out of her. He'd use that ridiculous statement in his closing. Cathy Tolliver had just handed him a gem.

Douglas looked over at the jury as he asked sarcastically, "Are you saying that it doesn't matter whether Ms. Rose set the fire on purpose? That you think she's guilty no matter what the facts show?"

"When we paid the claim, we didn't know that Ms. Rose threw her drink on the fire. She didn't disclose that information to me or to the Fire Marshal."

A shot of panic went through Douglas as his heart flipped flopped in his chest, and he suddenly felt weak at the knees. He knew immediately where she was going with it.

How do I get out of this?

If he asked her anything, it would give her the chance to clarify her answer and this case would be over. His client would be found guilty. If he didn't ask, Toro would, and the jury would hear the information anyway. He felt like a noose was constricting around his neck as he suddenly had trouble breathing. The thought occurred to him that maybe he could fake a heart attack to get out of this mess.

"May I have a second, Your Honor?" Douglas asked.

He walked over to the defense table, poured himself a glass of water and took a big gulp. Then he leaned in and whispered in his colleagues' ear.

"We're in damn trouble," he said to his assistant.

He didn't wait for a response. It would be better for him to deal with it now, when he could control the witness rather than turn it over to Toro and let him run with it all the way to the end zone. Toro probably would anyway, but at least he could try and throw some kind of smokescreen up in the air for the jury.

"Mr. Douglas," Judge Kelley said. "Are you finished with the witness?"

"No, Your Honor."

Judge Kelley tapped her wrist like it had a watch on it.

Douglas took a deep breath. "Did you ask Ms. Rose about the accelerant?"

"Yes."

Wrong question.

"Ms. Rose thought the glass was water, isn't that correct?"

"That's what she says, but it still doesn't matter. It's still insurance fraud."

He couldn't ask her to explain why. That would be a disaster. *I need to sit down before I make things worse.*

"No further questions, Your Honor."

I should've quit while I was ahead.

* * *

"Any questions, Mr. Toro, on redirect?"

"Yes, Your Honor."

Toro stood to the podium. Cathy let out a huge sigh of relief. Douglas had opened the door, and she had driven a bulldozer through it and dug a hole for Wanda and her attorney to crawl in. Now she needed to pour as much dirt on it as possible.

"Why is it insurance fraud regardless of Wanda Rose's intent when she poured the gin on the flames?"

Cathy knew exactly what to say. "Because she didn't disclose it. The State of California has adopted the Pure Comparative Negligence standard for paying insurance claims."

"What is that standard?"

"Damages are divided by percentages based on the claimant's level of responsibility. Ms. Rose was not entitled to a full reimbursement of the damages. Had she admitted to me or to the Fire Marshal that she had poured her gin on the flames and contributed to the fire's destruction, then her damages would've been reduced by her level of responsibility."

"So, it's insurance fraud to not disclose all of the information?"

"Her policy actually states that if she fails to disclose even one piece of relevant information, then we have the right to deny the entire claim. In reality, Ms. Rose is not entitled to any reimbursement for the claim, even though she has been paid for it. Since she disclosed the information after the claim was paid, Miles Fire & Casualty is entitled to a complete reimbursement."

"Your Honor," Toro said. "I want to re-play a portion of the audio of Ms. Tolliver's conversation with Ms. Rose in her townhome from the day she was wearing a wire."

"I'll allow it."

The audio was already cued up because the voices came over the speakers immediately.

"It's strange how fast that fire spread," they could hear Cathy say.

"That was my fault," Wanda said. "Stupid me. I poured my glass of gin

on it."

The next thing they heard was Wanda saying, "I guess I shouldn't have said that." And then some giggles.

The audio shut off and Toro continued, "Wanda Rose admitted that the fire spreading was her fault, did she not?"

"That's what I heard her say."

"As an insurance claim's investigator that tells you that she has a liability for some of the damages, does it not?"

"It does. And then when she says I shouldn't have said it, it shows me that she knew not telling me was wrong. Of course, she didn't know it was being taped so she could deny having said it later."

"Objection," Douglas said. "As to what Wanda Rose knew."

"Sustained."

"I have no further questions," Toro said.

"Neither do I," Douglas replied with a hint of resignation in his voice.

Judge Kelley said, "The witness will be excused."

"The prosecution rests," Mr. Toro said with emphasis.

"Mr. Douglas, do you plan to call any witnesses?" Judge Kelley asked.

"No, Your Honor."

"We will break for the day and begin closing arguments first thing in the morning. The jury may be excused for the evening with the thanks of the court."

Wanda and her attorney skulked out of the courtroom like a beaten fighter. Once the cameras were turned off, the prosecution team, along with Cathy, erupted joyously. Hugs were all around as Cathy was nearly giddy.

"You did well, Cathy," Toro said to her.

Today had gone as well as anyone thought possible.

* * *

The next morning

Roy Douglas finished his closing arguments, and now Toro would take his turn. Douglas did his best to rehabilitate his client but really didn't hit what Cathy would consider any home runs. He had no real defense for why Wanda Rose covered up the fire. Her motivation was obvious, which was what made it insurance fraud. She hid the information for financial gain. As it turned out, probably in the hundreds of thousands of dollars in that Cathy figured Wanda's contributory portion was thirty to fifty percent of the total claim.

The Fire Marshal had testified that Wanda probably could've put the fire out on her own if she hadn't thrown the gin on it. If fact, she might not have even suffered the loss of the necklace.

For the most part, Douglas didn't go after Cathy in the way that he had in his opening statement. Probably because Cathy came across as believable in her testimony. He would've looked foolish trying to make her out to be a criminal when the jury could see for themselves that she was anything but that.

* * *

This part of the trial was enjoyable to Cathy. Her testimony was over, and she could relax and watch Toro work his magic on the jury. Toro had a real opportunity to win this case, and he knew it. This was a big moment for him, and she could sense his nervousness.

In their morning meeting, Toro said he was going to hit the issue of the stolen identity first.

Once they returned to the courtroom, Toro began by thanking the jury again for their service.

"When you go back into the jury room, you're not asked to leave your common sense outside the door," he said.

Toro had calmed down the dramatics and Cathy thought that was a good idea.

"Wanda's ex-husband, Norman Hurst, may he rest in peace, had a copy of Wanda O'Neil's birth certificate. He believed that it belonged to his wife of twelve years. He also claimed that Wanda Rose was a stage name. If you look at the birth certificate, the date is November 5, 1912. The Wanda Rose in this courtroom claims her birthdate is November 4, 1912. But the defense failed to produce a birth certificate to that effect. If this is not Wanda's birth certificate you have to ask yourself why Wanda didn't tell Norman that fact. Wouldn't you? Wouldn't you say, 'Norman, you've got the wrong birth certificate. I'm not Wanda O'Neil.'?"

Toro brought back some of the dramatics for that exchange but more measured and more effective, in Cathy's opinion.

"That's what I mean by using your common sense. It's reasonable to assume that Wanda O'Neil is Wanda's Rose's birth name. Even her mother's name is Rose. That's too big a coincidence to be anything else but what it appears."

Toro walked back behind the podium and looked at his notes.

"Let's talk about the baptism records. Norman said that Wanda's mother died in childbirth and that Wanda went to an orphanage. The only orphanage in that area during that time was *Sisters of Charity*. The orphanage had a record of a Beatrice Rose Kennedy being baptized there just a couple days after Wanda O'Neil was born.

Common sense would tell you they are the same person since Rose Kennedy is the mother's name. How big a coincidence would it be if they weren't?"

Toro led out a laugh right behind the sentence for effect. He didn't pause long, though.

"Then we find the death certificate for a Beatrice Rose in New Orleans! Where was Wanda Rose living? New Orleans. The defense would lead you to believe that that is a coincidence. That defies common sense. The birthdate on Beatrice Rose's headstone is the same as Wanda O'Neil. The odds of that being a coincidence have to be astronomical. The only conclusion you can reach is that Beatrice Rose is Wanda Rose."

Toro now stood in front of the jury. As close as he could get. They were eye to eye. He could've reached out and touched the members of the jury on the first row.

He continued with his voice softened. "Beatrice Rose died. The death certificate says she died of mercury poisoning. Wanda Rose never recorded another album. Ladies and gentlemen of the jury, common sense would tell you that Wanda Rose is buried in that grave."

Toro pointed at Wanda. She was looking straight ahead. Emotionless.

"Two years later, that woman, whoever she is, married Dick Lawlor. What name is on the wedding certificate? Wanda Rose. The woman at the defense table divorced Dick Lawlor a couple years later and got two hundred and fifty thousand dollars in a divorce settlement. When that money ran out, she married Norman Hurst. She got twelve million dollars in that divorce settlement and bought the townhome in Beverly Hills. That money was running out. So, what did she do? Did she start a fire to collect insurance proceeds?"

Toro was really doing well. This was the best closing argument Cathy had ever seen. The jury was glued to his every word. While reading a jury is next to impossible, he seemed to be winning them over.

"I don't know if Wanda started the fire or not. The Fire Marshal didn't seem to think so. Okay. I'll concede that point. Wanda didn't start the fire on purpose."

That was a good concession. Makes the jury think he was reasonable. Toro had spent the first minutes talking about common sense. If he had tried to make the jury believe Wanda somehow caused the fire on purpose, he would look like he was the one not using common sense. Now the jury might believe him when he reaches more reasonable conclusions.

"That doesn't mean she didn't see the fire as an opportunity. When the fire started, she probably panicked as most people would. I know I would." Cathy saw a couple of the jurors, nod in agreement.

"Maybe Wanda thought she was throwing water on the fire. Doesn't matter. She concealed that fact, so she committed insurance fraud. She even admitted that it was stupid, and she shouldn't be telling Cathy about it. In other words, she should've kept lying about it because it might affect the settlement she had just received."

Toro was raising the intensity in the room. His voice got louder. The arm movements more animated. The closing seemed to be heading toward a climax.

"Next, Wanda Rose saw an opportunity to claim that the necklace was stolen. She didn't say anything about a stolen necklace the night of the fire.

Why not? Let's use common sense. Her story defies all logic. She had a necklace worth a hundred grand lying on her bathroom counter. And she doesn't notice it missing for an entire week! Wanda Rose gathered up pictures off the walls and saved them. Pictures of her with various celebrities. Yet she doesn't save a hundred-thousand-dollar necklace.

"Common sense would tell you that that is not how a normal person would react to that situation. Any of us would've rushed into the bathroom and checked on the necklace if it had really been on the counter. The necklace wasn't on the counter. It was in the safe. Secure. It was not affected by the fire."

Cathy didn't believe that the necklace even existed. But Toro's narrative fit better with his common-sense theme.

"Wanda has a week to think about it. So, she concocts a scheme. She can claim the necklace was stolen by one of the firemen. She calls Ms. Tolliver and claims the necklace is missing. One week later! It's not believable. Don't fall for the defense's tricks. They think you're not smart enough to see through the ruse. I believe you are. I believe you're going to bring back a guilty verdict on all counts. Common sense demands it."

Toro backed away from the railing and went back to his podium to check his notes. It seemed like he was wrapping things up.

"One final point, and then I'm done. Wanda Rose is a singer. The greatest female jazz singer of all time. Why won't she sing?" Toro walked over in front of the defense table.

"Her ex-husband said he never heard her sing. Not in twelve years. Even though he asked her to. Begged her. Pleaded with her. She always had an excuse. 'I've got a cold. My throat hurts. I don't know the words to my own songs.'"

Toro's tone had turned highly sarcastic when he mimicked her words.

"She wouldn't sing for Cathy Tolliver, even though it would've proven her innocence. You all heard the tape. Ms. Tolliver challenged her to sing.

Dared her to sing. Prove you're Wanda Rose! And she wouldn't do it."

He faced Wanda, who still wouldn't look at him.

"You heard the excuses. The one excuse was laughable. 'I don't know the words.' Are you kidding me? Wanda Rose doesn't know the words to her own songs? She can't sing one note just to prove her innocence?"

Toro walked in a quick manner back to the railing. The pace of his words was coming out like a speeding train.

"She doesn't sing because she's not Wanda Rose!"

His back was to her.

"Why won't she sing? Why won't she prove her innocence? Because Wanda Rose is dead. That woman sitting at the defense table is an imposter!"

Suddenly a noise filled the room.

A voice.

Singing.

A familiar voice.

Wanda Rose.

Everyone in the room stopped what they were doing.

Where was it coming from?

The judge sat forward in her chair. Several people in the audience leaned forward, straining to see what was happening.

The sound seemed to be coming from the defense's table. But the rich melody had filled the entire room and was echoing off the walls.

It was like a Wanda Rose record was being played over the speakers.

The singing was soft at first.

Then it got louder.

The sultry, smooth, deep, rich tones of Wanda Rose were unmistakable.

Wanda stood to her feet and her voice was louder. The acoustics of the room bounced the sound from wall to wall. From ceiling to floor and back again.

I'll Never Stop Loving You was the song she was singing. That was the same song Norman played at his house.

Cathy couldn't believe it.

She really was Wanda Rose.

25

The dazzling singing of Wanda Rose said more to the spectators in the courtroom and to the jury than a thousand words could express by even the most skilled lawyer. A trial has turning points, and this was a monumental one.

For two long days, Wanda sat in her chair listening to the prosecution accuse her of not being Wanda Rose. Now she stood at that exact same spot and shoved it back in their eye, having had enough.

Her eyes were closed, her arms crossed over her chest.

With seemingly no effort, she mesmerized the throng of spectators with the soulful and unmistakable sounds of Wanda Rose only heard in recordings and tapes—never in person—for more than forty years.

Things are not as they appear, she had told Cathy. A truth that had never been more self-evident than at that moment.

Rather than try and figure out how she got it so wrong, Cathy allowed herself to become immersed in the singing. It reminded her of the night she and Norman sat in his study with the lights dim, and the same beautiful, rich, sultry tones filled that room. Like it permeated the courtroom on this May morning.

If possible, Wanda sounded exactly like the record.

How is that possible if she hasn't sung in forty years?

Before she could fully consider that thought, Cathy was shaken back into reality when Toro began to shout, "Judge make her stop! She's testifying! Order her to stop!"

The judge hesitated.

Wanda kept singing.

The defense attorney remained in his seat. He had no reason to say anything. Every note Wanda sang, told more than any argument he had leveled in her defense in the entire trial. Even the jurors were looking at Toro with contempt. He had mocked this woman and accused her with such conviction and had been dead wrong. A fact that had to be obvious to everyone in the courtroom and those on the other side of the camera.

Cathy was at the head of the list. She had misjudged Wanda Rose almost from the beginning.

How could I have been so wrong?

The judge responded to Toro's pleas in a tone more like an admiring fan than an arbitrator. "Thank you, Ms. Rose. You may take your seat," she said sweetly.

As quickly as the singing started, it stopped, and Wanda sat back down with the same dispassionate expression.

The spectators erupted in applause.

The judge gaveled it down, but it took several seconds before it stopped.

While Wanda probably felt some satisfaction, the ordeal had obviously taken its toll. She appeared numb, vacant, like her mind was elsewhere. The blank stare evident of dark secrets unknown only to her. Maybe she had thought back to a dark time when she lost her voice and refused to sing for anyone or for any reason.

Until today when her freedom could be taken away from her. Perhaps the thought was similar to the idiom. *She won't sing if her life depended on it.*

Today, Wanda Rose's life did depend on it.

And so... she sang.

Beautifully.

Her accusers were stopped in their tracks. All the arguments about birth certificates, baptism records, and grave headstones, all grew strangely dim as her voice became front and center in everyone's mind.

Toro appeared to regain his composure. "Your Honor, I move for a mistrial," he stated emphatically.

"You've got to be kidding," Judge Kelley said.

"It's totally inappropriate for a defendant to testify during closing arguments."

"You egged her on, counselor. You're the one who dared her to sing. She obliged. You'll have to live with it. Motion for mistrial is denied. Sit down, Mr. Toro."

"I wasn't finished with my closing argument."

"You *are* finished!" the judge said. "Sit down. It's time for the jury to get this case and render their decision."

Toro skulked back behind his table and muttered under his breath.

Rather than sitting down, he said to the judge, "At least instruct the jury that they are to disregard Ms. Rose's singing and are not to consider it in their deliberations."

"I can't unring the bell, Mr. Toro. We all heard her sing."

"Your Honor, it's your duty to instruct the jury to ignore facts not in evidence."

"As you wish, Mr. Toro. Ladies and gentlemen of the jury pretend that you didn't hear Ms. Rose sing," she said. The words dripped with sarcasm.

A laugh went through the entire crowd, including every jury member whose demeanors ranged from a grin to full-on laughter. As if the singing was damaging enough, Toro had just made himself look foolish.

Cathy wondered if this meant their entire case was lost.

* * *

The prosecution had a room designated specifically for them and their witnesses to congregate during breaks and while the jury deliberated, like now. The room had a conference table, comfortable chairs, and a sofa. Snacks and beverages lined a credenza along the wall. Above the credenza hung a picture, ironically enough, of a rose garden.

The mood of the room was solemn, as if they'd already lost. Toro was in chambers with the judge, no doubt presenting further arguments for a mistrial. No one expected him to be successful. The jury was in a room not far from where they were congregated, and the team talked about what they might be saying.

Cathy tried to nibble down a snack but wasn't hungry.

The door burst open and Toro entered.

Livid.

So mad, it looked like he wanted to throw something.

"Kelley denied my motion for a mistrial. Big surprise!" he said.

"That was to be expected," Dylan Chandler, the assistant DA said. "We'll have to take it up on appeal, if we lose."

Toro was almost shouting. "I blame you!" he said with his arm outstretched and a finger pointed right at Cathy.

"Me? What did I do?" she answered.

"You said she couldn't sing. That she wasn't Wanda Rose. You made me look like a fool out there."

"How was I to know?" Cathy retorted, in shock at the accusation. "Norman was the one who told me she never sang for him."

"Obviously, she still does sing. You don't sound like that after forty years if you aren't singing every day."

Cathy fought back with a vengeance enraged by the accusation. "I'm just telling you what Norman told me! You heard the audio tape. I challenged her to sing and she wouldn't. I don't know why, but for some reason she quit singing for other people after her last album in 1944." Chandler tried to calm Toro, but he wasn't successful.

"This is a disaster," Toro said. "That clip will be played on the news over and over again. I look like an idiot standing there with my mouth wide open, listening to her refute everything I said over the whole trial."

"Everybody needs to calm down," Chandler said. "We haven't lost yet.

The jury can still find her guilty."

Toro retorted, "There's not a bat's chance in hell that they'll find her guilty of the identity fraud. Even the judge called her *Ms. Rose* and thanked her for singing for the court. What judge does that? A male judge wouldn't.

I knew a woman judge would come back to bite us in the ass."

Cathy was appalled to hear that kind of talk about a sitting judge from officers of the court. She had to speak up. "Wanda should be found not guilty on the identity fraud. She's clearly Wanda Rose."

"She should've never been allowed to sing. The judge should've stopped it the second she opened her mouth. We would've won if she had."

"Won?" Cathy said. "Sending an innocent person to jail is not winning in my book. Justice is winning. I, for one, am glad she sang. I'm glad the truth came out."

"You weren't the one who put in all those man hours preparing for the trial. You weren't the one who looked like a moron up there in front of the cameras when I claimed she couldn't sing when she could. I'm embarrassed."

"I'm sorry you were embarrassed!" Cathy shouted back, sarcastically. Her eyes watered from tears which filled her eyes. That's how mad she was. "Apparently, how you look on camera is more important than the truth! You think you're embarrassed. I've got to go back and face my boss. He's not going to be the least bit happy with me."

The ramifications of that fact hit Cathy all at once. Dawkins would never let her hear the end of it. He wanted the file closed a long time ago. Cathy had pressured him and skirted his instructions until she got the case to this point. In some ways, this was her fault. She was blinded by zeal and personal ambition. Wanda Rose was the victim of what was known as overzealous prosecution. They overreached when they charged her with identity fraud with no real proof.

Dawkins was right as well. She had let her emotions get the best of her and saw what she wanted to see. Ignored the facts right before her eyes.

The only consolation was that Wanda would not be found guilty of identity fraud. Or at least she hoped the jury reached that conclusion. At least Cathy wasn't devoid of ethics like Toro, who would rather send an innocent person to jail than lose a case and hurt his re-election bid.

She suddenly despised the man.

His chauvinism had been overlooked because he was on her side. Now, she realized that she should've been on the side of justice all along and stood up to his rude and crude remarks. She wouldn't let him get away with it now by criticizing Judge Kelley because she was a woman.

Before she said something else she regretted, Cathy excused herself and left the room. The stench of greed and ambition in the room sickened her stomach. She needed some air. For two hours, she walked outside the courthouse and then up and down the inside corridors. Never venturing too far away, because she had to stay close in case the jury came back with a verdict.

She didn't have to wait long. A buzz suddenly filled the hallways as the press and spectators started running around in a frenzy. People filed back into the courtroom.

That could only mean one thing—the jury had reached a verdict.

* * *

A courtroom was like a roller coaster. Ups and downs. Twists and turns. Every human emotion was present in one way or another. If not visibly, at least inside the people in the room.

Nothing compared to the moment when a jury reached a decision. The drama of that moment is intense and even the movies don't do it justice.

For some, the emotion was anticipation. They had no skin in the game other than a curiosity in knowing the outcome. For the accused, it probably bordered on sheer terror. Cathy couldn't even imagine what Wanda Rose was going through, even though her expression was the same.

When Wanda entered the courtroom, she looked at Cathy and smiled. Cathy wanted to crawl under her chair, even though she didn't see a hint of anger or vindictiveness in the gesture. The only thing Cathy knew to do was look away in regret.

When the judge entered the courtroom, the room grew eerily silent. The only noise Cathy heard other than the judge going through some formalities, was the pounding of her heart in her ears. She wanted to hold her breath, but they came shallow and fast, and she had no control over them. It must be what a panic attack felt like.

If Cathy could've bolted from the courtroom and slinked off to a deserted island away from the madness, she would've. When the verdict was read, the press would demand Cathy's response to the verdict.

Then it hit her.

In some ways, she was on trial. There wouldn't have even been a trial if not for her. The jury was about to render a verdict on her work. She would either be vindicated or reprimanded. While she wouldn't lose her freedom, the verdict was a reflection on her competence. Dawkins would certainly see it that way. The thought only increased her trepidation.

This must be what Wanda is feeling.

Cathy would soon know her fate.

The jury filed in. Nothing could be assumed from their expressions.

They seemed relaxed, like their jobs were finally over.

"Has the jury reached a verdict?" the judge asked.

A man stood. The foreman. "We have, Your Honor."

Out of eight women and four men, Cathy wondered why a man had been chosen as foreman. The tentacles of societal biases and norms reached even into the halls of justice.

"Please read the jury form as to the three counts."

Count one was the fraud for the fire. Count two was the fraud for the necklace. Count three was the identity fraud. There was no way they'd find Wanda guilty on count three. If they followed the law, they'd find her guilty on count one. Count two was up in the air as far as Cathy was concerned.

"Would the defendant please rise," the judge said while looking at her copy of the verdict. The outcome wasn't apparent on her face.

Wanda rose slowly. Like she had aged ten years from the trial. Her demeanor still hadn't changed. She stared straight ahead. Not even looking the jury's way.

The foreman began reading from the form. "On count one, we the jury find the defendant... guilty."

A gasp went through the courtroom. Cathy felt a huge breath expel from her lungs.

"On count two, we the jury find the defendant... guilty."

The murmur in the crowd became so loud, the judge resorted to her gavel.

Wanda hadn't changed her position nor her demeanor.

"You may continue," the judge instructed.

"On count three, we the jury find the defendant... not guilty!"

Applause erupted in the courtroom. Several reporters scurried out of the room. The judge didn't seem happy as she banged the gavel several more times and shouted, "Order in the court! Order in the court! I will have order!"

Cathy barely noticed. Her mind processed all the information, at least to the extent she could in that short period of time. The jury had decided to vindicate her.

Why am I not happy about it?

She tried to will a sense of relief to come over her. But she couldn't. Even with the not-guilty verdict, this was a big win for Miles Fire & Casualty. The publicity around the trial meant that it went all the way to the top of the company. They couldn't buy that kind of advertising. And the judge would order restitution. The company would be paid back for its entire loss.

Cathy would be a hero.

Why didn't she feel like one?

All this time, she had dreamed of this day. Dreamed of hearing the words, Wanda Rose is guilty. Now that she had heard them, it felt empty. A letdown. Like she had somehow let herself and others down. She'd done her job, and she'd find satisfaction in that.

But as Wanda Rose was led out of the courtroom in handcuffs, Cathy couldn't help but feel sadness instead of jubilation.

Things were not as they appeared.

They still weren't.

Those words haunted her in the depths of her soul.

What else is not as it appears?

She still didn't know the whole story.

Will I ever know?

26

Back at the office, a huge party awaited Cathy. Every coworker took turns congratulating her, patting her on the back, and praising her spirit and tenacity. The office seemed genuinely giddy. Especially Dawkins, who was out of character with his huge grin and celebratory mood. The home office would no doubt give him the credit. They had no way of knowing that the outcome happened in spite of Dawkins, not because of him.

What Dawkins didn't know was that Cathy was about to reveal something that would dash his hopes of using her victory for his gain. All she would have to do was endure a couple of his sexist toasts before she'd drop a grenade in the middle of the festivities.

Dawkins actually had champagne on order to be delivered in the event of a positive verdict. Several buckets of chilled champagne filled one half of the conference table and, once Cathy arrived, the bottles were opened immediately, and the bubbly started to flow.

Dawkins got the celebration going with a couple of benign remarks. A few kind words were even said about Cathy. Then he congratulated everyone in the room, although Cathy wasn't sure why.

He said, "Our entire office should be proud of this accomplishment.

Every one of you had a hand in this victory for Miles Fire & Casualty.

And you should be proud of your efforts to bring this about."

What?

Cathy had no idea what in the world he was talking about. For a year and half, she felt like the long ranger left to fight the battle on her own. He wouldn't ruffle her feathers. Not today. Not when she was about to announce her resignation in front of everyone.

The art auction was in three weeks. The curator said that if Wanda Rose was found guilty, he had a buyer for the painting who was willing to pay four-hundred-thousand dollars for it. As tempting as it was, Cathy was inclined to let it go to auction and see if it would possibly go higher. The buyer would be there if the auction didn't meet a reserve.

Either way, she would give Dawkins her two weeks' notice as soon as the party was over. The letter was already typed and in the drawer of her desk. The merrymaking was a bonus because it gave her the opportunity to embarrass Dawkins in front of everyone rather than just give him the letter privately in his office so he could spin it for his own gain.

Cathy would have to wait until later to drop her bombshell. Dawkins didn't invite her to say anything. Instead, he raised his glass and said,

"Gentlemen, start your livers."

The crowd began to drink in earnest.

A boisterous laugh filled the room as the champagne started to take effect. Cathy mingled some but mostly hung out with Laura and a couple of the other ladies who didn't drink. Laura already knew Cathy's plans and kept giving her looks of reassurance.

After a half hour of socializing, Dawkins got everyone's attention. "I hope you've enjoyed our little party, courtesy of our very own Ms. Cathy

Tolliver. Here's to the man of the hour!"

He pointed his glass at Cathy. The group applauded dutifully. Cathy had her arms folded and glared at him.

He sensed it. They had a love/hate relationship, and now was not the time for the hate to win out. "I'm sorry. I mean *woman* of the hour," Dawkins said giggling. "My apologies. It was a slip of the tongue."

She actually didn't have a glass to raise which Dawkins obviously noticed.

"Cathy doesn't drink. As most of you know. She's a Chris...tian." He elongated the word for effect.

Cathy looked at Laura and rolled her eyes. Dawkins was a little buzzed. Not drunk, but she could see the effects of the alcohol on his demeanor.

He continued. "I don't know why. But I love alcohol. Just like the Bible says we're supposed to."

Cathy caught Laura's eye and their mouths both gaped open at the same time.

"They say alcohol is man's worst enemy," Dawkins said as his arms flailed in an exaggerated manner. "Jesus said to love your enemies. So... I love to drink!"

"To drinking!" everyone in the room shouted except for the few who were offended by the joke.

Cathy whispered to Laura, "Wouldn't you like to just throw a glass of it right in his face?"

"Don't stoop to his level," Laura said.

"I won't."

"You be nice," she warned.

"I will. I promise."

Cathy motioned to Dawkins. "I'd like to say a few words."

"Listen everyone." Dawkins said. "The Queen desires to address her subjects. Hail to the Queen!" He raised his glass again as did most of the people in the room who turned their attention toward her.

Cathy waited for the din to die down and said, "Thank you all for being here today. I really do appreciate it. As Mr. Dawkins said, this was a team effort. I appreciate everyone who helped me along the way. You know who you are." No reason not to be magnanimous.

An applause filtered around the room like the wave at a football game.

"Thank you," Cathy said, as she bowed her head slightly. "Being at court today was quite an experience. Most of you probably didn't know that Mr. Dawkins had to go to court recently."

A howl went through the room as they started to heckle him.

Cathy raised her hands to silence them.

"The judge said, 'You've been brought here for drinking.' Dawkins replied, "Great! Let's get started."

The room let out a roar. Judging by the huge smile on his face, Dawkins liked it and raised his glass again.

Cathy took a deep breath.

Here goes.

"I have something important to tell everyone. I've been with Miles Fire & Casualty for twelve years. I can't say that I've loved every minute of it because I'd be lying."

A number of people grinned. Cathy looked over at Laura whose smile gave her moral support.

"But I've learned a lot and wouldn't trade my experience here for anything. We all know that the world of insurance is a rat race. The problem is that even if you win the rat race, like we did today, you're still a rat."

She looked right at Dawkins when she said it. His smile immediately turned to a scorn as his eyes narrowed in anger and his jaw clenched.

Cathy continued. "Even though we won the case today and the jury found Wanda Rose guilty, and she was... I guess, I still felt like a rat."

Cathy choked back the tears. She was determined not to cry in front of everyone.

"I was wrong about Wanda. She is the real Wanda Rose. Evidenced by her singing today in the courtroom. Which I'm sure all of you saw. The thing about it is... it made me wonder what else I've been wrong about over the years. People whose lives I've ruined with false accusations. We're supposed to search for the truth. Sometimes, when we think we've found it, we really haven't. Someone once said to me, 'Things are not always as they appear.' That's a lesson I learned in a big way today."

The room remained silent, to the point that Cathy could hear an ambulance drive by on the street, even though they were several floors above it.

"I can't do this anymore," she said as her voice shook. "As of today,

I'm officially giving my two weeks' notice."

A groan went throughout the room.

She purposely did not make eye contact with Dawkins. "But I would like to propose a toast," she said as she brushed back the tears with her hand.

"It's not really a toast. Since Mr. Dawkins quoted Jesus, let me as well. Jesus said these words, 'Blessed are the merciful for they will receive mercy.' I'm glad we won the case. I really am. But I hope Wanda Rose finds mercy."

"Hear, hear!" Several people said and raised their glasses again.

"That's all I had," Cathy said.

Dawkins jumped in, "On that down note, let's get back to work."

He walked up to Cathy. "In my office. Now."

On the way, Cathy got the letter of resignation out of her desk and sat it in front of him as soon as she walked into his office. She didn't even bother sitting down because she didn't plan on being there long.

"What the hell was that?" Dawkins said angrily.

"I'm quitting."

"Why now? The company's going to give you a promotion and a raise." "I don't care."

"I care. You up and quit, and it'll make me look bad to the bosses. They love you."

"That's not my intention."

"You need to reconsider."

"My mind is made up."

"I knew you couldn't cut it as an adjuster! I should've fired you the day I laid eyes on you. A woman can't do this job. You just proved it."

"Then fire me, and I'll leave today."

"I don't want to fire you. But if you're going to quit, then clear out your office now. If you do, then you'll have proven me right."

"It's not about being a man or a woman. It's about ability. Not sex. I think I proved that today. I feel sorry for you that you can't see it."

"You'll be back. You need this job. I can't promise it will be here when you come crawling back for it."

Cathy stood and walked out the door, cleaned out her office, and walked out the door of Miles Fire & Casualty for the final time.

* * *

Later that afternoon

"I quit my job today," Cathy said to Matt, the cute boy she had met in New Orleans who helped her find Beatrice Rose's death certificate. He was the first person she called to tell the news.

What did that mean?

She sat on the couch of her condo and ate ice cream. Her comfort food after a stressful day. The television was on, and the six o'clock news had just started. Pictures of Wanda Rose, Toro, and Roy Douglas all appeared on the screen as they gave their thoughts on the jury's verdict. The red light on the VCR machine confirmed the episode was recording so Cathy could view it later.

"You did the right thing," Matt said. "Does this mean you're going to move to New Orleans?"

Cathy chuckled. "I have no idea what I'm going to do. I just know I had to get out of there and away from that man."

"I hope he didn't ruin it for all of us men. We're not all like that, Cathy."

"I know. That's what I keep telling myself."

An image suddenly appeared on the television screen. A picture of a man Cathy recognized.

"I've got to go!" Cathy said and disconnected the phone before Matt could say anything.

She turned up the volume to the television.

"A Beverly Hills Fire District 3 fireman was arrested Tuesday for stealing items from homes while fighting a fire," the news anchorwoman said.

Cathy sat forward on the couch with the remote still in her hand and stared at the picture on a split screen. The anchorwoman was on the left and a mug shot of a man was on the right-hand corner. He was the man Cathy interviewed about the theft of the Wanda Rose necklace.

A firefighter.

"Court records show that Vinny Giordano, 38, allegedly stole several items from a residence in Beverly Hills. His unit was called out to a fire. The next day, the homeowner reported a number of items missing including a watch that had been in the family for years. That watch was later recovered by an undercover officer who purchased it from *Easy Pawn Gold and Jewelry* shop on East seventeenth street in downtown Los Angeles. The homeowner later identified the watch as the one missing, and video security footage from a neighboring business showed Giordano enter the pawn shop the day after the fire."

This is unbelievable.

The news anchor continued. "In the arresting officer's probable cause statement, he said that this is not the first time Giordano has acted. A search of his home found other items that homeowners believed were destroyed in their fires. The Beverly Hills fire department issued a statement. 'If these allegations are true, then Mr. Giordano violated the public trust and the solemn oath we take as firemen. It is a black eye on the entire department.' The fireman was fired from his job and is out on bail. His next hearing date is scheduled for July."

Wanda was telling the truth about the necklace.

* * *

The next day

Cathy no longer worked for Miles Fire & Casualty and was no longer on the Wanda Rose case, but her investigation had begun anew. She was determined to get to the bottom of it. The fireman's arrest had raised serious questions in Cathy's mind that she couldn't shake. Not only did Wanda not lie about her identity, there was a good chance the necklace really did exist. If she could find proof, maybe she could help Wanda get the conviction overturned. At least as it related to the necklace.

Common sense said she should walk away and leave well enough alone. But she wasn't wired that way. She was a person who liked to know things. If she didn't find out the truth about Wanda Rose, it would bother her for the rest of her life. The problem was that she didn't know where to begin. The file was back in the office, including the box Norman had given her, so she had to work without her notes. The fact that she hadn't made copies before she turned in her keys left her kicking herself.

The first thing she did that morning was go to the library and research everything she could about Wanda Rose. She didn't find anything she already didn't know. She did make another copy of the picture of Wanda singing with Tommy Dorsey in one of the encyclopedias. The same one she found in the New Orleans library. The caption under the picture gave her a lead. The picture was from a television special produced, recorded, and later aired by NBC.

Cathy called NBC and made an appointment to meet with someone in archives. They knew Cathy's name and her role in the Wanda Rose's trial and were more than willing to oblige as long as Cathy agreed to appear on a news show at a later date and discuss her role in the Wanda Rose affair. Something she was reluctant to do but agreed to anyway because she didn't have any other leads to investigate.

An employee of NBC, Tuesday Harding, was the person assigned to help her. According to her, Tuesday had worked in the archives for years and knew the records as well as anyone.

"What are we looking for?" Tuesday asked.

"Any footage of Wanda Rose. She performed with Billie Holiday, Tommy Dorsey, Duke Ellington. There has to be footage of her singing with them. Or at least I hope there is."

"That's a tall task."

"I know, and I can't thank you enough."

For two days they searched.

Their strategy was to find a recording, document it, set it aside, and then look at them all at once. At the end of the search, they only found three.

Tuesday set up a viewer that allowed them to watch the footage and work with it. Fast forward and reverse. Zoom in or out on an image. Brighten a dark picture. They could even record it onto a VCR tape.

The first footage was the one of Wanda singing with the Tommy Dorsey band. The picture in the encyclopedia came from it. They viewed it several times, but Cathy didn't see anything of value to her investigation.

The second footage was of Wanda and Billie Holiday taking turns entertaining a crowd in Las Vegas. The date was 1944. The same year Wanda recorded her last album.

When the third tape was cued up, Cathy nearly fell out of her chair. Wanda was on stage, in a sparkling blue dress. Around her neck was a necklace.

"Can you zoom in on that necklace?"

When she did, the image became grainier and lost its focus. Still, the features were unmistakable.

Oval shaped.

A large, blue sapphire in the middle.

Diamonds all around the sapphire. At least a dozen of them.

That had to be the necklace.

"Can you make me a copy of the tape and also print out a still picture of the necklace?"

"Of course," Tuesday said.

A few minutes later, the task was done.

"What are you going to do with it?" Tuesday said.

Tuesday had watched the trial along with scores of others. They discussed the role the necklace played in the trial, and Cathy imagined that she had already put two and two together.

"I'm going to go see Wanda Rose."

* * *

Cathy sped to the prison, lucky that she didn't get a ticket. Once inside, a man greeted her at the counter.

"I need to see Wanda Rose," Cathy said as she tried to catch her breath.

"You can't," the man in uniform said.

"I know it's after visiting hours, but I have to talk to her."

"She's not here."

"Where is she?" Cathy assumed she'd already been transferred out to a higher-security prison.

"Judge let her out on bail, pending appeal."

Cathy forgot to say thank you as she sped out the door and over to Wanda's townhome. All the way over, she rehearsed what she was going to say. When she got there, she rushed up to the door with the video tape in hand. Wanda didn't answer on the first knock, but the lights were on, and she could hear movement on the other side of the door.

She knocked harder. So hard it hurt her hand. "Wanda. Please open the door," Cathy said. "I need to talk to you." No response.

"I know you're in there. I heard you. I'm the last person you want to see. I get that. But I have evidence that will help you. Please let me in." The door cracked slightly.

"Go away," Wanda said as she peeked around the door to where Cathy could only see part of her.

"Give me five minutes," Cathy implored. "Please. I have to show you something."

"Do you think I'm stupid? I fell for your trick the first time. I'm not falling for it again."

"I'm not wearing a wire, if that's what you think. I promise. You can pat me down if you want."

"Like your word means anything to me."

"Please Wanda let me in. I know about the necklace. A fireman stole it. I can help you."

The door opened all the way, and Cathy bolted through it. They stood in the hallway. Cathy wanted to go upstairs so she could show her the tape.

"Do you have a VCR machine?" Cathy asked.

"Of course," Wanda said.

"I've got something I want you to see."

They went into the family room which was attached to the dining room adjacent to where the fire started. The site of the two major confrontations the two of them had had over the last eighteen months.

Wanda put the tape in the machine and hit *play*. The screen flickered, and the image of Wanda singing came on the screen.

Cathy noticed Wanda grimace slightly.

"Stop it right there!" Cathy said, ignoring the strange look Wanda had given the tape upon seeing herself.

Wanda hit *pause*.

Cathy walked over to the television and stood next to it. "Is that the necklace?" she asked excitedly.

"Yes. That's the necklace."

"The one stolen by the fireman?"

"I thought you didn't believe a fireman stole it."

Cathy told her about the news report and arrest of Vinny Giordano. She explained to her that this was new evidence. Her attorney needed to present it to the judge before sentencing. Cathy knew enough about the legal system to know that technically Wanda wasn't guilty of anything until the judge entered the order with the conviction. Until that time, her attorney had several legal maneuvers he could use.

Cathy tried to sound encouraging. "The judge will have to grant you a new trial. Maybe even throw out the conviction altogether. If you want, I'll testify on your behalf."

"Why are you helping me?"

"Because I was wrong. I feel bad about it. You are Wanda Rose, and I couldn't see it because of my own stubborn blindness."

A strange look came over Wanda's face as her lips and eyes contorted.

She slumped back in her chair and began to wring her hands.

Then she stood.

Then sat back down.

Tears had formed in her eyes. Her lips quivered.

"What is it Wanda?" Cathy asked. "Is there something you want to tell me?" Cathy knelt at her feet and put her hand on Wanda's to comfort her.

"I'm not Wanda," she said faintly almost under her breath.

"What do you mean?" Cathy said as Wanda pulled her hands away from Cathy's.

"I mean what I said. I'm not Wanda."

"Who are you?"

"I'm Beatrice."

27

1929

Beatrice lay on an old wooden altar in the basement of the parish church built as a wing to the orphanage. Her hands and feet were bound, leather straps ran across her chest and thighs acting as a harness to restrict her movement to no more than an inch one way or the other. Her muscles cramped from the atrophy.

Aside from the frequent beatings, the worse part of her makeshift bed were the splinters from the wood that had entered under the skin on the uncovered areas of her arms and legs and the heels of her barefoot feet. While the impulse to move and change positions was overwhelming, each time she did, something happened to make her situation even more uncomfortable.

If that was possible.

Her mouth was dry and parched but the hunger had long since left her to the point that she didn't notice it anymore. Bread and water were the only things she had eaten in the two weeks she'd been confined to her torturous dungeon.

Or at least she estimated it had been that long.

The cellar was without windows, and she judged the time by when her tormentors returned. Twice a day. Morning and late afternoon by her estimation. The calculations were made with a degree of certainty since she could hear the daily morning mass in the chapel above her, the sounds of which found their way through the cracks and crevices into her dark and dank prison cell.

Or as Sister Rita called it, her chamber of learning.

Not punishment.

Instruction, the vile woman had called it on more than one occasion.

Beatrice, "Bea" as she had been called the entire sixteen years of her life, even though she hated the shortened name, moved her head from side to side to at least feel some movement in her body. A small consolation, but she could lift her head and look in every direction, so she had something to do to pass the time rather than stare at the ceiling.

She'd give anything to shower and put on a new set of clothes. Hers had been soiled on more than one occasion. When Sister Rita and Ivan, the creature who came with her to perform their sadistic rituals, Beatrice was unstrapped from the table, allowed to stand, and permitted to use the bucket in the corner of the room to relieve herself.

That might be the worst part. Them watching her. Stripping her of all privacy and dignity. That and the vile stench of the bucket combined with the rank smells of the mildewed walls. At least her tormentors noticeably suffered from the ungodly stench when they came to provide her "instruction."

Not just instruction. An opportunity for repentance.

If she did repent and atone for her sins, she would be freed from her plight and could rejoin the other girls. There she could sleep in her own bed, take a shower, brush her teeth, eat two meals a day, play in the courtyard, and go to school, where she'd get real instruction. The only thing she enjoyed at the orphanage. Beatrice was a good student and sopped up every bit of knowledge she could glean from the classroom.

Each time, she refused to repent. Her resolve and obstinance increased with every new demand to adhere to Mother Superior's directives. The intensity of the cruelty increased as well, as Sister Rita ordered Ivan to put her back on the table where she would beat her with a cane.

Beatrice always climbed back on the table willingly before the hideous creature could touch her. If she hadn't, Ivan would force her on. She'd never let him put his hands on her. She'd rather die. So far, he had never touched her or participated in the beatings.

At some point, she realized, she'd have to fight back, even if it were against Ivan. Escape was her only option to get out of there alive. She was biding her time and waiting for the right moment. It had to be soon, or she wouldn't have any strength left to fight.

All of this pain and suffering because she wouldn't sing.

Two weeks ago, the orphanage had dignitaries from the community attend the morning mass. God had gifted Beatrice with the ability to sing like an angel, Sister Rita said. She was paraded in the front of the congregation at every opportunity like an act in a carnival show. They said she was singing for God, but they were the ones who relished in the accolades she secured for them, and the rector's offerings overflowed as a result. People came from everywhere to hear her sing. Attendance at the mass had never been higher, judging from the overflow crowd.

That particular day she refused to sing. Sister Rita demanded she obey under threat of punishment. Beatrice walked to the front of the church when the music started. Instead of singing, she crossed her hands and sat down on the floor. Two of the sisters forcibly carried her out of the chapel, to the amusement of the other girls and to the embarrassment and horror of the nuns.

Beatrice was beaten and thrown in the basement. When she continued to refuse repentance and absolution, she was strapped to the table. Her hands and feet were struck repeatedly with a wooden stick. Food and water were reduced to only meager rations. When she looked down, she could see her ribs.

It didn't matter what they did to her. She vowed to never sing again.

Not for anyone, ever.

Today, her oppressors were late.

The sounds from the morning mass had ended long ago. That was her biggest fear. That they would forget about her, and she would die a slow and painful death. Or the lone kerosene lamp in the corner which cast a dim light over the room would somehow catch fire, and she would burn to death before anyone could come.

In some ways, death would be welcomed. In other ways, she was only sixteen and had her whole life ahead of her. She dreamed of a different life. That's how she got through it. Her mind wandered to far-away places. Mountains and beaches. She'd been to Europe and Asia and every other continent in her mind. Most of the time she, thought of parts unknown in the United States. Places she would go to get away from there. As far south and west as possible. When she was thinking about those places, she felt peace.

Otherwise, she would've gone crazy.

When she did leave that place, she'd never step foot in a church again.

Eventually, they would have to let her out. As soon as they did, she'd run away. The thought occurred to her to tell Sister Rita she was repentant and would sing and then run away before she was forced to. That was a last resort. She had to find another way.

Then she heard the footsteps.

Two sets.

Ivan's were the louder and heavier ones. The hideous man was at least six foot six. His right arm was bigger than his left. He walked with a permanent limp. Most of his teeth were gone, but his head was full of jet-black hair. The goiter on the side of his neck was bigger than a melon, and his right shoulder protruded out like a rock on the side of a mountain.

Ivan tended to all of the maintenance at the orphanage. She'd seen him a thousand times but had never heard him utter a word other than a grunt. Sister Rita never came alone. If she had, Beatrice would overpower her and escape. Beatrice could never best Ivan. He was too big and strong. She could outrun him, though. But he always stood between her and the door. Somehow, she needed to distract him. Wait for the right opportunity, and when her bindings were released, risk her way to freedom.

If there was a God, maybe he would help her. Surprisingly, she wasn't mad at God. Surely, he didn't approve of what Sister Rita was doing to her.

The big wooden door opened with a familiar creak which allowed more light into the room from the torch Ivan was carrying. As was his ritual, the first thing he did was set the water bucket on the floor and refill the kerosene lamp so it would provide light until they returned, and he could refill it again. At least she wasn't left in total darkness.

Sister Rita stood inside the door and stared at Beatrice with her nose covered to block the stench from the room. "How are you today, my dear Bea?"

For two weeks, Beatrice held her tongue and refused to answer even the simplest question. Not only would she not sing, she wouldn't give her the satisfaction of talking to her. The only thing that could possibly come out was anger and bitterness, and she wouldn't give Sister Rita the satisfaction of seeing her pain.

Ivan released the bindings.

Once free, she struggled to her feet. Her knees wobbled as she tried to get her balance. Standing on her feet was painful as the wounds from the beatings had not healed, although the cold floor offered them some welcomed relief.

A dose of panic shot through her as she realized her strength was fading at a rapid pace. She doubted she even had the energy to overpower Sister Rita if it came to it.

This might be how I die.

"Child, it's time for this to end," Sister Rita said sweetly. "Are you ready to confess your sins and ask for absolution? I will freely give it to you. If you ask."

Beatrice did her best to stand upright and make eye contact but her muscles were contorted, and she could only stand hunched over with her left heel off the ground as it was too painful to put her weight on the sores.

Beatrice refused to speak.

She stared back at Sister Rita, emotionless.

Mother Superior said the same thing every time like a broken record. "If you will sing for me, Bea, I will release you from your bindings. You can rejoin the other girls. Don't you want that?"

For the first time in two weeks, Beatrice decided to speak. "You can keep me here until I die, but I will never sing for you again. Ever. As God is my witness. I will never sing for anyone again."

Sister Rita suddenly bolted toward Beatrice and slapped her across the face. The sound echoed through the chamber like a bullet ricocheting off a rock.

Beatrice could taste blood. "You might as well kill me," Beatrice said as she turned her back to her as a sign of disrespect. Also, so she couldn't hit her in the face again as easily.

"You have a sister," she said.

What Sister Rita said stopped her like a concrete wall would stop a bullet.

"What?" Beatrice said. "You're lying. You told me I'm an only child."

"Your mother gave birth to twins. She didn't want either of you. That's why she brought you here. Your sister's name is Wanda. She was adopted the first week. The couple didn't want two children. Just one. They chose her over you. That was providence. She was the good child. You are the wicked seed. Like Jacob and Esau. God loved

Jacob and hated Esau. God loved Wanda and hated Beatrice. That's why Wanda received the blessing of a family. Your behavior proves it."

"If you're lying to me, I'll kill you!" Beatrice could no longer hold back the hatred.

Sister Rita responded, "See what I mean. Your heart is filled with evil. I wash my hands of you. There's nothing more I can do. I condemn your soul to hell. Ivan put her back on the table."

"I haven't used the bucket," Beatrice said.

"And you never will. You will remain strapped to the table until you die. We'll bring you enough food and drink to keep you alive. That's all. Eventually, God will free you from your suffering, and you will be taken. God have mercy on your soul. Ivan, she is yours to do with as you wish. Take her as if she were your wife. Let's see how she likes that. Both of your souls are damned anyway."

Ivan grabbed Beatrice by the arm.

She screamed.

He lifted her up like she was a rag doll and set her on the table. Sister Rita left the room and closed the door behind her. Beatrice began flailing her arms and legs to fight back. The pain seared through her body with each movement.

Ivan put his finger to his mouth and made a sound like he was trying to quiet her. He stepped back from the table. Beatrice sat up, not sure if she should try to run. He had a look of compassion. His eyes were drooped, and he let out moans like he was in pain.

He pulled a piece of bread from his pocket and handed it to Beatrice. She took it in her hands and devoured it. Some crumbs fell to the floor and she stooped to retrieve them not wanting to lose a single bite. Ivan walked over to the bucket of water, picked it up, and brought it back to the table.

Beatrice gulped it down so fast she started to cough.

The water was cold and soothed her throat. When she was sated, there was enough water left to splash on her face and hair. The cooling stream brought a feeling of euphoria over her. Ivan handed her a rag. She used it to wash her wounds.

Why was he being nice to her? Did he still intend to take her? Was it like he was courting her before he forced himself on her? Was it because she smelled so bad?

His eyes seemed filled with compassion as his eyebrows constantly furrowed.

"Wait here?" he said.

Beatrice could feel her mouth fall open. He spoke! When she recovered from the shock, she said, "Don't leave me," as she suddenly trusted him and didn't want him to leave.

"Stay here. I'll be back," he grunted. His voice was deep and strong. He sounded like a bullfrog croaking out words.

He closed the door behind her, but she was not bound. She didn't hear the familiar sound of the lock fasten as she had so many times before.

Beatrice struggled to her feet. She wrapped the rag around the most injured foot and hobbled to the door. She pushed it open.

Should I escape?

He told her to stay there, but this was her chance for freedom. Why would he leave the door open? Was it so she could leave? Do I trust him? Should I wait for him to come back? How far would she get with no clothes, no money, and with her injuries? She didn't even know how to get to the outside.

Ivan did. He had keys hanging from the belt of his pants.

She decided to wait. Mostly because she had to get to Sister Rita's office. She didn't believe her when she said she had a sister. And she wasn't leaving until she found out the truth.

* * *

Ivan returned, but only after what seemed like two hours. When she heard the footsteps, her heart raced until she saw his huge presence walk through the door. The wait had been excruciating.

Her patience and trust were rewarded. He had waited for everyone to go to bed. Ivan took her under his arm and led her to his quarters where she showered and put on a freshly washed set of clothes he had taken from the laundry. The shirt and pants were loose fitting from all the weight she'd lost, but they felt soft against her skin.

The shoes actually fit. While they were rough on her feet, they would work. He also brought some gauze and ointment from the infirmary, which soothed her wounds. Once bandaged, she could walk on the soles of her feet with the pain lessened.

Beatrice still didn't know why Ivan was helping her. The fact that he was and had the presence of mind to find her clothes and medicine shattered every misconception she had of him. Seeing him working at a distance, all the girls had been afraid of him and mocked him for his strange appearance. Not knowing that he was as gentle and good hearted as a lamb.

When Beatrice insisted on going to the offices. He had vehemently resisted. "You need to get out of here as soon as possible. Someone could wake up and find you."

"I have to find out if what Reverend Mother said about my sister is true."

"It's too dangerous. They'll have us both thrown in jail."

"I have to know. I'm going with or without your help."

They waited until the middle of the night. Ivan led Beatrice through a series of back hallways to the administrative wing. Even though no one was rustling in the buildings, they still had to be quiet. Each step for Beatrice was painful, but she barely noticed because of the energy that pulsed through her veins and pushed her on to the office in the hopes that the wanted files were there.

The office was locked, but Ivan had a key. He stood outside the door as the watchman while Beatrice found the file cabinet.

Locked!

A bolt of fear shot through her like an electric current.

There had to be a key somewhere. Sister Rita would probably carry it with her. Beatrice wasn't leaving there without looking through those files, even if she had to break the lock. She thought about asking Ivan, but there his keys led to the office and places that he cleaned. He wouldn't have any access to the private records of the orphanage.

Beatrice opened the top drawer of Sister Rita's desk but found nothing. The side drawers weren't hiding keys either. She ran her hands under the desk to see if maybe they were there.

Then she spotted a plant on top of the file cabinet that seemed out of place. Searching behind the plant, Beatrice found a set of keys.

Please open the file cabinet.

She found herself praying more than at any time in her life. Even in her captivity. She had never wanted anything more than she wanted her sister's file.

The key worked after she jiggled it a couple of times.

Her file was easy to find. They were in alphabetical order and Beatrice Rose was written on the outside tab. But where was her sister's file? She didn't have a last name. All she knew was that her name was Wanda.

There was no Wanda Rose in the file cabinets. Beatrice opened her file and flipped through for any clues. She found that her mother's name was Rose Kennedy O'Neil. A sense of sadness came over her from having learned her mother's name.

Why did she give us up?

Sister Rita said she didn't want them. Beatrice refused to believe that, but there was no time to consider it now. The most important thing was that she had a possible last name.

O'Neil.

Flipping through the files, she found a file with Wanda O'Neil written on the tab. An elation came over her unlike any she'd ever experienced before. A stamp on the outside read in big red letters, ADOPTED.

It had to be her. Her heart skipped a beat then felt like it did a somersault in her chest. Two hours ago, she thought she was an only child.

Now she found a file that confirmed she had a twin sister.

"Please! Please God! Let there be an address."

The light was dim on purpose so no one would see a light on in the offices, but it hindered her ability to read the fine print. She strained to read the information. Inside the file were adoption papers. Signed by Bel and Irene Scurlock.

2917 Prosser Lane. Camden, New Jersey.

Her sister lived in the same city all these years! That is, if they were still there. What are the odds that they hadn't moved? It's been sixteen years. She had to go there and find out.

Beatrice closed the file cabinet and put both her files under her arm. Later, when she was alone, she'd study them further and glean more information. This was a start.

She should leave, but curiosity got the best of her. Another door led off of Sister Rita's office. Beatrice tried to open it, but it was locked. She went back to the potted plant where she had returned the set of keys.

Her fingers fumbled with them as she tried to hurry. The first three keys didn't open the door to the secret room. When she got to the last one, she said another prayer. This time the key fit. The door opened. Beatrice sat the files down on the desk and picked up the kerosene lamp and shone it into the darkness.

She let out a gasp.

The room was lined with shelves full of riches. Piled almost up to the top of the ceiling. Coins. Jewelry. Paper money. No doubt wealth accumulated through the years. Beatrice took a few coins from one of the bins and stuck them in her pocket.

She needed money, but she wasn't a thief. She only took enough to help her get a new start. Compensation for the times she sang for the congregation.

A glint caught her eyes. Something reflected from her light and cast a starry display on the wall.

She walked over to the shelf to see what was making the glinting glow. *A necklace.*

It had a blue sapphire and diamonds. They were causing the reflection.

She picked it up carefully and gazed at it. Never in her life had she seen anything so beautiful. Nothing that elegant had ever touched her hands. Suddenly, there came a sound outside the door.

Sister Rita's voice. "Ivan, what are you doing?"

"I'm cleaning. Just finishing up."

She heard what she thought was Ivan locking the door to the office from the outside.

She was trapped!

Beatrice dimmed the lamp.

Carefully, she closed the door where the riches were kept and returned the keys to their spot behind the potted plant.

She picked up the two files, put them under her arm, and eased over to the window. Once open, she slipped out and began to run, ignoring the pain in her feet that cried out for her to stop. Her mind willed herself to keep going until she was outside the gate of the orphanage. The coins clanged in her pockets. She prayed they wouldn't fall out.

Once outside, and on the deserted street, she stopped to catch her breath, now labored from the effort. It didn't seem as if anyone had followed her.

Then she noticed her hand was clutching something.

The necklace!

She had forgotten to put it back on the shelf.

28

1985

"What happened next?" Cathy asked Beatrice. "Did you find your sister?"

Cathy's emotions hung on every word. The story she'd worked so hard to uncover had unfolded before her eyes.

"I did find Wanda," Beatrice replied. "I found her house and went there that morning. I didn't know if she still lived there, but I had to find out. Between the houses across the street, was a place to hide. Imagine my shock when Wanda walked out of the house with books in her arms and started walking down the street. I knew immediately Sister Rita had told me the truth. We looked identical."

If Cathy had waited, Beatrice would've told her, but her inquisitive mind wouldn't let there be a single pause in the dialogue. She had to ask, "What did you do? Did you walk right up to her and say, 'hello I'm your long, lost sister.'?"

"I didn't even have to say anything. As soon as she saw me, she knew. We both could've been looking in a mirror."

"I can't imagine walking down the street, minding my own business on my way to school with not a care in the world, and then *bam*, I see someone who looks just like me."

"It was a weird feeling for both of us. Although, Wanda *did* have a care in the world."

"She wasn't happy at her home?"

"Well... she was adopted. There were already two girls in the house. You do the math. She was the odd one out. The biological kids treated her like Cinderella. The mother was a wicked hellcat according to Wanda. She couldn't wait to get out of there."

"So, what happened?"

"I showed her our files, and we decided to skip town together."

"Just like that?" Cathy snapped her fingers.

"Just like that. Wanda was thrilled to learn she had a twin sister. They never told her about me. Her adoptive parents did tell her that our momma died giving birth to her... us. That was new information for me. Sister Rita said she gave us up because she didn't want us. That woman was evil as well."

"I met Sister Rita," Cathy said.

Wanda's painted-on eyebrows went halfway up her forehead.

"Where... when did you meet her?"

"At the orphanage. She's still alive."

"You are a persistent little devil, aren't you?" Beatrice said with a grin. "I figured Rita died a long time ago."

"She's on her last legs. Anyway, back to the story. You and Wanda decided to leave New Jersey."

"We had a little bit of money from the coins I took from the orphanage. We figured that would get us out of town to start a new life. When her parents left the house for work, we went in and packed two bags and left. Wanda had enough clothes for both of us. We were basically the same size."

"Her parents must've been worried, sick."

"Wanda left a note but didn't tell her parents where she was going. That's when she decided to change her name to Wanda Rose to match mine so they wouldn't find her. And, she was sixteen, so technically, she was an adult and could leave on her own."

"Where did the two of you go?"

"As far away as possible."

"Did you take a bus? Jump on a freight train?"

"They didn't have buses back then. Or if they did, we didn't know where to catch them. We hitched rides."

"That must've been scary."

"Not back then. People were happy to give us rides. We got as far as the Mississippi river, right at the Arkansas line, and then turned south. We thought we were far enough away from New Jersey that no one would look for us there. When we got to the Gulf of Mexico, we couldn't go any further south, so we settled in New Orleans."

"Where Wanda signed the record deal?"

"Wanda could sing as good as or better than me. They tried to sign both of us as a sister act, but I told them I couldn't sing. Which was a lie. I *wouldn't* sing. Because of Sister Rita. The rest is history. Wanda became a big star. And I watched from the sidelines."

Wanda stood from her chair catching Cathy off guard. "Let me show you something."

She walked over to the VCR and turned on the tape of Wanda singing with Tommy Dorsey. At one point she paused it and motioned for Cathy to look at the television screen. "See that," she said.

Cathy moved in closer.

"That's me sitting in the audience."

"Wow! I see it now," Cathy said. "I didn't even think to look in the audience."

"I was with Wanda for most of her performances. Then she married the record producer. That was a disaster. He used her to further his career. Wanda was all starry eyed. Thought she was in love. I married Bobby Brice about the same time. He wasn't much better. We divorced a few years later."

"That's why you said the name, Bobby, when you talked about your ex-husband. I thought you weren't Wanda, and that's why you forgot the name."

"I panicked as soon as I said it. But you gave me a chance to clean it up."

"Wait a minute!" Cathy said as a sudden thought came to her. "You're supposed to be dead. I saw your headstone in the graveyard. I even took a picture of it."

Then Cathy panicked like she'd walked in front of a cement truck.

Wanda didn't answer right away which added to her trepidation.

"Is Wanda the one buried in your grave?" Cathy asked nervously. Almost dreading the answer, she knew was about to come.

Tears formed in Beatrice's eyes. "Yes," she said. "Wanda died and is buried in the grave with my headstone."

"You killed her?" Cathy erupted in fear and anger. "Mercury poisoning.

I saw the death certificate." She started pacing around. "You did steal Wanda's identity! How could you kill your own sister?"

"It's not what you think. I can explain."

"I've heard enough. I have to get out of here." Cathy bolted toward the stairs.

Beatrice was closer and as quick as a cat and blocked her way before she could take the first step down. Cathy tried to push her way past her, but Beatrice was surprisingly strong and grabbed her arm in a vise grip.

"Let go of me," Cathy said. "Are you going to kill me like you killed your sister? Like you killed Norman?"

"Let me explain."

"I've heard enough!"

Beatrice pushed Cathy back roughly and almost knocked her to the ground. "I'm not going to kill you. But I will tell you the whole story if you'll go back in the living room and sit down!"

"Why should I believe one word that comes out of your mouth? All you do is tell lies."

"I can't make you believe me. But I can tell you what happened.

Aren't you the least bit curious? You've come this far. Might as well know the truth."

If Cathy's heart was beating any faster, it would've leapt out of her chest. Only three times in her life had she felt like her life was in danger.

All three times were in this house.

I should've never come here.

She thought she was doing a good thing, helping Wanda... Beatrice.

One thing Beatrice said was true. Cathy was curious. "Okay. I'm listening. Tell me what happened to Wanda. Then tell me what happened to Norman. I know you had something to do with his death as well." "I was with Norman the morning he died. I'll tell you that story too." Wanda walked to the kitchen.

Beatrice no longer blocked the exit. Cathy had an opportunity to leave, but her investigative curiosity wouldn't let her.

When Beatrice returned, she had two drinks in her hands. One for her and one for Cathy.

Cathy was thirsty.

Is it safe to drink?

Not until I know what happened!

* * *

1945

New Orleans, LA

"I got here as quick as I could," Beatrice said to Wanda. "What's wrong?" When she got the call that Wanda was sick, she rushed over to her house.

Wanda was in her bed. Curled up in a fetal position. Moaning in pain. When Beatrice left her the afternoon before, she was fine. Now she looked like death.

"I'm dying," Wanda said to Beatrice.

The words cut through Beatrice like a knife. That wasn't possible. In her mind, Wanda was as healthy as she was.

"What are you talking about?" Beatrice blurted out. "You're not dying.

Don't be ridiculous."

Wanda clutched her stomach.

"What hurts?" Beatrice asked. "Did you get food poisoning from something you ate?"

Wanda let out a deep and agonizing moan. "The pain is unbearable."

"That must be it. I'll call the doctor."

"The doctor was already here. He said I only had a few hours to live."

"What are you talking about? It's only food poisoning. No one dies of eating bad pizza." Beatrice had seen a pizza box on the kitchen table when she walked in.

Tears were building up in Beatrice's eyes. She couldn't believe the words she was hearing. "You're not going to die. You can't. I need you. Let me get you to the hospital."

"The doctor tried to get me to go, but I wanted to stay home and wait for you to get here. He said it wouldn't make any difference, anyway.

There's nothing they can do. I'd rather die at home."

Wanda suddenly let out another tormented moan.

"Doctors don't know anything!" Beatrice said. She panicked now. "Let me help you up."

"I can't move." Wanda clutched her stomach. "My throat is burning. Can I get a drink?"

Beatrice's hand shook as she got a glass and went to the sink and filled it halfway with water. This didn't make sense. Wanda was only thirty-two years old. She had her whole life ahead of her. The two of them were inseparable and had big plans. Wanda's career was booming, and she was in demand everywhere. Her last album sold more than a million copies.

How can I live without her?

Beatrice rushed back to her bedside and lifted Wanda's head so she could take a drink. She cried out in pain as the liquid touched her throat.

"What's wrong with your throat?"

Wanda closed her eyes and just moaned.

What's going on?

"What happened to you?" Beatrice said as she carefully laid Wanda's head back on the pillow.

"Tell me what happened!" Beatrice implored.

When it seemed like the pain had eased some, Wanda pointed to the dresser. A vial was turned over on top of it. Beatrice walked over and picked it up. The vial was empty but let out a metallic smell. Beatrice quickly put it back down and wiped her hands on her pants leg.

"What did you do, Wanda? What is this?"

"The doctor said it's mercury."

"Where did you get mercury?"

"A lady on Bourbon Street gave it to me. After my gig last night, I walked home, like I usually do. She was on the corner. I was so tired. She said the elixir would give me energy and strength. And make me fertile."

Beatrice and Wanda had tried to have kids but were unable to. Something they were both troubled by.

Wanda continued. "She told me to dab some behind my ears and to drink the rest."

"Oh... Wanda. Why would you do such a thing?"

"I don't know. I didn't think it would hurt me."

Wanda doubled over again in agony. Like she was in labor. The pain came in waves. One minute she could talk, the next she was in anguish.

Beatrice felt a tide of guilt. Last night, she was supposed to be with Wanda, but was tired as well and stayed home. She never would've let her take something from a voodoo woman on the street, much less drink it.

How could you have been so foolish?

What can I do? There must be something?

If the doctor said he couldn't do anything to save her life, what could Beatrice do? The stark reality of the situation hit her like walls that had just caved in around her. In a way, Wanda was her whole world. Without her, life as she knew it, would crash down around her. She had lived the first sixteen years of her life without her sister, now she was faced with living the next forty or fifty years without her. The tears smeared her makeup as she took Wanda in her arms and clutched her tightly.

"You can't die," Beatrice said. "I won't let you. You can't."

For several hours, Beatrice cared for Wanda and watched her fade away. Her eyes became cavernous. Red circles formed around them. Painful blotches formed on her face, arms, and legs.

All Beatrice knew to do was to sing to her sister. She was the only person who Beatrice would sing in front of. The songs seemed to bring Wanda comfort.

Wanda would try to hum along but nothing would come out of her mouth other than a slight tone, barely above a whisper. As it got near the end, she could only mouth the words.

What does this mean?

Wanda Rose can't die.

Does she have to?

A thought came to her. She quickly dismissed it. Then it came back again like a circling hawk over a prey.

I can be Wanda Rose.

"No!" she said aloud to herself.

Wanda finally fell asleep. Maybe she was in a coma. She never woke up. Beatrice stroked her hair and put a cold compress on her head. Then stood and paced around the room. Riddled with anxiety. A horrendous thought bounced around in her mind like a rock that skipped across the water.

Wanda lived in a beautiful mansion in the rich part of New Orleans. Beatrice could barely afford a flat in the lower parish. Wanda had expensive clothes and jewelry. Money in the bank from her last divorce settlement.

Wanda tried to help Beatrice with money, but she always refused the help.

Wouldn't Wanda want me to do this?

Don't be ridiculous! You'd never get away with it.

Beatrice was brought back to reality when Wanda's breathing became labored. She rushed back to her side. Beatrice could tell that Wanda was fading fast.

"Don't die yet!" she said to her. "You can't die. I'm not ready to lose you."

All previous thoughts had dissipated. All Beatrice could think about was the horror of losing her sister—the only person in the world she had ever loved. Now her best friend was leaving her. Forever. And there was nothing she could do about it.

Beatrice clutched Wanda in her arms. Nothing held back the tears now. The pain so overwhelmed her that she could no longer speak. Her words were no more than moans as she embraced Wanda and rocked back and forth as she could feel the life slowly ebb from her.

At some point, she noticed that Wanda wasn't breathing. She lowered her back onto the bed and listened for any signs of life. Wanda's eyes were closed, and she looked peaceful. The pain was gone. At least Wanda's pain was gone. Hers was only beginning. Grief washed over her like hurricane flood waters.

Beatrice couldn't move. She sat on the edge of the bed sobbing. Doubled over in her own pain. In her torturous dungeon, she had never suffered like she was suffering now. Time was no longer part of her reality. How long she cried, she hadn't a clue. It went long past when the tears had dried up.

Finally, Beatrice forced herself to stand. She brushed her eyes roughly. She had things to do.

Wanda would never want to be found in her current condition. Beatrice got a wet rag and cleaned her up. Put her in one of her nicest dresses. Fixed her hair and makeup. Silly. But this would be her one last act for her sister. That's how it should be. Wanda should die in the way that she lived.

Glamorous.

Elegant.

A star.

When she was satisfied, Beatrice dialed the number for the hospital. She gave them the address and told them her sister had died. The hospital said they'd call the coroner's office.

He arrived a couple of hours later.

"What happened to her?" the coroner asked. "Has she been sick?"

Beatrice walked over to the dresser and pointed to the vial. The coroner picked it up and smelled it. His face contorted and he jerked his head back. "That's mercury. Where did she get this?"

"A woman on Bourbon Street gave it to her. Told her to dab some behind her ears and then drink the rest."

"Those damn voodoo women. This is mercury. It's highly lethal when consumed. She's the third person in the last month who died from the same thing. Mercury poisoning. The stuff is lethal."

"The police need to get those people off of the street," Beatrice had the presence of mind to say.

"I agree. Do you want to stay or go while I prepare the body?"

"I want to stay with her. She's my sister."

"I see the resemblance."

For the next twenty minutes, he went through his processes and prepared to remove Wanda from the house. When he finished, he said, "Is there a place we can talk. I need to get some information on the deceased."

Beatrice led him to the kitchen where they sat at the table. He took out what looked to be a death certificate and started to write on it.

"What is the decedent's name?" he asked.

She hesitated.

Finally, she said, "Beatrice Rose."

29

Cathy said to Beatrice, "So, you were found *guilty*, for faking the theft of the necklace, even though you were innocent, and you were found *innocent* for identity fraud even though you were guilty."

"Kind of ironic, isn't it?" Beatrice said with a grimace and a slight grin at the same time.

"That's our legal system for you." Cathy said, soberly. "Hard to believe you kept the secret all these years."

"I never thought I'd get away with it. I gave the coroner the wrong birthdate for the death certificate. I gave him Wanda's birthday. November fifth. Mine is November fourth."

"I knew there had to be an explanation for the discrepancy in the birthdates. I never could figure it out."

"We were born ten minutes apart," Beatrice said. "I was born right before midnight and Wanda four minutes after midnight. Our mom died later that morning."

Why was Beatrice telling her all of this? It seemed like she wanted to unburden herself from the load she'd been carrying all these years.

Beatrice continued. "That's why I had to steal the birth certificates in Camden. I knew you wouldn't give up until you found the truth. I took them back to my hotel room and burned them so no one would ever see them."

"I should've left the family secrets buried," Cathy said pensively. Not that she ever imagined saying those words. She was born to be an investigator. To discover the truth. But... there were probably some truths better left in the graves. It seemed like this was one of them.

One truth was still undiscovered that she wouldn't let go. "What happened to Norman?"

An eerie pall fell over the room.

Not that she expected Beatrice to tell her. Baring her soul for identity theft which she could never be tried for again, was different than confessing to murder.

"I was there," Beatrice said in a somber tone. Macabre like. "Hiding in a car off the driveway. I saw you drive away."

Cathy was stunned. All of a sudden, she wasn't sure she wanted to hear all the gruesome details.

"I thought you'd never leave," Wanda said as she seemed to force a grin and at least lightened the tension in the room somewhat.

"I tried to leave," Cathy answered. "Several times. Norman wanted me to stay, so I did. We sat in the study and listened to your records. I mean Wanda's records."

She still couldn't get used to not thinking of her as Wanda Rose even though she had known for a long time she wasn't.

"I brought some Vodka. His favorite."

"He told me he quit drinking the day your divorce was final."

"He told me the same thing. He did have a drink with me, though. Several actually. I guess I made him fall off the wagon. That's my fault. I wanted to get him drunk, so he'd tell me what he told you."

"The police detective said it appeared he'd been drinking and that contributed to his fall."

"We got a little tipsy. Norman started talking about old times. One thing led to another."

Wanda's face became noticeably red.

"What happened?" Cathy asked, which she immediately realized was none of her business.

"I'm a lady. I don't kiss and tell. I mean... We're both old. Norman was eighty-eight. It's not like we could do much. But we did the best we could. It felt good to be that close to someone again. Especially Norman."

Cathy thought it best to not ask anything further. Some things were better left unsaid.

Beatrice continued. "Norman wanted to do the deed upstairs. I tried to talk him out of it. He insisted. He wanted to be in *our* bed."

Cathy saw that bed. The four-poster queen bed with the velvet bedspread with an "N" and a "W" on it. *It should have been an "N" and a "B."* While she understood it, something was inherently wrong about what Beatrice had done, deceiving Norman in that way.

"I loved Norman. You don't have to believe me, but I did. Still do. There have only been two people in my life who I loved. Norman and Wanda."

Cathy started to ask, *why did you kill him then*, but thought better of it. Wanda had opened up, which was obviously hard for her to do. If Cathy made it confrontational, then she might not ever know what happened to Norman.

"Later that night—afterwards—I told him everything,

Beatrice continued. "The whole story. About Wanda and that I was Beatrice. I think he already suspected."

"I think so too. I'm not sure if it mattered to him. He told me you were the only person he ever loved in his entire life. I believed him."

Tears welled up in both their eyes. Beatrice turned her head away to hide them and put her hand, the knuckle portion to her upper lip just under her nose to try and hold them back.

"We fell asleep. The next morning, we woke up together. Norman said he was going to fix us some coffee. I told him I was going to take a shower."

Beatrice's hands balled into a fist and she banged them against her lap, several times. Cathy could only imagine the pain the memories were causing.

"I never should've let him," Beatrice said roughly. "The old fool. When

I got out of the shower and got dressed, I came out of the room, and Norman was at the bottom of the stairs. Damn Esmeralda. Those stairs were like an ice-skating rink. I almost fell down them trying to get to him."

Is she telling the truth?

Was she concocting a story for Cathy's benefit? To create reasonable doubt if it ever came to that. It never would. Cathy couldn't even testify about it. What Wanda told her was considered hearsay.

"Norman lay in a pool of blood," she said, her voice cracking. "I was too late. He was clearly dead. His body was already cold. His cane was next to him."

The tears became sobs. "I cried for weeks. Still do sometimes... when I remember."

Cathy couldn't stop being a skeptic. "They said his cane was found at the top of the stairs."

"I put it there. I had to make it look like an accident. Which it was! I took my glass from the night before that was still in the study, and I washed it. I cleaned the upstairs bathroom and washed the towels and made it look like I had never been there. I wiped away the fingerprints the best I could. What do I know about it? There's no way I could get them all."

"The investigators never even looked for prints. They assumed he fell, and the case was closed as an accident."

"That's what it was. An accident."

Cathy wasn't sure. The one thing she did know was that Beatrice and God were the only ones who knew the truth. She hoped it was true. Otherwise, it would bother her for the rest of her life. Cathy could even see herself pursuing it.

Should she out Beatrice?

But how could they possibly prove it. Beatrice would claim she never said it. She wasn't wearing a wire. It would be her word against Beatrice's. Even then, the only thing a jury could convict her of was not notifying the authorities about the dead body.

What if Beatrice was lying, and she really did kill Norman? *Doesn't he deserve justice?*

But that's what she thought she did before when she investigated the insurance fraud. All she did was make things worse. Everything she thought about this case was wrong. The necklace did exist. A fireman did steal it. Wanda wasn't Beatrice. If everything she thought was wrong up until now, what made her think she wouldn't get it wrong again and harm Beatrice even more.

So, she decided to believe it. That would bring closure. She needed it. God would have to bring justice to the situation and sort it out in his own way.

The painting.

The only loose end. That would bring her closure. The art gallery planned to auction it off in three weeks. Then the whole Wanda Rose affair would be closed forever, in her mind.

Sometimes she felt like Beatrice had a sixth sense about her and knew what she was thinking because she said, "What did you ever do with the painting?"

"An art gallery is going to auction it off in three weeks."

"You can't do that!"

The intensity in which she said it startled Cathy. "Why? Do you still want it? Make me an offer."

Beatrice hesitated. Cathy wasn't sure why.

"I'm so relieved you didn't sell it. Pull it from the auction."

"Why?"

"There are two paintings."

"I don't understand what you mean."

"Behind the portrait of me is a valuable painting by Dylan Roisin. A French impressionist painter. I hope I said his name right. It's on a canvas attached to the back of the frame."

"I've never heard of him."

"He was a lesser known impressionist artist during the time of Rembrandt, Monet, and the others. Norman's first wife bought it for close to a million dollars."

Cathy's mouth flew open.

"I know. Norman was furious. Anyway, it hung above the fireplace until my portrait was completed."

"Is it still worth a million dollars?" Cathy asked.

"Norman said it was worth three times that."

Cathy couldn't believe the words coming out of her mouth.

Three million dollars.

"I asked Norman that night what happened to the painting. I figured he sold it. Norman said it was attached to the back of my painting. He had a mischievous grin on his face when he told me about it. The sly fox already had changed his will to give it to you."

Cathy gripped the arms of the chair to keep from falling out of it. "Why are you telling me this? You could've bought it at the auction, and no one would've ever known."

The thought suddenly occurred to Cathy that Beatrice was trying to buy her silence. More hush money. To keep her secrets. Anger started to rise inside of her all over again.

Beatrice shrugged her shoulders. "Norman wanted you to have it. I guess kind of a slap in the face to me. I don't blame him. I hurt him badly. I didn't even realize it until that night. He still loved me. Even after all I had done to him. I admit it. I married men for money. That makes me a gold digger. Guilty as charged!" Her arms were animated as she said it. Guilt was written all over her face as her lips were pursed and her shoulders slumped.

She continued. "Before, I did want to buy the painting and not tell you about the second one. Not anymore. I have enough money to live two more lifetimes. My days of living a lie are over. They have to be. It's too great a burden to bear."

Her tone got somber again. Cathy believed her. It may be foolish, but she did.

"Do you still want the painting? The one of you?"

"I'll buy it from you," Beatrice said. Her eyes lit up. "I loved that painting. It reminds me of my sister. And Norman. Does that sound strange?"

"Not at all. If what you say is true, you don't have to buy it from me.

I'll give it to you."

"I'd feel better if I paid you what it's worth."

"We can work that out later," Cathy said with a wave of the hand.

A silence came over the room as they both didn't seem to know what to say next.

"So, what happens now?" Beatrice asked. "I guess you're going to tell the judge that I'm not Wanda."

"Your secret is safe with me."

"Why would you do that?"

"Why would you tell me about the painting? You and I are coming to an understanding. I don't know what good it would do for me to tell anyone. The judge is probably going to dismiss the charges for the necklace, anyway. The jury found you not guilty on the identity fraud. You can never be tried for that again. Doesn't matter what I say to the judge. As to the other charges, clearly you were telling the truth, and the necklace was stolen from you. That's a legitimate claim. Miles Fire & Casualty owes you that money."

"Put in a good word for me with your boss. Dawkins. I don't think he likes me."

"He's not too happy with me right now, either. I quit."

"You quit?"

"A couple weeks ago. Cleared out my office. My word is dirt there. I do think you'll have to pay back some of the proceeds for the fire. The comparative negligence part. I'd estimate that to be about twenty to fifty percent. The company owes you at least half of the fire claim."

"That's better than paying all of it back. Do you think the judge will really dismiss my charges?"

"I'm not a lawyer, but I don't see why not. You have the video tape of the necklace. You can have that copy and take it to your lawyer," Cathy said pointing at the VCR machine. "The fireman was arrested. You'll get the necklace charge thrown out for sure. I'll help you if you need me, although I can't imagine why you would."

"Thanks."

"At the very least, if the judge doesn't dismiss the guilty verdict outright, you'll only get probation. I can't see her sending you to jail."

"But if I tell her that I'm really Beatrice, then she might."

A bolt of adrenaline shot through Cathy. "You can't do that!"

"Why not? I'm not really Wanda."

"Yes, you are!"

"I just spent the last hour telling you I'm not."

"Hear me out." Cathy leaned forward in her chair. "You and Wanda were identical twins. She's as much a part of you as you are of her. Maybe you shouldn't have taken her identity. I don't know. Who am I to judge? I might've done the same thing. The point is that you are Wanda Rose. As long as you are, her legacy is still alive. Why tarnish it because you made a mistake?"

"Over the years, I did sometimes feel like I was Wanda. Like a part of her was still inside of me."

"That's what I'm saying. Not only do I think you should continue to be Wanda Rose, I think you should start singing again."

"I can't do that. You know why."

"You have to! You were born to sing. You can't let what Sister Rita did to you stop you from using the gift God gave to the world."

"It did feel good when I was singing in the courtroom."

"That's what I mean. The world needs Wanda Rose. When she died, you let her voice die too. You need to bring her back to life."

Cathy stood. "Sing Wanda! Carry on her legacy. I think that's what she would've wanted."

"I know it is. If she'd only lived long enough for us to talk about it, I think she would've wanted me to continue as Wanda Rose."

"I can see that. If I had a twin sister, that's what I'd want."

"It wasn't about her possessions, Cathy. I swear it. I didn't do it for the money. I would've inherited everything anyway. The house. The clothes. The jewelry. You're right. Subconsciously, I wasn't ready for my sister to die."

"I think, deep down, you did it because you didn't want Wanda Rose to die either. This was your way to live vicariously through her. Now you get a fresh start. Maybe God used this big mess for a reason. With your newfound fame, you can record albums. Make appearances. Make a Wanda Rose greatest hits album. Sign a new recording contract. Start a Las Vegas show. The Blue Rose Returns!"

"I do have a dozen calls from agents on my message machine who want to sign me. Even the Johnny Carson show called and wanted me to appear. Can you believe that?"

"You should do it! I'll be your biggest fan."

"What about you?" Beatrice asked. "What are you going to do?"

"I'm going to New Orleans!"

"What's in New Orleans?"

"A cute boy and lots of Neapolitan ice cream."

The Spy Series

Save The Girls

The Ingenue

Saving Sara

About the Author

TERRY TOLER is the author of the Jamie Austen and Alex Halee book series along with The Eden Stories. He is a minister, public speaker, counselor, and retired entrepreneur. Impacting the lives of people worldwide through storytelling has become one of his passions in life. He can be followed at terrytoler.com.

www.ingramcontent.com/pod-product-compliance
Lightning Source LLC
Chambersburg PA
CBHW020211260626
47156CB00002B/322